CAUGHT

With stories by
Karin Huxman
Michelle M. Pillow

Contemporary Romance

New Concepts   Georgia

Caught is an original publication of NCP. This work has never before appeared in book form. This work is a novel. Any similarity to actual persons or events is purely coincidental.

New Concepts Publishing
5202 Humphreys Rd.
Lake Park, GA 31636

ISBN 1-58608-693-6
The Commitment © copyright 2004 by Karin Huxman
Mountain's Captive © copyright 2004 by Michelle M. Pillow

Cover art (c) copyright 2004 by Eliza Black

All rights reserved, which includes the right to reproduce this book or portions thereof in any form whatsoever except as provided by the U.S. Copyright Law.

If you purchased this book without a cover you should be aware this book is stolen property.

NCP books are available at special quantity discounts for bulk purchases for sales promotions, premiums, fund raising, or educational use. For details, write, email, or phone New Concepts Publishing, 5202 Humphreys Rd., Lake Park, GA 31636, ncp@newconceptspublishing.com, Ph. 229-257-0367, Fax 229-219-1097.

First NCP Paperback Printing: 2005

We offer a 20% discount on all new Trade Paperback releases ordered from our website!

Visit our webpage at:
www.newconceptspublishing.com

THE COMMITMENT

By

Karin Huxman

Chapter One

A foot kicked her. Miranda Symons jerked awake. She had no clue where she was, or who the heck snored next to her.

Frantically, she tried to focus. First things first--where was she? Obviously in a bed--not her own.

The top of a blond head emerged with a snort from beneath the deep blue satin sheets beside her.

Oh no. She gasped and looked down, hoping for the visual clarification. Thank goodness, she was clothed. Not fully, but as her Granny would say, the fancy long johns "covered the law." Except she couldn't remember where the red satin outfit came from.

Another snort from the person beside her. A male head appeared as the sheets slid down. She watched in a kind of horror as his bare shoulders followed his head. Firm, tanned biceps and finely muscled forearms came next. Holding her breath, she watched his left hand flail about. A gold wedding band winked at her.

Her nightmare had come true. She found herself in bed with a married man. Not any married man, her sister's ex-husband and her own current boss.

Her throat constricted. A quick physical assessment assured her that they hadn't made love, had sex, done the horizontal polka. At least she was reasonably sure she'd know that. Wouldn't her body remember even if her headache-wracked mind refused to answer her frantic pleas for reassurance?

Drake McLain stirred again and flung a hand until it rested against Miranda's breast. Gingerly, she reached to remove it. She stopped in mid-reach. A golden twinkle teased her from the fourth finger of her left hand. She groaned and flopped back on the pillow.

It was worse. She was married to the Devil.

A shaft of sunlight arced through the separation of the heavy drapes. It hit Drake square in the eyes. He bolted upright. The sheets pooled around his waist. Miranda stared at his tanned torso. Her gaze ran from light golden hairs on his chest to the hint of the same where the sheets met his lower body.

Unless he wore some pretty skimpy underwear, Drake McLain was nude--in bed--with her.

She fervently wished she were the kind of prissy girl who could faint. She held her breath as Drake blinked and rubbed his head until the silky waves of hair stuck out in all directions. Slowly, he turned his head until his eyes met hers.

Miranda didn't give him any time to think. She jumped out of bed nearly revealing the rest of him. "What on Earth are you doing here?" she demanded. "Get out, now."

His gray eyes closed for a brief instant. When they opened again, Miranda saw a calculating gleam in them. A gleam similar to the one she always saw right before he demanded, and got, his way from his mother, her sister, and his employees.

"I'm pretty comfortable right here," he drawled. "Seems to me you were content enough to have me around last night. As a matter of fact, I'm sure I remember you clinging to me, begging me not to leave you."

"You are an evil man." Miranda managed to bite the words out. "From where I stand, you took advantage of me last night when I was feeling about as depressed as I've ever been. I trusted you and look where it got me."

"Actually, I'd rather you told me where we are." He looked around the room and frowned. "And why am I naked? Unless you undressed me and I woke up before you could take advantage of me?"

"Drat. Fine. If you won't leave, I will." She spun on one heel and lost her balance. The room swayed around her as she landed on the plush pink rug with a muffled yelp. The yelp turned into a screech as she saw her own reflection in the huge mirror that hung above the bed. More details of the room became clear as the room lightened with morning.

The bed, which she'd only registered as being covered in slippery satin sheets, appeared to be round. A small, glass-topped table accompanied by two chairs looked okay, until she saw that the chair backs were heart shaped and upholstered in red fabric.

The same red fabric lay in a puddle on the floor, obviously the bedspread somehow tossed aside in the night.

On one of the twin nightstands, Miranda spied a discrete sign next to a coin slot. A timed vibrator for the bed.

An empty champagne bottle lay on the carpet under the table. A second, half empty bottle stood in a room service ice bucket. Two cheap, plastic champagne flutes rolled off the bed as Drake moved.

She looked at him, at the evidence surrounding them, at the rings they both wore. Her brain stumbled to a conclusion. It hurt. "I think we're in Las Vegas."

"Yup. The Little Love Hotel, if memory serves me."

Temper flared in Miranda. "Just how many women have you brought here?"

"Jealous so soon? Tsk, tsk. Not a good way to start a marriage."

"A marriage. It can't be true. I mean, I don't remember ..." A flash of memory assailed her. It showed a neon lit building front flashing the words "Instant Weddings." Drake was holding her hand as they stood side by side in front of a strange little lady dressed in a muumuu or caftan or something. Tufts of purple frizz stuck out of the woman's wildly colored turban.

"A little hair of the dog?"

She opened her eyes to see Drake, draped in blue satin, hold a plastic glass to her. Without thinking, she gulped back the now flat champagne and grimaced.

"Yuck, it's going to take more than that to make this all disappear."

"Disappear? Sweetheart, you ain't seen nothing yet," Drake drawled.

He sauntered towards the bathroom door, trailing the satin sheets like some kind of ceremonial robe. Just before he shut the door behind him, the sheet dropped to the floor giving Miranda a glimpse of tight male buttocks and muscled legs.

Heat flashed through her. She drained the final drop from the glass and searched for anything else to clear her throat. Well, almost anything. The greenish water in the flower vase grossed her out, and the melted water in the ice bucket held a lone fly that was performing a feeble backstroke. Double yuck.

Fine, she'd order room service. Married or not, at the very least Drake owed her breakfast after what they'd gone through last night.

Mortification induced heat flamed her face as more bits and pieces of the past twenty-four hours floated out of memory and marched lewdly in front of her mind's eye. It hadn't been a nightmare after all. She vaguely remembered getting slightly drunk, more than slightly, and propositioning Drake. Hell, she'd have to be raving to do something like that.

Somehow they'd decided to take the Millennium Tech company jet and fly to Las Vegas. The flight was fuzzy, though she did remember giggling a lot and sitting on Drake's lap after take off. She squirmed as her body reminded her of the exhilarating combination of comfort and erotic excitement.

Her head throbbed once more, the pounding reverberating through her. It was as if ….

The knocking on the door ceased. "Room service," a voice called out.

Miranda glanced toward the bathroom door. She heard the shower running. The knocking resumed. She staggered to her feet to open the door before the noise incurred permanent damage to her brain cells.

"Yes?" She opened the door to a toga clad young man with an incredible tan who stood beside a wheeled cart.

He flashed an Osmond-white smile at her. "Good morning. Here's the breakfast you ordered last night."

Miranda stepped out of the way as Toga Boy wheeled the cart inside. He whistled tunelessly. The cart squeaked. A carafe of what she hoped was hot coffee stood beside a pitcher of orange juice. Three silver domed serving dishes covered the rest of the top surface. Plates, cups and flatware were stored below.

Wordlessly, Miranda trailed after Toga Boy and watched him set utensils and food dishes onto the glass topped table. Every now and then the bottom of his "clothing" swished. She stared as he leaned over. Cartoon character boxer shorts--the man was wearing boxer shorts adorned with fat cartoon cats under his uniform. She snorted.

"Ma'am?" He turned, a quizzical smile on his lips.

Miranda collapsed onto the bed howling with laughter. What else could happen?

Toga Boy stared at her and backed away. His sandaled feet caught in the thick nap of the carpet. He fell backwards into Drake who was coming out of the bathroom. Tears fell down Miranda's face. She held her stomach as she watched the tangle of arms, legs, togas and boxers enmeshed with the virulent violet shade of Drake's robe.

The writhing, cursing mass finally disengaged and became two individuals. Toga Boy scampered from the room without waiting for a tip. His outfit twisted this way and that. The last Miranda saw of him was the back of the boxers running out the door.

Her stomach hurt with laughing. Her final giggle turned into a hiccup as her gaze collided with Drake's. She couldn't decipher the emotions that roiled in his eyes, but the silver gleam that caught her brought her hand to her throat.

Drake glanced at the table, now set with food and drink. "Are you hungry?" His voice throbbed low.

Miranda scrambled across the bed, trying to put more distance between them. Somehow, this man seemed much more dangerous than the Drake she woke up with. His hair was damp and tousled. The robe molded to his body, proving in detail that he was naked underneath. His hands were clenched into fists, which he suddenly jammed into the small pockets of the robe, only serving to tighten the material around his body.

Miranda was desperate. She despised Drake McLain for any number of reasons, but right now she was at a definite disadvantage. Better to play whatever game they were playing. She needed to know the ground rules before she could figure out how to break them.

First she needed to improve her position. Food might help. Her stomach was queasy; she never had learned how to drink champagne without getting a headache. She wanted real clothes. Something thicker than the slick little outfit that both covered and revealed.

"You know, I could eat something." She gestured toward the table. "Smells good, doesn't it?"

Drake stopped his advance and swiveled towards the food. "Join me," he ordered.

"Sure, why not?" Miranda took the long way around the bed so she wouldn't have to brush past him. She shouldn't have bothered. He came around to hold her chair for her.

She stared at the thick, white china plate in front of her in a vain attempt to ignore the way Drake's closeness affected her senses. She hated him, right? Then why was her stomach clenching at the brush of his robe against her arm? Why did the scent of him, clean from the shower, call to her even more than the fragrance of the coffee?

Damn, she must be sick. That was the only reason she was thinking of him as a sexy man, instead of the power hungry brute she knew him to be.

Food--She shrugged off the lingering effects of sleepy confusion mixed with a spine tingling emotion she was not even going to try to decipher. The first domed dish held croissants. They steamed as if fresh from the oven. Her mouth watered and stomach growled. Good, that meant it was hunger causing her strange reactions to Drake. Here was something she could handle.

The first pastry went down with fresh butter and hot coffee. Amazing how refreshing calories could be to a stomach, which had recently been shriveled with hunger, caused by ... heartache.

No, she didn't want to think about that. Miranda forced herself to pour juice with a steady hand. Forced herself not to think about the reasons she had pretended to seduce Drake last night. Flushing with the memory of that damning phone call from her now former fiancé, Jack the Jerk, she knocked the lid from the second plate. The rich aroma of hot scrambled eggs and honey cured bacon wafted to her nostrils.

For a half an instant, she enjoyed it. Then, her shaky stomach rebelled.

"Excuse me," she blurted. She had a brief glimpse of Drake's face, mouth open in surprise, before she slammed the bathroom door shut and gave in to misery.

Her humiliation was now complete.

* * * *

Miranda's face was an unpleasant green as she raced from the table. Shouldn't have given her that last glass of champagne, Drake thought. He heard the fan come on and turned back to his breakfast and the complimentary newspaper, thankful to have something to focus on other than Miranda's distress.

The newspaper didn't help. No matter how hard he tried to concentrate her face kept swimming in front of his eyes. Those deep dark eyes of hers trying to be at once pleasing while failing to hide the pain that was all too evident. Something truly awful must have happened for her to come to him, of all people, for comfort. It was just her rotten luck that he had been vulnerable himself last night. Too vulnerable to hold back what had been festering inside for years.

He gave up any pretense of reading. Against the backdrop of the fan, he heard faint sounds of rushing water. Hoping the shower would help her feel better he looked around for his clothes.

His conscience was getting the better of him. He darned well needed to have all his wits about him when she came out again. Pretending to have married her was low. Getting her drunk enough so she couldn't see through the sham was lower. Even with the enormity of those two events looming along the horizon he planned about to stoop even lower.

He was going to use her for a selfish act of revenge. Better yet, revenge against Lucy, who happened to be Miranda's sister as well as his ex-wife. His heart beat faster with anticipation.

He looked at the headboard of the decadent bed. Good, the special camera he'd hidden was still there. He was afraid she'd knocked it loose.

All he needed was one well-developed picture of Miranda in a compromising position with him and part one of his self-prescribed mission would be complete.

Once again, conscience stabbed at him. It was Lucy and her new boy toy he wanted to hurt, not Miranda. Sure, Miranda had stuck up for her sister all through the brief time of their marriage. Her loyalty must have been severely strained between family and Millennium Tech, his company, during the messy divorce. That he employed her must rankle. He admired loyalty, even when misplaced. Still, Miranda remained his best shot to ensure that Lucy got just what she deserved. Lucy wanted the spotlight; he was about to aim it directly at her.

He spied Miranda's clothing in a heap on the seat of a red velvet fainting couch. With a swift move, he wadded the jeans and shirt into a ball then stuffed the ball between the headboard and the wall.

By the time the bathroom door jerked open, Drake was back in his chair sipping a third cup of coffee. He was glad he was sitting down. The purple robe she wore hit her at mid thigh. Nice thighs. Cinched in at the waist, the soft fabric both hid and accentuated curves her regular workday clothes mocked by their utilitarian drabness. With her hair slicked back from her delicate features and no make up to cover the soft sprinkling of freckles, she looked like a water sprite just emerging from a pool deep in a dark forest.

A familiar throbbing pulled at his groin. He stifled a groan. This, he admitted to himself in a brief moment of clarity, could be a mistake.

Something innocent surrounded Miranda, something he'd never quite noticed before. A quality of vulnerability that she never revealed around the bustling office in which they worked showed itself now. They often had a "take no prisoners" attitude in the business. Miranda had never shown an ounce of emotion when heatedly debating a prospect or sale. The ultimate corporate player, focused and cutthroat.

Her current hesitation threw Drake off balance. He forced himself to hide it. He'd reassess this side of Miranda later.

"Sit down before you fall down," he barked louder than he intended.

She flushed and moved on unsteady feet to the table. He didn't dare hold her chair for her this time. The evidence of his physical response to her would fall out from between the folds of the robe as soon as he stood.

Wickedly he wondered how she'd react to that surprise.

Miranda nibbled a wedge of toast. "Let's get this farce over with. I want to go home."

"Farce?" Drake was determined to follow through with his original plan, even though his desire had just shifted.

"This marriage." She waved a ringed hand.

The dull gleam on the fourth finger had him biting back a grimace. The least he could have done was buy a proper wedding ring.

"But Sweetheart, you promised to love, honor, and all that other stuff. I always thought you were a woman of your word."

He sipped at his coffee as he fought with conflicting emotions. The quest for revenge had faded into an urge to protect this woman from ... himself.

Miranda shot a glare in his direction. He held the newspaper up as if to deflect a hit. Never forget, he reminded himself, she's the best contract breaker in the business.

"I refuse to compromise either my personal or professional reputation by going along with this sham. I want an annulment now." She slammed the flat of her hand against the table making the china rattle.

Enough. Drake folded the newspaper and set it down. "No annulment. We are man and wife. Besides, I wouldn't want my child born to a single mother."

Miranda paled and sank back in her chair. Her eyes opened wide, saucer like. "We didn't ... I mean, I don't remember ..."

She turned her head from side to side. Drake nodded in counterpoint.

"But," Miranda sputtered, "I was dressed when I woke. I'd know, surely I would, if you and I had had sex."

Drake leaned across the table and took one of her limp hands. "We did more than have sex, dear wife. I made love to you until you begged for more."

She jerked her hand away. "I do not believe you." Each word was enunciated through clenched lips.

"Your choice," Drake shot back. "One way or another, I'm keeping my side of the arrangement, at least until we know one way or the other." He felt himself growing hard again, wishing they *had* spent the night making love.

He needed another cold shower.

A fine seashell pink color replaced Miranda's pallor. "A month, six weeks tops. No one, absolutely nobody, must know."

"Too late," Drake murmured as the sounds of running feet and muffled voices carried through the door.

"What on earth do you mean?"

The door burst open. Miranda's sister pushed her way past a harassed looking man in a rumpled shirt and ugly green and pink tie. Drake allowed himself a small smile.

"I took the liberty of spreading the happy news of our nuptials while you slept."

Miranda groaned and grabbed her head with both hands.

Drake eyed his ex-wife. "Good morning, Lucy. Coffee?"

Chapter Two

Lucy glared at Drake, and then her gaze pierced Miranda. One elegant foot tapped rapidly against the carpet. Her sculpted lips curled into a snarl. Miranda's otherwise calm, cool sister reminded her of nothing less dangerous than a rattlesnake poised to spring.

"I ... I'm sorry, Mr. McLain," the sweating manager stammered. He wrung his hands. "She insisted, I mean, she said...."

"Be quiet, idiot. Leave." Lucy dismissed him with a flick of her wrist.

He turned and barreled into Jack Langfeld, a.k.a. Jack the Jerk, Miranda's most recent intended. The two collided in the narrow doorway, looking like they were auditioning for a Broadway vaudeville show. Miranda chanced a look at Drake. A dimple danced on his cheek. He was enjoying this, she realized. She was biting her lower lip, trying to figure out what to do, when Lucy reached into the thrashing bodies in the doorway and extricated Jack.

Miranda covered her mouth and tried in vain to hold in a snicker. Drake waggled his eyebrows at her. That did it. She exploded into laughter. Drake joined her. Through the tears streaming down her face she saw the trio in the doorway stiffen and turn towards her. Finally free, the manager fled; the door slammed shut.

Jack and Lucy stood with arms crossed identically, inciting more howls of laughter from Miranda. Twin frowns graced their faces, making her think of the phrase "monkey see, monkey do."

I'm hysterical, she thought as more giggles poured out. She gave in to them. They were better than the crying jag she'd fought off earlier.

At last her mirth wore out. Twice in one morning was too much.

Drake's laughter subsided into a final chuckle. He pulled two additional cups from the lower shelf of the service unit. "Coffee?" he offered Lucy and Jack again.

Somehow his cultured voice incited another short burst of laughter from Miranda. He winked at her. The intimate act checked her giggles. Pulling herself together, she sipped the tepid coffee left in her own cup.

Electric silence filled the room.

Jack cleared his throat. Miranda lifted her head and stared at him. He had a weak chin, she realized. What had she seen in him? The blue eyes she'd found compelling just yesterday now appeared watery and vapid. A thin line marked where his lips should be.

"Miranda," Jack said. "I demand an explanation."

Anger stirred in her. "Tough luck. I don't owe you anything."

He took a step back. "But just yesterday you told me you'd always love me. Now I find you here with ... McLain." His voice deepened on the last word making it sound as if the name itself conjured doom.

Miranda raised an eyebrow and allowed herself a cold grin. "Yesterday you broke off our engagement. I don't know why you think you have any say in how I conduct my affairs."

She chanced a glance at Drake. His face was smooth and non-committal. On the other hand Jack's face was beaded with sweat. Lucy wore her "about to explode" look.

Jack crept forward. "Maybe I made a mistake."

Miranda threw up her hands. "What do you expect me to do?"

Jack strode to Miranda. He knelt beside her. She held herself under strict control as he grasped her hand in his pale, moist one.

"Come back to Colorado with me," he cooed. "We'll get married as soon as you want. I promise."

CAUGHT 13

Miranda stood and pushed her index finger into Jack's chest. "Forget it. I'm tired of being told what to do. I'm tired of being manipulated. From now on I'm making my own decisions."

"But, Miranda." Jack lurched to his feet.

"Besides," she wiggled her left ring finger in front of his nose. "I'm already married."

Lucy pushed forward. She spoke to Miranda, but her gaze was glued on Drake. "A ring on your finger doesn't make you married, whatever you may think. I'm more than a little surprised. I never took you for the romantic type."

"Maybe it's time everyone stopped putting me into a little box marked 'Miranda's type' and started realizing that I have wants and needs of my own that go far beyond the board room."

Drake's soft, deep voice cut through the tension. "What do you want, Miranda?"

She turned to him and caught her breath. For an instant as she stared into his silvery eyes, she thought he might even be sincere.

Lucy stepped behind Miranda and spoke rapidly into her ear. "Don't you remember anything? This man was a tyrant during our marriage. You don't have to do this to prove anything to me."

"I'm not you," Miranda said, gentling her voice. She took Lucy's hands in her own. The fact that her sister was trembling shook Miranda for an instant. Did Lucy still have feelings for Drake?

"I just want you to be happy," Lucy whispered.

"Thank you. Now, go home." She softened the words with a hug. "Take Jack with you."

"This has got to be the most stupid, irresponsible thing you've ever done," Jack sputtered at Miranda. Lucy took his arm and hauled him toward the door.

Drake stood. Miranda was sure he was the only man on earth with the ability to loom threateningly while wearing a purple satin bathrobe. Her heart clenched as she watched Drake stride to where Jack stood trapped between the door and the approaching groom. Or was it doom?

"Apologize," Drake drawled when he was nose to nose with Jack. Miranda held her breath.

With the door at his back, Jack had nowhere to run. "I'm sorry, Miranda. I was mistaken." His voice shook.

"Miranda McLain is my wife." The menace in Drake's voice was apparently sufficient. Jack nodded, reached for the doorknob and made his escape.

Lucy remained a moment longer. In that heartbeat of time,

Miranda understood a truth she hadn't realized before, Lucy feared her ex-husband. Her elegant, sophisticated, beautiful, younger sister had left her marriage with Drake for reasons Miranda now questioned.

"Call me when you get home," was all Lucy said as she departed.

"You bet I will," Miranda muttered to the blank door.

A hand closed on her shoulder. She whirled around and stumbled, falling into Drake's arms.

His face was a breath from hers when he said, "Tell me, Miranda. What do you want?"

His arms tightened around her, bringing her barely clad body into intimate contact with his. The slippery material of their robes transferred heat from his chest to hers. She was aware of her heart beating a rapid staccato.

Desire flamed in his eyes. Unwanted echoes surged through Miranda.

When he dipped his mouth to take her lips, all she could do was whimper in confused delight.

The wonder of it was that Drake's kiss did not repulse her. She expected revulsion; instead liquid warmth streamed through her with the stroking of his tongue against her own. Pleasure warred with will.

She felt his hand trace fire along her back. They sank together to the floor. Something warm and firm pressed against her thigh as the robe she wore fluttered open. Drake left her mouth to nibble her earlobes, first one side then the other. His hands cupped and stroked her breasts until she moaned with the delight of it.

The sound was her undoing. Miranda Symons moaning? She froze. Drake murmured something at once gentling and titillating against her stomach.

Her stomach? How had she allowed him to get that far? A rush of panic replaced lust.

"Stop. We can't. I can't." She pushed with both hands at his shoulders. "Drake," she wailed.

Abruptly, he rolled off her and faced away. For an instant he sat very still, then he stood and strode into the bathroom without glancing at her. Miranda heard the shower start.

Tears pricked her eyelids. She didn't know whether she was madder at him for kissing her, at herself for enjoying it, at herself for stopping him, or at him for stopping. What a mess. She rubbed her face briskly and climbed to her feet. Her body

CAUGHT

tingled. The robe gaped open. She shivered and scanned the room for her clothing.

Sunlight glanced at a sharper angle through the draperies. It blinked off something shiny tucked into a small shelf in the bed's headboard. Miranda pulled the drapes open and took a closer look. The sight of her clothing stuck behind the headboard distracted her from her investigation. She grabbed the wrinkled clothes and pulled them on. With a bit of physical armor, she'd be better able to face Drake and whatever else he had up his sleeve.

Relief filled her as she felt the small bi-fold wallet in the back pocket of her jeans. It hadn't fallen out. With the contents, her driver's license and a credit card, she was a free woman--if she wanted to be.

Her loafers stuck out from the lavender and red horror of a bed ruffle. With a small bounce, she sat on the edge of the bed to slide them on. Something fell from the headboard, hit the mattress beside her, and landed on the floor.

Black, compact, a tiny red light glowed on it. A hollow ache began in the pit of Miranda's stomach as she picked up the miniature video camera. She recognized it as a component of a prototype security system Drake had recently installed in specific high technology sections of the office building where they worked. Small and non-intrusive, no one would know they were being recorded, unless they knew what to look for. Of course, the employees knew. The point was to discourage stealing of technology. Drake didn't trust anyone.

Evidently, Drake had been taping them during the night. Her hands shook. The damning piece of machinery fell to the floor again.

Why? Why videotape their wedding night? She grimaced. Not much to record for posterity if her memory served. She still didn't know how she came to be wearing red satin. Okay, forget the red satin for now.

Blackmail? For some twisted reason of his own, was Drake planning to use this against her? Why? How?

Sudden silence from the bathroom propelled Miranda into action. She grabbed the camera, took one last look around her honeymoon suite, and quietly left. If Drake was interested enough to follow, then he would. Damn the man.

Tears threatened once again as she hailed a cab from the heat of the Vegas sidewalk.

"The airport, and hurry," she told the driver.

With the camera in her hands, she willed away tears. This was her time to take action. Right now she wanted nothing more than to be home in her cozy apartment and think. She had a lot to consider before she saw Drake again.

* * * *

Drake gritted his teeth and spun the steering wheel of his forest green SUV. Snow treads gripped the slushy goo covering the street. The vehicle spurted mushy cold stuff into the air as he sped into the parking lot of Miranda's apartment complex.

He hated snow. For the tenth time that day, he cursed the weather, the season, and the reason he was out in it in the first place.

Miranda.

The change from the comparative warmth of Las Vegas to the bright frigid air here in Colorado Springs added to his irritation. If she hadn't run out on him, they'd be on their way to Bermuda or Jamaica by now.

The cheerful voice of the radio announcer said, "Highs today in the mid-twenties, with a wind chill of minus five."

Drake stabbed at the off button and came within inches of crashing into Miranda's car. The happy fire engine red color perversely irritated Drake even more. His foot slid into a pile of unmelted snow as he stepped from his car. To add insult to injury, Miranda stepped out of her apartment in time to witness his discomfort.

A huge, four-legged form followed her. It stopped and sniffed at the air, and then fixed it's gaze directly onto Drake. Drake imagined it came right out of the Sherlock Holmes tale, "The Hound of the Baskervilles." With a straight-from-Hell growling bark combination, the beast hurled itself at Drake.

"Pumpkin," Miranda called out. The animal dragged her a couple of steps before the leash sprang from her hands.

Snow flew as Pumpkin ignored the shoveled walks and made straight for Drake.

Drake had a fraction of a second to wonder why this gray spotted beast was named "Pumpkin." Six inches of icy slush encased his foot. The weight of his own body held the car door shut. There was nowhere to run.

Don't wimp out in front of Miranda. He was sure this would be his last conscious thought.

At the final second, he straightened his back and shut his eyes. Braced for death, or at the very least, dismemberment.

Instead of teeth and claws, Drake shuddered as a heavy weight

CAUGHT

hit his chest. The car did an admirable job of holding him up.

He opened one eye. Loud, raspy panting accompanied the grinning canine that stared into Drake's face. Panic subsided, or at least the fear of tragic death. Suffocation was a more definite possibility now. The combination of dog food breath and constant pressure on his chest made breathing a challenge.

Abruptly, Pumpkin's face and body retreated. Drake allowed his knees to bend a fraction, and then Miranda's face replaced the dog's. The dog had looked friendlier. A frown creased his "wife's" forehead.

"You," she sputtered.

Clearly she was overcome with emotion. Drake tried a smile. He'd been told he had a charming smile.

"Hi, Honey. I'm home."

His foot was beginning to petrify with cold.

Miranda's eyebrows turned into jet-black wings as they rose into the empty space where the frown had been. Surprise looked good on her, Drake thought, along with the pink pursed lips and cheeks rosy from cold and temper.

"Go away," she sputtered some more. "I have nothing to say to you." She turned and jerked Pumpkin from his interested sniffing of the tires of Drake's car. Then, with casual indifference, the dog lifted his leg, as dogs will do, before moving off.

"Miranda, wait a minute." Drake tugged at his numb foot. The shoe remained stuck while his gray argyle sock, limp and wet, emerged. Miranda kept walking, fast. The dog strode regally beside her. The matching sway of their respective bottoms caught Drake's interest, and then he realized she was getting away before he had a chance to say his piece.

He reached down, tugged his slush-filled Italian leather loafer from the gushy stuff and winced as he jammed his foot back in. Limping down the slick sidewalk, he struggled to catch up with Miranda and the wing-footed creature.

A ground-level door opened as Drake hobbled by. A large, bald man, with the biceps of an ex-prize fighter bulging from a sleeveless tee shirt stepped through. His head turned from Miranda to Drake back to Miranda.

"Hey, Miranda," the mountain called. "Is this guy bothering you?"

Miranda turned and began walking backwards. Drake was impressed at the speed she maintained. She opened her mouth, but was pre-empted by a warbling voice.

"Miranda, honey, is everything okay?"

Drake jerked his head for the source of the tinny sound. An older woman, a handful of mail in one hand, a wooden cane in the other, crossed the parking lot towards Drake.

Making speed backwards, Miranda called out, "Yes, he is bothering me, Ted. I'm okay, Mrs. Whitman." With a small wave and an evil grin she turned and moved up to jogging speed.

Puffing with exertion, Drake slowed, then stopped. He had to. Mrs. Whitman had crossed his path and remained in the center of it. The man, this Ted guy, was closing in from behind. One turkey-sized hand slapped a rolled up newspaper against a thigh that would rival the thickness of a California redwood.

Mrs. Whitman shook her cane at Drake. "Who are you? Some kind of pervert or something?"

"No, ma'am." Drake tried out his charming smile on her. Her frowning face relaxed fractionally. He smiled wider. "We had a disagreement. You know, a lover's spat." He winked at her.

"You don't say." Mrs. Whitman tapped one combat booted foot against the cement.

"Yeah, you don't say." Ted's deep voice reverberated through the back of Drake's skull.

Drake's smile faded as he turned to face the barrel chest of Miranda's gladiator. Charm--this guy probably didn't understand the meaning of the word. He stood as straight as he could, trying to reach chin level of this giant.

"Actually, Miranda and I were married over the weekend." He tried backing away, but a snow bank stopped his progress. "We argued about where we would live. You know, I wanted to live at my place, she wanted to stay here." He spread his hands wide and gave them both what he hoped was sincere chagrin.

Ted stopped swatting his leg with the paper. Drake noticed it was "The Wall Street Journal." So much for his illiterate tree theory.

"Miranda didn't say anything about getting married." Ted turned to Mrs. Whitman. "She mention it to you, Alice?"

Mrs. Whitman raised an eyebrow and tapped her cane. After frozen seconds, she said, "Well, no, Ted. I don't believe she did."

"Didn't think so." Ted loomed closer to Drake. "Mister, we have laws about harassing people around here. You better leave. Now."

Mrs. Whitman tapped close enough to jab Drake in the chest with her cane. "Might be a good idea for you to listen to him." She leaned over and whispered, "Ted has a thing for Miranda. You wouldn't want to make him mad, now would you?"

Stuck between a rock and frozen snow, Drake conceded defeat. Temporary, but defeat all the same. It grated. He pulled together what little dignity remained and bid his farewell committee good-bye.

It didn't help one bit that Miranda and her beast turned the corner to re-enter the parking area as Drake spun out. Nor did the grin on her face or spring in her step go unnoticed. It merely added fuel to the fire that burned within him. The flame that told him he'd misjudged the woman. She was more than the corporate sum of parts he was used to.

And he wanted her.

Chapter Three

One small, sweet victory. Miranda savored the furious expression on Drake's face as he careened from the parking lot. Then her gaze found Ted and Alice Whitman standing together at her own apartment door, arms folded identically across anything but identical chests. It was clear they were awaiting her--and an explanation.

She breathed deep, enjoying the bite of frigid air. "Come on, Pumpkin. Guess it's time to face the music." The part Greyhound, part Saint Bernard responded to her gentle tug with his curiously graceful gait.

"Thanks, Ted, Alice, for getting rid of that weirdo for me." Miranda unlocked her apartment door and motioned her neighbors to precede her inside.

"That 'weirdo' claims to be your husband," Ted growled, not at all his usual calm self.

Alice settled into a flowered chintz armchair as if she belonged there. "Yes, dear. I realize your personal life is, well, personal, but maybe you could tell us something so we won't worry if he shows up again."

Miranda busied herself in the tiny kitchen on the opposite side of the counter. She filled a kettle with water and put it on the stove to heat for tea before venturing an answer. What could she say? The truth was embarrassing, humiliating even. Lying was out of the question.

Ted paced the length of her tiny living room. Alice waited with her usual patience, hands folded in her lap. These people were more than neighbors--they were her friends. With the exception of Lucy, they were the only family she had.

"It's kind of complicated," she said. She brought the tray to the coffee table and convinced Ted to sit down.

"Got nothing but time," Ted said. The porcelain teacup looked tiny in his massive hand.

Alice picked up her usual mug. It sported "Take No Prisoners" inscribed across it. She sniffed at the rising steam. "Earl Grey, my favorite."

Miranda hesitated. May as well just get it over with. "Jack called off our engagement yesterday. I drank too much and went to Las Vegas with Drake McLain and married him."

She desperately wished she'd spiked the tea.

Ted snapped his cup into the saucer so hard the delicate handle came off in his hand. It circled his index finger like a mutant ring. "I'll kill him," he rumbled.

"Which one? The ex-fiancé or the new husband?" Alice asked. "Honestly, Miranda, I never knew what you saw in that Jack person anyway. Weak chin."

Ted cracked his knuckles, a habit that set Miranda's teeth on edge. "Have a cookie, Ted." She shoved the plate into his hands.

He looked at her, the pain in his big eyes startling and hot. "If he ever hurts you in any way I'll take care of him." Without another word, Ted left. Awkward silence filled the turbulence of his wake.

Miranda dropped to the floor next to Pumpkin. The beast put his head in her lap and rubbed against her hand. He always knew when Miranda was hurting. She scratched behind his silky ears, comforting herself with the familiar.

The intensity of Ted's emotion made her feel small. "How long has Ted felt this way about me?" she asked Alice after a long stretch.

"Oh, quite a while now. He'll get over it. Every time you broke an engagement, he thought he'd have a chance. Now that you're married, well, he needs time to get used to the idea."

"Married." Miranda snorted. "I'm not used to the idea myself. The fact of the matter is," she felt heat creeping up her neck, "we never consummated the marriage. At least, I don't think we did."

"Seems to me that's something a woman would know," Alice remarked.

"I was a little out of it," Miranda muttered.

"Do you mean to tell me you don't want to be married to Drake?"

"I despise him. He made my sister's life a misery when he was married to her. Why should I expect different treatment?"

"The plot thickens," Alice said, eyes twinkling in the cool winter light coming through the window. "So, it's Drake the Devil you find yourself married to. Something tells me you haven't told the whole story yet."

The urge to confide in someone she trusted fought with her need for privacy. She fiddled with Pumpkin's ears. "There's this." She stood and went to her desk. "Look." She handed Alice the video camera.

Alice turned it over in her hands. "Looks like an improved version of Mitiko's latest surveillance camera." Her voice was now crisp, authoritative. She'd spent her working years with Air Force intelligence. Since retirement, she'd hid her sharp wit and keen intellect behind the "little old lady" facade. She enjoyed the surprise on people's faces when they found out about her earlier James Bond lifestyle. At least, those she chose to tell.

"Where did you find it?" Alice asked. She pushed a tiny switch. An inch sized laser disc popped out.

"Hidden in our honeymoon suite. And yes, you're right. It's the prototype camera Drake's been installing in our classified technology facility."

Alice cackled. "He videotaped your wedding night?"

"I don't think it's very funny."

"No, I'm sorry." Alice picked up her mug again. "Why?"

Miranda finished the question. "Video our wedding night? Beats me. I've been trying to figure that out since I left him in Las Vegas."

Alice tapped her chin. "I wonder if it could be --"

Rapid pounding on the door interrupted her.

"Who could that be?" Miranda turned the doorknob. She stumbled forward as Drake jerked the door open all the way.

"Thank you," he said, though Miranda plowing into him muffled the formality.

The way her body vibrated at the inopportune touch of his hands on her shoulders, steadying her, had her pushing him away.

"Let go of me." She may have pushed, but if anything his grip tightened.

"Not until you agree to talk to me." Drake's lips were compressed into tight lines, his eyes obsidian cold.

"I hate you," Miranda managed to say. "Come in." He released her and she stumbled back.

Alice stood and gathered her coat around her, but not before Miranda saw her hide the camera within the heavy folds of leopard print cloth. The idea that Alice would be working to figure out the contents and intents of the recording offered Miranda a huge shot of encouragement.

"You know," Alice remarked as she headed for the door, "communication is the foundation of all happy marriages." She sent her best "little old lady" smile at Miranda and Drake and tottered through the door, closing it behind her.

"At last, someone I agree with," Drake grumbled.

He rolled his shoulders as Miranda had often seen him do in the boardroom after winning a subtle point in a contractual dispute. Good, if he thought he had the advantage she'd make use of his overconfidence. Maybe play with it just a little, and then go for the jugular.

Oh, yeah.

"There's hot tea. Would you like a cup?" Her best hostess voice served her well.

Drake raised an eyebrow, and then pulled off his still soggy shoe. "Thank you."

"Cream and sugar?" Or perhaps a dash of arsenic?

"Both, thanks." He took the offered mug, which was decorated with silly, colorful cartoon figures, and the slogan "Time to Play" printed in huge ballooning letters.

Miranda sat across the coffee table from him and took his measure. Strain that might be simply fatigue was evident in the lines around his lips. He hadn't changed clothes. Hadn't taken the time to do more than find a place to turn his car. Her plan to play "cat and mouse" fizzled in the face of his presence and her own curiosity.

"Why did you come back?" she asked, her voice quiet.

"As your neighbor so correctly said, we need to talk."

Miranda shook her head. "We need to do more than talk."

"Oh?" His eyes lit when he smiled. Something deep inside Miranda did a slow somersault. She found she needed to take a deep, calming breath before continuing.

"First of all, I want an annulment. Then, I want to know why you married me to begin with."

"Most women would want the question answered before taking such drastic action."

She leaned back and folded her arms across her chest. "I'm not most women."

"So I've heard." He mimicked her pose. "I understand you've

CAUGHT

been engaged three times. Seems to me you'd be overjoyed to finally get through the marriage ceremony without your groom running away."

The unexpected attack brought Miranda to her feet. His words pierced the vulnerable spot in her heart until she was sure he could see the blood seeping out. "Get out," she ordered.

"I'm quite comfortable right where I am. Now, lets talk about theft. Where is it?"

"I don't know what you're talking about." She clamped her teeth so tightly together that her jaw ached. Making the words come through clenched lips was an agony. She tried to un-ball the fists her hands had become. The trembling in her knees forced her to fight for control.

"We can play that game if you want to. Anyway," he leaned forward, "as long as we're married, it's not really theft. After all, what's mine is yours."

"Quit talking in riddles, McLain." Maybe he'd let something, some reason for the hidden camera, spill.

She's stalling. Drake recognized the brushing-back-the-hair motion as one used at work when she hadn't decided the best course of action. How far could he push her?

"A small video camera is missing. It was a prototype; used mini-disc technology. I had it with me when we checked into the hotel in Las Vegas. I discovered it was missing after I also discovered my brand new bride had deserted me." He leaned back and sipped at his now tepid tea. "I imagine you'd draw the same conclusion as to where it went."

"Why take something so valuable on a personal trip?"

Drake shrugged. "To try it out. I thought we might like pictures of our honeymoon to show the kiddies some day."

Direct hit. Drake watched a pink flush creep up Miranda's neck until it disappeared into her hairline. She'd found it all right, and in that damning place pointing at the bed.

"We're not going to have children. I refuse to continue this marriage. In fact," she narrowed her eyes, "I haven't any proof that we are married."

"Would a signed certificate do?" He pulled an official looking document from his jacket pocket. "How about a photo of us, the happy couple?" The hideous picture showed more of the fake official than Drake or Miranda. Just as well. Drake watched Miranda pale as she looked at the documents. In the picture, Miranda's eyes were half closed and she had a sappy smile on her face.

She wasn't smiling now. "Why? I don't understand why you would want to maintain a marriage to a person who despises you."

"I decided we need each other. With your credentials and my business sense we can take the market by storm. When the possibility presented itself to make it a family business, it seemed like a good idea."

"You don't understand," Miranda shouted. "I hate you."

"Love and hate, two strong emotions. I've heard one is close to the other, almost interchangeable depending on the circumstances. Besides, your affection is unnecessary. All I need is your cooperation for the next four weeks."

"An arbitrary length of time. What's happening in the next four weeks that you need me as your wife?"

"Payback."

"I need more information."

"At the end of four weeks, if you still want it, I'll give you a divorce." Time to bargain a bit, let her think she had some maneuvering room.

Miranda paced again. When she stopped, her face was carefully devoid of expression. "Not good enough. I don't need your cooperation to get a divorce. I could go back to Nevada tonight and take care of it. Tell me more."

"You've forgotten, you might be pregnant. A month is enough time to know about that as well."

"I haven't forgotten anything," Miranda snarled. "I just don't believe you."

"Your belief in me is the last of my concerns. Now, do you agree to the month?"

"I want it in writing; signed by a credible witness," Miranda said. She dropped into a chair.

Drake allowed himself a small, internal shout of glee. The first part of his plan was in action. "One witness, whom we can both trust to keep the details of the arrangement secret." He nodded. "Okay."

"Alice will do it."

"You mean Grandma Moses?"

Miranda glared at him. "Don't make fun of my friends."

"Sorry." He considered her suggestion, could find nothing wrong with it. Certainly a friend of Miranda's would be more concerned about her reputation than his own reasons for the secrecy. "Alice will do fine."

Miranda jumped up and grabbed a yellow legal pad from the

counter. She began to write with a thick purple pen that Drake was sure had never seen the inside of her briefcase.

When she finished writing she thrust the pad at him and said, "Look this over while I get Alice."

"Delighted," he said to her back.

He read the short paragraph. It may have been written in purple ink, but the commas and dotted I's were in all the right places. Miranda agreed to maintain her marriage to Drake for thirty days from this date. At that time either party had the option of getting a no-contest divorce unless Miranda found herself pregnant. In that eventuality the contract would be revised.

Keeping a high tech business afloat was a never-ending challenge, Drake mused. He never thought he'd need the inconvenience of marriage in order to remain solvent. His expression hardened and his hands gripped the paper so tightly it rustled.

The fact that this move would have been unnecessary if Lucy and Jack hadn't conspired to buy out small stockowners here and there, grated on him. He wondered how long the pair had planned to undercut him. The day he'd found Jack's memo, unwittingly sent to Drake instead of to Lucy's private e-mail account, was the day Drake decided revenge might be best served cold but he wanted something hot as a side dish.

Miranda was the perfect foil. Sister to one conspirator, ex-lover of the other, he could use her to bring them both down. If he lost her in the process, so be it.

A stab of conscience grazed him as Miranda returned with Alice. According to his in-depth and discrete investigation, Miranda had no idea of the extent Lucy was mired in debt, or how she planned to get herself out of it. Miranda made an unlikely pawn. Pawns, often underrated in the game of chess, just as often proved the winning piece. He planned to have the piece on his side when the last move was made.

"Here's the agreement I told you about," Miranda said to Alice as she plucked the pad from Drake's hands.

Alice placed a pair of wire-framed glasses on the bridge of her nose and took the pad to the window where the wintry sun shone through. Miranda tapped her foot. Drake sipped his cold tea.

When Alice finally turned back to the room, a small frown joined the myriad lines on her forehead. She tapped at the paper with a finger. "This will never stand up in a court of law. I suppose you both understand that?"

"Sure it will," Drake said. "It's a personal agreement, not a business one. No one is pressuring anyone to sign."

Alice ignored him and focused on Miranda. "At least put in a line about not taking anything out that you didn't bring in, dear. You didn't sign any kind of pre-nuptial agreement, I suppose?"

Miranda rubbed her nose. "Not that I remember."

Alice hesitated a moment longer, then wrote another sentence on the paper. She then signed it. "Here, I've made a small change. About the best that can be done if neither of you want to use a lawyer for this thing."

"Thanks, Alice." Miranda held the pen in her hand, point poised over the sheet. With a grimace, she affixed her signature to it then pushed the document to Drake. He signed and dated it as well, then stood, folded it and put it into his pocket.

"Hey, I want a copy of that. Alice should have one too," Miranda protested.

"I'll do it at the office tomorrow," Drake soothed. "Now get your things and let's go home." He couldn't wait for a glass of brandy. Now that his reason for being here was accomplished he was twice as cold as when he first walked in.

"I'm not going anywhere," Miranda insisted.

"You agreed to maintain our marriage. That implied cohabitation."

"I intend to cohabitate right here," Miranda stated. She folded her arms across her chest and lifted her chin.

"Another little spat," Alice said with a sigh. "I'll leave you to work this out. Just remember that compromise is the basis of a sound marriage." She patted Miranda's cheek and left.

"You can't believe for an instant that I'll live here?" Drake demanded. He looked around him, for the first time taking in the cozy living area, tinier kitchen and the door that must lead to the bedroom. "We'll be in each other's way every second. You can afford a bigger place on the salary I pay you."

"How I spend my money is none of your business," Miranda shot back. "I've agreed to your silly marriage solely because I'm unsure of what really happened on our so-called wedding night. I refuse to uproot myself further so as not to inconvenience you. I'm staying here. What you choose to do about it is your business." By the time she finished, her voice had risen to a shout.

Moving closer and keeping his voice soft, Drake said, "It seems compromise would be a good idea."

She trembled but didn't back away. Were those unshed tears glistening in her eyes? She turned away before he could be sure.

"This is home," Miranda insisted, her voice tight with emotions that Drake couldn't begin to understand. For some reason he couldn't put a finger on, he wanted to understand.

The Miranda of the boardroom was gone, leaving this fragile, vulnerable woman in her place. A woman Drake uneasily understood that he wanted to know better--better than the Miranda who worked with such professional efficiency. This woman lived in a small, one bedroom apartment when she could easily afford an elegant condominium. Plants vied for window space, framed pictures glinted from every surface, and fat pillows took up space on the couches and chairs. That dog looked at home in the middle of the braided rug.

This was a woman secure in her home. If he wanted her cooperation, he'd better give in a little. Besides, he liked it here. The observation surprised him. He tamped down the warm emotion and turned Miranda to face him. Her swollen lips trembled, but the look in her eyes undid him. Glaring and strong, yet at the same time huge and entreating.

He was her husband, sort of. Perhaps he should take a moment to remind both of them of that quasi fact.

The expression on her face turned to panic as he touched her lips with his. Sweet, she tasted soft and hot and sweet, Drake mused.

He delved deeper, holding her arms against him to keep her from pulling away. She gasped. He took it as an encouraging sign until a hard hand descended on the back of his neck and yanked him away.

"I think it's time you left, mister," the behemoth snarled. He spun Drake around and out the door before anyone else had a chance to speak.

Wow, Drake thought, you really do see stars before you pass out.

Chapter Four

"Tough weekend, boss?" Nicole asked.

Drake ignored his executive assistant's question. An echo of a headache throbbed from the bruise on the back of his head. He was glad Miranda had a protector in Ted; he just wished Ted didn't feel the need to protect her from *him*.

"Make these changes to my personnel records, please. Fax the change in beneficiary to my insurance company today." He tossed Nicole the address and telephone number changes then angled away, keeping her face in the corner of his eye to judge her reaction.

Her double take followed by a tiny gasp gratified his warped sense of humor. The news would be around the building within minutes of him entering his private office. No need to send out a staff memo. Nicole's efficient use of e-mail, fax, and telephone would get the job done in half the time.

Whistling, Drake sauntered into his office and shut the door. He mentally ticked off the "get the news to the office staff" memo on his virtual priority list. That should shake up a few people around here. Maybe flush out just the person he wanted--whoever had been working with Jack.

* * * *

In Miranda's department a floor below the executive level, a rising and falling wave of excited voices filled the vast room. Only "pod" dividers broke up the sound. As she entered, heads popped up and down past the orange and blue dividers. An even more remarkable silence replaced the babble.

Miranda narrowed her eyes and strode into her office. Kevin, her assistant, stood just inside with a mug of her favorite hot coffee in one hand, a stack of papers in the other, and a curious gleam in his young brown eyes.

"Thanks." Miranda took the coffee and papers to her desk.

Kevin shut the door and waited.

She flipped through the stack of memos and hoped he'd go away. Nope, still there. Rats, she'd have to tell him something.

"I supposed you've heard the news?"

"I heard a rumor. Any truth to it?"

Miranda sighed and waved him to a chair. Though only twenty-three years old, Kevin had been with her long enough to know she could count on his reticence. He wouldn't betray a confidence.

"Tell me what's going around," she invited.

"Scuttlebutt is that you eloped with the boss."

"Eloped," Miranda repeated. "That's too romantic a term for what happened."

Kevin leaned forward. A frown marred his handsome features. His hands clenched the arms of the chair. "He didn't hurt you, did he? I don't care if he is the boss. If he laid one finger on you, I swear I'll—"

Miranda held up a hand to stop his sputtering. His defense of her was touching, but under the circumstances, embarrassing. "He didn't hurt me, Kevin. It's true, we are married, but only for a little while."

"Why? I thought you hated the guy." His nostrils flared as he leaned back in the chair.

Heat rushed to Miranda's face. She turned to the window hoping he couldn't see her flush. "I suppose you heard what happened with Jack?"

"The broken engagement?" Kevin's voice gentled behind her. "I never liked him, anyway."

A feeble laugh escaped Miranda's lips as she watched fleecy clouds speed across the winter-blue sky. "I thought I liked him enough to marry him, and that he felt the same about me. We all thought wrong." She turned back to the room and flashed what she hoped was a reassuring smile at the young man. "To tell the truth, I'm relieved that the engagement is over. Did you ever notice that Jack is a chinless wonder?"

"So, you're okay with that?"

"What, his weak chin? I could care less."

"I mean that rumors are going around that Jack is already involved with someone else."

Cold fingers traced across Miranda's neck. She sank into her chair before her knees gave out. Good thing she'd drained her coffee mug, otherwise the thud she gave it would have spilled what was left. She rubbed the tight spot between her eyes. "You listen to too many rumors." A lame try at humor, but the pained expression on Kevin's face told her this was yet another rumor that was all too true.

"My sources are pretty accurate." Kevin's voice both sympathized and implied a question.

Miranda made a quick decision. "Don't tell me who your sources are. I don't have the time or energy right now to deal with it."

Kevin leaned his hands against her desk. His dark eyes searched hers as if trying to decipher her mood, trying to decide how far he could stretch the comfort of their working relationship. After a moment, he straightened and stepped back.

"Sure, boss. Whatever you say. Would you like me to send a formal memo to your staff stating your new name and position?" His voice became the brisk, efficient one of the man she relied on to keep the office running smoothly.

The last part of his statement caught in her mind. "New position?"

"According to my source, not only did you marry McLain, a promotion to Vice President of Acquisitions is yours as well. Congratulations. Looks like you're moving upstairs." With an almost military crispness, he turned and left the room.

As soon as the door closed behind him, Miranda picked up the phone. How dare Drake promote her without her permission? She punched the numbers that would put her through to his office. What was he thinking?

"Mr. McLain's office. This is Nicole. How may I—"

Miranda cut her off. "This is Miranda Symons. Put me through to him."

A full three seconds of dead air vibrated across the telephone line before Nicole said, "I'm sorry, Mrs. McLain. Mr. McLain is unavailable at the moment."

"Tell him I need to talk to him as soon as he becomes … available," Miranda snapped.

The minute she returned the phone to its cradle she regretted being so irritable to Nicole. After all, it wasn't Nicole's fault if McLain was busy. But, what if he'd told Nicole to tell Miranda that so that he wouldn't have to talk to her?

"Arrogant, son-of-a –" She stalked across the room. If the mountain wouldn't come to her, she'd take herself to him.

She got as far as the door before she realized what she was doing—giving him the advantage. The action of seeking him out rather than waiting for him to come to her implied need. Or at least, she considered, his arrogance would interpret it as such.

Her hand twitched on the doorknob. No. She added up the scores, his and hers. The marriage itself, his. The consummation, she grimaced. His, if that videodisk offered proof. Living arrangements, at last a point in her favor. She smiled at the vision he'd presented just that morning. Sprawled across her living room couch because she refused him her bed, he'd been distractingly sexy …. Until Pumpkin had licked Drake's chin. His expression of wide-eyed horror had brought another giggle to her throat.

She relaxed her shoulders as she strolled back to her desk. Letting the office know before she had a chance to break the news was a non-issue, no points. The people they worked with would have to know sooner rather than later.

So far, Drake led two to one. Time to get busy.

"Kevin," she called into the intercom. "Let's get to work."

She'd start by ordering that new stationary and making sure accounting knew about her promotion. It may not be permanent, but she intended to make as much use of it as she could. An office on the penthouse level ... that had a nice ring to it.

Kevin entered, folders and steno pad in his arms. Miranda rubbed her hands together and grinned at him. "Let's look at those samples; after that, get me the manager of space in the executive suite. You and I are moving up."

Kevin hesitated for just a second, and then sat in his usual chair. He gave her a small salute. "Whatever you say, boss."

Several hours later, Miranda rubbed the back of her neck. Boxes and papers covered her desk and the surrounding floor. Moving the contents of her office was proving to be more of a headache than she had anticipated. More so when it coincided with juggling phone calls, faxes, and personal visits of congratulations.

Flowers from business associates held sway on the credenza. She'd have to hold a moratorium on accepting any more until she moved. Flat surfaces were at a premium.

Compound that with interviewing the several people in her division she thought deserving of the promotion to her current office, and keeping business going as usual .... No wonder she pulsed from her head to her toes.

She closed her eyes and wondered if it was too soon for another couple of ibuprofen. She heard the door open behind her; it rustled as it brushed against cardboard boxes.

Without opening her eyes, Miranda said, "Kevin, why don't you go to lunch. Bring me back soup and a bagel, please."

Strong hands stroked her shoulders, caressed her back.

"Stop it, Kev–" She spun around, tripping on slippery packing paper. Drake's devilish grin caught her off-guard. She promptly fell to the floor.

Drake knelt to offer her a hand. His eyes glittered. "Does Kevin make a habit of massaging his boss' back?"

"Don't be an idiot." Miranda brushed off her skirt. Her blouse was askew; she knew her hair was a mess.

"I'm thinking that you should leave him here to help the new department chair. You can hire someone new when you move upstairs."

"No way. Kevin comes with me." She glared at him. "What do you want?"

He folded his arms, tightening the fabric of the well-fitted suit across his shoulders. "I want a lot of things, but I'll settle for lunch with you."

Miranda moved back to the relative safety of her desk. She waved at the chaos surrounding her. His suggestion made her snicker. "You're kidding, right? I've got a full day even without the moving hassle you forced me into."

"Forced?" Drake raised an eyebrow. "I didn't hear you object. As a matter of fact, I've spent the past hour with my space guy upstairs shuffling offices and executives in order to accommodate you."

"You want to give me a promotion just because I wear you name, then you have to be prepared for an inconvenience or two."

"You have assured my 'inconvenience' on several counts. Now, how about lunch?"

He strode towards her. The movement would have been much more forceful, Miranda admitted, if he hadn't had to skirt boxes and paper every half step. She sat on the edge of her desk swinging one leg and wondering about her next move. His apparent pique had to be from more than just her piddley little move upstairs.

A frisson ran up her spine. The sensation set the small hairs on the back of her neck on end. The fact that she hated him had nothing to do with how he made her feel. Fragile, needy, emotions and feelings that were out of character with the image she sought to project at work. She'd never be able to keep up with the competition if she allowed him to see her vulnerability.

When he reached her, she lifted her chin. "Sorry, Drake. As I said, I've got too much to do. Look around. I'd be shirking my responsibility if I just left."

He stood close, too close. Her foot brushed his pants with an intimate swish each time it swung out and back. He leaned in. Her nostril quivered with the scent of him, pine and musk and, she stifled a giggle, dog.

"You're a vice president now. Hire this chore out and come to lunch with me."

His voice gentled as it twined through her. His mouth, a bare whisper away, the warmth of his breath touched her lips when he spoke.

She couldn't help leaning closer. Mesmerized and hating herself for allowing the temptation, she put her hands against the broad expanse of his chest.

"I ... I can't," she gasped.

"You can." His mouth captured hers in a brief, heat-seared kiss. She trembled as he straightened. His eyes, she couldn't meet his eyes. Could not let him see how hatred warred with lust within her. Because it couldn't be anything more than lust, this heat that shot through her each time he closed the distance between them.

"Well?" His voice cooled.

Kevin answered from behind Drake, where Miranda couldn't see him. "Phone call for Ms. Symons, I mean for Mrs. McLain."

Miranda strove to keep her voice cool, businesslike, but the sounds came out uneven, like an adolescent boy whose voice was changing. "I told you, not unless it was important, Kevin."

She struggled to find a clear path around Drake. He didn't budge, making her want to shove him out of her way. Except she didn't dare touch him for fear of the reaction he caused in her.

Kevin persisted. "She said her name is Alice and that you would want to talk with her."

"Alice?" Drake looked from Miranda to Kevin.

"Alice?" Miranda echoed. There was only one reason Alice would call her at work. She flashed Kevin a grin. "Thank you, Kevin. I'll take the call. Why don't you go have lunch now."

He left the room, closing the door with a discrete thud.

Miranda forged a path back to her desk and picked up the phone. She kept her back to Drake as she listened to Alice's dry voice.

"I've borrowed a video disk player, Miranda. You'd better come have a look as soon as possible. I suggest you leave your husband out of it for now."

Miranda kept the anticipation out of her voice. "I'll be there in fifteen minutes."

"Let me guess," Drake drawled, ice replacing fire in his eyes. "She managed to find a disk reader. Did she tell you what it showed?"

"I'll let you know." Miranda grabbed her purse, slung her coat across her shoulders.

Drake stepped into her path. "You mean you're going to leave in the middle of this chaos?" Sarcasm dripped from his voice.

Miranda waved a hand. "Of course. I'll just leave word for Kevin to hire movers for the job. That's what vice presidents do, isn't it?"

"I'm coming with you."

On her guard, Miranda made a darting motion around him. The cramped space was to his advantage. She could not get by unless he wanted her to.

"No. I don't want you with me when I watch this." She kept her voice firm but felt her chin tremble.

"Why not? I think it would be fun."

Anger flared through her. "I think it would be a travesty of what a wedding night should be." Her words sliced the air between them. Hurt and embarrassment were sure to be pictured on the video. The last thing she needed was Drake watching her every reaction as she viewed him seducing her. She was done being humiliated by Drake McLain.

"Sorry you feel that way, darling. I remember it much differently."

She gritted her teeth. "Get out of my way." If she didn't get away from him soon she was either going to scream or cry or hit him. None of those actions would do anything but amuse him and lose points for her.

Drake opened his mouth again, but a hammering at the door followed by Nicole and a flood of other employees stopped his response.

Nicole, breathless, managed to gasp, "Mr. McLain, all the internal communications in this part of the building are dead. We can't find Mr. Beardsly."

Beardsly was the chief of internal communications. The phones, intercoms, everything must be down for Nicole to rush in like this.

Miranda took advantage of the opportunity.

"You'd better go clean up this little emergency, dear," she cooed at Drake. "I'll be waiting at home." She waded as gracefully as possible through the stuff on the floor.

"Miranda," Drake growled.

Miranda turned in the doorway and flashed him her best sultry smile. Employees stared at their bosses.

"Don't be late." She winked then made her escape.

* * * *

Fifteen minutes later she sat on the leather sofa in Alice's neat apartment clenching her nervous hands together. Alice fiddled with some fancy electronic equipment she'd placed on top of her television set. Wires snaked from the video camera Miranda had taken from her "honeymoon suite" to the box on the TV.

"Did you watch it already?" she asked as Alice came to sit beside her.

"Just enough to see that it had recorded something. I thought you'd better be with me. Just in case there's company business on here, not just Drake's monkey business."

Miranda felt her face flame. For some reason the whole situation took on a tragi-comic color. She laughed and relaxed. "Thanks, Alice."

Alice gripped one of Miranda's hands. "It's what friends are for, dear. Now." She pressed a button on the remote.

Chapter Five

White, black, and gray visual static filled the television screen. The scratch of electronic white noise rustled from the speakers. She blinked, and as if the camera blinked with her, the screen snapped to a wide-angle view of a bedroom. The round bed and garish colors matched the hotel room in Las Vegas where Miranda had awoken from her "wedding night."

The camera angle looked down on the bed from behind where the pillows would be. It encompassed a clear view of the two doors, one leading to the corridor, the other to the bathroom.

The picture blinked again. Now Miranda saw the door to the corridor open. Drake, carrying a large bundle, walked into the room. Toga Boy, or his twin brother, followed with a single small suitcase. He kept glancing at the bundle in Drake's arms. Miranda looked closer. She gasped. The bundle was her.

"Are you sure she doesn't need a doctor?" Toga Boy's voice came through high and thin.

Drake deposited the sleeping Miranda on the bed with a care that made the watching Miranda swallow hard. "My bride overindulged in champagne. Don't give it another thought." He reached into his pocket then handed the boy what Miranda assumed was a tip.

"Yes, sir. Congratulations, sir. Thank you, sir."

A big tip.

Toga Boy handed Drake a key card and exited.

Miranda watched Drake turn the extra locks on the door home. A fierce jitterbug commenced in her stomach as he approached the figure on the bed.

Here it comes.

He loosened his tie with slow, thoughtful movements, all the while staring at Miranda's unconscious figure. Then, for a brief instant, it appeared that he looked directly into her eyes. His intense stare unnerved her. It wasn't until he moved closer and reached out a hand that Miranda realized he was checking the camera.

The breath she had held sighed out of her. Alice patted her hand. "Would you like me to leave for the next few minutes?"

Mutely, Miranda handed Alice the key to her apartment. She kept her gaze fixed on the screen.

"Call me when you're done." Alice left Miranda alone with recorded history.

She froze the video as soon as Alice left. The screen showed Drake's face with startling clarity. She could even see that he needed a shave. She shivered and placed the remote onto the tabletop with a snap.

Despite the below zero wind chill outside, a trickle of sweat tickled the valley between her breasts. Dread rocked her. What if it was true? If they had made love and conceived a child, life as she knew it was over.

The next few minutes would drive the course of the next month, maybe the rest of her life. Drake's steady gaze from the screen mocked her. Its cool, unemotional stare dared her to go on, to learn the truth.

Fine. Leaning forward so as not to miss anything, Miranda clicked on the play button.

Nothing changed. For a second she wondered if she'd pressed the correct button. Then Drake blinked and backed away. She saw him look down at her image on the bed. Amazement filled her as she watched his expression soften. Maybe she imagined that part, because the next thing he did was pull that damned red satin thing out of a bag.

She wanted to turn away, shield her eyes, anything, but a perverse fascination held her transfixed. Her hands trembled causing her to drop the remote. She left it on the floor, unable to take her eyes from the screen for even the second it would take to pick up the small rectangle of plastic.

Holding her breath Miranda watched Drake peel away the clothes of the Miranda who lay unconscious on the hotel bed. It was not the slowness preceding seduction, though. He did it with a care and gentleness that she would not have believed possible if she hadn't seen it herself.

Respect. Miranda perceived a measure of that emotion as Drake finished the job. His hands hadn't roamed over her breasts or bared any part of her without a degree of modesty she never had fathomed in the man.

After he finished changing her, he went into the bathroom for a time. When he came out Miranda held her breath. His nudity showcased a brash, masculine form she'd always seen encased in business attire. Averting her eyes was the natural response from years of seeing him as her boss, then as her sister's husband. She fought it. As she did, the perspiration on her body chilled making her shiver.

If she didn't hate him, she'd be attracted to the man.

He crawled into bed, pulled a satin sheet to his chin, and stared at the ceiling. Miranda couldn't read the expression on his face from this angle. What was he thinking?

He reached out a hand to the bedside lamp. The room went dark.

End of Act One.

She slumped back as tension released her. Her brain rolled over the realization--he hadn't raped her or seduced her. She couldn't be pregnant. At least not so far.

At that point the screen flickered to life. Veiled sunlight fell through the hotel windows, enough light to see her own form stumble from the bed and fall to the floor. This was when she'd awoken. No point in watching the rest. She knew the rest. If, as she suspected, the fancy digital camera had an automatic on/off capacity based on movement, she was safe in saying she could not be pregnant. Alice would confirm her guess about the camera.

She reached onto the floor for the remote and smacked her head on the coffee table as someone knocked on the door.

"Ouch. Come in."

Alice entered. "I should have waited for your call, but curiosity got the better of me. Well?" The sofa cushions dipped minutely as she focused her gaze on Miranda's face.

Miranda rubbed her head. "First, tell me that this camera is equipped with an automatic off arrangement if it doesn't sense movement within its range of view."

"Oh yes. I believe after two minutes it's programmed to go into power save mode. Once a movement is detected by tiny motion sensors the record function starts automatically."

"Good. Here, see for yourself." Miranda rewound the video and watched Alice's reactions throughout the short playback.

"Well." Alice fiddled with her eyeglasses.

"Exactly." Miranda's voice hardened. "He lied to me. But

why?"

"Why did you stop here? There must be more, like the morning after," Alice said.

Miranda flushed. "There's more, but nothing I don't remember. I got up. Drake woke and told me his version of what happened. I ... I went into the bathroom. Lucy and--"

Alice interrupted. "You left Drake alone in the room while the camera was recording?"

"Yes, not for long. I was indisposed."

Alice quirked an eyebrow upward.

"Okay, I had a hangover to fight off. I don't want to be indelicate." Embarrassment flooded Miranda once more.

"Never mind that. Let's see what Drake said or did while you were out of the room. We might find the missing piece to this puzzle."

"Why didn't I think of that?" Miranda mumbled. Anxiety returned. She turned the television and video back on.

They watched; Alice with a permanent quirk of the eyebrow, Miranda sinking lower into the cushions. In the end, all was as Miranda had remembered.

Miranda got up to go back to her own place. There was nothing else to see here.

As she opened the door, Alice asked, "I wonder why he called Jack and Lucy?"

Miranda shrugged, disheartened, and left. Back in the comfort of her own home she could not help but think, why indeed? She was still puzzling it through when she heard the apartment door open then slam shut.

"Get down and quit slobbering."

Through the singular rasp that signified the happy panting of the dog, Miranda realized her husband was home. Just what she needed.

She peered at him over the back of the sofa. "Who let you in?"

"I live here, remember? You gave me a key." He remained at the door, pinned there by the loving Pumpkin. "How about calling off this horse?"

Horse indeed. Miranda considered letting them bond some more; for some reason Pumpkin had taken a liking to the man. More bonding wouldn't be fair to the dog. Sooner of later Pumpkin would come to understand that Drake wasn't a very nice human. Until that happened Miranda would enjoy the way the big canine greeted him at every opportunity.

Her head throbbed. "Pumpkin," she said. A muffled thud

CAUGHT

indicated the dog had dropped back to all fours.

Drake straightened his jacket and stalked to the sofa. He spoke to Miranda, but his eyes strayed to the television screen. "Have a nice afternoon?" His tight-lipped voice indicated an odd mixture of amusement toying with annoyance. "Did you learn anything interesting?"

Miranda glared at him. The image of his naked body striding with purpose towards the hotel bed flickered through her memory. She turned her back on him, settling back into her seat before he could get of glimpse of the heat she felt rushing to her face.

"Show's over," she stated. The throbbing in her head began anew.

A tickle on her neck had her turning until she faced him. His face rested on the back of the sofa, on her level. Impossible to ignore. She forced herself not to flinch.

His breath touched her again. Its warmth answered the heat she'd been feeling.

Wait, she didn't want to appreciate anything about this man. He was the enemy. Not a sexy man with nicely sculpted lips or eyes that crinkled when he twitched his nose.

She needed more than the back of the sofa between them. Something a little bigger, like a galaxy, would be better. Something full of vacuum so she wouldn't be able to hear the rich timbre of his voice or smell the subtle wintergreen on his breath.

She shushed that nagging little voice inside her that insisted that it wouldn't matter how much distance she put between them.

With the remote firmly in hand, a hand that was not trembling she was happy to note, she backed off the sofa and stood. Drake straightened as well; his gaze never left hers.

Pumpkin's head swiveled from Miranda to Drake as if trying to decide if he should get involved. Miranda flicked her hand as she said, "Pumpkin, down." Sighing, the dog flopped to the rug.

Pulling anger around her to cover the other strong emotions that welled up inside, Miranda began a direct assault. "You lied to me. We never made love. I can't be pregnant."

Drake crossed his arms. His eyes narrowed. He spoke not a single word in his own defense. For some reason his silence fed Miranda's rage like oxygen fed flame.

"You," she stabbed a finger in his direction, "made me stay married to you and I want to know why, right now."

He'd only heard that icy control in her voice in the boardroom.

Had always been glad it had been turned toward anyone but him. A shiver ran up his back as he considered his options. If it came down to whether or not to continue lying to her and hope he could pull it off, or tell her the truth and gain an ally.

All he knew about Miranda in the several years of their association came down to this moment. What did he know of her true character? She was bright, brilliant in fact with a quick grasp of facts and an intuitive feel for the best way to go.

Loyalty, a trait she held in untold quantities and an uncanny ability to separate business from family. That had been made crystal clear the year he and her sister had been wed. Miranda had never tried to take advantage of that personal connection at work. It had been nothing but business at the office. Very little socializing after hours, though. At the time he'd been too involved in trying to make a marriage then hold the shreds of it together to wonder at that. Somehow Miranda had remained loyal to both her sister and him as her boss even when their marriage had disintegrated. Why she hadn't packed her bags and found a different job was a mystery he wasn't sure he wanted to unravel right now.

Miranda listened with an intensity that made the speaker feel that he was the only important person on the universe. This one just one of the reasons she was so well respected and liked by those who worked under her. And why she was held in such high esteem by her business associates.

Well, the one thing he was surer of than her loyalty was the fact that he could trust her. He knew his business, his secrets, the most important parts of his life as far as work went was safe with her. He had no reason not to trust her with this.

She had every right to know.

What a Boy Scout.

Except watching her pace the floor, arms akimbo, face flushed, she looked anything but like a boy.

She was everything her sister was not. Everything he had wanted in Lucy but had failed to find.

What would she do when he told her the truth?

He moved so that Pumpkin lay between him and Miranda. Best to have a buffer in case she tried one of those Tae Kwon Do moves on him.

"Corporate espionage."

She threw her arms up in the air. "I'm still waiting." Then her eyes widened. "What did you say?"

"Someone inside is stealing from me, or was. Stealing

technology."

She stopped pacing. "What has that got to do with marrying me?"

"Stocks, too. Buying stocks here and there in small bunches that would be overlooked by the casual observer, but taken as a group starting to become a good sized chunk of company assets."

Her eyes narrowed. "Again, and I'm beginning to hate what I think is coming, what has this got to do with marrying me?"

"Logic rather than lust." He knew he'd pay for that little lie later. Right now a lot of lust was involved. "You own a large number of company stock. I need control of it. I need you to stay with the company because of your expertise and know how. QED."

"You need me. Or rather what I represent." She tapped the tip of her nose with the tip of one finger. Her thoughtful look.

"Yes." Time to tread carefully.

She blinked, twice. "You could have gained control over more stock without marrying me. Any number of individuals would have helped you out." Her voice slowed.

He nodded but didn't say anything. She was close to working it out. It was amazing to witness her deductive skills at work. He inched a little further away.

"This is about something more than money, though. Even you wouldn't marry for just ... that...."

Here it comes.

"Lucy!"

Bingo.

Chapter Six

He expected her to throw knives at him. He even had a sofa pillow fisted, just in case he needed some kind of shield. Instead he watched her rage dissolve into the kind of chuckling bad B movies had people in insane asylums make.

Pumpkin let out a soft huff of sound. Drake relaxed his hand on the pillow but kept it close just in case. He waited.

The phone let out a shrill ring, then another. All three of them started. Drake waited for Miranda to answer it, but she didn't. On the fourth ring the machine answered. After Miranda's voice explained what the caller should do, Lucy's voice came on.

Fate had a strange sense of timing.

"Miranda. Call me as soon as you get home. It's--it's important." Sniff. "Call me, okay? Bye."

"So, is this about revenge on Lucy? Because if it is, you have a weird way of punishing her by marrying me. She's more concerned about my welfare than about herself." Miranda's voice held a quiet calm.

"It's about trust. How much can I trust you, Miranda?"

"What's that got to do with Lucy? She was your wife."

"And now you are my wife. Can I trust you more than I could trust her?" He already knew the answer to that, but did she?

She sank into a barstool, crossed her legs. "Tell me what else."

Now she was in information gathering mode. Good, she'd moved past emotional much sooner than he thought she would. He relaxed a couple of muscles.

"A few weeks into my marriage to Lucy, I received an email from a competitor."

"So? That happens everyday."

"This one had been misdirected, addressed incorrectly. It started, Darling Lucy, and ended with lots of dollar signs and instructions for a meeting." He remembered the empty ache of the moment he had realized his bride was deceiving him. He forced the muscles in his jaw to unclench.

Miranda blanched. She whispered, "You must have misunderstood. Lucy adored you. She would never …."

"So you and everyone else were led to believe. Even me." Sucker. "She denied it when I confronted her, but by the time I did that, I had proof. As you know, the divorce was messy."

Pumpkin chose this moment to stand, stretch, and rub his head against Miranda's leg. She scratched his huge ears in an absent-minded way. Drake could use that kind of comfort right now. He could use an answer, too, to a question he'd never come out and asked her.

"Why didn't you leave the company then?"

She shook her head. "I can't believe you're asking me that now. Look, Lucy told me you left her. How do I know what you're telling me is the truth? Why would she lie to me?"

He chose the easiest question to answer. "Pride, regret, fear, who knows? You'll have to ask her."

Nothing Drake said made any sense. Miranda remembered with vivid clarity the day Lucy showed up at her doorstep in tears claiming Drake had left her, called her an ice cube.

Heartbroken for her sister, yet wondering how to hold onto her job while hating her boss, Miranda had listened to Lucy pour out her heart.

Everything Lucy had said rang true. Hadn't Miranda warned Lucy against a relationship with someone as ruthless as Drake? In business he *was* ruthless. Miranda had never known him as a private individual until Lucy's surprise announcement of marriage.

Even after the marriage the newlywed couple had emitted an aura of togetherness that led Miranda to believe all she'd heard about Drake was wrong. Over time their appearances together at holiday meals and public functions had diminished. Lucy became gaunter. Drake, if possible, became even more difficult to please at work.

Had Drake verbally abused Lucy as she'd told Miranda? The things Drake said now made her wonder if what Lucy had told her was the truth. Miranda loved her sister. She also knew that Lucy's air of vulnerability and elegance had been carefully crafted through years of practice.

No. Miranda couldn't believe that Lucy would lie about such a big thing. She glanced at Drake. For the life of her she couldn't figure out a reason for him to lie either. He never cared what people thought of him. In fact, she was sure he relished his reputation as a scoundrel of sorts. A Rhett Butler for this century.

The whole thing left her dizzy. An uncomfortable sensation grew in her, a sensation that she was being led along a path she would not chose for herself.

Another thought struck her. "Lucy wanted a houseful of kids. You couldn't supply them. Is that what this is about?"

He snorted. "I was the one who wanted children. Lucy decided it would stretch her figure. She couldn't be bothered."

"You're wrong. She told me she wanted to get pregnant as soon as possible."

"Sweetheart, she always told you exactly what you wanted to hear. Then she did just what she pleased anyway."

"What do you mean?"

"I think it's you who wants a houseful of rugrats. Lucy went along with the idea so you wouldn't make a fuss about her marrying me." He closed the gap between them. "She told me how you argued against the marriage. That only made her more determined to go through with it. After all, marrying the richest guy in town would have a been a huge step up for your sister, wouldn't it?"

Miranda's throat tightened. He stood too close. It was as if all the air in the room weighed more than her lungs could take in.

"After she had me," Drake continued, "she had complete access to company records, employee transfers, money. She had me fooled for a while. I wanted to be fooled. She shed a bright light into my life." His eyes lost their focus. "It took me months to figure out it was just a cold reflection fed by greed and ambition."

To Miranda's relief he backed away. "Have you got anything to drink? I can't bare my soul without scotch."

"What ... what did you do?" Miranda whispered.

His eyes were back to normal. "Nothing. Not a damned thing."

Miranda opened the cupboard above the stove and pulled out a dusty bottle of single malt scotch she'd been given for a holiday several years before. The strongest drink she indulged in was an evening glass of wine.

As she filled two glass tumblers with ice and poured the smoky golden liquid, she decided this was as good a time as any to try strong drink. What Drake had revealed, if it was true, changed everything while at the same time clarified her relationship with her sister.

Relationship aside, Lucy had always had a small problem with the truth. Miranda had thought she'd outgrown it once adolescence had passed, like outgrowing acne. If Drake was right, Lucy's little character flaw had simply become more refined.

The whole thing gave her a sour ache somewhere near her heart. The heavy weight of disappointment held her immobile.

She didn't hear Drake come up behind her. She jumped when he reached past her and took one of the glasses.

"I take mine neat." He fingered the ice cubes out and let them clink into the metal of the sink.

Miranda found herself mesmerized by his action of licking the moisture from his fingers. It was innocent yet imbued with sensuality.

Stop it.

She forced her gaze away and tried to move back into the living room. Drake blocked the way. It was a very small kitchen. Unless he moved or she vaulted over the counter, he had her trapped.

He took a deep drink. Nervously she did the same. The fiery liquid paralyzed her throat. It looked like iced tea but tasted like hellfire with an attitude.

Tears sprang to her eyes as she gasped. "Damn, from the way people talk you'd think this stuff at least tasted good."

Drake took the tumbler from her shaking hands and replaced it with a towel. "It's an acquired taste. The next sip will be better."

"Maybe later, once my throat's healed." Miranda splashed water on her face. "Back to your sad tale," she demanded.

He sipped his drink while leaning against the archway to Miranda's only route of escape. He knew it, too. She could tell by the way his eyes glinted.

"It ended simply and ugly enough. Sort of like a soap opera. I found her in bed with another man."

Miranda slumped into the nearest chair. "On, no." Her mind reeled. This was just too much for one day. Before she had time to consider the consequences, she blurted out, "I'm surprised you left either of them alive."

In a flat, hard voice, he said, "What makes you think I did?"

She opened her eyes wide at that.

He drank some more. "I'm no murderer, though by the time I was done with him, he might have wished to be dead. Lucy left that night. I divorced her within the month. I'm sure she's trying to get control of my company as some sort of revenge for not overlooking her behavior and allowing her a large divorce settlement."

Miranda shook her head. "She's not smart enough for that." As the import of her statement struck her, she clapped a hand over her mouth.

Drake grunted as he sat across from her. He swirled his glass in a wet circle on the tabletop. "You're right. This is too sophisticated for her. It's got to be an inside job."

"That's why you think she's in cahoots with an employee? Just to get back at you?" She stood, leaned against the table, glad that her shaky knees didn't have the entire job of holding her upright. "Has anyone ever told you that you have an enormous ego?"

Without thinking, she took another sip of her drink. After a moment of horror she realized she'd live through it. The stuff had a soft, almost sweet flavor. She tasted again, a larger mouthful this time.

What had they been talking about?

"I don't believe I've ever heard anyone use the word 'cahoots' in casual conversation," Drake said. "You are a unique individual, Miranda."

The intensity of his gaze made her mouth dry. She gulped the rest of the liquor hoping it would alleviate the tightness in her throat, assuage the heaviness in her chest.

"It's a perfectly good word," she stated. "Would you like another drink?" His glass was empty.

He nodded. She poured for both of them, wondering why it was hard to focus her eyes. She sat.

Drake's fingers grazed hers when he took the glass. She focused on his action, and then glanced at his face. The air between them seemed to crystallize. Panic swept through her as she realized how very much she was attracted to him. She couldn't seem to think straight when he was around.

What had they been talking about? She was angry with him because--because--ah!

"You didn't really make love to me," she accused.

Anger mixed with hurt. Maybe she hadn't been worth his time. Lucy was what he wanted, not plain down-to-earth Miranda.

"No, I didn't." The words sighed from his mouth. Miranda had to lean closer to hear him.

"Why not?" To her dismay tears formed in her eyes. She blinked to clear them.

"Despite what you've heard, I'm not a monster. Making love to you while you were unconscious would have been unconscionable."

She appreciated his clever play on words. "I never knew you to have feelings before."

This whiskey was really good. It slid down her throat like warm chocolate.

"There's a lot you don't know about me."

She blinked. When she opened her eyes, he'd vanished. "Hey, where'd you go?"

Hands dropped onto her shoulders. Miranda spun around. Her drink sloshed. Drake leaned across and took the glass from her hand.

"I'm not going to miss this opportunity to make things right." He dragged her to her feet. The last thing she saw before he kissed her was the blaze of passion shooting at her from his eyes.

Chapter Seven

At first dizziness and shock kept her from fighting. Crystal

CAUGHT

sharp awareness slammed into her. Wherever he touched, she burned. From where his lips attacked hers to the trail of fire his fingers blazed down her arms, her back, her buttocks, the burning left tremors of desire in their wake. Tremors that threatened to rock Miranda's deliberately constructed world.

She pushed against his chest. It was like pushing on granite. He held her tighter. The intensity of his mouth on hers changed. Where at first it demanded she kiss him back, it now gentled and asked.

She stopped pushing. Stopped thinking. She allowed herself to enjoy the warm softness of his lips.

Someone whined. Pumpkin. Thank goodness. Miranda had had a horrifying moment thinking it was her moaning and whining with desire and delight and pure lust. As she thought this, and thought it might be time to put an end to this kiss, Drake shifted the tenor of his mouth once more.

Now Miranda did gasp. She held onto his shoulders for balance. His lips opened against hers. His hot tongue probed. His teeth nibbled until she opened her mouth against the onslaught.

That cost her. Up until that moment she could have pulled away, put some distance between them. Probably. Later, when she'd take the time to think about it, she tried to convince herself it was true.

Deep need pulsed through her. This time it was her groan that escaped as she tried to breathe. Drake's growl echoed it. The primal noise matched the way his hand strayed to her breast as his other found the bottom of her skirt. He pulled the fabric up until his fingers reached the soft skin of her inner thigh through her hose. She writhed against the strictures of fabric.

His hands--she wanted them everywhere.

He unbuttoned her blouse all the while deepening his kiss. When he had her throat and shoulders bared, he removed his mouth from hers. Shivers shot through her as he licked at her earlobes nibbled her neck, made his way to the softness where her breasts began.

At the same instant his mouth reached her cleavage his clever fingers stroked the moist fire he'd created below. Miranda couldn't decide whether to melt or to scream. She had too many clothes on. She wanted skin to skin; heat against heat. Nothing else would do.

She reached to unbutton his shirt. Damn buttons. Her fingers fumbled with the small pieces of plastic. In her growing need she grabbed and pulled hard. The shredding of cloth and the patter of buttons dropping onto the tile floor faded into the background as a deep-seated tremor burst through her.

His mouth found her nipples through the lace of her bra as his fingers encouraged the first slamming orgasm to rock her. She cried out. Her voice almost undid him as she arched against his body with the force of her release. Before she finished cresting he stopped the frantic touching. He lifted her as she moaned. As he carried her to the bedroom he had an irrational hope that the damn dog would stay out for a change.

Miranda's eyes fluttered open as Drake laid her on the bed. Her face, soft and flushed, lips parted, stopped him. She'd given herself to him unselfishly. He wasn't sure he should complete the task.

The throbbing in the lower part of his abdomen gave him notice that he *did* want to get on with it. Fierce self-control was the only thing that kept him from lowering his trousers and taking Miranda now while she was soft and pliable and oh so sexy.

He curled his fingers into hard fists. His earlier reasons for wanting her had melted away. Now he wanted her to want him. When had his feelings shifted from cold planning to warmer caring? He couldn't think about that now. Now he had to get away from her before he did something both of them would regret.

A soft swish of fabric stopped him before he got to the door. Miranda's hand touched his sleeve.

"You can't leave yet," she whispered. Her eyes, huge and liquid, held him captive.

Warm light from the living room spilled through the bedroom doorway. Her body glowed. Drake hesitated.

This time she put her arms around his neck and kissed him. Her tight nipples touched his flesh where his shirt hung open. White heat shot through him. For a brief instant he was unable to move.

He waited for her to break away, to laugh at him. Waited for her to push him out the door. He waited through an eternity of need for Miranda to somehow end what he had started. He waited for her to cast him out of her life. His heart pounded.

Her hands crept under what was left of his shirt. Then his shirt was on the floor.

He stopped thinking. He picked her up and carried her to the bed. Her legs lifted and wrapped around him as her kisses deepened.

He'd never make it. He'd embarrass himself before he got his pants off. Perspiration broke out on his forehead as he settled her on the bed. He fumbled with his belt; groaned with relief as his trousers and briefs hit the floor.

He plunged into her. Her moist wetness sheathed him, clenched around him. He gritted his teeth, determined to make this more than an animal coupling.

Miranda moved against him, gyrating her pelvis to take in more of him. It undid him. With a hoarse shout he came.

Through the haze of his pleasure he was aware of Miranda's deep, rhythmic orgasm. Time defined itself to that moment of shared intimacy. There was nothing else in the universe except her touch, her body and his together.

Reality returned when something cold and wet touched the leg Drake had dangled over the edge of the bed. He jerked away then looked. Pumpkin's drooling face frowned at him from the floor. Disapproval arced from the dog's clear brown eyes.

Drake shook his head. Pumpkin had no idea what was going on. He was a dog.

Miranda shifted beneath him. Great, not only had he just ravished her, now he was pressing the life out of her. He rolled off with reluctance. She felt soft and warm and infinitely better than the cool sheets that caught his backside.

He was afraid to say anything. What could he say? "Let's do it again?" Or what about, "Guess we consummated that, now."

He stifled a groan as his loins relayed to his brain that they weren't quite ready to quit.

He stared at the ceiling and tried not to think about it.

Miranda's voice, quiet and devoid of emotion, zeroed in on the one thing he should have remembered. "I don't suppose you used a condom?"

He shook his head.

"Then you got what you wanted, didn't you? You did it without taking advantage of me."

Her cool voice held neither judgment nor censure within the fabric of the words. That got to him. Shame and elation fought for space within him. Shame because he had planned her seduction, and got it. Elation because her response had been so much more than he expected.

She had wanted him, had given herself to him when all he asked for was her body. He'd felt her soul come to him in that rare moment of clarity when they were joined.

Had she been aware of it? Did she know how her sweet

surrender shattered his plans and thrust him into a dervish of emotions he thought he'd cast off along with his bad marriage?

The silence between them pressed against his chest. Turning toward her, his breath caught in his throat. With eyelids half shut she was curled to face him. One hand cupped her cheek. Her free arm stretched along the curve of her silhouette, enhancing every line beneath the sheet.

Words of apology stuck in his throat. "I'm going to need more than thirty days," he said as he gave in to the heat that rose through him.

Miranda's eyes flashed open. "Why?"

He rolled closer, gratified when she didn't pull away. "Because I want more of this." He took her into his arms and kissed her again.

Her tense resistance faded away. He knew he'd won a major battle when she opened her mouth and her legs to him. He slowed the pace of his lovemaking. He wanted to do it right this time.

Moving her stroking hands away from him, he lifted back the sheet. Goose bumps appeared on her arms. Her nipples peaked.

"What?" she murmured as she watched him.

He hushed her with a gentle kiss on the mouth then directed a body-length caress along her. The goose flesh disappeared. She kept her eyes open.

He began this slower seduction at the top of her face. Flicking tiny kisses across her brow, over the corners of her eyes, around the edge of her mouth, and up the tip of her nose. Her lips curved up.

Next he touched an earlobe with the tip of his tongue as he brushed a nipple with his fingers. She arched into him. He came close to ending it then.

Deep breaths. This time he wanted it to be perfect, unrushed. Deliberate.

Dipping his head, he ran his tongue along her neck until he reached the hollow of her throat. He cupped the other breast and stroked that nipple with his thumb all the while kissing Miranda's neck and throat, moving down to her shoulders and upper arms.

She moved against him again, moaning. Her hands stroked his head. As Drake moved down her body she writhed beneath him. When his fingers found the moistness between her legs she arced to meet them, crying out. He pulled away; determined to pace it. Instead he gave his mouth to her breasts as he placed his body between her thighs.

Her damp pubic hair rubbed against his belly as he kissed and sucked first one nipple then the other. Her hands rubbed his shoulders with a primal rhythm. She burned with the need of him. Shards of desire emanated from every cell as he tortured her with his mouth, his hands.

When his lips deserted her breasts she sobbed. His mouth kissed down her torso trailing flames along her length. She touched his head. When he turned his face to hers, the blaze in his eyes burned hot. He returned to torture her skin.

Lucid thought left her as his mouth sought the nub of her femininity. She grasped handfuls of sheets as his tongue stroked her. Panting, she pulled his head away.

Inside. She had to have him inside her.

For an instant he held back. Just as her body began to tremble with the wave she could no longer resist, he entered her. A long stroke completed her, and then propelled her into the warmth of a universe that was now composed of only the two of them. Infinity waited.

Chapter Eight

Miranda welcomed the darkness of her new office when she arrived. The sun waited below the horizon but its promise started a golden glow in the eastern sky.

On a subliminal level she was aware of the executive appointments of this room. But even the corner view couldn't distract her from the reasons she had arrived so early. Her little apartment had been invaded; she needed someplace where she could be alone to think. This small domain was her best bet. For a little while anyway.

She threw her coat and briefcase onto a chair before sinking into place behind her new desk.

What had she done?

For starters, she'd slept with, correction - had sex with - Drake. He'd wanted consummation; he'd gotten got it. He was husband in fact as well as in name.

She rubbed her forehead as images of herself plastered to him last night--had she really begged him to make love to her?--flashed through her mind. Last time it had been champagne yet he'd been decent enough to keep his hands off. Last night whiskey had been her downfall.

Blaming the liquor was too easy. The cold fact remained that her anger at Drake's deception had blossomed into something else as he told her his side of the story of his marriage. She wondered who was right, Lucy or Drake? Her future depended upon this pivotal question.

Drake's business conduct bordered on ruthless, yet never untruthful. He didn't lie. He had no reason to lie about his personal life. Of course she hadn't known much about that until he'd married her sister. Even then, he'd been close-mouthed. Probably because she remained employed by him.

He had fired Jack on the same day Jack broke off his engagement to her. The next thing she knew, she was in bed with Drake at a no-tell motel in Las Vegas. Were the incidents connected? Even in her exhausted state she was astute enough to realize that somehow all of these pieces fit together.

Lucy was the key. That seemed ridiculous. Even though Miranda loved her sister deeply, Lucy's interests revolved more around clothes and her new career as a dental assistant than anything sneaky. Unless money was involved.

Lucy, younger by three years than Miranda, had developed an early talent for bending the truth so that it benefited her. As much as Miranda loved her sister, she also knew that Lucy wouldn't hesitate to lie if it suited her.

Except for gaining Miranda's sympathy, why would Lucy lie about the reasons for divorce?

Exhaustion dogged Miranda. What little sleep she'd had last night did nothing for her. Right now she needed answers.

It was close to seven o'clock. Lucy should be stirring. Time for a breakfast meeting with little sister. Miranda left a note for her assistant and headed for her car.

* * * *

Lucy lived in one of the newer condominiums on the northeast side of town. The sun was well up and shining through a thin layer of clouds as Miranda slid up the ice encrusted steps to the door. Three minutes and two rings later she heard the bolt lock rasp open. Lucy's pale face met her.

Lucy's upswept hair and picture perfect make-up was in odd contrast to the plain dental assistant scrubs she wore; yet she made even those look perfect. Her elegant model's body would accept nothing less. Her clunky shoes were the only part of the uniform that didn't suit her style. Guess she had to make some concessions to the job.

"Miranda, what are you doing here?" A delicate frown creased the space between her eyes.

"Freezing my butt off," Miranda replied. "Can I come in?"

Lucy glanced over her shoulder then back. She licked her lips. "The place is kind of a mess right now."

Miranda stared. Who was this stranger wearing Lucy's face and clothes? Her Lucy would have been eager, happy to see her. Another frigid blast blew up her long wool coat. "I promise not to look. How about a cup of coffee before we both need to be at work?"

After hesitating just a bit longer Lucy stood back so Miranda could enter.

"I haven't got much time. We have early appointments today." Lucy hurried Miranda through a messier than normal living room and into the kitchen.

The coffee carafe was half full. Since Lucy didn't seem inclined to be gracious this morning, Miranda poured herself a lukewarm cup and set it into the microwave to heat. Lucy busied herself with loading the dishwasher. Normally chatty, she stayed silent, chewing her lower lip and glancing at the clock.

What was she so nervous about?

The microwave chimed. Miranda enjoyed her first hot drink of the day. The familiar flavor settled her. She shrugged off her coat and made herself comfortable at the counter. Lucy kept her back towards Miranda while rinsing cups under the steaming faucet.

Stalling, Miranda realized, as if she knew Miranda wasn't there for a pleasant social visit.

At last Lucy dried her hands. "I really do have to get ready for work."

Miranda sipped, using the time to gather her wits about her. She may not have the opportunity to ask questions again, at least not while Lucy was so flustered.

"I want to know the real reason you and Drake got divorced," she said without subterfuge. "Why did you show up with Jack the other day in Las Vegas?" She refused to blush at the memory. Thanks to the tiny recording she knew the truth behind that scene.

"We went all through my reasons months ago. He was cold, abusive. I couldn't love him like that." Lucy paced.

"Funny, he told me a different story."

"Of course he did. Did you expect him to tell his new bride the truth about what a bastard he is?" Lucy's voice snarled. "You should have paid more attention to me. He's going to hurt you just like he hurt me." Her eyes glittered. Then she flushed and turned back to the sink.

Miranda went to her sister. Regardless of the truth Lucy's distress brought out Miranda's maternal instincts. When Miranda touched her, Lucy's shoulders stiffened.

"I didn't think my marrying Drake would affect you so much," Miranda said, taking a stab in the dark. "Are you still in love with him?"

Lucy whirled to face her. "No. It's not that. I just worry about you." Again Lucy's gaze strayed to the clock. "I'm sorry, but I really need to go. Keep my warning in mind, okay?"

"You don't need to worry about me. I've been handling Drake longer than you."

A strangled laugh escaped Lucy. Her gaze locked on something behind Miranda. "You have no idea what you've gotten yourself into."

This wasn't getting her anywhere, just more frustrated. Miranda had to ask just one more question before she left. The same question that had gone unanswered before. "Why were you and Jack together when you came to Las Vegas? I didn't think you even liked him."

Lucy flushed a deeper shade of rose. She didn't answer the question; instead she pushed past Miranda into the living room and pulled on her coat. "Let's go."

As Miranda followed she noticed more details about the rooms than before. She noticed that a good deal of the clutter in the living room did not belong to Lucy. As a matter of fact, Lucy didn't own a briefcase let alone a tan cowhide number like the one that leaned against the sofa.

Miranda sniffed. That's what had bothered her before but she hadn't been able to identify it. Now she recognized the faint odor of cigar smoke in the air. A tented pile of newspapers covered the small coffee table. A tumbler with a quarter inch of liquid in the bottom kept the newspaper company. Miranda twitched aside the paper. An ashtray containing a chewed on cigar stub was hidden beneath.

"Since when did you take up cigars?" She raised an eyebrow at her sister.

"Oh, I try lots of different things these days." The corner of Lucy's mouth quirked up and down. When had she developed a twitch?

"Sure."

A single brown loafer, a man's shoe, lay angled sideways near the door to the bedroom, as if it had been cast off in a hurry. A red and black sweatshirt had been tossed on the arm of a chair.

An uneasy suspicion formed in Miranda's mind. All of these man's things had a familiar look to them. They reminded her --

The door swung open. Miranda turned. She and Lucy said, "Jack," at the same time.

Except for his eyes, Jack stood motionless. Those beady blue marbles rolled in the sockets, first looking at one sister then switching to the other. Miranda saw him swallow. His jaw tensed, and then he put his keys into his pocket and strolled into the room.

"Looks like Miranda has discovered our little secret." He kissed Lucy on the cheek.

Miranda felt her thinning strands of composure slipping. Lucy went from flushed to porcelain pale in a heartbeat.

"Secret?" Miranda's voice came out in a whisper.

Jack scratched the back of his neck. He unzipped the expensive leather jacket. "Lucy asked me to move in with her."

Miranda fought dizziness. "Three days ago you and I were engaged."

Jack had the grace to look at his feet, caught. "Now you know why I called that off. Sorry you had to find out this way."

"Sorry?" Incredulous, Miranda stepped toward her sister. "How could you?" she asked Lucy.

Lucy turned away without answering.

"I think you should leave now," Jack told Miranda. "I won't have you harassing Lucy. Besides, I have a job search to begin." His mouth pursed with the bitter taste of his last remark. It illuminated what Drake had told her.

Confusion coursed through Miranda, tinged with anger. "Is Jack the reason you divorced Drake, or rather why he divorced you?"

Not meeting Miranda's eyes, Lucy nodded.

I'm going to throw up if I don't get out of here, Miranda thought. Without saying another word she grabbed her coat and purse and pushed past Jack to the door. His smirk made her do something she'd never done in her life. She slapped him across the face just before she left. The satisfaction of seeing the red marks of her fingers on his face and the shock in his eyes justified the tingling in her hand if not the act itself.

The ache in her chest refused to go away.

Keeping her mind on the increased traffic, Miranda focused on driving, refusing to replay the scene she'd just lived through. She didn't know where she was going until she pulled into her parking space at work.

Jack's appearance at Lucy's place, his words and actions, sickened her. That she'd been attracted to such a slimeball spoke about her ability to sense character. She'd have to work on that.

Now that she knew at least part of the truth about Jack, how was she going to face Drake? How many other people at work knew that Jack had been cheating on her? A stray memory surfaced. It was of arrested conversations accompanied by sideways glances as she entered the break room.

She leaned her head on the cool steering wheel. Probably everyone knew. Great.

The pain of humiliation at the hands of her beloved sister left her gasping. She wondered whether the howl trying to escape her throat was going to be hysterical laughter or hysterical weeping.

Three broken engagements and one unconscious marriage. She was doing just great.

The car was cooling off. She couldn't sit here all day and stew. She sat up and squared her shoulders, swallowing the howl for now.

She'd do what she always did when life threw her a curve ball. She'd somehow find a way to get on base. Never a quitter, she had to admit that she'd never felt more like just dropping everything and moving to someplace where no one had ever heard of her. Antarctica would do. A billowing snowy gust blew past the car. She changed her mind--Easter Island. At least it was warm there.

Putting confidence and determination into her every move, Miranda left her car and entered the building.

Chapter Nine

The intercom beeped. "Your wife just arrived, Mr. McLain."

"About time," Drake grumbled. Where the hell had she run off to without waking him first? After the passion of the night before he expected, okay hoped, for a more pleasant morning than waking up to a bed containing Pumpkin rather than Miranda.

He suspected that Pumpkin had been happier to see him than Miranda would have been. He wouldn't mind so much if the dog had better breath. The sloppy doggy kisses were a little much, too. Taking the dog for his necessary walk had given Drake a whole new appreciation of Miranda's endurance. Nobody walked a greyhound. The dog ran you.

Miranda hadn't been at her old desk or the new one. He tried hard not to care. He tried hard not to think about the fact that maybe she regretted their intimacy of last night.

He tried especially hard not to think about whom she might have gone to cry to.

He slammed a fist onto his desk. The feeling of possessing her had crept over him last night when they at last finished making love. He'd held her while she slept. She was his now in every sense. Nobody took what was his. One way or another he'd bind her to him.

A flash of light on his computer screen stopped his introspection. A small window opened. Finally. Someone was accessing the company stock portfolio program.

Since it was privately held stock only employees and their families were allowed to buy and sell it. There had been more shares traded than usual of late. Someone was buying a lot of stock.

If he had a disgruntled employee manipulating stock in an effort to have more leverage on the board, Drake needed to know about it. Millennium Tech was his brainchild, his company. Every employee benefited from the new patents his or her discoveries brought in. Drake was determined to hold onto the control that brought them that measure of security.

A few keystrokes later had Drake gritting his teeth in frustration. Whoever had logged onto the stock portfolio program, logged off before Drake could track him. It could be a her, he mused.

Miranda marched in without knocking. A driven, forceful executive in a suit had replaced the soft, passionate woman of last night. He put away his disappointment and prepared for battle.

Her question surprised him.

"Why did you fire Jack?"

A flash of heat shot through him. Had she left their bed to run to Jack? "It's no longer your concern." He struggled to keep his voice cool, controlled.

She placed her hands palm down on his desk and glared at him. "It is my concern if he called off our engagement because you fired him."

Rage settled over Drake in the guise of icy calm. He had to make her forget Jack. He stood and cradled her face between his hands. Her eyes opened wide. When his lips crushed down on hers a satisfying shaft of desire and conquest rushed through him. He claimed his woman.

Her sweet mouth gave in to his as if it had no choice. Then she pushed him hard enough to break his hold.

"That's not going to work this time," she spat out as she wiped the back of her hand across her mouth. Her hand trembled.

"It was worth a try," Drake answered. His rage was replaced by gratification of her reaction.

"If you're done proving your manhood, answer my question," she shot back at him.

Her single-mindedness both pleased and irritated Drake. He had first hand knowledge that she applied that trait to her personal life. It made for intense intimacy. Right now he wished he could distract her. But maybe this should be dealt with without further delay.

"Sit."

She crossed her arms, more glaring.

"Please sit," he amended.

She did so, but kept her arms crossed.

"I caught Jack stealing technology. He didn't know that I'd installed those nifty new cameras. You remember those little cameras? Like the one you pilfered from our honeymoon suite?"

Miranda refused to rise to the bait. "Jack had no reason to steal from Millennium Tech. Why would he? This was the best job he ever had."

Her defense of Jack grated on Drake. "Maybe he got greedy. Money is the biggest motivator when an employee steals. The second biggest is desire for power. Take your pick."

"What does that have to do with Lucy?" Miranda's voice was close to a whisper, like she was talking to herself.

"Unless they've suddenly become partners, I don't see that it has anything to do with your sister."

Miranda started pacing, a sure sign that her brain was working overtime trying to put pieces of a puzzle together. "Did you sign over any stock to Lucy as part of your divorce settlement?"

"My lawyer worked out most of the details." Ugly suspicion began to grow. His mind worked out the possibilities. He didn't like them.

"While you were married did she take much interest in the company--how it worked, who it hired, that kind of stuff?"

"At first she didn't seem to care much as long as it brought in lots of money." Drake fought to keep the long buried bitterness out of his voice. "After a while I was pleased that she'd want to accompany me when I came in over the weekend to work. I even had security make up a key card for her." His voice trailed off. He joined her pacing.

Miranda stopped. She put her hand on Drake's arm. He looked down at her, into her eyes. He didn't like what he saw there, something soft, like pity.

Her voice, gentle as spring sunshine, asked, "Who did you find Lucy in bed with?"

"Not Jack."

She nodded. "Who?"

"Jones, Bob Jones." He clamped his jaw tight.

Jones Industries was Millennium Tech's closest competitor. Lucy had known that. Drake had never discovered what Jones had offered her. Whatever, it had been had been enough to coax her into bed; the bed Drake had found them in that afternoon.

He forced the mental image from his mind.

Miranda nodded. She sat. "Jack, Lucy, and Bob Jones, there must be a connection. Once we find it we'll know what's happening to the stock."

Glad that she didn't want to rehash the end of his precious marriage any longer, Drake took his chair again. "What's the connection between Jack and Lucy?"

Miranda squirmed. Without meeting his gaze, she said, "He's moved in with her."

A small wave of sympathy washed over him as he realized where she'd gone that morning. "You found him at Lucy's this morning?"

She nodded. All Drake felt was anger at Jack and Lucy for hurting Miranda, not for the folly of their living arrangement.

Miranda's chin sank as she said, "I'm worried. Lucy did not look happy. She should have been ecstatic since she must be the other reason Jack dumped me. She always won in the guy department."

Drake ignored that last remark. "We need a plan," he said over steepled fingers.

Miranda shook her shoulders. Drake watched her chin come back up as she focused on action. Then he saw a twinkle form in her eyes.

"I've always wanted to be a spy," she said. "Here's what we're going to do." She leaned across his desk and outlined the beginnings of a plan.

He loved it.

Chapter Ten

Miranda struggled with her strappy high heels. She pasted a smile on her face. Now she remembered why she had spent years avoiding these business club dinners. Getting dressed up to be nice to people who, during regular business hours, were happy to cut your company's throat just went across her ethical grain.

As if reading her mind Drake lifted his highball glass in a toast in her direction.

Okay, so networking was important even if it wasn't her cup of tea. She put up a hand to tug the stray wisp of hair out of her face, but stopped when she remembered that the hairdresser had lacquered it there on purpose. Wispy was sexy, she'd been assured.

Why was it, she silently fumed, that men could come to these things without changing from their business suits? For some insane reason women were expected in "cocktail" wear. The temperature was in the low twenties and dropping with a wind chill designed to freeze an Eskimo and here she was in her ridiculous strappy little heels, her ridiculous strappy red dress, and her ridiculous strappy hairdo. She felt ridiculous.

Why had she let Drake chose her clothes for tonight?

With as much dignity as she could muster in the tight dress, Miranda tottered to the Ladies Room. Before engaging the enemy she may as well refresh the fire-engine red lipstick that matched the dress.

At least the restroom was quiet. An older woman in a well-cut blue evening suit sat at the far end of the mirrored counter.

The plan was all Miranda's idea, well mostly. She and Drake had decided to start attending these social business functions together as husband and wife. During the course of this evening she was supposed to meet Bob Jones as if by accident. She had wanted to wow him with her intelligence. Drake thought the red dress would get his attention faster.

She made a face at her reflection before applying the lipstick. Drake was probably right. She hated it when he was right.

CAUGHT 61

Sighing, she adjusted the new push-up bra before wobbling back to the dining room. Time to start hunting.

Several male heads turned as she entered the room. She straightened. Maybe she should try enjoying the attention. In the past Lucy had been the head turner in the family where as Miranda hadn't even tried.

She surveyed the room. Many faces belonged to men and a few women whom she'd met over the conference table. According to the attendee list, more faces belonged to individuals with whom she spoke regularly over the phone but had never met in person.

Where to start? She tapped her fingernails against her evening bag.

"I see McLain likes to keep it all in the family," a deep voice said from her right.

Miranda fought the urge to jump. As the import of the words sunk in she fought the urge to hit the man who spoke. Her throat dried when she turned and recognized her irritant to be her prey.

Swallowing the sharp retort about Drake's choice in wives, she smiled and said, "Have we met?"

Bob Jones's dark eyes swept her from painted toes to lacquered head then back again. His gaze stopped somewhere below her chin. She assumed he was admiring her new décolletage. In an effort to start a conversation she held out her hand.

The movement must have distracted him enough to bring him out of the daze. He took her hand. "I'm Bob Jones. I've been looking forward to meeting the newest Mrs. McLain."

"Why is that, Bob? And please, call me Miranda." She practiced batting her eyelashes but nearly lost a contact lens in the process.

"I've heard about your business acumen. I had no idea you were also lovely. Congratulations on your marriage." He squeezed her hand. She tugged it away, restraining the urge to wipe it against her dress.

"Thank you."

"May I buy you a drink?"

"White wine, thank you. I am thirsty and I don't see Drake anywhere."

Actually Drake was only ten feet away, but his back was turned. She wished he were standing here offering her a drink instead of this pathetic excuse for a playboy.

Bob returned with the stem of wine. Miranda smiled her thanks and gulped. The cool tingle along the back of her throat calmed her nerves. She glanced over and around Bob. Drake quirked a questioning eyebrow in her direction. She managed not to stick her tongue out at him. No doubt her current companion would consider it a come-on to him.

After another sip for courage, she turned back to Bob. "Tell me more about your company. I understand it's one of Millennium Tech's biggest rivals."

Bob leaned closer, as if to divulge a secret. "We are Millennium Tech's only rivals."

Miranda backed up, holding her drink in front of her like a shield. "Our only rival here in Colorado Springs, but what about the rest of the Front Range and Denver? We have quite a large presence both north and south of here."

Bull's-eye. Bob's smooth charm slipped. He narrowed his eyes and pressed his lips together until they were white. The he regained control. "That's the nice thing about being an upstart company," he replied. "No place to go but up." He set his now empty glass on a nearby table. "Another glass of wine, Miranda?"

The shivers that crept up her spine as he purred her name were nothing like the hot fever Drake inspired. She couldn't wait to go home and shower this conversation away.

"I think I'll just nurse this along. I don't have a very good head for alcohol."

She hoped he couldn't hear her teeth grinding together as she smiled back at him. By now he had her backed against the wall. The strong, sweet cologne he wore invaded her nostrils. Its cloying scent made her dizzy. He was too close.

He put a hand against the wall beside her head. The closer he leaned, the more trapped she felt.

"How about lunch tomorrow?"

"Bob, I'm a married woman. Why would I want to have lunch with you?" This game was definitely wearing on her. If he came one inch closer she'd take action.

"I think we could have an interesting exchange of ideas about Millennium Tech and what the future holds in store for both our companies."

"That's more Drake's line than mine," Miranda protested as she tried to slide away. A table prevented her escape on one side, Bob's huge arm on the other.

"Drake doesn't like me." Bob's eyes gleamed as he stared hard at her.

That did it. She bumped into him and spilled her wine down

the front of his suit.

It had the desired effect.

"Why you!" Bob jumped back as Miranda made her getaway. She was almost out of the corner, just looking over her shoulder at the commotion of Bob being dabbed at with cloth napkins by a small army of wait staff, when she ran into a solid object--a warm, large, familiar, solid object.

"Being your usual charming self?" Drake drawled as he steadied her with both hands.

She shrugged off his hands. "That man's a slug. I don't know what Lucy saw in him." She shuddered. "Can we go home now? I've had enough fun for one night."

"This was your idea. Did you find out anything from Casanova?"

Miranda glared at him as he found her coat in the coatroom. "He wants to have lunch with me tomorrow. What do you want to bet he wants to do more than discuss the future of our mutual companies?"

Drake raised an eyebrow. "I'll bet another four weeks added to last night."

She flushed. In their rush of passion, fueled by emotional pain and whiskey, neither of them had thought to use birth control. The chances of her becoming pregnant were slim but not impossible. She'd give him four more weeks. She'd also make sure she kept her distance from him until then. And no more whiskey.

"Aren't you worried about me having lunch with that slimeball?" The idea irritated her already raw sensibilities. If Drake could care just a little, show some sensitivity to the woman he claimed as wife, and with whom he had consummated the agreement with such passion.

"Not concerned in the least." He helped her into the car and walked around to the driver's side.

"Why not?"

"A couple of reasons. One, you are not Lucy. I know you. I can trust you." He started the car and pulled away from the curb with a growl of power and a wave of slush.

His face was only visible in the occasional glare of a passing set of headlights or the infrequent streetlight. She saw enough to know his jaw was set.

"What's the other reason?" she asked.

"I'm going to wire you for sound." He chuckled. "Just like in the spy movies. No secrets, Miranda. That's got to be part of our deal, too."

"You don't trust me," she accused, hurt by the thought.

"As I said, I trust you more than I trusted your sister. That's not much. But I have reason to know you have integrity and honesty."

"Swell."

He remained silent after that. Miranda didn't press him again. Once more she played the part of good old Miranda. Honest, trustworthy, kind to animals. Just once she wished he would think of her as more than a means to an end. Last night didn't count, couldn't count. Neither of them could be held responsible for their actions.

That was stupid. They were both adults. She remembered as if she were reliving it the surprise and desire she saw in his eyes as she took off her clothes and offered herself to him.

Don't forget that you despise him, she told herself. An ache grew in her stomach. An ache that was for more than the supper she'd missed or for the nerves that had passed.

She was so busy pondering her options that she didn't notice the direction in which Drake drove until the car stopped. She moved to open her door. Drake was already at her side. When she saw where they were, she almost fell out of the car.

"Take me home," she demanded.

"I'm tired of sleeping on your damned couch. Last night doesn't count. We didn't sleep much."

Miranda couldn't think of a snappy retort to that. He had spent the night in her bed. Sleep had taken only a small percentage of the time.

Drake took her arm and propelled her up the three stone steps to his front door. "At least take a look at the arrangements I've made before you say no."

A reasonable request until she remembered, "Pumpkin needs me to walk him. My plants must be watered and talked to every day."

Warmth flowed over them as Drake swung open the carved wooden door. A scratching against the floorboards greeted them, accompanied by the astounding sight of the huge dog skittering towards them along the polished floor. As he draped his paws against Drake's shoulders in a doggy show of affection, Drake managed to say, "I've take care of Pumpkin. Your plants are in the living room. Your clothes are upstairs."

"You had no right," Miranda stormed. She tossed off her wool coat and grabbed Pumpkin's collar with both hands. "Down," she ordered. The dog pushed off from Drake and landed lightly for such a big animal. He followed wherever his new master went.

Drake brushed dog fur and slobber from his coat then shrugged out of it. "It's just not working for me to stay at your place all the time. Besides the inconvenience to me, it sure as hell looks funny to my associates."

"Like who?"

"Batgart for one. The CEO of Batcorp is wondering why I'm not home at night to return calls. We have a major investment in their good will. I have to be available."

"And your cell phone is where? That's just not enough to justify this move without asking me first."

Drake rubbed the back of his neck. When he moved down the hallway Miranda had little choice but to follow. He let them into a large kitchen. She watched him open the refrigerator and pull out a beer.

"Want one?" he asked.

"No." She tapped her foot. "I want to go home."

"You said you'd help me find out who's been fooling around with company stock. You're the one who convinced me to take advantage of our domestic arrangement while it was in force. No one will believe we are happily married if we live apart, and no one in their right mind would believe that you prefer staying in that tiny apartment when you could live here." Exasperation colored his voice. He slouched on a stool that stood adjacent to the large center counter.

Miranda sighed. "I like my little place. I have neighbors who care about me. People I like. What do I have here?"

"Just me," Drake said. His face was a mask.

Nodding, she wandered around the large room. It smelled of garlic and cinnamon in an appealingly comforting mix. If she didn't know better she'd swear this was a kitchen designed for a gourmet chef.

The island counter where Drake sat was on casters that locked or unlocked with clever latches. A large wooden cutting board sat beside an array of knives in all shapes and sizes nestled into the top of a chunk of wood. A variety of pots and pans and kitchen utensils hung from a ceiling rack. Ropes of chili peppers, garlic bulbs, onions in baskets, and other green things she couldn't put a name to hung from the ceiling.

A large stainless metal door hung on one wall. Through the small pane of glass Miranda glimpsed what appeared to be packages of frozen food. The stove had gas burners. Long counters ran along each wall.

She completed her circuit of the kitchen, arriving back to face Drake who had remained motionless during her inspection.

"Who's your chef?" she asked.

"You're looking at him."

"You cook?" The idea struck her as ludicrous.

"Didn't Lucy ever tell you how much she loved coming home and finding me in the kitchen?" Drake crossed his arms.

"Did she?"

"Did she what?"

"Love to come home to find you puttering around in the kitchen?"

"I don't putter. I create."

"I don't believe it. Drake McLain, CEO chef. What next?" She sank onto the stool across from him, unsure of whether to believe him or not.

"Everyone needs a hobby. Yours is taking care of Pumpkin and Alice and your plants and that giant who thinks he's your personal bodyguard. I cook."

"Okay." Bemused and more than a little hungry, she hadn't eaten much at the social hour, she couldn't think of a better retort. At that moment her stomach answered for her.

Drake grinned. "I think that's my cue to prove my culinary worth, Mrs. McLain."

"Don't call me that." Miranda's response was automatic.

"It suits you." Drake went to the refrigerator. "You may as well get used to it. That's what my housekeeper is going to call you when she meets you in the morning."

"I'm not going to be here in the morning."

Drake moved to the center island, selected a large knife, and began to slice, dice, and chop until he had a pile of fresh cut vegetables in front of him.

"Don't count on it."

He moved to the freezer and disappeared into a cloud of frost. When he emerged the square box he held was dusted with snow. After brushing it off he opened it to reveal an exquisite layered cake.

"Ice cream cake for dessert," he explained. "By the time we're ready for it, it will have warmed enough to cut. Right now I'd need a chain saw to cut through it."

Miranda rotated on her stool every now and then as she followed his progress through the kitchen. What he ended up doing was a more than fair display of *Tappan* cooking, like she'd seen at her favorite Japanese restaurant. He tossed knives around as if it were second nature. The moment of truth, when he lit the fiery sake with a wooden match causing a whoosh of flame, had her on the edge of her seat.

At last he piled two plates with the deliciously scented stir-fry and led her through a swinging door into a small dining area. The circular table was set for two as if he'd thought this through ahead of time. The table was in an alcove encased by windows that overlooked the Front Range. During the day the view would be stunning. At sunset she wagered the view would take her breath away.

He held her seat then sat in the facing chair. All she could do was stare at him. His face glowed as if he'd just had the time of his life.

"Well?" He frowned. "I should have asked what you wanted. You hate stir fry, don't you?"

She answered by putting a forkful into her mouth. Delicious. She shut her eyes to savor the explosion of flavors on her tongue as she chewed. When she opened her eyes she found Drake staring at her. "It's great," she said.

"I'm sure you're embarrassed that your big, tough, wealthy husband cooked it for you." His statement came out flat--a challenge.

"The only thing that embarrasses me is that I can't cook this well. From now on you have kitchen duty." She gulped from her water glass; what she'd just said implied that she'd be staying.

"I'll hold you to that. Wait until you see what I can do with eggs at breakfast." His dimple deepened.

"Just for tonight," Miranda stated. "One night. I'm too tired to argue anymore."

Drake nodded and drank a tiny cup of sake. She wasn't sure, but Miranda thought he looked pretty pleased with himself.

He was more than pleased. One night would lead to two, then a weekend, then the next week, and then she'd be so comfortably entrenched that she wouldn't want to leave.

Watching her enjoy the meal he'd prepared, sitting across from him in his house, filled him with more content than he'd felt in a long time. He'd had damned little contentment with Lucy.

Lucy. Time to stop comparing the sisters. How could two such different individuals share the same gene pool and upbringing? They were as different as fire and ice. He much preferred Miranda's honest to Lucy's glamour. Miranda's deep-seated intellect to Lucy's charm.

Miranda looked delicious in red.

Which reminded him of his other hunger. The one she'd satisfied so unexpectedly last night. He wondered how much was the alcohol. He knew for damned sure she wouldn't have been a willing partner in her own seduction if she'd been sober.

Shifting in his chair, he poured another tiny cup of warm Japanese wine. "Would you like some sake?" he offered her.

She lifted on eyebrow, and then surprised him by crossing her eyes. "No thanks. I'm swearing off alcohol for a while."

"The morning after's a real bear, isn't it?"

Her blush started at the low neckline of her dress. Fascinated, Drake wondered how far in the opposite direction it went.

"I don't like to be out of control." Miranda sat straighter.

"Doesn't bother me a bit." He raised his cup in mock salute. He enjoyed watching as the embarrassment in her eyes shifted to annoyance. She narrowed her eyes at him.

"Don't think it will work again, Drake."

"I won't even try. I much prefer knowing a woman wants me for who I am, not for the whiskey she's drunk." He meant it to be sarcastic but the caustic tone of his voice made him flinch. Miranda threw down her napkin.

So much for a congenial dinner together.

"Drunk or sober it will take more than a miracle to find me in bed with you again," she shouted. She stalked out of the room.

He leaned back and waited.

Two seconds later she returned, flames in her eyes, mouth tight and tense. "Where the hell is my bedroom?"

Chapter Eleven

Miranda's first night at Drake's house was a bust as far as he was concerned. Instead of a rerun of the wild passion of the previous night, icicles shot from her eyes as she slammed the bedroom door in his face.

He had four weeks to melt icicles.

Instead of Miranda sharing his king-sized bed, Pumpkin snored on the rug on the floor beside him.

In the morning he found a piece of white notepaper at her place at the table instead of her. The note said, "Had some things to do before work. Will see you there." Polite, bland, passionless except for the thickness of the dark lines of her script.

Her absence disgruntled him. Until that moment he'd been unaware of how much he'd been looking forward to seeing her across the table from him again.

"She didn't even wait to see you this morning," he said to Pumpkin, who followed him everywhere. The dog even stood outside the shower door while Drake showered. At first the big brown eyes staring at him through the frosted glass disconcerted him. He became glad of the company soon enough.

He cut his morning routine short. He wanted his wife. More troubling, he wanted her to want him.

Rose and gold mist reflected the last of dawn's radiance on Pikes Peak. Fresh snow glazed the road making the morning sparkle. He was on the way to her. For the first time in years he enjoyed a frigid winter morning.

Her parking space at Millennium Tech yawned empty. It was early yet. The executive suite echoed with his footsteps as he strode across the hardwood floor.

He glanced into her office. The room and the position he'd created just for her was as empty as his stomach.

Where was she? She was as reliable as the sunrise, as the fact that it would snow in March.

"Get a grip," he mumbled. She must have gone back to her apartment for something he forgot to pack. He held that as a talisman against the worry that nagged at him. He turned on the computer. Soon he was engrossed in reading and answering email.

On the edges of consciousness he was aware of the sounds of the building waking up around him. He grunted his thanks as his assistant put his ritual morning coffee at his elbow. By that time he had the stock market quotes displayed on the screen. He studied what he saw there, then switched to the company stock system.

Something was wrong. More shares of private stock had been manipulated than when he last checked yesterday. An expert had shuffled them. He was being undercut.

He needed to talk to someone.

He needed Miranda.

* * * *

"He's a pig-headed jerk," Miranda said to Alice over coffee. She didn't care that she was late to work. She only knew that she needed to touch base with someone familiar.

Alice smiled around the steam from her mug. "Because he

wants you to be comfortable in his house?"

"You're on his side?" Miranda asked. Her voice squeaked a notch higher.

"I am not taking sides, my dear. Just trying to see both of them."

"It's just that everything is moving too fast. And now," she stopped. As far as Alice knew the last time Drake and Miranda had slept together had been on their so-called wedding night. Miranda thought of it in capital letters, The Night of the Missed Conception.

Now conception was a definite possibility. Unless she wanted to spill her guts, admit her less than appropriate behavior, to Alice, she'd better stop talking about Drake. Except that Alice probably thought she and Drake were still married because Miranda wanted them to be. After all, why the month long commitment if it was unnecessary?

Now it was necessary. She didn't want to admit that to her best friend.

What a mess.

Alice patted Miranda's hand. "It will work out just fine. Drake seems like a reasonable man. Just talk to him."

Miranda sighed.

"Tell me about this stock thing again," Alice prompted.

Miranda was only too happy to change the subject. She hated telling the part about Lucy's possible role. The part about her own broken engagement and how she'd learned about the reasons was embarrassing. But a funny thing happened as she told Alice everything she'd learned since that night in Las Vegas. She no longer felt protective of her little sister.

Her heart twisted at the thought that Lucy's choices, while not ones Miranda could approve of, were her own. Miranda's sympathies were fast approaching Drake.

Lucy had manipulated both of them.

"But," Miranda said to Alice as she had insisted to Drake, "Lucy doesn't have the technical or financial knowledge to manipulate stock or to steal technology."

Alice tapped her chin. After several silent minutes staring at the wall, she said, "You said something about this Bob person. He and Lucy had been involved and now he wants to have lunch with you?"

"He was lusting after lunch with me, until I spilled a glass of wine all over him," Miranda remembered with heat.

"A little spilled wine is nothing to a man who thinks he can still get what he wants. And if that something is in the form of his rival's wife and control of his rival's company, he'd probably forgive a lot more."

"You're right. It's important to get his guard down so I can find out what he really wants." She suppressed a shudder. "I suppose I can call him and offer him lunch as an apology for that accident."

"Good girl. What does Drake think about all this?"

"It's a big game to him. He's going to wire me like in spy movies."

"That's an excellent idea." Alice nodded. "Have you thought about how you will steer the conversation once you and Bob are alone?"

"Well, no."

A grin twitched at the corners of Alice's mouth. "I'll bet Drake has."

"Maybe. You sure are enjoying this." Miranda glanced at her watch. She couldn't remember a time when she'd been less enthusiastic about going to work. "I need to get to the office. I left the house before Drake woke this morning. If I know him, I'll have more explaining to do."

"I'll come with you," Alice said. She retrieved her coat from the closet. "I have a little experience with this 'spy stuff.' Going into lunch with a script will help you be more convincing. I'll see what I can gin up."

Even though she was pleased with Alice's offer, Miranda was still anxious about seeing Drake. Would he be angry that she'd left without more than a note? Worse, would he not care at all?

The second possibility worried her more than the first. Any emotion was better than none.

Drake's receptionist directed them into his office as soon as they stepped from the elevator. If Drake was anxious about Miranda's earlier disappearance he had a funny way of showing it. He sat behind his desk, telephone clasped to one ear while he hammered at the keyboard of the computer with his free hand. The only emotion he showed was a gleam in his eyes as Miranda and Alice entered the room.

Brief silence followed the end of his phone call. Then Drake directed his gaze at Alice. "Good morning. How's the book coming along?"

Miranda sank into a chair. What book?

Alice answered Drake, "I'm close to the end. The bad guys are about to get what's coming to them." She sat without waiting to be asked and crossed her ankles, the epitome of proper. "I'm here with practical advice today. Miranda tells me you plan to wire her for a meeting?"

Drake moved around his desk, leaning a hip against the edge. "Yes, but we didn't have a chance to pound out the details."

"I have some experience in this area; it may as well be put to use. Don't ask how I know. If I tell you," she smiled with grandmotherly sweetness, "I'd have to kill you."

"A woman after my own heart," Drake replied. "I have an expert on the way to set up the equipment. Your advice on the actual operation is appreciated."

"Good." Alice pulled a notebook and pen out of her voluminous purse.

"First, Miranda needs to make the phone call to Jones asking to meet her for lunch so that she can apologize for dumping her glass on him." Drake handed Miranda a three by five card. "I've made some notes on what you should say."

Miranda studied the words on the card. Heat crept up her neck. "No way. I can't say this to that creep."

Alice craned her neck so she could see what Miranda was reading. "Oh, very good, Drake. *Treat him* has such a seductive ring to it. Miranda, you must practice cooing a bit more."

"I don't coo," Miranda grumbled. She read a bit further. "The Oyster Palace? Why there?"

"Because, my naïve wife, oysters are sexy food," Drake drawled. "He'll be drooling and willing to tell you anything if you follow my script."

"What, exactly, do you want me to get out of him today? I'm hoping this is the one and only time I'll have to play this game. Spying is bad for my nerves."

"You have nerves of steel," Drake stated. He crossed his arms. "One more thing, I've got a special outfit for you to wear. One that will both carry the mike and make up for any verbal mistakes you make during your face to face."

"Not another tight red number, I hope. Maybe some sensible shoes this time, too."

Drake's eyes gleamed. "You're going to love it."

The level of deceit Drake was prepared to rise to in order to nail this guy astounded Miranda. Not only that, he didn't seem at all put out that it was Miranda's reputation he was putting on the line.

"Again," she said, "what exactly do you intend to accomplish from this meeting." Though she'd been eager to get to the bottom of the stock and technology scheme, she needed to know just what the stakes were now, today, and to her.

"Wheedling," Drake said. "See if you can get him to admit that his relationship with Lucy was more than just in the sack. And try to find out if he has any connection with Jack."

"What should she offer in return," Alice asked?

Drake turned to her. "I wanted your advice on that, seeing as you've dealt with this kind of thing before."

Miranda listened, feeling more and more like a lamb being led to the slaughter. Alice and Drake were deep into their discussion when a discrete knock on the door announced the wiring expert. When he joined the conversation, Miranda sneaked out.

Kevin met her in her new office suite. She looked around, pleased that earlier chaos had been replaced with the shining order she preferred.

Kevin handed her a small sheaf of telephone messages. He said, "I've made lunch reservations at The Oyster Palace, per Mr. McLain's instructions."

Miranda stared out the window. Kevin's reflection stared ghostly from behind her. "Get Bob Jones on the phone for me, please." She could see him open his mouth, and then shut it. The door clicked shut when he left.

The card with Drake's notes was crumpled in her fist. The bright winter sunshine failed to warm her. The intercom buzzed. Show time.

"Mr. Jones on line one, boss."

"Thanks, Kevin." She took a deep breath and picked up the phone.

"Bob," she cooed; she could do it if she wanted to. "I'd *love* to buy you lunch. My treat."

Chapter Twelve

Miranda wanted a shower after that conversation. Talk about an acting job. She pushed the intercom button. "Please tell Mr. McLain that everything is set. He'll know what I mean."

"Right away," Kevin's voice came through.

Miranda turned back to the window. The spectacular view failed to cheer her. The bright winter sunshine failed to warm her. Marrying Drake had changed even these simple pleasures for her. The job change was a nice change, not so the change in her relationship with her sister. Up until now that had been the most important relationship in her life. Her marriage had thrust her into a situation in which Lucy was the enemy.

Family ... Lucy was all the family Miranda had. She patted her flat stomach. Maybe that had changed, maybe not, but the whole incident was putting a whole new spin on how Miranda looked at her life. A child, the possibility made her warm with a type of pleasure that came as an unexpected gift.

She shook her head and turned her thoughts back to the company problem and how to discover the nature of who was buying stocks and how.

Her company stock might be the key to derailing Jack and Lucy and Bob. How much of it, how much of her future, dare she put on the line? Who would take the bait?

Most importantly, should she tell Drake her idea?

After her lunchtime espionage she'd decide. She'd also see Lucy again. There had to be more going on than met the eye. Lucy had lied about her role in the divorce, why stop there? Her motivation, that's what had Miranda puzzled because she couldn't figure it out.

A knock disturbed her reverie. Alice entered with a hanger of clothing draped over one arm and a nest of wires cascading from the other.

"What's all this?" Miranda asked.

"This is your lunch time illusion, Mata Hari." Alice's eyes twinkled.

"What's wrong with my suit?"

Drake strolled through the doorway, hands in the pockets of his slacks, tie loosened. Sexy, Miranda thought, and damned happy with himself.

"Your suit is fine for business." He looked her trim winter wool suit up and down. "But this will get you the results we need from lunch." He swept the plastic from one of the garments. A deceptively simple black dress with an extraordinary designer's label was thrust at her.

"You have just enough time to change," Drake said. "Then they'll wire you." He turned to Alice. "Come back in fifteen minutes."

When Drake and Miranda were alone, she fumed at him. "I'm tired of being pushed around. Get out so I can change."

He tossed the expensive dress across the back of a chair and closed in on her. "Wouldn't want to send you into the face of danger without a reminder of who I am and why you're here."

She leaned against her desk, arms crossed. "Reminder?" The intent expression on his face took her breath away. She hoped her knees would hold up.

Drake stopped inches from her face. Heat emanated from him. It coiled around Miranda. She fought its mesmerizing spell.

"Stop," she gasped.

He blinked. "Why? Aren't I good enough unless you've had a drink or two?" His lips tightened.

Was it possible she'd hurt him?

"Hardly." She slid around him and went to the dress. Picking it up she appreciated the drape of the cloth, the simple, elegant cut. She hoped she could live up to it.

"I would have locked the door." Drake faced her, his hands in his pockets again as if nothing had happened. Miranda felt the shift in his mood. The change in his posture, his blank expression, told her a lot.

"That's not the point." She lay the garment back down. "The purpose of our marriage is to use both our strengths to flush out the evidence against Jack and Lucy about the technology espionage and the stock buy-outs. Not to continue to add to the period of time we're married by a month here and there."

"You deny the attraction?"

Frustration boiled out of Miranda. She slapped the top of her desk. "Attraction is not the point." She paced like a trapped animal. "I plan to live a lifetime with the man I marry, committed to him and our life together for more than a finite, prearranged period of time. You cheapen it with your stupid innuendoes. I agreed to stay with you on a very slim condition."

She stopped her angry pacing and whirled to face him. Her voice dropped. "Wouldn't you prefer a marriage based on love and trust than whatever you thought you had with Lucy?"

A muscle along his jaw jerked. Other than that she couldn't see that anything she'd said had made an impact. Silence stretched between them, taut. At last he held up the dress.

"Regardless of your feelings, you have a job to do. When you're changed I'll send Alice in." He sauntered out of the office.

Miranda drooped into a chair. Talk about a confrontation. That one had fixed nothing. Wasted breath. Fine. She'd play spy girl as agreed. But she refused to stay another night under the same roof as him. Let people talk. She didn't care. She'd swallowed her pride more than enough of late. It was past time to stand up for herself. The place to start was with Drake.

Twenty minutes later Miranda thought she looked more like somebody's mistress than a spy. The dress had just the right combination of tightness and drape to look sexy yet approachable. Dignified yet seductive, and blessedly much less obvious than the red cocktail dress. How could Bob Jones refuse this bait?

"You'll do," was all Drake said through tight lips as he circled her after Alice and the electronics guy finished the wiring job.

"The microphone is in my necklace. These earrings hold a tiny receiver," she babbled. The way Drake stared, hungry and angry at the same time, unnerved her. "Let's get this over with," she demanded.

Drake nodded. She waited for him to help her into her coat but he walked out in front of her.

Now what was wrong? She couldn't figure this guy out. He ran hotter than the Sahara, and then colder than the Antarctic. If anyone had told her a month ago that she'd be in a personal relationship with him, she'd have laughed so hard she'd be crying. No one could get close to this man. She knew better, now. She'd do her damnedest to deny further intimacy between them.

Self-knowledge was supposed to liberate. Why did she feel so miserable as she followed Drake to the elevator?

* * * *

Alice chatted nonstop during the short drive to the restaurant. In a way it soothed Miranda's tattered nerves. Drake maintained his icy silence.

She shrugged off the vague unease caused by his attitude. She needed to focus on lunch and her role.

Role, she snorted. Between last night's red dress and today's simple elegance she felt more like an actress than an executive. Perhaps she was in the wrong profession.

She considered how the roles might be reversed had they been on their way to meet a female instead of Jones. But this outfit would look silly on Drake. Her mind drifted with that piece of idiocy until she caught Alice glancing at her, one eyebrow raised. Miranda smothered a giggle.

Drake broke his silence. "Glad you find this so funny."

How much more clipped could a man's voice be without cutting off his tongue?

"It's either laugh or cry at this point," she replied. "The details are fuzzy, but wasn't this your idea?"

His hands white-knuckled the steering wheel. "It'll work." The words came close to strangling him. "But," his eyes blazed as he took his gaze off the road for an instant and skewered her. "I swear I won't be as nice to you as I was to your sister if things progress further than we planned."

Miranda saw twenty vivid shades of red. How dare he? "Stop the car this instant."

"Is something wrong?" Alice asked.

"Damn right there's something wrong. Drake says he trusts me. He put me into this situation and now is putting conditions on a scenario I may have to improvise. Yes. Something is definitely wrong."

She put her hand on the door handle. "I swear, if you don't stop right this instant I will open the door while we're moving and jump into the street." Her breath came in deep gasps.

Was it possible for a face to become more mask-like? Drake ignored her demand.

"Think of the scandal, Drake. Won't that be good for business-- new bride can't stand sitting next to her husband and jumps out of a moving car?"

"Miranda, dear, don't do anything rash," Alice counseled. She reached forward to touch Miranda's arm.

"I agree, don't do anything rash," Drake said, his voice switched to that irritating drawl that made Miranda want to scream.

"Oh Drake, I'm not sure that was the best thing to say," Alice said.

"Rash is what got me into this mess to begin with," Miranda retorted. "I'm sure my dear husband knew exactly what to say," she said to Alice.

"My hand is on the door, Drake."

Drake sped through a yellow light.

"Drake, don't you think you should slow down and talk about this?" Alice's voice of reason sounded from the back seat.

The tension left Drake's shoulders. Through her anger Miranda recognized his "I've almost won" posture.

No way. Not this time. She fumed in silence until they reached a cross street where Drake had to slow down.

She jerked the door handle, prepared herself for the fall, and pushed.

Chapter Thirteen

Nothing happened.

Miranda pushed again, and again, and finally used both fists on the door that stubbornly refused to open. He'd locked her door with the switch on his side.

She watched a grin curl around one side of Drake's mouth. "I hate you," she muttered.

Alice settled back into her seat. "That's better."

"It's not better." Miranda subsided against the door, seething and giddy at the same time.

The restaurant was just ahead. Drake pulled into the parking garage and turned off the engine. Against the ticking of the cooling car Miranda struggled to control her heart rate. Whether or not Drake trusted her, she had to go through with this. Her future was at stake as much as Drake's or that of Millennium Tech.

She glared at him. "The next time I tell you to stop, I expect you to listen."

He quirked an eyebrow at her.

She took a deep breath, one battle at a time. "Let's get this over with."

At Drake's push of a button all the car doors unlocked. He nodded to Miranda. The grin that crinkled the corners of his eyes caused that knot to form in her stomach again.

"I'm glad you're buying me lunch," Alice remarked as she opened her door. "Espionage and marriage counseling is a tiring business."

"Dangerous, too," Drake added. He led Miranda and Alice to the entrance of the restaurant. "We're early, as planned. Alice will go in first. When Miranda enters she will insist on a table nearby. That way Alice can provide assistance if needed. It will be a bit more handy and natural than me storming through the door.

Miranda nodded. Too late for second and third thoughts now. It was crunch time. Her hands were clammy inside her gloved even thought the temperature hovered near the freezing mark.

She said to Drake, "You'd better leave now. If Jones sees you hovering, all bets are off."

Alice agreed. "Once Miranda is seated I'll do a sound check." She patted Drake's arm. "Don't worry. Everything will be just fine."

"Fine," Drake repeated, his face a mask again.

CAUGHT

Miranda shook herself as Alice entered the restaurant and Drake turned to go back to the car.

He didn't get far. "One more thing." He pulled her to him and kissed her hard and fast. When he set her away from him, his eyes blazed at her. Their breath hung in little puffs between them. "I trust you."

Stunned, Miranda watched him stride away. His kiss did more than take her breath away. It sent her mind reeling. It took every ounce of will power she possessed not to follow him.

He *did* trust her. Being told that was nearly as compelling as the kiss. Both combined to weaken her knees.

She glanced through the restaurant window. From this vantage point she could see Alice seated at a small table near the center of the cozy room. In order for this to work, she had to focus. Hard as it was, she must shake off the enigmatic spell Drake kept binding her with.

With an effort she closed her mind to everything except the required conversation and actions she must take over the next ninety minutes.

Breath, she commanded her lungs. Then she opened the door - Act one, Scene one.

* * * *

Drake started the car's engine. Both the radio and recorder were tied in to the car battery. This way he could keep it charging and stay warm.

With one ear he listened to Alice and Miranda's sound check. He heard Miranda tell the maitre 'd that she was meeting a friend. She ordered a cup of hot tea. Then the real wait began.

He glanced at the clock on the dash then at his wristwatch. Jones was late. Would he show up or back out at the last moment?

Just as Drake was beginning to think this was one of the worst business decisions of his career, he heard Miranda whisper, "Here he comes."

During the next hour every demon Drake thought he had exorcised after Lucy's betrayal haunted him. The receiver attached to Miranda's microphone made every word she uttered sound breathy and seductive. Bob Jones came off as slick, arrogant, and overconfident.

"You told her your trusted her," Drake muttered, disgusted with the wealth of emotions roiling within. "Get a grip."

It took a lifetime for the two diners to get to dessert. He heard Miranda tell the waiter, "Just coffee for me."

Jones ordered a chocolate strawberry cheesecake, not a taste sensation Drake associated with a man. Jones' words stopped Drake's stray thought.

"I wanted something rich and sweet," Jones murmured. The voice was so cloying Drake imagined it gumming up the speakers.

Laughing, Drake relaxed against the cold leather seat. In his mind's eye he saw Miranda cutting poor, unsuspecting Jones off in mid-seduction. She'd never fall for that sweet, rich routine.

The next words he heard her say throbbed through him. "That looks delicious. May I try a bite?" She practically purred.

Drake straightened. He gritted his teeth. She knew he was listening. This was for show, that's all. A damned convincing show.

And the show was almost over with nothing to show for it. He had nothing on Jones. He needed something concrete about business. Something he could dig his teeth into. Something he could wrap his hands around and squeeze --

Miranda's soft voice interrupted Drake's fantasy. "This lunch was your idea, Bob. I think you had something in mind other than food."

"I heard you like to cut to the chase. Excellent. But not here. Too public."

"You realize that that is the only reason I'm here. I can't afford to jeopardize my reputation." Miranda's voice held just the right note of curiosity and reticence.

Damn, she was good.

"Of course," Jones said. "Your reputation is the very reason I sought you out. No one would suspect—"

Miranda cut him off. "Please get to the point. Drake expects me back at the office soon."

"I have a business proposition to offer you. It could be very lucrative."

"I'm intrigued. Tell me more."

Drake allowed a small grin to move his rigid lips. This was what he'd been waiting for.

Jones said, "All I can say is that my source of information within Millennium Tech has dried up. I need a new source. I think you'd be perfect for the job."

Silence and a bit of static held Drake captive. Then the clink of porcelain against porcelain came through. Miranda must have taken a sip of coffee while considering Jones' proposal.

"Come on, Miranda," Drake muttered. "Take the bait."

The steel in her voice caught him, and no doubt caught Jones, off guard.

"I don't like being used, Mr. Jones."

"Bob, please call me Bob."

"What makes you think I would even consider your offer?"

"The fact that your are here with me so shortly after your marriage indicates that all is not what it seems between you and McLain."

"Maybe." A long pause. "I'll need more information before I make a decision. Money is irrelevant, there are other matters of more importance to me at this time," Miranda murmured.

"I understand."

Drake wished he could see Jones' face. Was it sneering or smiling or a mask of concern? He wished this odd luncheon were over. He needed to see Miranda's face, know that his trust in her was well placed.

Miranda spoke again. "Before I meet you again, tell me who your source inside Millennium Tech was."

"No names. Not now. But I will tell you it was someone you knew, ah, intimately."

Drake uttered a sharp curse. With a name on tape he could have prosecuted, or at least he could have gone to the authorities with something more than a gut feeling and inconclusive evidence. Now he'd have to let Miranda go through with another meeting with Jones.

He didn't like that one bit.

He heard Jones and Miranda part company after setting another meeting time and place. Alice's voice came on. "She's out, so is he. I'll meet you in a few minutes."

* * * *

Miranda slipped into the car beside Drake. "I'm glad that's over." She rubbed between her eyes. "I don't think I make a very good femme fatale."

"You were adequate," he replied. He disconnected the recording devices from the car and stowed them away.

"Gee, thanks for the glowing review."

"You didn't get the information I need to send someone to jail," Drake grated.

"It's not like I didn't try. What did you expect me to do? Sleep with him on the spot?"

Drake growled. Miranda couldn't decide if it was a sound of warning or something else.

Alice opened the back door and climbed in. "Communicating

again? Wonderful."

Drake started the car and began the drive back to Millennium Tech. "She's going to have to meet with him again."

"Unwise," Alice said. "Jones may come across as bland and unimaginative, but there's something about him that I don't trust."

Miranda nodded. The last thing she wanted was to be alone with that slimeball again.

"Trusting Jones has nothing to do with it," Drake said. "Getting tangible evidence is the only reason we're doing this."

"We?" Miranda turned to Alice. "I know the outcome of this plan is the good of the company and all, but I think Drake should be the one to make a fool of himself the next time. This was it for me."

Drake growled.

Tapping her front teeth, Alice said, "You know, a different strategy might be more effective."

"Like what?" Anything but another vamp number, Miranda hoped.

"If you want to know without a shadow of a doubt who sold technology to Jones, a different kind of bait would be more useful." Alice was silent for a moment, and then her quiet voice said, "I take it you have an idea who you want?"

"Yes," Drake said.

"Who would that be?"

Tense quiet filled the car.

Drake pulled into the parking garage at their office building, parked, and turned off the ignition. Into the ticking silence he said, "Jack and Lucy."

Miranda's throat tightened at the coolness of his voice. Though she knew Lucy was one of his suspects, that Jack might be involved as well made her ache.

"Is that why you fired Jack?" Her voice sounded stretched and tight to her own ears.

Drake nodded. His voice was more than a little fierce when he said, "You were too good for him."

Alice cleared her throat. "I could have told you that."

Though Miranda heard Alice's statement, her awareness remained centered on the man beside her. His gaze caught hers across the cooling air, warmed her with the intensity that always roiled just beneath his calm surface.

"Is that why you fired Jack?" she asked again, meaning something completely different.

She waited as she watched Drake swallow twice. He wrenched his gaze from hers.

"Lunch break's over," he said.

The two women followed him, a solitary figure striding forward. By the time they reached the executive suite Miranda had decided to ignore the feeling that Drake had deliberately not answered her last question. Besides, what did she hope to gain by an answer? Their marriage was doomed from its not-so-auspicious start. She already knew a good deal of his reasons for marrying her. The fact that Jack was involved up to his thinning little eyebrows surprised her, but not as much as it should have.

Alice followed Miranda into her office. They removed the microphones and other spy paraphernalia. When she'd changed back into her business suit, Miranda took a moment to appreciate the new space. Her assistant must have bribed the custodial staff to move all of her personal and business affects up here so quickly. That young man deserved a raise.

Drake was all business when Alice and Miranda joined him in the conference room.

"New plan." He ran a hand through his hair. "I'm giving you just the bait Jones will want, Miranda. Technology. But you'll have to get him to divulge his inside source first. Without evidence I can't prosecute."

"Just what kind of technology are you going to tempt him with?" Miranda asked.

"The best kind. Something so new and revolutionary he's only heard little tiny breaths of it." Drake grinned. "So new it doesn't even exist. You and I will invent it tonight."

Chapter Fourteen

"This is crazy enough it just might work." Alice drained her cup and pushed away from the boardroom table. The surface was strewn with papers, from computer printouts to doodled legal pad remnants.

"It is crazy," Miranda agreed. Her stomach rumbled. Long hours had passed since her lunch with Jones. They'd spent the afternoon and into the evening planning this elegant trap.

Drake said nothing. He sat at the end of the table staring into space and tapping a pencil. His quiet intensity encouraged

Miranda more than anything else had during this intense day. The staring and pencil tapping presaged a winning strategy. It always did. Why should this be any different?

At that moment Drake shifted from staring at the ceiling to staring into Miranda's eyes. His penetrating look mesmerized her. She felt heat between her breasts. All thoughts of business and espionage fled her mind. Images of Drake and what he'd done to her, in her bed, rushed to fill the void. As if she were experiencing it again, she felt the insistent pressure of his lips on her mouth. She tasted the smoky essence of his whisky-coated tongue as it coaxed hers.

Locked into his gaze she swallowed. A muscle in his cheek twitched as if he knew her thoughts. Struggling not to whimper Miranda forced herself to look away--at the floor, the table, the remains of the crumpled coffee cups--anywhere but at Drake.

A droning filled her ears. She realized it was Alice speaking. "So as long as that's settled I'll talk to you later."

"Oh sure. Thanks for your help." Miranda hurried to stand.

"I haven't had this much fun since I retired," Alice said, the twinkle evident in her clear blue eyes. "Drive safely you two. Looks like more snow coming down."

After Alice left, Miranda stood in front of the plate glass window. White flakes danced in the glow of the orange-yellow streetlights far below. She shivered. Warm hands cupped her shoulders. She resisted for a token second before giving into their comfort.

Drake massaged Miranda's neck and shoulders. The tension that had built throughout the day drained away under the pressure of his strong thumbs and hands. Her eyes drifted shut. She relaxed into him. The way he touched her made her forget why they were together.

He nibbled her neck. She inhaled a faint ghost of his aftershave. He moved to an earlobe. His thumbs rubbed away her earlier anger and anxiety.

Miranda opened her eyes. What she saw made her gasp. Their ghostly reflection in the glass showed a woman on the brink of saying, "yes," to the man behind her.

The effect was like stepping into an icy stream. She straightened away from Drake, pulling her professional mantle around her as she moved. It was the only way she could keep any distance from this man. At the same time a little niggling voice inside taunted her, "You don't *want* any distance. Coward."

She managed to ignore the voice for now. It would return

louder and more insistent as she tried to sleep later.

Drake remained facing the window.

Good, think cold thoughts, she aimed at him.

The look he gave her when he finally turned around was anything but cold. Banked fires gleamed from his eyes to hers.

The Board Room was too small. She had to get away from the hypnotizing effect Drake had on what was left of her intellect.

That's not intellect, the little voice inside her jeered.

Miranda shook away the thought. "I'm ready to call it a day. Pumpkin will be desperate for his walk and I'm hungry. I'll meet you back at your house."

"You were great today," Drake said.

Miranda paused in the act of pulling on her coat. Earlier hurt rushed back. "You might have said that sooner."

"I should have."

His gentle tone mollified her. "Not overdone, then?"

"No."

"Good. I'll see you later?" She hated the question at the end but couldn't help adding it.

"Yes. I'll follow you home."

Home. Miranda buttoned her coat and pulled on her lined leather gloves. It wasn't her home or their home. It was his home. She'd best remember that. When her thirty days was over she'd be leaving it and him.

The flutters in her stomach at the thought were hunger induced. At least that's what she told herself as she drove through the snowy night.

* * * *

The wind howled. Pumpkin shifted uneasily on the rug beside Miranda's bed. Miranda snuggled under the down comforter. The electronic number on the clock on the bedside table read two-fifteen in a red that was straight from hell fire.

Her body wept with exhaustion. Her mind raced through the events of the day and plans for the next day.

She tossed to her other side; fluffed the pillow. A grainy pattering of icy pellets sounded like bony fingers as the wind drove them against the window. Since midnight the storm had increased in intensity.

Pumpkin moaned. Restless, he put his head next to Miranda's on the bed.

"I give up, too, boy." She flung off the covers, pushed her feet into slippers, and shrugged into her robe. "Let's go see what we can find in the kitchen. A cup of hot chocolate would taste good right now."

The childhood days when hot chocolate was all she needed to go back to sleep were long gone. She had to try something, though.

A sliver of light showed under the door to the kitchen. Hesitating for just an instant Miranda pushed open the door. Pumpkin preceded her inside. He did not hesitate as he lumbered directly to Drake.

Miranda's breath caught in her throat as she looked at Drake. In a gray college sweatshirt, worn jeans, and sneakers he looked anything but the successful executive.

He oozed sex appeal.

She resigned herself to a sleepless night.

"I hope you don't mind if I raid your refrigerator," she said as she reached for a mug.

"What's mine is yours," he said without looking up from scratching Pumpkin's ears.

Silence, punctuated by the sounds of the storm, accompanied Miranda as she went about heating milk and adding cocoa and sugar.

This would be a perfect time to talk to Drake. To let him know her concerns about their relationship. To tell him how making love the other night had affected her much more deeply than she ever wanted it to. This would be the perfect time to tell him.

Tell him what? That she was falling in love with him? No.

She leaned against the counter as she sipped her drink. His head, hair tousled and chin needing a shave, was inclined toward the magazine on the table in front of him. One hand scratched Pumpkin's large head. An unbidden memory surfaced. It reminded her of the pleasures that very hand had given her.

Miranda gulped then choked as the hot liquid seared her throat.

"Are you all right?" Drake's eyes bore into her as the cough subsided.

Her mind screamed *no* at the same time she nodded. "I, um, guess I'll go back to bed." She rinsed her mug and set it into the sink for morning. Her hand shook as he came up behind her.

His body's warmth radiated toward her. She focused on not arching back to meet it. His breath glanced across the nape of her neck. The tiny hairs tingled and danced.

She held her hands clasped together, determined not to reach around for him. When his arms came around her, she gave up. She turned to face him.

What else could she do? Whenever she fought the desire to be in his arms, desire won.

In spite of his high-handed ways she'd fallen in love with him. Even so, pride demanded that the last thing she should do was allow more intimacy.

He didn't kiss her. Except for that tick in his left cheek you would think his face was carved from stone.

"What will you do when the thirty days are up?" His voice throbbed low and deep across the scant inches between them.

She put a hand to her abdomen. "It depends."

"What if you aren't pregnant?"

She swallowed hard. "It depends," was the only thing she could think of to say.

To her surprise he did not pull her closer, didn't try to kiss her or touch her or do any of the things she knew she shouldn't want but wanted all the same. He regarded her with those gray eyes. A slight frown creased his brow. He took a step back, then another.

If Miranda didn't know the man better she'd think he was unsure of something. Impossible. Drake had the original license for "sure of himself." He never showed weakness. Retreating was out of character, like water running up hill. At any other time it would be amusing.

His next words sobered her. "We should remain married regardless of your condition."

"Words every romantically-notioned girl wants to hear," she said. Her fingers grabbed at the counter behind her. "Why?"

He stopped pacing. "You know the answer."

Irritation gave her strength. "I can think of any number of reasons. All to your benefit. Let's see, how about so you won't look like a fool for losing a second wife who just happens to be the sister of your first?"

"I don't care what people say." His toneless voice should have warned her, but she was on a roll.

"Well, there's all my stock and vaunted business expertise. You'd hate to lose all that, wouldn't you?"

"True." He took a step in her direction.

She backed to the door. "Then there's the fact that I know more about you now than I did a week ago. That makes me too valuable to let me go. That's the real reason, isn't it, Drake? I know more of your personal and professional secrets than anyone does. That scares you. You know that knowledge is power. It makes me quite the hot commodity in today's market. Don't you agree?"

On that parting shot she reached around her for the doorknob.

Unfortunately she'd lost track of Pumpkin while she was shouting. Instead of smooth porcelain, her hand met wet dog nose. It distracted her.

In the instant she took to look down at Pumpkin and wipe her hand against her jeans, Drake had her. In one quick movement he trapped her against the door.

At least I reached the door, she thought with a panicky sense of humor. She fought against the delightful ache that possessed her as Drake's hard body pressed against her.

She looked into his eyes. They were storm-dark with emotion. A tremor ran through him.

He's afraid, she realized.

"Why don't you want me to leave?" she whispered.

"For all the reasons you so succinctly stated."

"And?"

He stared into her eyes. His gaze dropped to her lips. She licked them wet.

Then he changed the way he held her. The subtle shift made her breath quicken.

"And?" she asked again.

"Because," he growled, "we haven't made love while sober yet." His lips claimed hers.

Drake felt Miranda's initial resistance fade, then vanish all together. He'd almost lost his composure, his will to keep her off guard. Now with her soft moans against his mouth and her hands grasping his shoulders, he struggled with a different type of composure. He pulled back and rested his forehead against hers.

He wanted her. He needed to possess this woman who stood toe to toe with him and gave as good as she got. The fact that he would lose himself in her terrified him. He kept his thoughts to himself. To reveal such weakness wasn't his way. Never had been. Why change now? He'd learned this lesson the hard way.

Pumpkin whined. He butted his head against Drake's thigh in an effort to wedge himself between Drake and Miranda. The movement knocked them close together. It forced Drake's thighs to rub against Miranda's. Her soft breasts pushed against his chest. He was aware of the peaks, hard where they pressed against the fabric and him.

The look she gave him, hot, needy and slightly frightened, melted the last of his resolve. She put her hands on either side of his face before she reached up to kiss him.

With a groan he drowned himself in her taste, her scent, the feel of her soft rounded body pressed against his need.

He picked her up. Their mouths pressed together. Her legs came up and wrapped around his waist. Pushing her against the door, he reached beneath her robe. The bunched up fabric of her nightgown was in the way. He shoved it aside.

The groan she uttered when he reached the moist warmth of her womanhood made him harder. He'd explode if he didn't have her soon.

The floor would have to do.

Chapter Fifteen

Drake lowered Miranda to the floor. Everything was going great until Pumpkin decided he didn't want to be left out. Drake came close to losing his grip on Miranda as he struggled to push away the dog while continuing his seductive assault on her.

Pumpkin growled. He poked his nose into Drake's cheek. Drake's feet slid out from under him. The next thing he knew, he was at the bottom of a heap with Miranda and the dog collapsed on top of him.

So much for seduction.

Miranda hiccupped then squealed. "Get off, Pumpkin." Her voice came out breathless, hoarse.

After Drake helped push the dog away he took a deep breath and looked at Miranda. Her flushed face, swollen lips, and bright eyes had him reaching for her all over again.

"I think Pumpkin came to my rescue just in time," she said. Her calm gaze belied her rapid breathing.

Drake's heart plummeted. He was sure that if he had the chance to make love to her again, sober without anything to "blame", that she'd agree to stay with him.

Damn that dog.

The offending beast chose now to lie down. He kept his gaze on Drake and Miranda.

Probably happy to keep us separated, Drake thought. Just what he needed, a jealous dog. He'd gotten Miranda away from her apartment complex full of nosy neighbors. He'd brought the dog along because she wouldn't have stayed a single night without him. Now what happens? Instead of being grateful for his good fortune the huge hairy beast sabotaged Drake's one chance in days to seduce his wife.

Drake got to his feet, lending a hand to Miranda as he rose. Her wrinkled brow had him grinning. She grinned back. As the idiocy of the situation hit them both, laughter followed.

"This dog is better than a chastity belt," Drake gasped when he stopped laughing long enough to speak.

"A virtual knight in furry armor," Miranda said. Another bout of giggles overtook her.

Drake stepped closer. He reached for her. "Let's try that again."

She stopped laughing. The hand she placed against his chest was firm. "No. I was serious when I said it was a good thing Pumpkin stopped us."

Cold air, a draft perhaps, touched the hands Drake had reaching for her. He looked down at her left hand that lay on his chest. The rings pressed against him and at the same time held him away.

"We're husband and wife. Why shouldn't we?"

She stepped back. "It's all a ruse, Drake. I don't like being played with."

"I'm not playing house with you." More than sexual frustration colored his voice, deepened its tone. He couldn't tell her how important she'd become to him. If he told her, she'd laugh it off. He couldn't chance it.

"Then what were you doing just then?" She turned a now angry face away from him and headed for the door.

"What do you want, Miranda?" It was the only thing he could think of to say. Miraculously, she stopped.

In a quiet voice, she said, "I want a marriage based on love and respect, trust and friendship. A marriage where making love is an act of completion, not an act of sex. I want a marriage where making love is the icing on an already gourmet cake. That's all I want. I won't settle for anything less."

With her back straight she left Drake standing alone in the brightness of the stainless steel kitchen. Pumpkin followed her.

Sudden tightness caught the back of Drake's throat. He'd never felt more alone.

* * * *

After a night of listening to the wind blow, Miranda was glad to hear the nagging beep of her alarm clock. A glimpse outside showed her at least a foot of new fallen snow. The sun shone fitfully through low clouds. Wind blew feathers of frozen particles against objects in its path.

Thankful for the wool pantsuit hanging in the closet, she dressed then took Pumpkin outside to take care of his morning business. Hot coffee greeted her in the kitchen. Drake's presence consisted of a grunt when she said good morning. He looked like he'd been up for hours, his face had a tight, strained appearance even though he looked just as sexy like that as when he was relaxed and composed.

It seemed that Pumpkin had been the only one to get a decent night's sleep. She amused herself with a ridiculous image of Pumpkin dressed in a pinstriped suit.

"What have you got to be so happy about?" Drake grumbled. He didn't give her a chance to answer. "Here are the phony specs for you to entice Jones with.

Miranda took the sheet of paper from him and sat in the chair across the table. Much of it was derived from their meeting yesterday with Alice. The paper held facts and figures and the briefest of proposals for developing new computer software reliant on micro disk technology. It was even printed on Millennium Tech logo stationary. Drake had put hours into this piece of paper that was meant to trap his competitor. A tiny line in the footer of the paper caught her attention. It showed that the file had originally been created over a year ago. Nice touch.

Frowning, Miranda freshened her coffee and returned to the information in front of her. Analysis was her forte, this information intrigued her.

The rasping bark of Pumpkin asking to come in broke her concentration. She looked up to see the unlikely sight of Drake, in dress shirt and tie, wiping down the snow-covered dog with a thick towel. His hands rubbed until Pumpkin was mostly dry, and then he bent to clean the snow from between the dog's pads.

The care lavished on her dog mesmerized Miranda. Except for the unforgettable night they'd spent together, she'd never experienced his tender side.

Heat crept up her neck as she thought about that night. So much sheer passion. Was that what had been missing in her other relationships with men?

Answering warmth began between her legs. At just that moment, Drake turned his head and caught her watching him. The warmth in his eyes mimicked the very real sensations of her body.

She licked her lips and almost gave herself whiplash as she refocused on the paper in front of her. Words swam around making no sense. What had she been thinking of before she had looked at Drake?

Breathe, she commanded.

Technology and timing--that was it. But Drake had changed a few of the details that they'd hashed out with Alice yesterday. Forcing her voice not to show any emotion, she asked, "Just what are we trying to give away?"

Drake came to loom behind her. She felt the heat from his body only inches away from her back.

"It's something I've worked on, off and on, for a while. No big deal. I had to make it look like something we already had in the works or Jones would be suspicious."

"I had no idea you worked the technical side of the business, too."

"I couldn't very well run a successful business without knowing all aspects, could I? I've got to know every detail about our products before attending trade shows or conventions in order to attract customers and keep current clients happy."

Interested more in Drake than in the specs in front of her, Miranda turned in her chair. Mistake. The move put her nose on level with the center of his trousers.

She fought off another blush. "When did you step away from the design work and focus on the business end?"

"A couple of years before you came on board."

"And this?" She waved the paper at him.

"A hobby, just something I fool around with from time to time."

"This is breakthrough work, Drake. I can't agree to put something too important to both you and Millennium Tech on the line." It was true. This design was brilliant if she was any judge; and she was.

Drake leaned over her shoulder. The clean scent of him made her nostrils flare. It was all she could do not to lean into him.

He said, "The stakes are already high. If you do your job right, nothing is at risk."

"If I blow it?"

"Don't."

The single word chilled her. Its simplicity said volumes about who was taking the biggest risk in this venture. It also spoke loudly that he trusted her not to fail. She had a reputation for working well under pressure, but the stakes of this project were higher than she'd ever imagined. Millennium Tech's future, her future, and Drake's future all revolved around her giving Bob Jones a convincing performance later today.

It wasn't fair that Drake should be taking the biggest risk. Her personal integrity was on the line, but this was Drake's whole life. What could she contribute that would sweeten the deal with Jones? How could she insure that he wouldn't be able to say no to her proposition?

For the first time she didn't refuse Drake's offer to drive her to work. They listened to the weather report and early news as Drake navigated the freshly plowed streets.

Miranda used the quiet to make a decision. A decision that she had to keep from Drake or it wouldn't work. If he suspected anything, he wouldn't let her do it. She'd put her own shares of stock up for sale. Jones would be the only person to know. If that didn't sweeten the pot for that slimy creature, as well as flush out Jack and get some damning evidence on him, she didn't know what would.

She was almost relaxed when they pulled into Drake's parking slot. He ruined her calm by asking, "How are you feeling these morning? Any queasy stomach, exhaustion?" The dimple in his cheek flashed at her.

She allowed humor to chase away her initial irritation. She could give as good as she got. "Not yet. By the way, did you know that twins run in our family?"

His jaw dropped.

She kept the memory of that look on his face with her all morning.

She had little time to enjoy her new executive suite. In between getting up to speed on her new job responsibilities she had to put her stock on the market without tipping anyone off--including her efficient assistant.

The third time Kevin interrupted her computer work so that she had to minimize her computer screen in a rush, she snapped. "Would you mind knocking?"

He dropped the papers he'd been carrying, then scrambled to pick them up. "Sure, boss. Sorry, I thought you wanted to keep the same routine."

Miranda rubbed the back of her neck. She'd hurt his feelings; it was clear in the confused look in his eyes. "I do want to keep the same routine. Just give me an hour of uninterrupted time, would you? No phone calls, no visitors, nothing."

"Can I help you with something?"

She summoned up what she hoped would pass for a reassuring smile. "Not right now. Thanks. Just keep it quiet for a while.

"No problem."

"Thank you." Miranda sighed after he shut the door behind him. This stock thing needed more concentration than she'd anticipated. Almost done, though. Then she could take a break.

Fifteen minutes later it was finished. She'd set the bait. Now all she had to do was dangle it in front of the greedy nose of Bob Jones.

Chapter Sixteen

Immersed in a tricky acquisition plan, Drake didn't notice the time until an alarm on his computer beeped. He'd programmed it to notify him whenever company stock came up for sale.

He looked up from the papers on his desk and stared at the computer screen. He frowned at what he saw. A chill blanket settled in his chest. He tapped at the keys, needing more data, hoping for a different answer than that displayed before him. Miranda's shares, all her stock, had been put up for sale.

The black and white figures on the screen mocked him as a testimony to his gullibility. She had tricked him into marrying her, then into seducing her. He'd begun to think he could love her.

It looked like blood had won out after all. She had thrown in her lot with her sister and that miserable excuse for a man, Jack.

The enormity of his conclusion weighed on him. It made sense. The audacity of her scheme left him breathless.

It took a few moments of incredulity for the idiocy of his conclusion to surface.

The Miranda he knew, or thought he knew through years of working together, never came across as an underhanded traitor.

He made a conscious effort to unclench his fists. Paper rattled. He looked down to see that his hands had mangled the merger papers spread across his desk.

Flexing his hands he forced himself to consider other reasons for Miranda's actions. Maybe she needed cash. No, he paid her well despite her less than luxurious apartment. He wondered how she spent her salary if not on a fancy condominium or house. Money and greed was the most common reason for crime. Everything he knew about Miranda screamed that he was on the wrong track.

Maybe she had a secret life--a secret husband in a different state. His head pounded, then he dismissed the idea as pure fantasy. Primal possessiveness filled him. She was his. Besides,

CAUGHT

she wasn't the type to have a secret life. He laughed at the notion, glad to put it away.

He prided himself on being a good judge of character. Remembering how first Lucy then Jack had tricked him made the pounding in his head return.

Images of the recent past with Miranda flashed through his mind. The silliness of her trying to seduce him and his unguarded reaction to it; the wedding that she still believed had been real. She would have to know the truth sooner or later. He imagined her reaction to the news, his lips curled.

His groin tightened as his mind leaped to the brief flash of red satin he'd slid her into on their wedding night. He'd stared at her as she'd snored lightly, innocently. He'd been plotting to use her and felt a sense of relief that the camera idea had failed. Using her that way would have done irreparable damage.

He could not hurt her, ever. Perhaps that was why he'd touched her with more care than efficiency when changing her into that red outfit. To say it took more willpower than he thought he possessed not to run his hands across her warm, soft skin when she had been at his mercy was a memory he tried to forget.

The lovemaking, the way she'd truly seduced that night at her place, her passion had startled him. He wanted more of that. He wanted more of her.

What she thought of him as a person, not just as a boss or co-conspirator, had become of pivotal importance.

A cool bead of sweat tickled his brow. His feelings for Miranda overshadowed everything.

He glanced at the stock transaction on the computer screen.

Nicole's voice intruded through the intercom. "Mr. McLain, the meeting is ready for you."

"Thanks." Drake's reply was automatic. Miranda would be at that meeting.

Until he knew for sure what she was doing, he'd avoid her. Wanting to trust her, even telling her that he trusted her, was insufficient. Knowing beyond a doubt--that was necessary.

A weight he suspected was his cooling heart settled in his chest. He made arrangements for a trusted associate to buy Miranda's stock for him.

Loneliness followed him to the meeting. Miranda's smiling face tortured him for the next two hours. He brushed her off when the meeting was over; noticing how her smile became a question became a frown. Hurt crept into her eyes. He swallowed hard.

For the first time in as long as he could remember, work refused to solace him. When he couldn't take it any longer he left, giving the car keys to Nicole to keep for Miranda. The taxi ride home passed in a blur.

Pumpkin kept Drake company in the kitchen where he tried to cook himself into a better mood. It didn't work. He gave that up as the sun went down. Miranda had not come home. The sky was dark with the last bloody streak of sunset the only relief.

Drake went to the bedroom Miranda used. The perfume bottle on the dresser, her robe across the end of the bed, a novel on the bedside table all managed to make this impersonal room cozy, warm, and imbued with her.

Pumpkin lay on the rug. Drake sat on the edge of the bed.

"I miss her." Drake's voice cut the quiet air.

Pumpkin lifted his large head and twitched his ears. With a soft whine the dog set his muzzle on Drake's knee.

"You too?" Drake scratched Pumpkin's silken ears. It soothed him.

"You know, I stopped trusting people a long time ago. That thing with Lucy just reinforced what I already knew--everyone looked out for herself. Why should I stop thinking that way now?"

Pumpkin licked Drake's wrist. Drake was aware of the dog's chocolate brown eyes following him as he wandered around the room.

"She's unlike anyone I've ever known." He opened her closet door. His nostrils quivered at the combination of the scent of cedar panels and Miranda's scent that lingered within.

"She listens to what I say. She likes my cooking. I don't intimidate her." He went to the window, wishing the headlights glowing in the distance heralded Miranda's arrival. But they kept on past the house; nothing cut across the darkened landscape below.

"How can we work things through if we're never together?"

The dog's gaze gave Drake a silent agreement.

He'd confront her this evening. This on again-off again marriage business had worn thin. He'd just have to win her over with wit and charm and passion. Then, when he had her melting in his arms, he'd tell her that they weren't really married.

Pumpkin whined.

"If she's pregnant, she'll have to marry me for real. Won't she?"

The dog blinked.

"You're right," Drake commented. "She'll kill me, sue me for child support, then kill me again. I guess I wasn't thinking straight when I hired Cherisse the Caftan Queen to pretend to marry us. How did I know I was going to fall in love?"

He stopped. In love? Where had that come from? It sure hadn't happened on their wedding night or in the immediate aftermath. Somewhere between meeting her ditsy neighbors and fawning canine companion and after that night of passion he'd fallen in love with his pseudo-wife. Damn.

Where the hell was she? No note. No message on the machine. No indication of where she was. He needed to see her, find out if she could ever trust him enough to consider making their arrangement less than temporary.

The problem that he'd been dealing with, fighting with, fighting against, crystallized. He needed Miranda the way a drowning man needed air.

Somehow he had to find a way to convince her to trust him. Maybe she couldn't love him back, at least not right away, but showing her that he trusted her with his business, with his life, with his heart, would go a long way towards building that kind of trust.

He slapped his hands against his knees. The dog tilted his head.

"First things first," he said to the dog. "I'll make her a full partner. I can start putting that in the works from here."

He moved to the desk. It was neat and tidy, just like Miranda.

A white slip of paper just this side of the closed drawer caught attention. Curious, he pulled at it. A to-do list in Miranda's purple ink handwriting. Just like her to write a list. He moved to put it down when the curved letters begged for his attention. Incomplete words that he could only guess at comprised part of the list. Her own personal shorthand, Drake imagined.

The listing, *talk to Lucy*, was underlined twice. A star marked the cryptic phrase, *do S thing*. Next was, *get rid of Bob idea*. Drake laughed at that. She hated the meetings with Jones even though they'd been her idea. He wondered how she intended to end the tryst scheduled for tomorrow night?

The final entry answered his question, at least in part. He read it and swore. *Tell Drake the plan.*

Pumpkin followed him at a lope as he rushed from the room. Drake was too distracted to notice until he stopped outside at the car.

Pumpkin stood at the passenger door of the spotless car. "Why not?" He let Pumpkin in. The only way the dog could fit in the front seat was to sit on his haunches. Drake considered for a minute then reached around and fastened the seatbelt around Pumpkin, getting a kiss on the nose for his trouble.

"I sincerely hope I don't get stopped by the police tonight," he muttered. He headed toward the apartment where Miranda had lived. Maybe her friends could tell him where she was.

He was done waiting.

Chapter Seventeen

"I was going to tell him my plan about the stock tonight," Miranda wailed. "But he wouldn't talk to me today, then he left work early without me. I think he's finally lost interest."

Alice sat across from Miranda at the tiny table in the kitchen. "Let me see if I understand this. You decided to put your personal company stock up for sale in hopes of speeding things up?"

"Yes. I'm tired of playing Mata Hari. That James Bond stuff leaves me with a headache."

"Stop whining for a minute and consider what you've done." Alice's sharp tone took Miranda by surprise.

"I thought I was making a sacrifice in proportion to Drake's," Miranda said. "I was so tired after a long night of not sleeping that I knew I had to do something to show him he could trust me. He's put everything that he's worked for on the line." Her mind raced as she tried to figure out why Alice was frowning at her.

"Who oversees company stock purchases?" Alice asked.

"I suppose, eventually, Drake ... Oh, no. He saw my stocks up for sale before I had a chance to tell him." Frustrated and angry with herself, she didn't even know she had tears in her eyes until she wiped them away.

Alice nodded. "You'll have to explain it unless you'd prefer him to speed up the divorce."

Miranda sat up straighter. "The divorce?"

"Well, that's what you wanted all along, right? If he is so angry at your perceived treachery he'll grant you a divorce before the thirty days are up. Pregnant or not, I can't see that man remaining married to you after this."

Miranda remembered the pain in Drake's eyes when he had told her why his previous marriage had ended. Though unable to believe Lucy would treat him so callously, the hurt she'd sensed in Drake was real.

A soft knock at the door had her heart jumping to her throat. Had Drake tracked her here? She swallowed hard as Alice went to open the door. Ted's huge form surprised her, and then she remembered that she'd seen him packing his car when she'd arrived.

"Just thought I'd stop by to say so long." Though he stood in front of Alice, his gaze was riveted on Miranda.

This was almost as hard as seeing Drake.

"Call me when you get settled," Alice said. She hugged him.

"Sure." He hesitated, and then turned to the door.

"Where are you going?" Miranda asked. She walked to within a yard of Ted and looked up into his hard, honest face. She was sure his leaving was her fault. She also knew that nothing she could say or do would stop him.

Ted stared into her eyes. They stood like that without speaking a word for several long minutes. At last Ted grinned. "Massachusetts. My sister lives in Plymouth."

His smile released her. She moved into the circle of his arms and hugged him. Her throat tightened. She cleared it. "I'll miss you. What will we do without you?"

"I'm sure you'll do just fine. Be happy Miranda." He left. The quiet of his wake was sad, but contented.

"What do you suppose he meant by that last comment?" she said to Alice as she found her coat.

"He's deeper than you suspect. And he probably knows you better than you think." Alice's remark was just about as cryptic as Ted's.

She'd think about it later. "I've got to get some straight answers out of Lucy before I see Drake again. Thanks for helping me put this into perspective, Alice."

Miranda stepped into the frigid night, glad for the clear night. In her current mental state driving on snowy roads would be a recipe for disaster.

* * * *

No sign of Jack's sports car in the parking lot. Good, she'd have Lucy to herself.

In the months since Lucy and Drake split up, Miranda had rarely found her sister alone for more than five minutes. Now after learning what she had from Drake and Bob Jones, Miranda was left to wonder again at the degree in which Lucy was involved in the plot to steal technology and stock from Millennium Tech.

Shrugging off the discomfort anticipated because of the coming conflict, Miranda dodged frozen patches of snow until she reached the steps leading to Lucy's door.

Lucy opened the door just as Miranda put her hand up to knock. Her sister's appearance shocked her. Lucy wore a baggy pair of pants topped with an even baggier sweatshirt and a drab down vest. Her golden hair was pulled into a ragged ponytail; not the glamorous mane Miranda had alternately envied and taken delight in over the years.

The biggest change was the expression of wary exhaustion that showed in the lines running from the corners of Lucy's mouth. A faint bruise around the left eye had Miranda breathing deeply. It looked like Lucy had been punched.

"I should have known you wouldn't leave well enough alone," Lucy said with a weariness that matched her appearance. "You may as well come in. My ride isn't here yet."

"Where are you going?" It was the most innocuous thing Miranda could say. Anxiety overrode all other emotions. She struggled to control it as a knot of fear grew in her stomach.

"Out of town," Lucy answered. She waved a languid hand toward two suitcases. An overnight bag squatted next to the door.

"Vacation?" Miranda asked with a chipped brightness that sounded false even to her.

"Why not?"

"Just curious. You've never had a mid winter vacation before, not counting your honeymoon trip to Aspen. Of course, you never did like to ski."

Lucy ignored Miranda's opening. She pulled a cigarette from an open pack as she sank onto the surface of the coffee table.

Miranda looked around the room. Signs of wear echoed Lucy's appearance. A film of dust dulled the surfaces that Lucy generally kept sparkling, due more to pride in her belongings than in any fervor of cleanliness. It echoed her appearance.

It looked like no dusting or vacuuming had occurred in weeks. Stubs of cigarettes and ashes overflowed saucers and half-full coffee cups on every flat surface. A quick glance into the kitchen showed the same unusual neglect there.

A sour smell pervaded the apartment. If despair had an odor, it was this one.

The oppressive silence grated on Miranda. She sat where Lucy couldn't ignore her. "Tell me the real reason you divorced Drake. He wasn't the monster you claimed, was he?"

Lucy looked away through a wisp of acrid smoke. She grimaced then she crushed her cigarette into an already full ashtray. "You must know by now that he's different at home than in public. Why are you so set on knowing the details of my failure?"

"So I don't make the same mistakes." Miranda surprised herself with the honesty of her answer. Though she and Drake had married under less than ideal circumstances, she'd come to like and respect him. If she were to be totally truthful, she realized in a moment of painful clarity, she might admit to maybe falling in love with him.

Maybe.

"You never make mistakes," Lucy snorted.

"Yeah, right. You're talking to a three-time loser. Or have you forgotten three failed engagements?" She couldn't help the bitterness that seeped into her voice.

"You recovered nicely."

Miranda stifled a ridiculous urge to laugh. "I'm not sure that marrying your cast-off husband can be called recovering nicely." She kept her tone gentle. Unexpected vulnerability surfaced in Lucy's shaking hands.

"What happened with Drake?" Miranda asked.

Lucy pulled another cigarette from the pack. She put it between her lips but didn't light it. Instead she took it out of her mouth and began to systematically shred it. The pieces of paper, filter, and tobacco drifted to the floor.

"He ... I ... " Her hesitation caught at Miranda's heart. The Lucy's clear blue gaze met Miranda's. "He loved too hard." Her voice hitched.

Miranda's heart pounded hard in her chest. Maybe she didn't want to hear this after all. She spoke around the lump in her throat. "I don't understand."

Lucy looked away, and then turned her red-rimmed eyes back to Miranda. "He wanted more from me than I could give him. He wanted me, totally and in every way, committed to him. I discovered that I couldn't give him what he wanted. I was a grave disappointment to both of us."

"Didn't you know what he was like before you married him?"

"I always managed to keep him at arm's length."

"But why?" Bewilderment filled Miranda.

"Why marry him when I didn't love him? Prestige, money, take your pick."

"I'm sorry, Lucy. I thought you loved him. I couldn't imagine any other reason to marry him or anyone."

"Couldn't you?" Lucy shot back, her eyes hard and icy.

Heat rose between Miranda's breasts. "Three out of four times I was ready to marry for what I thought was love." She picked her words with care. "I didn't plan to marry Drake; it just sort of happened."

"Then why don't you just sort of get a divorce if you hate it so much?"

Miranda ducked her head. The flush reached her cheeks. "There's the question of whether I might be, um, you know, pregnant." The last word came out in a whisper.

Eyebrows pulled together in an elegant frown, Lucy leaned close to Miranda. "Pregnant?" she whispered. She reared back and shouted, "Pregnant!" She paced and mumbled.

I've pushed her over the edge, Miranda thought.

Lucy swung around the room, her face an amazing wreath of smiles. She pulled a cigarette out of the pack again, started to light it, then snuffed it out in rapid succession. "Bad for the baby," she said.

"You aren't angry?" Miranda asked, a bit stupefied by Lucy's reaction.

"I'm going to be an aunt," Lucy crowed.

"I said *might*. Don't start knitting booties yet. What about Drake and that whole mess?"

"Drake was the worst possible person for me. That doesn't make him bad for you. Oh, I have some reservations, but don't you see? He never allowed the possibility of getting me pregnant after our wedding night. Maybe he had an idea of how it would end. Though he kept up the pretense of marital bliss, he made sure he was protected. The man takes no chances."

"There's more going on than Drake's and my relationship," Miranda said. She had to bring this up, sweep everything into the open.

Lucy stopped her buoyant pacing.

Miranda took a deep breath. "There's the stock you took out of the marriage. How did you manage that little trick if Drake is so careful?"

"Damn. How much do you know?" Lucy slumped into a chair.

"A lot, but not enough. How deeply are you into this with Jack?"

Lucy paled at the direct question. She turned on the lamp on the table next to her. Miranda saw the full extent of the bruise on her temple.

"I'm more dangerously 'into it' than you can imagine. You aren't the only one Jack fooled. I have no luck with men at all."

"Runs in the family." Miranda bit her lip.

"Yeah."

"The only way I can help you is if you tell me the truth. What's going on?"

"I'm way past the stage where anyone can help me." Lucy sighted. "It started shortly before I divorced Drake. He asked me what I'd like for my birthday. In a moment of idiocy I asked for Millennium Tech stock instead of something more liquid."

"Why?"

"I knew our marriage was going down the tubes. I also knew that it wasn't his fault as much as it was mine. Even so, I guess I wanted a small piece of him to keep. The stock was a gift, not part of our pre-nup agreement. Sounds pathetic, doesn't it."

"No." Miranda covered Lucy's hand with her own. "Not pathetic, kind of sweet in a crazy kind of way. But I think the stock was more expensive than you realized."

Lucy took a shuddering breath. "Bob Jones started sniffing around soon after the transaction would have been posted wherever it is that they post that kind of thing. He managed to convince me that Drake was not only a monster but also a poor businessman. I was too good for him. I'll regret my actions for the rest of my life."

"You slept with Jones."

"Yes." Her shoulders slumped with the weight of her confession. "I'll never forget the look on Drake's face when he opened the bedroom door. He covered the hurt up with the coldest rage I'd ever witnessed. Jones didn't have much of a chance to defend himself. Drake punched him in the nose and threw him out the door."

A chill pervaded the room. Miranda shivered. "What did he do to you?"

"Nothing. That's the hell of it. He had every right to yell and carry on and be as pissed off as anyone. But he just looked at me as though I were less than an insect he'd just stepped on. When he turned and walked out I knew that divorce was my only alternative. I could never live in the same house as Drake again."

Miranda squeezed Lucy's hand once, let go, and asked the next painful question. "How does Jack fit into the picture?"

Lucy flushed a brilliant crimson. She met Miranda's gaze. "I apologize for that. It caused you a lot of pain."

Miranda's throat tightened. Jack's canceling their engagement had sent her straight into Drake's arms. Cause and effect.

She touched Lucy's hand again. "You did me a favor. At the time it hurt like hell. I didn't know that it was about you and Millennium Tech until Drake and I had come to an understanding about the fate, or the state, of our marriage."

"You didn't suspect even when Jack and I arrived together in Las Vegas that morning after you were married?"

Miranda shook her head. "I was pretty hung over. Drake kept pulling the rug out from under my very unsteady feet that morning."

Lucy raised an eyebrow. "How, exactly, did you and Drake get together? Neither of you ever made that clear."

"Later," Miranda insisted. "The more immediate problem is to get you away from Jack and bring with you any evidence of stock tampering and technology theft."

"I hadn't thought of anything more than running away," Lucy admitted. "Last night Jack lost his temper. After ... after he slammed out of here I decided to leave."

"This is *your* apartment."

"It doesn't matter. I have to get away."

"We'll go straight to the police and have him arrested for assault," Miranda stated. In light of her sister's injury, stock and technology took a backseat.

"Not yet." Lucy narrowed her eyes. She stared over Miranda's shoulder. "I know. Jack kept back-up disks here. I think I can put my hands on them. Wait here."

She left Miranda in the living room, moving with a purpose Miranda hadn't sensed in her in a while. When Lucy returned she held a small black computer diskette. Her smile was reserved. "Here it is. This should have everything that Drake needs to prosecute."

Miranda stood to hug Lucy at the precise moment the door slammed open. Jack lurched inside. He shut the door with an unnatural gentleness.

* * * *

Lucy, Jack, Miranda--the names and faces floated behind Drake's eyes as he drove toward Lucy's apartment. When he pulled into the parking lot he couldn't decide if he was relieved or angered at the sight of Miranda's car. A sporty green Mercedes coupe was parked beside it. Its engine ticked with heat as Drake walked past. He was glad Alice had convinced him to leave Pumpkin with her. One less thing to distract him, she'd insisted.

He hesitated a moment before knocking. A moment that would play over and over again in the years to come. The sounds of voices, muted but angry, came through the door.

His hand was on the doorknob when the sharp crack of a pistol shot propelled him forward.

Chapter Eighteen

The gun in Jack's hand shone with a silvery lethalness. Miranda's breath caught in her throat. Her heart pounded hard twice before it settled into a faster rhythm.

"I had a feeling you wouldn't leave well enough alone," Jack said to Miranda. "Pretty soon it won't matter. Most of the information is downloaded." His gaze and the barrel of the gun swerved toward Lucy. "But it looks like my darling is cheating on me."

Miranda took advantage of his momentary inattention to calm herself. She shifted her weight. The irrational gleam in Jack's eyes combined with the tremor of his hand suggested a man on the brink of losing control.

She calmly pocketed the data disk.

"Lucy was just congratulating me," she told Jack, hoping to regain his attention. Lucy made too good a target for the bastard. Miranda was big sister enough to want to keep her sibling out of harm's way. Even if Lucy had brought it on herself. Blood did tell. Miranda allowed a moment of pride in her sister.

"Congratulate you on what?" Jack asked.

The black maw of the muzzle swung back to Miranda. She swallowed past the dry lump in her throat; forced a smile.

"I'm pregnant." It was a lie but it got his attention.

"Too bad Lucy won't be around to play aunt." He turned to Lucy again. "You were going to run out on me. What did you plan? To cop a plea in exchange for immunity?"

Lucy wrung her hands. She glanced from Jack to Miranda to the evidence of her planned flight waiting patiently by the door.

Hoping to distract Jack again, Miranda swayed. She put a hand to her head. "I'm not feeling very well," she murmured.

Instead of getting Lucy out of range of the gun, Miranda's ploy brought her sister to her side. Jack now had both of them within his sights.

"Never mind that," Jack growled. "Hand me the diskette. I'm disappointed that you chose to spy on me, Lucy."

Miranda reached into her pocket. It seemed for a second that life and death, her own and her future's, hung in the balance. She hesitated. Jack cocked the hammer. She noted the sheen of perspiration on his forehead and hoped his finger didn't squeeze the trigger prematurely.

The cool square of plastic that held enough evidence to convict Jack touched her fingers. She slid it from her pocket.

"Is this what you're willing to kill for?" she asked.

He didn't answer, just reached out his hand.

Now or never. She flung the diskette with a quick flick of her wrist. "Catch," she shouted.

"Bitch," Jack screamed. As he reached for the diskette, the gun fired.

Miranda saw the plastic square hit him in the head as Lucy flung herself between Miranda and the bullet.

"Lucy." Miranda caught her sister as she fell. A bright patch of crimson stained Lucy's sleeve.

Savage anger roared through Miranda. With all the strength and training at her command, she launched a reverse roundhouse kick to Jack's head. He hit the floor like a marionette whose strings had been cut.

The red rage cleared from her eyes. She looked up to see Drake standing beside Jack's crumpled form. A mixture of bemusement fought with fear in the way his eyes glittered and his hands made fists then relaxed.

He stared at her. His expression was unreadable. Why was he here? She blinked back tears, more happy than she could say that he *was* here.

Lucy's groan sliced through the silence. Miranda hurried to her. "Call an ambulance," she said to Drake. With a negligent glance at the fallen Jack, "And the police."

The next few hours were divided between the hospital and the police station. Lucy's wound was minor. Her emotional injuries would take longer to heal. After a long bedside talk with her, Miranda was sure she'd make a complete recovery on both fronts.

Night had become morning and then moved to late afternoon by the time Miranda and Drake were done at the police station and hospital. They stepped into the waning light of the day and breathed deeply. After hours cooped up with doctors and detectives the frigid air refreshed Miranda's tired body. For the first time in hours she relaxed.

She stiffened as Drake spoke. "I'm starved. Come on, I need to cook something. Alice will have returned Pumpkin by now."

She searched for some emotion on his face. As usual his handsome façade hid his feelings. She'd hoped he would have learned to let his guard down with her by now. It hadn't happened. After all they had been through together with the technology theft and the heartache of the truth Lucy had told, after all that Drake still didn't trust her.

She wanted to weep in defeat.

Instead she followed him to his car. He drove back to Lucy's apartment where Miranda's car was parked. She followed him home. His home, she reminded herself. Not hers, not really.

Her fatigue as so great that Pumpkin almost knocked her over with his joyous greeting.

"Down," Drake ordered. The dog whined and groveled and wriggled with delighted restraint.

Miranda rubbed Pumpkin's belly, grateful for an excuse to avert her gaze from Drake. She didn't want him to see the tears that threatened. When she stood she had her emotions under control.

She steeled herself to face him. "I'm taking my clothes and Pumpkin and going home."

The trace of a smile that had softened Drake's mouth vanished. His stare was like trying to look through a window that had been barred and shuttered.

This was harder than she thought it would be. She forced the rest of the words out. "I'll be taking a leave of absence starting tomorrow and driving down to Mexico for a divorce."

Had she imagined it or had Drake's shoulders slumped a fraction? No, it must have been the light. His continued silence unnerved her.

She moved to go around him to the stairs. He shifted. She tried again. Again, he blocked her path.

"Your thirty days aren't up," he said through tight lips. "I thought you'd honor this commitment."

"You got what you wanted, answers to who was stealing from you. I fulfilled my commitment." Her voice had a honed edge to it.

"There's the second half of the agreement."

A wave of physical and emotional exhaustion swept over Miranda. She melted to the floor followed by Pumpkin. Drake loomed over her. She didn't care. She was too tired to care about what her thought of her right now.

"I'll take a pregnancy test before I go through with the divorce. Will that satisfy you?"

"It's too soon to be sure."

"Maybe. I'm not certain. Besides, it was only one time."

Like the sun coming out from behind a storm cloud, Drake grinned. Miranda's heart did a slow somersault.

"One night, you mean," Drake said. "More than one time as I recall."

No response was adequate. Tendrils of all that night had encompassed threaded through her mind. She suppressed a sob into Pumpkin's soft fur. "What do you suggest?" she mumbled.

"Oh, a pregnancy test sounds good. I'll take a leave of absence and drive down with you. Mexico is just what I need this time of year."

"Swell." Her word hit his retreating back. She watched him until he disappeared around a corner. The sounds of pots and pans clanking away came from the kitchen. He was whistling.

Miranda sighed. This wasn't going the way she had planned. "Come on, Pumpkin. Let's go pack." Pumpkin stood with her, but when she started up the stairs he hung back. His head swung from her to where Drake had gone. His doggy loyalties were divided.

Miranda knelt next to him. "I know just how you feel. Come on."

With one more wistful glance toward the kitchen, Pumpkin ambled up the stairs behind her.

Chapter Nineteen

Whose dumb idea had it been to drive to Mexico? They were stuck in northern New Mexico waiting for road crews to clear the highway after a late winter storm.

He looked across the café table at Miranda. A shaft of clear winter sunlight caught her cheek as she turned her face to the window. For an instant the glow burnished her skin with a cool beauty that took his breath away. The sun scuttled behind another swiftly moving cloud, but Miranda's face maintained the glow.

He loved that glow. He loved Miranda. It had happened

CAUGHT

without even trying. From the moment she'd tried to drunkenly seduce him to this moment on their way to a quick divorce for a non-marriage, he'd learned to trust her. Trust and growing respect had turned into love. How could he let her go?

He rubbed his forehead. Sometime before they reached their destination he had to tell her that they weren't really married. That would make her mad as hell.

He needed a drink.

"More coffee?" the waitress asked.

Startled, Drake knocked his mug flying. "Sorry." He fumbled after it as it skittered between the waitress' legs and toward the counter.

He was so intent on recovering the mug that he didn't notice all eyes were on him until he returned to the table. Miranda had a hand over her mouth. Her eyes twinkled as he took his seat.

"What?" he asked. A shift caught his eye. He glanced around. As he did, talk picked up where there had been silence. The diners returned to their meals.

Miranda giggled. "That reminded me of Toga Boy."

Drake stared at her. Maybe the stress was too much for her. Clearly she wasn't thinking straight. He decided to play along. "Toga who?"

"At the hotel," she flushed and looked away. "In Las Vegas. The room service waiter wore a toga. Don't you remember?"

"Yes." His voice sounded hoarse. He had to tell her. Taking her hand, he started, "Miranda, there's something you need to know."

She turned an unusual shade of green, held her hand to her mouth, and bolted for the ladies restroom.

"I wasn't going to say anything bad," he said to the waitress who stopped by with the ever-present coffeepot.

"Would you like me to go check on her for you?" She smiled.

"This is like a bad dream," he muttered. To the waitress, "Let's give her a minute or two. I don't want to embarrass her."

"No problem. You know, nausea goes away after the third month."

"What?"

"Your wife, she's pregnant, isn't she?" The woman left Drake for another caffeine-starved customer.

Drake stared after her. Could Miranda be pregnant? It hadn't been thirty days since they'd made love. Maybe a couple of weeks. He started counting back in his head then gave it up. Remembering the box he'd picked up at a pharmacy before leaving Colorado Springs, he grinned. It was part of the deal.

Mexico, here we come.

Pale and shaky, Miranda returned to the table. She sipped her water and blessed the fact that the dirty plates had been removed. For some reason the scent of leftover tuna patty melt had turned her stomach.

Drake was looking at her funny again. In that possessive, hungry way that made her stomach flip-flop. It had nothing to do with nausea.

"The roads look clear," she said. "Let's get going."

The sun on the fresh snow dazzled their eyes. By the time they made Albuquerque the snow had melted into the surrounding high desert.

Miranda dozed. She jerked awake now and then; just long enough to appreciate the desert swathed in the light of the full moon. When they stopped for the night she was surprised, and a little annoyed, when Drake deposited her gently on one of the two double beds in the motel room. She was alone in the bed when she awoke in the morning.

Guess he didn't want her after all.

Nausea gripped her. She stumbled to the bathroom hoping the fan was loud enough to keep her retching from Drake's ears. When she came out the room was empty. By the time she was dressed, Drake returned with coffee, orange juice, grapefruit, and blueberry muffins.

She was grateful that the juice and muffin stayed down.

"How much farther?" she asked.

Drake handed her the highway map. Her heart fell as she saw how little distance was left before they make the Mexican border and Cuidad Juarez. The border town was as far as they needed to go to finalize anything.

Drake was oddly solicitous all day. He adjusted the temperature controls until she was comfortable. He asked her to choose a CD to listen to instead of telling her which one to grab. He even stopped at the first rest stop along the highway without her asking.

His behavior, combined with the odd grin that never left his face, made Miranda more than a little sad. She'd fallen in love with Drake the Devil. She'd lost the opportunity to reveal it. If she said anything now he'd laugh all the way back to Colorado.

Somehow she'd get her life back together. How she'd do that without Drake was a mystery. There was no other way, of course.

She turned her head to the window as an unplanned tear leaked from her eye.

The border crossing was as tedious as it was uneventful. At last Drake pulled up to the address that Miranda had given him. She'd found this attorney on the Internet. She just hoped the divorce could be accomplished with a minimum of fuss and bother. Her heart couldn't take any more uncertainty.

She took a deep breath and forced a smile. "Shall we?"

"Just one more thing." Drake pulled a small brown paper bag from under the seat. It contained a home pregnancy test.

She gasped. "You're kidding."

He shook his head. "Part of the deal, Miranda. It hasn't been quite the thirty days we agreed on, but long enough I think."

"You're not kidding."

"Correct." He handed her the box. "Put this in your purse. You can take care of it inside."

Her hands trembled. She grabbed the box, struggling for calm. The past two weeks had already given her the answer that Drake was looking for. This would confirm it.

Then what would she do?

In a daze she walked into the cool lobby. Drake checked in with the receptionist while Miranda found the restroom. The test strip showed her exactly the answer she expected.

She's very pale, Drake thought as Miranda rejoined him. Tenderness overwhelmed him. The words he'd held back escaped his mouth before he considered the consequences.

"We don't have to go through with this."

She swallowed hard but met his gaze without flinching. "We had a deal, remember?"

Heat broke out on his forehead. A dribble of sweat tracked down his back though the ceiling fan beat steadily away at the warmth of the day. His throat was as dry as the desert through which they'd driven.

He tried again. "You don't understand. We don't have to get a divorce."

The quiet tip-tapping of the receptionist at her word processor ceased. Some faucet dripped in an unknown room somewhere. He heard his own heart beating as he watched Miranda's eyes open wide. The corners of her lips trembled.

"I think you'd better spell it out for me. Before you do that, don't you want to know the results of the test?"

"Yes, I mean, no." He couldn't believe how hard this was. "Just listen a minute. The test results don't have anything to do with what I need to say."

Tiny creases appeared between her eyebrows. Drake wanted to kiss them away but knew that if he tried any attempt at an explanation would be lost.

Taking her silence as consent, he took a deep breath. "We aren't really married." Forestalling her reply he rushed on. "I hired an out of work actress to be the Justice of the Peace. You were so drunk, I didn't think you'd notice. Now I wish I'd gone ahead with the real thing." He dropped his head in his hands, wondering how hard she'd hit him.

After a silent count to ten he peeked between his fingers. Her mouth gaped open. Her nostrils flared with each quick breath. The paleness of her face worried him, as did the tremor of her lips.

"I never wanted to hurt you, Miranda."

A smile lit her lips. "Tell me again."

"Huh? Oh, the out of work actress."

"No, you idiot. The other part."

"The part about...." Realization hit him at the same moment her smile gave way to laughter. "I wish I'd gone ahead with the real thing."

Her laughter quieted, and then went away. "What do you mean by that?"

"I...." He knelt on one knee in front of her. "I mean, marry me, Miranda." He didn't know what he'd do if she refused. "I can't imagine my life without you in it."

She turned her head away. A silver droplet rolled down her cheek until he caught it on a fingertip.

"Why?" Her voice was only loud enough for his soul to hear.

Answering in the same vein, "Because I love you." Anguish rammed into him. What if he was too late, or if she didn't care? "What do you want, Miranda?"

"You." She looked back at him. This time the tears in her eyes glistened and sparkled as she smiled. "Are you sure you want a ready-made family, complete with Pumpkin?"

"I wouldn't have it any other way." Then her words hit home. "You are pregnant." Joy burst through him.

"Oh, yes. And I wasn't kidding when I said that twins run in my family. They tend to skip a generation. It may be our turn."

"I can't wait." He turned to the receptionist.

The grandmotherly lady was sobbing into a handkerchief. She said, "Bueno," over and over again. When she had her emotions under control, she escorted Drake and Miranda into the lawyer's office.

CAUGHT

* * * *

The hotel's honeymoon suite was waiting when Drake and Miranda arrived. As they rode the elevator up Miranda whispered to Drake, "I don't have anything, you know, special to wear. A wedding night deserves something unforgettable."

Thinking about the red satin jumpsuit he'd crammed into his suitcase at the last minute, Drake whispered back, "I've got the perfect thing."

"A toga?"

"What?"

She winked.

THE END

MOUNTAIN'S CAPTIVE

By

Michelle M. Pillow

Chapter One

"Devon, I'm here." Chloe Masters looked dazedly around the Las Vegas hotel lobby. The brilliant lights of the strip glared through the hotel's massive front windows but she hardly noticed through the dark lenses of her designer sunglasses. From her place on the phone booth floor she could see the feet of numerous tourists sauntering past. Not one of them distinguished her as the drunk, miserable woman who crouched in the corner of the small cube. "I made it."

"What took you so long? Your flight got there four hours ago. I know because I called the airport to check."

Chloe flinched as Devon Wentworth's sobering voice boomed out of the phone. Devon had a way of talking too loud when she was agitated.

"Devon, you have to understand. I wanted to enjoy my last night of freedom," answered Chloe with a slight slur, as she closed her eyes against the overbearingly bright lights that peeked through the edge of her glasses. "I walked around the casinos trying to regain my composure. You wouldn't have me making a bad impression, would you?"

"Why, what are you wearing?" Devon's authoritative voice inquired sharply. "Please tell me it's not sweatpants. I was afraid that you were going to do something like that. That is why I bought you that little white dress."

"What does it matter?" Chloe snapped in return. "I don't care what he's wearing."

"It matters because this is going to be your new life." Devon softened her tone before continuing. "Chloe, I went to a lot of trouble arranging this for you, despite what it might do to my reputation if it was found out. I would be scorned out of every prestigious law firm in New York. My career would be over. We have been through this. I can't change your father's will."

"I know, Devon. Believe me, I know. It wouldn't be his if you could," Chloe interjected. "You're a good friend to me."

"I gave you every chance to back out and you said that you were confident that you wanted to go through with it." Devon sighed in frustration. Chloe could hear the honking of horns behind her friend's voice.

"Tell me again," Chloe paused and gulped, "about him."

"He's everything you requested--adequate looking, smart, and by his background check we know him to be loyal and discreet. He also comes from old money, so he won't have a use for yours. Though I don't know how much he's worth exactly. His financial information is well protected." Devon's voice cut out. "Damned cellular phones! Chloe are you there?"

"Yeah, I'm here," Chloe slurred.

"Hmm. The best part is he also agreed to the prenuptial." Devon's stout voice vibrated in her hand. She was using her most professional courtroom tone. "You haven't been drinking, have you? You know you can't hold your liquor. What will Paul think if you go to him intoxicated?"

"I just had a little on the plane." Chloe gave a short laugh as she set down her glass of scotch and soda. "And a few in the casinos."

"Stop. I can hear the ice tinkling in your glass. You're going to need your wits about you. You don't want him to think you are a lush and back out, do you? He's your only chance."

Chloe moved her head away from the phone to make a childish face at the receiver. She readjusted herself on the floor and blinked heavily when a group of tourists wearing bright yellow jackets passed too close.

"Chloe, are you listening to me?" Devon sighed again in exasperation.

"Yeah, I'm here." Chloe took another drink, this time crunching on an ice cube as she reached the bottom of the glass. A piece of her wayward blond hair fell over her eyes. As she swatted at it, her watchband got caught in a tangle. "Damn it."

"Chloe?" Devon's voice cut out again. "What'd you say? I didn't hear you."

"Nothing."

"Fine," Devon huffed before lowering her voice and slowing her words. "Now, Chloe, I want you to dial Paul's room and tell him that you're there. Then I want you to finish what you went there to do. Ten years will be over before you know it. When it is, you'll have your freedom back and this nightmare will be over. Until then, maybe you could come to an arrangement with him."

"Yeah, I know and with the right plastic surgeon I won't look half bad in ten years." Chloe set the empty glass on the ground. "I'll call you tomorrow with the horrible details."

"Fine. Remember, it's room three, five, eight. Got it? 358." Devon sighed, refusing to dignify her friend's ill humor with a comment. "Congratulations and good luck."

"Yeah," Chloe mumbled against the phone and hung up.

"Yeah, good luck," she mumbled to herself. Chloe shook her head and hugged her knees to her chest.

She took a deep breath before ambling slowly to her feet. The liquor had taken more of an effect on her then she had realized. She was drunk and didn't care. Somehow, she knew that it was one of the reasons why she had picked Vegas--free liquor. The other reason was the quick and painless ceremonies offered by the numerous chapels.

Pausing for a moment, she let the numbing effect of the liquor take over her mind. She closed her eyes, wishing that Devon would call her back and tell her she didn't have to go through with it. But she knew it would never happen, just as she knew that she couldn't turn back.

Chloe made a beeline through the blur of the crowd to the white courtesy phone. She stared at it, wondering if she should run and get on a flight back to New York. If she did, no one would know of her selfishness. Well, no one but herself. Taking a deep breath, she realized that there was no other choice. She had to do it. There were a lot of people depending on her.

Chloe picked up the phone and held it to her ear. She tried to punch the buttons, but her fingers shook so badly that she dialed the wrong number. Hanging up she cursed. "Come on, Chloe. Three, Five, Eight. Time to be a big girl."

She picked up the phone and tried again.

"Hello," an irritated masculine voice answered.

Chloe gasped at the low rumbling sound. Shivers racked her spine as she pulled the phone back to look at it in stunned amazement. Paul sounded nothing like she had imagined. That one word echoed bravely in her head, capturing her voice in her throat. Swallowing over the lump that formed behind her tongue, she breathed heavily and put the receiver to her ear.

"Room service?" the voice questioned sharply.

Chloe closed her eyes as the sound fell over her like a stirring caress. She didn't know what to say. Her breath came out in uneven pants as she tried to speak. Her body felt like it was on fire.

"Hello?" the voice asked in growing curiosity in response to the nearly obscene breathing. Chloe could almost hear the interested smile in his reverberating tone, as he whispered, "Who's there?"

"Yes, it's me. Sorry I'm late. I'm in the lobby now waiting for you. I need you to come down so we can do this." Closing her eyes to the hollowness that threatened to consume her, she ignored the pleasure she derived from hearing his voice. Chloe swallowed hard. "I'm wearing a white dress."

She hung up the phone with a decisive clink so she couldn't back out. Almost falling to the ground in uneasiness, she narrowed her eyes and turned to the elevators. Spotting a waitress passing through the lobby, she absently waved her over and swiped a drink from her tray, not caring what it was.

Downing it in three large gulps, she set the glass back down with a thud. The waitress looked at Chloe in confusion, but smiled when the woman drunkenly threw a fifty-dollar bill on her tray and grabbed another drink.

With a wave of her liquor-laden hand, Chloe dismissed her. But the glass never made it to her lips. Looking across the lobby dimmed by dark sunglasses, she froze.

Gasping, she set the glass down by the phone, untouched. She tugged insecurely at the tightly fitted hem of her short skirt. A disturbingly piercing hazel-green gaze met her from across the crowded hall. She suddenly felt very exposed. Lifting the glasses from her eyes, she winced as the light hit her vision. The sounds of the busy lobby faded completely, as she started toward the closing elevator door. Her heart raced, beating a fearfully erotic rhythm through her veins.

"This can't be Paul," she muttered under her panted breath. She suddenly wondered why she didn't insist on seeing a picture first. "He's too big."

Dazedly, her hand moved to the dip of her exposed cleavage. She could feel the rounded tops of her own breasts and quickly pulled her hand away. Unable to stop her feet, she took a hesitant step forward. Cocking her head to the side, she stumbled to a stop and waited for him to come to her.

Paul's stride was relaxed and sure as he confidently came through the crowd to reach her. He wore a business suit, very appropriate for what they were about. His brown hair was neatly pulled back into a ponytail, falling to his shoulders in soft waves. A smile curled on his lips as his eyes dropped over her in appreciation. His penetrating gaze exuded sexual prowess and intent. Chloe shivered, never having been looked at as if she were about to be devoured.

As he stopped in front of her, she swallowed audibly and tried to smile. Paul towered above her head so she was forced to lean back to look at him. Instantly, her eyes found his parted lips-- firm and inviting. Drunkenly she swayed. Her knees weakened.

"Oh, hey," he said with a short laugh. "Are you all right?"

Chloe shivered and briefly closed her eyes. He put his hand on her elbow to keep her from falling over.

Yes, she thought when she heard the disarming voice from the courtesy phone. *This is definitely Paul.*

When she opened her eyes, she noticed how close he had drawn to her. She could see the beginnings of evening stubble on his strong jaw. Breathing in his earthy scent, she answered weakly, "Yeah, I--"

Paul suddenly grinned, a naughtily delectable movement. His voice drew into a low, husky murmur, as he asked carefully, "Are you here about the contract?"

"Yeah," Chloe sighed in relief. She was glad to have her mind on something she was able to comprehend. The emotions fluttering though her brain were causing too much havoc. "I was afraid you weren't the right man."

"No, I'm afraid I am," he stated with a smile. "You're not disappointed are you?"

Chloe saw in his eyes that he already knew she was anything but. Glancing over his shoulder, she shook her head and mumbled, "No, of course not. Though, you're not what I expected."

"So, where do you want to do this?" His eyes daringly dipped over her form.

"I have a car waiting outside if you like," she returned. He smiled and nodded his head. Looping his arm through hers, he kept her steady as he led her outside. Belatedly, she added, "We could go there."

Chloe felt his heat soaking into her skin like a sudden blaze of tempestuous fire. Her midsection lit with liquid heat in response. Suddenly, she became all too aware of the heady desert air on her breasts and legs.

CAUGHT

"I must admit I have never done this before," he said. "I mean over a paid contract."

Chloe laughed lightly in confusion and pointed at the awaiting limousine. "Well, Paul, I...."

"Everest," he interjected.

"Oh," she frowned, confused. "I'm sorry, I...."

"Don't mention it," he dismissed her mistake easily with a wave of his hand.

Paul Everest Lucas, thought Chloe. She couldn't help herself as her eyes strayed to his athletic backside. He leaned over to open the limousine door for her. *Interesting name for a very interesting man.*

As the car began to move, Everest leaned over her seat and hit the window button to block out the driver. Chloe tilted her chin in surprise. His thick neck came close to her cheek and she saw the steady beating of his pulse under the smooth texture of his skin. Then, as he sat back, he began to remove his jacket. Chloe watched in avid interest. The car jolted over a bump and she gasped in surprise.

"You don't mind if I get comfortable, do you?" he asked. Setting his jacket aside, he took off his tie. His lips lined with a devilish smirk and his eyes glittered with promise. "I've been in business meetings all day."

"No. Of course not," she answered. Turning to the mini-bar, she poured them each a glass of champagne and handed one to him. Drinking it a little too quickly, her gaze stayed boldly on him as he undid the top button on his shirt.

"I have to tell you that I have had a little too much to drink tonight," he admitted. "So you must forgive me if I'm not too chivalrous."

"Yeah, me too." The limousine bumped and champagne spilled over her chin and down her throat. Chloe licked her lips, watching as his mouth parted in moist offering.

"Come over here," he said, finishing off his drink with one swallow. The glass slipped from his fingers onto the floor. With a low rumble coming seductively from his throat, he motioned her to him.

Captured by his penetrating gaze, Chloe obeyed the command. Opening her mouth, she was about to speak as she sat next to him. She had no time for words. His mouth crushed passionately to hers. Chloe gasped in surprise as she felt his tongue instantly in her mouth. She could taste the stout hint of expensive whiskey on him. His hands grasped her shoulders to keep her from backing away.

"You're a damned sexy woman," he growled against her mouth, as he continued with his deep kiss.

Her fingers shook at the admission, loosening their hold on her champagne glass. Small drops of liquid dripped onto his back before the glass fell to the car floor. It noisily clanked into his discarded glass as the car started and stopped. Everest didn't even notice.

Forcefully, he pushed her to lie back on the seat. His tongue traced over her teeth, exploring her and demanding she explore him with a returned kiss. Discovering the taste of champagne on her neck, his mouth followed the delicious trail. His hands found their way to her legs. Running his fingers over her calves, he massaged them gently before working his way up to her inner thigh. "Those lawyers must know what they're doing, for the moment I saw you I wanted to rip your clothes from you. I'll have to remember to thank them."

"I," Chloe began, but couldn't finish. She was too drunk to think straight and his confident hands felt way too nice against her skin. Everest urged his hardened arousal against her. She was helpless against the firm press of his body, under the slanting of his mouth. Moaning, she ran her hands into his shoulder length hair, pulling it free of its tie.

He chuckled in careless enjoyment against her lips as he broke off the kiss. His hand strayed to her neck to pull the thin dress strap from her shoulder. Tugging it down over one arm, he unveiled her lacy white bra.

Everest groaned in masculine contentment and lightly traced a line over the curves of her breasts. When she sighed in approval, he circled her nipples into hard peaks, leaving them behind lace as he continued lower. Staring mischievously into her aroused eyes, he inched his hand up her skirt. The material bunched around her hips and he growled in delight. His eyebrows rose slightly as he found the matching white panties.

"Mmm," he licked his lips. He rubbed his fingers over the white lace covering her hot center. Chloe jolted in surprise. Chuckling, he nuzzled his face near the top of her breast. Tracing his tongue in a hot wave along the edge of her bra, he murmured hoarsely, "How about we take off our clothes?"

With an expert shift of his hips, his raised manhood was firmly placed against her inner thighs. Chloe moaned as he skillfully thrust himself along her in a slow, controlled stroke. Her hands found his masculine chest. Every inch of him was hard, unrelenting muscle. She fumbled to unbutton his shirt, moaning when she discovered his smooth, bronzed chest.

Giving up on the buttons, she was about to unzip his pants when the car lurched unexpectedly to a stop, startling them with a surprising jolt. Everest rolled off of her and landed on the floor with a thud, barely missing the glasses. Chloe sat up in astonishment, trying to cover herself.

"Are you all right?" she questioned when she had regained her wits.

Before he could answer, the limousine's driver lowered the window between them. Completely aware of what he had interrupted, he said with a chuckle, "We're here, ma'am."

Chloe nodded, taking a deep breath. Glancing longingly at Everest's protruding member pushing against his pants, she uttered, "Can you give us another minute?"

"I'm sorry, ma'am. I have another client to pick up later tonight. You only have about fifteen minutes here before I have to take you back to the hotel. They're waiting for you inside." The driver turned and stepped out of the car.

Quickly, Chloe covered herself. With a blush fanning her delicate features, she closed her eyes.

Everest growled as he crawled back up on the seat. Leaning to her, he stroked his thumb over the racing pulse at her slender neck. Reluctantly, he mumbled, "Well, I suppose we had best get business over with. Though, you'll be coming back to the hotel with me, right?"

Chloe nodded. Swallowing hard, she said, "I have nowhere else to be."

"Good," Everest sighed in relief. Then, taking a deep breath and then another, he asserted, "I need a drink if I'm going to be forced to wait."

He grabbed a bottle of hard liquor from the bar. Taking several gulps, he swallowed it to combat his raging desire. Then, handing the bottle to his companion's outstretched hand, he watched as she followed suit.

* * * *

The evening passed in a drunken haze as they left the limousine. Hastily, and with barely concealed carnal appetites, they rushed through the chapel ceremony. As the driver finally pulled up in front of the hotel, Chloe drew her lips back far enough to urge, "Take me to your room."

Everest complied with a throaty growl. He swept her up into his arms to carry her across the lobby. Ignoring the stunned faces of those they passed, he strode straight onto an empty elevator. Everest set her down only to claim her mouth with his.

"I haven't made out this much since high school. If I don't get you alone soon, I think I'm going to explode," Everest whispered with savage intensity. He trailed kisses to her neck as he grabbed a handful of her breast. Chloe groaned. It was the only response her heated body could manage. He continued in a drunken frenzy, "Damn, woman, you're driving me insane. I want to be deep inside of you so badly. I haven't been this hot in a long time."

As if to prove his point he ground his hardened erection into her softer belly. Everest fumbled unsuccessfully to unlatch her bra. Finally, the elevator door dinged and opened. Grabbing Chloe about the wrist, he pulled her down the hall. They ignored the gasps of dismay as they passed an elderly couple.

"That was a prostitute!" the woman shot to her husband. Then turning around to the disarrayed pair, she shouted, "You should be ashamed of yourself!"

"I would defend your honor," Everest began, stopping as he reached his door. Pressing his keycard into the lock, he pushed it open before saying, "But it would take too long. Hope you don't mind."

"Not at all," Chloe ignored the couple as Everest nearly flung her into the room before him. Not bothering with the lights, he narrowed his eyes to stare at her through the dimness.

"How about letting me see that sexy bra and panties again?" he asked with an insistent smile. He kicked the door shut behind him. Then, tossing his jacket from his body, he ripped open his linen shirt without bothering to unfasten it. Little white buttons scattered soundlessly to the plush carpet. His eyes found Chloe as she pulled her dress to her waist.

"Keep going," he encouraged. Licking his lips, he dropped his shirt on the floor.

Chloe shivered with desire as his fingers found his belt. His tanned, muscled chest gleamed in perfect masculine form like that of an Olympian god. His broad shoulders flexed with power. She knew that if she was dreaming, she never wanted to wake up.

Pulling the dress over her head, she spread her stance slightly. Her heeled shoes pressed into the floor. His eyes roamed heavily over her slender form. He took in her trim stomach and the pleasing effect of the push-up bra.

"I want to fuck you," he mumbled dirtily. He kicked off his shoes as his pants fell around his ankles. He then pulled off his cotton boxers to unveil his aroused manhood. "I want to fuck you so bad."

Chloe looked with wide-eyed awe at his proud form. She had never felt so free in her life. Too drunk to think about what was coming over her, she uttered, "Where do you want me?"

"Everywhere," he growled.

And in two steps he was next to her. Grabbing her breasts, he flicked her nipples out over the top edge of her bra so that he could take them in his mouth. Sucking hard against her flesh, he devoured her trembling skin.

Chloe ran her hands over his thick arms. She could feel the hard strength in him demanding her complete submission. Moaning loudly, she hollered, "Oh, God, yes!"

Noticing the nearby table, Everest knelt down before her. His hands glided over her hips to the thin sides of her panties. She caressed his hair as he slid the panties down her legs. Smiling at her trimly kept mound of hair, he could not help himself as he dipped his mouth forward to taste her.

Chloe jolted in pleasure as his tongue slipped between the lips of her slick opening. Groaning into her core, his mouth closed around her center nub to suck passionately at her sensitive femininity. Her hips bucked against him as she began to tremble. Her breasts ached as they arched forward. Beginning at her heeled shoes, his hands moved over her legs and hips.

"This," he began with a grunt that held much promise, "I will have to finish later."

Chloe moaned in protest as he stood. But soon her disappointment was forgotten as she looked into his commanding eyes. Eagerly, he whipped her around to face the table. He pushed her forward until she was standing before it.

"I've got to have you," he shot passionately, smacking her backside lightly before running his hand over her creamy skin. Reaching in between her thighs, he encouraged her legs apart. Persistently, he commanded in a coarse whisper, "Bend over. Now!"

Chloe did as he ordered. Her hands flung to the side, digging into the wood of the table for support. Her loins pulsated with the burning need for fulfillment. She didn't have to wait long. Everest grabbed onto her hip as he took himself in hand. Guiding his very ready manhood to her tight opening, he massaged himself into place, gliding easily in her natural hot fluids.

"Ah," Chloe panted, breathless in anticipation.

"Argh!" Everest hollered as he thrust his hips boldly into her. His manhood slid effortlessly within her tightened hold.

Chloe trembled as she felt his large shaft embed itself boldly inside of her. The muscles of her body lurched and clung around him in a soft, velvety caress. There was no escaping the hands on her hips. Everest controlled her movements, compelling her to his whim as he pushed himself in as deep as his body would go. She was helpless against the pleasure of his onslaught. She gripped the edge of the table as he moved with aching precision.

"Oh yeah, baby," he grunted as his hips found a fast, hard, thrusting rhythm. "That's it. That's what I want."

Chloe's breath came out in panted moans. Everest ground his hips in a furious tempo, mindless to everything but the driving need to end the torment she had put him through all evening. Her sexy body, her skin, her smell--all of it, combined with the invigorating day spent drinking stout liquor--was more than he could fight or control. He needed release. He needed to find release. He needed to get deeper--oh, yes, deeper....

"That's it, baby!" He groaned as he slammed himself against her willing body. His buttock muscles tensed with each bold thrust.

Chloe screamed as the passion built inside of her. Her blood pounded into a fervent pitch until all she could do was feel the power of the dominating man behind her. Never had she been so controlled. Suddenly, she tensed. Her core exploded with a violent force of gratification. Everest gritted his teeth as he held her fast to his member. Her moist center violently trembled all around him, kneading him past the point of sanity. With a loud, claiming growl, he released himself heavily inside of her.

As the savage climax subsided, they were left with the pleasing tremors of its aftermath. Leaning his head against her back, Everest placed his hands on the table next to hers and sighed in contentment. His member still lodged inside of her, he looked down over her back shadowed in darkness. The bright city light coming from a crack in hotel curtains outlined the curve of her buttocks. Slowly, he watched himself withdraw. The scene was just erotic enough to begin stirring his heated blood once more. He smiled wickedly.

Chloe stood. Turning around to face him, she was met with his satisfied grin. His eyes dipped possessively over her frame--past her dislodged bra to her high heeled shoes.

"You don't have to be anywhere tonight, do you?" he asked in a low tone.

Chloe let a catlike grin curl her features. She shook her head in denial.

"Good," he stated, before asking with a promising smirk, "Can I get you a drink?"

Chloe nodded, wondering at his glinting eyes.

"You might need it, because this is going to be a long night." Everest headed toward the suite's mini-bar setup next to a long mirror.

Chloe watched his naked backside and licked her lips. Already her body was urging her to go to him again and the bar, with its numerous bottles just waiting to be poured over his skin, looked to be as good a place as any. With a dazed shake of her head and a lustful glint in her eye, she followed eagerly behind him.

* * * *

A slight groan rumbled from Chloe's parted lips. She felt the soft caress of satin against her restless legs as her mind struggled to wake up. Her whole body was deadened from the neck down. It was as if she had just completed a marathon and someone had forgotten to tell her to train for it. Considering the amount of alcohol she had consumed the night before, she was doing remarkably well. She had half expected not to wake up at all this morning.

She opened her eyes to see the gold leaf ceiling. Closing them, she grunted in disapproval. Only in Vegas would there be a ceiling that gaudy. She took a deep breath and again forced her eyes open. This time she ignored the golden cherubs staring down from above and turned her head to the pillow beside her. It was empty.

Chloe glanced around the room in surprise. Finding that it too was empty, she sat up slowly and edged her way to the side of the mammoth heart-shaped bed. Her head pounded in protest. She had a lot to drink the night before. In fact, that was all she could remember doing the night before. It took her a moment to realize that she not only had a hangover, but she was also naked.

"Oh, no," Chloe groaned silently. "We didn't. Not like this."

She stood up and pulled the sheet around her aching body. She tried in vain to remember what Paul looked like and couldn't do it. For an instant she got a flash of a delectably solid chest and chiseled abdominal muscles, but the image was too hazy and definitely too masculine in its fantasy-like qualities to be real.

The hotel suite was quite elaborate--too elaborate for Chloe's tastes. She never found it advantageous to waste money on such luxuries. The suite had a living room, kitchen, partially stocked bar and full size bathroom. It had to be an expensive room, much more than she could justify spending. It could only mean that she was in Paul's suite.

"Paul?" Chloe's voice cracked and she cleared her throat. "Paul, are you there? Hello?"

No answer.

"Paul?" she tired louder.

Still she got no answer. Not that she had expected one. The room was too quiet.

Chloe took a deep breath and made her way to where her white dress was folded neatly on a table, along with her undergarments. She knew that she never would have folded her own clothing into such a neat stack. On top of the pile was a note.

"Thank you for an enjoyable evening. I had to leave early for a meeting. I believe the arrangements would have been taken care of beforehand. Feel free to take a shower and order room service." Chloe read the note out loud and then turned it over. That was it, not even a signature.

"Wonderful," Chloe laughed in amazement. "Just wonderful. Our first day of marriage and he's already abandoned me."

She decided to take the note's advice to take a shower, but declined to order food. Chloe rarely drank and was afraid that after last night if she tried to eat her insides would come out of her throat.

Tossing the note on the table she dropped the sheet and walked naked to the bathroom. She couldn't miss the irony that she wouldn't be able to recognize her husband's face if she was to try to pick him out of a crowd of two.

* * * *

"Devon Wentworth's office, please," Chloe said into the hotel room's phone. She drummed her bare feet lightly on the plush carpet. She had to give it to the people of Vegas--they sure knew the meaning of comfort. The shower she had used had been big enough for five grown men with spouts coming out at every angle and everything around her was soft and covered in velvet. "This is Chloe Masters."

"One moment please, Miss Masters."

CAUGHT

Chloe pulled the pink towel off of her wet hair. She held the phone with her shoulder as she brushed through her shoulder-length tresses with nervous fingers.

"Chloe?" Devon questioned immediately, sounding upset. "Where are you?"

"I'm in the hotel suite." Chloe frowned at the woman's worried tone. Devon had been one of her roommates in college. She was a good friend, but lately she had been getting overprotective. "The real question is--where's Paul?"

"What do you mean, where's Paul?" Devon sounded shocked.

Chloe stood up and walked over to her clothing. "He left me this note. It says I had to leave, order room service. And the funny thing is I can't really remember what he looks like."

"What are you talking about a note?" Devon queried. Her voice was puzzled and Chloe could imagine the frown that would be marring her perfect brow. "Paul has been calling me frantically all night. He said that you never got a hold of him. He thinks something happened to you. He's really quite worried."

"What are *you* talking about?" Chloe scratched her head in confusion. Spotting her oversized purse on the floor she picked it up and set it on the table next to her clothing. "I am in Paul's room right now. We spent the night together."

"You're in Paul's room?" Devon's tone was disbelieving.

"Yeah, only he isn't." Chloe sighed as she slipped on her underwear with one hand.

"What do you mean you spent the night together?" Devon questioned, her voice growing even more skeptical.

"All I know is that I woke up this morning naked and not in my room." Chloe sighed. Then, sheepishly, she added, "If you must know, I can tell. I haven't been this sore in a long time. It's as if I was doing gymnastics in bed. And there were more condoms in the trash can--and shower--than I care to admit to."

"Oh, no." Devon started to laugh despite her concern. "Chloe, that's not right."

"What?" Chloe asked, confused.

"Chloe, honey, listen to me very carefully." Devon took an audible breath before stating in a firm tone, "You didn't spent last night with Paul. He hasn't met you yet. In fact he said you never called him. He's still in his room as we speak."

"But, that's impossible." Chloe's knees weakened and she sunk to the floor. "Then, who?"

"Honey, I don't know. Can't you remember anything?"

"I remember calling Paul and telling him to meet me downstairs. Then I woke up alone this morning with a cheap metal band on my finger, which looks as if it came out of a toy machine." Chloe picked herself off the plush carpet and began searching her purse for an aspirin. "Devon, I had a lot to drink."

"Paul doesn't have to know a thing. I'll tell him my secretary gave you the wrong hotel name. You can still meet him today and get married. Everything will be all right." Devon tried to sound encouraging. "We'll just chalk last night up as a girl bachelor party."

"Yeah, you're right." Chloe laughed halfheartedly. Inside she trembled with uncertainty. "I just wish I knew where I was now. What if I am not even at the same hotel?"

"What room number are you in? Check the phone. It should be printed on the side. The hotel's name should be there, too." Devon turned to her professional calm. Being a top-notch attorney, she was used to dealing with high stress situations.

"Well, it's the same hotel. It says so on my robe. Just give me a second and I'll look up the room number. I'm trying to find my aspirin first." Chloe turned her purse over, dumping the contents on the table in frustration. She picked through the mess and found the bottle. "Got it."

"Well?" Devon questioned sharply.

"I meant I got the aspirin." Chloe started to move to the phone when she spotted a piece of newly folded paper amidst her belongings. "What's this?"

"What?" Devon's voice demanded. "What's wrong, Chloe?"

Chloe fingers quivered violently as she unfolded it. "Oh, my God.

"Chloe?"

Chloe stared at the paper as if it would start fire and disappear. "Oh, Devon. Your plan is not going to work. I'm married and it's not to Paul."

Chapter Two

Two Weeks Later

Chloe frowned in irritation. She pulled her sunglasses down over her eyes as the rental car bounced heavily on the mountain pass road. The sedan was the only car the rental lot had left. The rental agent had told her it was because many of the tourists were leaving Montana due to the heavy snowfall the state had experienced recently.

Chloe scanned the sides of the mountains, searching for avalanches. She couldn't imagine that they would occur too often, as the agent had suggested, or at least not this early in the fall. She guessed they only told people that so they would purchase the extra insurance when they made the rental.

It had taken her twice as long to drive across the mountain passes as she had at first anticipated. What looked like an hour's drive on the map actually had taken her closer to three, due to the dangerous curves. Chloe slowed the car as she came to a fork in the road.

"*Miner's Cove.*" She squinted and lifted her glasses to read the faded print on an old, rusted sign. "I guess it's that way."

Chloe turned the car to the left. From the looks of the landscape she guessed that her husband lived in the most un-populated area of northern Montana. She sent a brief prayer to heaven that he wasn't a backwoods hillbilly or a militia leader of some sort.

It had taken her the better part of two weeks to track down Everest Beaumont. Luckily, she had Devon to help her. Devon flew to Vegas shortly after Chloe discovered she married the wrong man. And with a few subtle bribes to the hotel staff, Devon found that the man on the wedding certificate did indeed exist and was a prosperous Montana businessman. At least that was to be assumed since a major corporation had paid for his hotel suite.

Chloe took a deep breath. She was running out of time. Her thirtieth birthday was coming up in a little over a month. That gave her four weeks to divorce one husband, marry another, and collect her inheritance from her father.

Coming quickly to a small town hidden within the mountain valley, she stopped the car in front of a small General Store. Miner's Cove was a modest town built into the side of a mountain. She was sure she had seen the exact same community in pictures of the old west. It was really a beautiful area, once a person got over the fact that they were out in the middle of nowhere.

Chloe had been raised in the hustle and bustle world of New York. She hadn't even seen the countryside until she was thirteen. By then, the wide-open area frightened her in its quiet serenity and she had begged her father to take her back to the city.

There was a light sprinkling of snow on the ground so Chloe grabbed her jacket out of the back seat. Making sure to take her purse, she locked the car door. A few of the local's watched her with avid interest. It was clear that they rarely had visitors. Chloe averted her eyes and walked straight into the General Store. Years in the city had taught her to mind her own business and these locals terrified her more than the city at night.

The small store stood in a lone brick building that actually was a grocery that doubled as a hardware store that doubled as a post office. Every imaginable item a person would need was packed onto the cluttered shelving until there was hardly room left for walking. As she pulled open the thick glass door, it jingled.

"Hello?" Chloe called, as she made her way toward the back. She grimaced softly as her jacket snagged on a protruding broomstick.

"Be with you in a moment, I will," an old voice answered her.

Chloe found the register. It was inconveniently located in the rear of the store, as not to allow for easy departure. She leaned on the counter and started to drum her fingers.

"There now, how can I be of help?"

Chloe smiled as an old man bustled from the back room. He was very energetic for his advanced years. Smiling kindly, she reminded herself that these people lived at a slower pace. Trying not to sound panicked she greeted him politely. "Hello."

"There now, who do we have here?" The man smiled as he scratched at his balding head. He was a compassionate looking person, with a round face and a cheery smile. Chloe imagined that if he grew a white beard he would look exactly like a skinny Santa.

"My name's Chloe." Chloe held out her hand.

"Just Chloe?" The old man laughed. "That will do, that will do. Are you lost, Chloe?"

"Actually it's Chloe Masters." Chloe scrunched up her face in confusion. "I mean, Chloe Masters-Beaumont."

"Beaumont, eh?" the man inquired, growing curious. "I'm Grandpa. Everyone just calls me Grandpa. You related to any Beaumont's around this way?"

"I am actually. I'm looking for an Everest Beaumont." Chloe to a deep breath before rushing, "I've been informed he lives around here."

CAUGHT 131

"Everest, you say?" Grandpa laughed again. "Could be I know him."

"If you could tell me where to find him," she began, only to frown when he cut her off with his chuckling amusement.

"Seems to me that I heard of a Chloe Masters," Grandpa broke in. "Could it be that you're her, the writer I mean?"

Chloe nodded, trying not to let her frustration show, "Yes, I am a writer."

"Well, I'll be. What are you wanting with Everest? He finally take my advice and write you a piece of fan mail?" Grandpa grinned delightedly and clapped his hands with glee. "That boy has me ordering your books as fast as they come out."

"Really," Chloe answered dejectedly. She grew apprehensive. Surely she wasn't married to a fanatical admirer. Her stomach began to churn with nausea. Over the weeks the sultry image of chiseled muscles had dissolved into scrawny arms with a machine gun and hatchet.

"Well, you never mind that. Everest has me ordering him all kinds of books." Grandpa smiled and shook his head. "What are you wanting with our Everest? Hey, is he going to be in your next book? Wouldn't that be something?"

"Maybe. I haven't thought about it. There's something I need to discuss with him." Chloe lowered her voice as the bell tinkled behind them at the front door. Two elderly ladies walked into the store. The man lifted his hand to them in greeting. Ignoring the women, she hushed, "Of a personal nature."

"Personal, eh?" Grandpa leaned forward, his tone growing suspicious. "How personal? You don't want to cause him trouble, do you? Are you in the family way?"

"No, I am certainly not. Please this is between Everest and myself." Chloe looked painfully at the two ladies and leaned closer. It was obvious that he wasn't going to let up. She whispered just so the old man could hear her. "I'm his wife."

"Everest is married?" Grandpa shot back loudly. "Well, I'll be! Did you hear that Gladys? Everest finally went and got himself a wife!"

Chloe flinched as Grandpa waved over one of the women who milled quietly near the entrance. Turning her pleading gaze to the old man, she begged, "No, please, don't ... do that. It's just a misunderstanding."

"Well, I never!" exclaimed Gladys. She was a woman in her late fifties who patted her bouffant hairdo into place as she approached in her waitress uniform. "He was just in town a couple weeks ago and didn't mention it."

"There is nothing to mention. It's a simple mistake," Chloe persisted. She gripped her purse to her hip in aggravation. "I'm here to get some papers signed to clear up the confusion. Honestly, it's all a misunderstanding."

"Divorce, she means." Gladys raised a disapproving eyebrow toward Grandpa, who nodded his head in silent understanding. "That's what they all mean these days when they call marriage a mistake. Can't seem to make them last. Not like we did, anyhow. Back in the old days we knew 'til death do us part' meant just that. You were going to be together until one of you croaked, in some cases longer."

Chloe backed away, feeling like she was cast into the middle of a bad fifties movie. Grandpa and Gladys stared after her. "Excuse me. I should be going. I really must find him."

"Wait a minute, child," said Grandpa before turning to Gladys. "You hush up. You don't know if that is the case. Maybe she's here to straighten things out with him. Could be she's here to make the marriage work."

Both of them turned their head to her in expectation. Chloe slowly moved back to the counter. She silently pondered the fact that both of them might be in need of a good hearing aide. This was not how she wanted the conversation to go. She hadn't planned on anyone finding out about the fake marriage. Everest would no doubt have a lot of explaining to do when she left. She was sorry for it, but there was nothing she could do about it now.

"I have a load of supplies I have to take up to Everest's place tonight. It's a good hour's ride from here. You're welcome to come with me in the jeep," Grandpa offered. "Your car won't make the trek into the mountains."

Chloe turned to glance out of the front window. Her car could be seen through the dusty pane of glass. Already snowflakes were covering the hood.

"That would be fine," Chloe nodded when she once again faced them. "And I'm afraid that the car is a rental."

"Anyhow, it won't make it." Gladys chimed in as if she hadn't heard Grandpa's offer. "And the only available room for rent is taken up by some photographer fellow. So you'd better take your luggage with you and stay the night there with Grandpa. Maybe it will give you some time to work whatever it is out. There's no need to resort to divorce quite yet. Everest is an upstanding man. He'll make whatever it is right with you. You'll see."

"What a splendid idea, Gladys." Grandpa nodded in approval. "Everest has plenty of room in that cabin of his."

Chloe gave a smile that she wasn't sure she meant. She didn't like the idea of spending the night in the mountains, let alone a log cabin. People disappeared all the time in the mountains. Anything could happen to her. Chloe shivered as she imagined being attacked by a hungry bear or getting bitten by a diseased tick. And if the wilderness didn't do her in, her husband just might. Either way, the prospect of roughing it in nature didn't hold too much appeal. She liked the relative safety of the city. Sure there was crime, but she knew how to protect herself against that. How did one convince a bear not to eat?

Seeing Grandpa's smiling face, it appeared as if a night in the mountains was going to be her only option. It's not like she had the time to be choosy about her accommodations.

"Fine, when do we leave?" she asked quietly. She tried not to let her apprehension show.

"I close up here in about two hours. Why don't you go grab something to eat at the diner until then? It's across the street. Can't miss it." Grandpa winked at Gladys.

"Very well." Chloe nodded with a sigh as she left the store.

"What are you up to, Grandpa?" Gladys gave him a suspicious look. "Did you know about this?"

"Not at all, Grandma." Grandpa leaned over and kissed his wife's cheek. "But, I'll find out tonight."

"I like her," Gladys put forth. "I wish there was a way we could get her to stay up there longer. Everest has been alone for too many years now. It isn't good for a man his age to spend all that time by himself. He should get out more."

"I quite agree." Grandpa smiled mischievously as he whirled his wife around in a dance. For a moment they swayed to a song only they could hear. Pressing his cheek to his wife's, he breathed heavily in contentment. "I'll take care of everything. Now, help me round up some extra supplies to take to Everest. We only got two hours and your old bones don't move like they used to."

"Oh, you!" Gladys swatted his arm and laughed as he chased her playfully into the back room.

* * * *

Chloe stared out of the diner window as she waited for her hamburger. It was about the only thing on the menu that the waitress seemed to know was in stock. She lifted her cup of coffee to take a drink and noticed everyone was staring at her.

"Hi." She nodded and tried to smile. "Nice town you have here."

A few of them nodded back. A few others grunted.

Chloe guessed that this was the place everyone in town got together to visit--only they weren't visiting. They were staring at her as if she was a political speaker ready to make an important announcement regarding the town mining company. And they didn't anticipate her speech to be good.

"So is it true?" her waitress asked with a cock to her hip. She gave a sly smile to the man at the counter she had been flirting with. His teeth were slightly bucked and stuck out when he smiled.

"Pardon me?" Chloe looked at the attractive woman. She wore too much makeup and hair spray, but was comely nonetheless. Chloe guessed she was one the few women her age in the town and from the looks of her bored expression she seemed to resent the fact that there weren't more men to choose from. "Is what true?"

"That you're married to Everest Beaumont." The waitress was chewing loudly on a piece of gum. Chloe wanted to snatch it from her.

Chloe took another drink of coffee, not knowing how best to answer. Biting her lips, she started to panic. How was it that everyone seemed to know her business already? She had only been in the diner for twenty minutes. Then, as she spied the woman who had been shopping with Gladys in the General Store, she grimaced in disdain.

"Are you?" An older gentleman at the counter joined the inquiry.

"Yes. But, it's a mistake--a clerical error." Chloe tried to remain calm. She felt like she was on the witness stand. "I am here to clear it up."

"So, what you mean to say is that you found out he lives out here in the boonies and you want no part of it." The waitress laughed heartily. A few of the other's joined her. "I can't say that I blame you."

"No, I didn't mean that at all. Your town is l-lovely," Chloe stuttered.

"How do you like that?" The older man again.

Everyone chuckled as Chloe turned red with embarrassment. She wished she were let in on the joke, though she got the feeling she was somehow the punch line.

"Leave her alone, Clyde," the waitress scolded before turning back to her interrogation. "Now, Everest is a cute one. Could it be that you're here to convince him back to wherever it is you're from? Not that he will go, mind you. Where are you from?"

"New York," Chloe answered weakly, feeling as if she had no choice. She took a sip of coffee wondering what the waitress' standard for cute was--a man with most of his teeth? She gulped as the bucked tooth lad leered a little too approvingly at her.

Dear God, she thought. *Please tell me I didn't sleep with something like that!*

"See, I told you. She doesn't want to be moved out here. She's used to that city living. What I wouldn't give to go to New York." The waitress gave a dreamy sigh. "Do you get to shop on Fifth Avenue?"

"Now you've done it." Clyde, the man at the counter laughed as he lit his cigarette. "Betsy will be asking to go with you before you know it, mark my word."

"Shut up, Clyde!" Betsy, the waitress, yelled.

The diner broke up in laughter as Betsy ran into the waitress station with an audible sob.

"Now you all leave that poor child alone. Shame on you!"

Chloe turned grateful eyes to Gladys who had just walked in. Her stern voice instantly drew respect from the gathered customers. She pointed her finger at Clyde and shot him a scolding look of disapproval.

"Last time you made her mad, Clyde Walton, I had to cover her shift for three days."

Clyde nodded his head as he gave her a defiant look. But, instead of answering, he turned back to his coffee and said nothing.

Gladys moved to join Chloe at her table. She sat down in the booth across from her without waiting to be invited. "Don't you mind them, none. They don't have anything better to do."

"Thank you," Chloe mumbled. She didn't know why the woman was joining her, not that she minded terribly. Chloe coughed as the smell of the smoke coming from the man at the counter drifted over.

"Not at all." Gladys smiled kindly as she began rearranging the condiments on the booth's table. "You'd see that they really mean well, if you'd get to know them."

Chloe groaned inwardly. "I am sure you're right. But there has been a terrible mistake. Our marriage isn't real. I don't want this to become inconvenient for him after I am gone. I shouldn't have said anything."

"Don't you worry about Everest. He's known these people his entire life. He won't have any problems with them." Gladys winked as Betsy brought a plate of food to the table. "Glad to see you didn't have the meat loaf. Well, I'll leave you be. Grandpa should be ready to go as soon as you are done."

"And just what is wrong with my meat loaf?" Betsy asked in a huff.

"Nothing, dear," Gladys chuckled in merriment as she stood up.

"Yeah, except you're supposed to kill the animal before you cook it." Clyde coughed, happy to have his two cents in.

Chloe smiled halfheartedly as Gladys joined an offended Betsy in the kitchen. She found it difficult to eat with so many of the locals trying to watch her out of the corners of their eyes.

"Waitress," she called, as she grabbed her jacket, "can I get this to go?"

* * * *

Chloe held onto the roll bar of the jeep as the vehicle jostled on the bumpy trail. She prayed Grandpa knew where he was going for she had yet to see anything that resembled a paved road. She would have taken the time to enjoy the scenery, but her eyes were beginning to freeze into her head.

"How much farther?" Chloe yelled over the wind. Grandpa's jeep didn't come with a top. The chilly air was making her breath come out in puffs of white fog and she thought she felt the water from her eyes freeze to her red, stinging cheeks.

"Just a bit further," Grandpa hollered back. "You see that cliff over there?"

Chloe followed his crooked finger and nodded. Miserably, she tried to control the shivers in her body. The cold didn't seem to be affecting the old man. Grandpa was well bundled for the weather.

"We had an avalanche there a couple winters back. See the clearing in the trees? That's how you can tell." Grandpa put his hand back on the wheel. "Everest was snowed in for two months without a telephone. Takes a certain kind of person who can live through that. Most people would grow crazy in the isolation. Not Everest, no sir. He comes from good stock. No telling when that thing will go again."

Chloe eyed the mountain in fright. It seemed the avalanche was the local horror tale. She turned to Grandpa. He seemed to think the fact that her husband was a loner who lived in the mountains should impress her. What it actually did was make her suspect her husband had indeed gone crazy years ago.

"I've seen many avalanches, been in one too. But that was a long time ago. One of the prettiest acts of nature you'd ever see. Well, that's as long as you aren't looking at it from the bottom of the mountain." Grandpa laughed gruffly. "Animals won't even go down that ravine this time a year."

Chloe smiled politely as she edged farther away from him.

"Everest's place is just over this ridge," Grandpa yelled as he pointed again.

"Why aren't there any roads?" Chloe asked, as she pulled her hair to her nape and held it in place.

"No need. Most people ride horses up here. They're more efficient in the snow." With a wink, he added, "And you can eat a horse if you had to. Everest had a horse up until a few years ago."

"Of course," Chloe mumbled, unable to believe what she was hearing. She gulped and turned pale. Weakly, she inquired, "Was that the year of the avalanche?"

Grandpa's teasing grin was lost on her, as he mused thoughtfully, "As a matter of fact, it was."

Chloe grasped nervously at the door handle wondering if she should bail.

"Yes, sir, there's no need for roads. Not many people live up here." Grandpa nodded his head. "And those that do manage just fine."

They rode in silence as Grandpa maneuvered his jeep up a steep incline. Chloe grabbed the roll bar even tighter, frightened that the vehicle would tumble over onto its back. When it leveled out again Chloe gasped in surprise for before her lay a cleared section of land surrounded by trees. In the middle stood a large two-story cabin, as elegant and as well kept as any country home she had ever seen. The soft glow of firelight shone dimly from a giant picture window. A long porch wrapped around the front of the house. To the side of the cabin was a barn where Chloe guessed her husband had kept his horse before he'd been forced to eat it. There was a small storage shed next to the barn and an old Ford pickup. If Chloe had her guess she would say that the Ford was from the 1950's, like everything else on the mountain.

"This is it," he announced proudly. Grandpa honked his horn in several short blasts.

"It's beautiful." Chloe breathed, amazed that something this elegant could be found hidden within the woods. She laughed with relief as she realized she had been expecting a sod house or some camping tents.

"Everest built it himself." Grandpa grinned with pride. "He just finished with the first floor this last fall. Well, actually there are only a few minor details left to do. But mostly it's finished. I think you should be most comfortable here."

Chloe took it to mean that Everest had the house built for him. She wondered how much one would have to pay a contractor to come out this far into the mountains, and what sort of man would even want to.

"Everest! Come out here, boy!" Grandpa hollered, slowing the jeep. "I've brought something for you."

Chloe darted her gaze away from the barn to stare at the cabin. She ignored Grandpa, unable to hear his friendly chatter over the pounding of her heart. She waited in breathless anticipation and fear. Her slight smile froze as she saw the vaguely familiar man open the front door. If his home had amazed her, the man himself astounded her.

A blurred vision of a night of passion came rushing back to her as if from a long ago dream. Her body shuddered in response. She could feel hands--strong and powerful as they commanded her flesh. She could feel lips pressed in places she rarely looked at. Blood stirred hotly in her veins warring with the insistent chill of the evening air. The mere sight of him took her breath away and she could understand fully how she had succumbed to him.

The jeep stopped in front of her husband and she stiffly moved to climb out, aware that his eyes remained curiously calm. He was a tall man, with bulging muscles underneath a flannel shirt. Chloe gulped, instantly thinking of the stereotypical handsome lumberjack. His strong arms were folded neatly over his chest, giving him the confident air of supreme dominance. He looked as if he worked hard to survive in the wilderness.

Chloe let out a slow, unsteady breath. Everest Beaumont was nothing like she had expected. She felt dwarfed standing in front of him. He was a massive man in size, looking like he could have been a professional body builder at one time, only to have given the occupation up long enough to let his rock-hard build mellow into a smoothly seductive sculpture of masculine perfection. Chloe found herself captivated by the hidden muscles of his broad chest. Men just were not made like him anymore. Seeing the amusement in his expression, she turned her eyes

CAUGHT 139

downward in distress. She hoped that she hadn't been too forward.

"Grandpa, what are you doing out here?" Everest gave the woman a questioning look, but didn't move. His firm lips curled slightly in a lazy smile. "I didn't expect you for another week."

Chloe shivered at his deep resonant voice. Her lips were suddenly dry. Growing unsteady, she fell to lean against the jeep.

"Just as well, I've got some venison in the freezer for you," Everest paused before adding, "Did a bit of hunting last weekend."

"There now, don't let the marshal hear that." Grandpa chuckled mirthfully. "He'll want some for himself."

Everest chuckled.

Clearing his throat, Grandpa nodded to his companion. "I told you I brought something for you."

Everest turned his attention to Chloe and smiled a wickedly handsome smile. He took a step forward, uncrossing his massive arms. Giving her an acknowledging nod, he held out his hand. "Everest Beaumont, ma'am."

"Chloe," she stammered in return. Lifting her finger in a polite wave, she didn't dare touch him. She was afraid to take his hand in her shaking one. She tried not to blush at the teasing light in his hazel-green eyes. He had noticed her mental perusal of him and let her know it with a piercing look that shot through her like a bolt of lightening. His hand fell to his side.

"That's strange." Grandpa scratched his balding head. His eyes narrowed in confusion. "I was under the impression you'd met."

Everest smiled kindly and shook his head. "Afraid not."

"Well, actually," Chloe interrupted. Her disheartened glance found the old man as she took a halting step toward Everest. "We did meet once. About two weeks ago, in Vegas."

The easy smile faded from his handsome face as she said the words. Recognition dawned on him. Clearing his throat in discomfort, he said absently, "Uh, let me help you with those, Grandpa. What have you got there anyway?"

Chloe pursed her lips as she watched him ignore her. As soon as he turned, she took a steadying rush of air. Everest Beaumont was not the backwoods, inbred man she had envisioned. He was a virile example of American masculinity. He was tall, strong and very handsome. He had warm, inviting hazel-green eyes and soft shoulder-length brown hair that was tied back neatly into a ponytail. He wore a red flannel shirt, tucked neatly at his waist into a pair of worn blue jeans over boots.

"Can I help?" she asked the men, hoping her voice didn't sound too weak.

"No, you just wait right there." Grandpa answered with a smirk. "This won't take us long at all."

Unsure, she watched the men carrying boxes of food and supplies into the house. She felt like a fool standing in the snow. It began to fall on her lightweight jacket. She wished that they had invited her in. The bitter cold soaking into her toes crept into her lower legs leaving her shivering uncontrollably. She wasn't prepared for an early winter. She hadn't packed for it. The jacket offered little protection against the elements, as did the business suit underneath.

Chloe wondered if she should bother with her luggage. Everest didn't appear overjoyed to see her. She speculated briefly that he might have someone living with him who would not be heartened by her presence. She hadn't even thought of that.

When they came back for their last load Chloe was still standing by the jeep. She hadn't moved from her place, too frozen to take a step. But, as she saw Everest's heated gaze glance pointedly in her direction, her body went completely numb until she could no longer feel the chill in her feet through the thin dress boots she wore.

"Everest, if you don't mind, Chloe and I will be staying on for the night. I'm not feeling right and don't want to drive," Grandpa said. He put a weathered hand to his chest and patted his heart. Chloe gulped. The men ignored her, as Grandpa continued, "Tomorrow, being Sunday, the store will be closed and I don't feel up to going to church with Gladys."

"Fine," Everest nodded slowly. He shot the old man a confused look.

"Help me with her bags, son." Grandpa winked at Chloe as he moved to grab her luggage. Taking the briefcase out of her frozen grip, he told Everest over his shoulder, "Haddy had someone staying at her place, so there was nowhere else for this young lady to go."

Chloe's mouth went dry as Everest gazed at her in silent expectation. Suddenly, she was grateful for the weather for it hid the blush that threatened her red cheeks. Snowflakes fell harder, blanketing him gently. He didn't appear to notice. Grandpa cleared his throat noisily to break the spell between them. Everest immediately stepped into action.

When Everest drew near her she could feel her body tremble in reaction. She caught the slight scent of cedar smoke coming off

CAUGHT

of him. He leaned over the side of the jeep. She turned next to him to grab her purse and laptop computer.

"I won't impose long," she whispered.

"Why don't you go inside?" Everest said as he passed her. "We can get these."

Chloe did as he instructed, wondering how she could have forgotten a night with a man like him. She stepped inside the door to his home, feeling like an intruder.

His cabin was simply decorated. A fireplace burned brightly, giving her the impression that it was the only source of heat in the house. It did a magnificent job. Before the fireplace was a bear skin rug, head included. She wondered if he had killed it himself. A wooden bench and matching chair surrounded the fur. And there was a beautiful old rocking chair with a thick knitted blanket thrown over the back.

Chloe stepped aside as Everest came into the house behind her. She could feel the heat radiating from his body.

He put her bags into a pile by the front door. His arms barely strained under their weight.

"You have a lovely home," she asserted politely, meeting his devilishly handsome gaze.

"Thank you," he offered in short reply. He gave her a brief glance of curiosity before moving to close the door behind Grandpa.

"There now," Grandpa said. "Why are we standing about?"

"Please, have a seat," Everest offered belatedly. His voice was a bit hoarse as he uttered in a low tone, "I was just working on some blueprints in the kitchen. I'll be right back."

"Always working," Grandpa scolded when Everest left the room. He moved to the wooden couch. "Why don't you warm yourself? He won't be too long."

Chloe didn't need to be invited twice. She took a chair next to the fireplace and held out her stiff fingers. Closing her eyes, she soaked in the inviting warmth of the fire. She willed her heart to slow its frantic pace as she thought of the quiet man she had married. Her knees weakened and she was glad to be sitting. Biting her aching lips, she stared into the lapping flames. It was going to be a long evening.

Chapter Three

Everest studied the woman sitting across from him. She was laughing politely at an anecdote Grandpa was telling. Truth be told, she was the last person he had ever expected to see in his home--or ever again for that matter. The fire crackled in the fireplace, lending a softened red glow to her blond hair. She was remarkably beautiful in a high class, city sort of way. Her black business pantsuit was a perfect match to the black leather briefcase Grandpa had carried in for her earlier. He had no idea what a high dollar prostitute would want with a briefcase.

A prop, maybe? Everest thought. He suppressed his lecherous chuckle, suddenly curious to see what kind of 'toys' she might carry inside it.

Everest smiled at his grandfather and wondered what the old man was up to. Grandpa was a wily one if you didn't keep an eye on him. Everest knew it had to be something, the old man had never complained of sickness a day in his life.

"There now, you two young people can stay up as late as you like." Grandpa sighed as he pulled himself out of his chair. "But these old bones need a bed. I'll see you in the morning."

Everest stood and moved to help his grandfather. The man jolted in surprise at the offer. Under his breath, Everest hushed, "Wouldn't want you to strain yourself, Grandpa, since you aren't feeling well."

"Right you are, dear boy." Grandpa chuckled delightedly.

"What is going on?" Everest hissed as soon as they reached the kitchen and were out of earshot. He dropped his grandfather's arm, knowing he didn't need support. "Why the extra supplies? You know I have enough up here to last two winters."

"Your grandma was worried about you. It isn't right for a man to spend so much time alone. You need a woman here. She'll liven up the place." Grandpa shuffled his feet toward the spare bedroom. It was where he always stayed on visits. "Besides, don't tell me she doesn't stir your blood a bit. Hell, if I was younger--"

"If you were younger, I'd throw you both out on your asses," Everest put in. "So be damned thankful you're old."

Grandpa guffawed and slapped Everest on the arm.

"What is she doing here?" Everest questioned sharply. "You aren't trying to play matchmaker with a woman like her are you?"

"So you do know her then?" Grandpa smiled. With a playful wink, he inquired, "How well?"

"Grandpa, she is a Vegas prostitute." Everest sighed, unabashed. "The guys from Chilton Enterprises sent her to sweeten the deal with me."

"Is that why you came back early?" Grandpa shot in surprise. "She doesn't seem like a prostitute to me."

"Believe me, she is." Everest groaned at his grandfather's hearty laugh. "A high dollar one at that. Let's just say that, if I had been unsure, she'd have been able to convince me to sell out."

"Must have been some night for her to follow you home," Grandpa asserted a bit proudly. "Maybe you should keep her on for the winter."

Everest groaned. "It'd be a waste of money."

"You can afford it, and a woman is the best way to waste it if you ask me." Then, with a gentle chuckle he shooed his grandson away. "Now quit talking to an old fool and go. You better find out what she wants. We'll catch up in the morning."

* * * *

Chloe waited impatiently by the fireside as Everest helped the man to his bed. They had been sitting quietly for about an hour. Grandpa had held most of the conversation, having a self-claimed billion stories about the mountains--from fly-fishing to Rocky Mountain spotted fever outbreaks, bear attacks to snow peaks shaped like naked women.

She wanted to say so many things to Everest. She wanted to explain her presence. But she had felt uncomfortable talking in front of the chatty old man. It had been made clear at his shop that he wouldn't have welcomed any word about divorce. And it really was a private affair, no matter that the whole town of Miner's Cove already knew their business.

Chloe really felt terrible about the town's knowledge of the marriage, especially since she was there to end it. Grandpa especially seemed to genuinely care for Everest. And she could well imagine how horrible gossip would be in such a small place. There would be no escaping it.

"Are you cold? You've been shivering all night." The words were gentle as they washed over her from the doorway.

Chloe jumped as she heard Everest address her. His voice was low and husky, like a seductive song. Her midsection heated with a curious fire. She cleared her throat, amazed that he had taken the care to notice her discomfiture. Shyly, she said, "No, I'll be fine. I'm just not used to this weather."

"You're not really dressed for the mountains," he noted, as he took a seat across from her. His gazed narrowed and traveled over her slenderness. "I'd guess this is your first visit here."

Chloe nodded, unable to speak. She wished she were drunk, although she rarely partook of liquor. Without the aid of alcohol she would never have had the courage to go to him. Her husband really seemed to fill up a room, and now that they were finally alone she didn't know how to begin.

Everest studied her for a moment. Then, boldly he stated, without embarrassment, "Are you pregnant? Is that why you're here? Except for that first time, I used protection. Actually several--"

"No," Chloe broke in with an apprehensive cough. The great blue orbs of her eyes widened in surprise. Why did everyone assume she was with child? In truth, she hadn't thought of the possibility until Grandpa had said something. "I don't believe so."

"Then you were sent here by Chilton," Everest concluded, as he crossed his arms and leaned back in his wooden chair. "Sorry you had to waste your time. Tell them I'm still not interested in their proposal."

"I'm sorry, I don't understand." Chloe cocked her head to the side in puzzlement.

"I said the answer is no. I don't wish to sell. Ever." Everest studied the baffled woman in front of him. She was lovely in her confusion. His loins began to lift and fill with a primal need and he considered hiring her again for the night--might as well, as long as she was there.

"I'm afraid I do not know who Chilton is," Chloe answered. "I don't know what you're talking about."

It was Everest who was confused now. "Then what are you doing here?"

"That's a nice welcome." Chloe huffed, letting the stress get to her. "Are you this friendly to all your guests?"

"I apologize. I don't get many guests out here," Everest asserted coolly in return. He uncrossed his arms and leaned forward to put his elbows on his knees. He gave her a lazily seductive smile. His eyes glittered with a dangerously hot meaning. "Just the occasional clients."

Boldly, he watched her. She thought she might explode from the intensity of his lustful gaze. Chloe pushed her thighs together to keep them from aching. It didn't work. His smile sent chills up her spine as she imagined just what it was they could have done on their wedding night. "No, I apologize. I realize I'm uninvited."

"Let's start over." Everest relaxed as he leaned back on the chair. He enjoyed the sweet torture of waiting. Not paying his words much heed, his eyes drifted over the slender length of her throat to her pulse. He stretched out his legs and crossed them at the ankles, before questioning, "What brings you so far from Vegas?"

"I am not usually in Vegas," answered Chloe. It was becoming evident he had no idea about the marriage. "In fact, two weeks ago was my first time there. I don't think I care for the city--too many lights and overdone glamour."

"I agree." Everest had to admit she piqued his curiosity. "So you travel a lot in your profession?"

"Sometimes. Mostly I work out of my home in New York." Chloe smiled, relaxing at his easy conversation. "I can concentrate better there. I think it's the familiar surroundings."

"Really," Everest mused. He didn't remember anything being wrong with her concentration. Then again, he had been very drunk. The boys at Chilton had plied him with liquor trying to loosen his resolve. He hardly remembered anything from that night. Only that he had awakened completely sated with a beautiful stranger.

"Yeah," she continued. "I used to have a cat that would watch me, but she died last year. I haven't been able to replace her."

"Really?" Everest cleared his throat. For the first time, he seemed disconcerted.

"Everest is an interesting name." Chloe felt it better to change the subject. She didn't know why but she got the impression that her comments made him uncomfortable. Maybe he didn't like pets.

"My parents loved to climb mountains. I was conceived the same night they finished climbing Mt. Everest." He smiled sadly in thought. "They died in a rock slide in Colorado five years ago."

"Oh, I'm sorry."

"Don't be. They died together doing what they loved." He lightly shrugged his shoulders. "How about you? Do your parents know what you do for a living?"

Chloe wondered at the strange question. Millions of readers knew what she did for a living. She thought that maybe it was his idea of a joke. He wasn't smiling. "My mother died when I was born. I never knew her. My father passed away three months ago. We weren't very close. He was a workaholic and let's just say that I am my father's daughter."

Everest sat up and shifted uneasily in his chair. "About that, I'm sorry I left so suddenly. I had an early meeting and a flight to catch. I didn't wish to wake you."

"That's okay. Though, I don't understand what that has to do with my working." Chloe adjusted herself on the rocking chair. For wood, the chair was really quite comfortable.

"Is this about money?" Everest sat up at the sudden insight. "Are you here because you didn't get paid?"

"What?" Chloe's jaw dropped in shock.

"How much do you usually get for a night?" Everest continued, unaffected by her pale face. "I don't know what's fair. I usually don't solicit prostitutes."

"I--I," Chloe stuttered. She shook her head unable to finish.

"Is that why you seem so nervous? It's all right. I'll pay you what I owe you. I don't keep a lot of cash around, but I can write you a check." Everest smiled politely. Then, an interested light entered his steamy eyes. "I might like to hire you again tonight. That's if you don't mind making this a working vacation."

"B--but," she stammered.

"I'm sorry you had to come all this way to get your money. I would have believed you if you had written first. I honestly thought that you were taken care of by Chilton," Everest continued unhampered. "But, as long as you are here--"

"I am not a prostitute!" Chloe shouted. She stood up in mortification. Her limbs shook in outrage. He thought she was there to collect a debt! Her chest heaved, drawing his eyes to the feminine mounds. He licked his lips.

"I don't understand." Everest stood up to tower over her. Chloe backed away, intimidated by his overbearing size. "We did spend the night together, did we not?"

"Yes." Chloe spouted in anger. His offensive offer left her shaken--partly in insult but mostly in excitement.

"Then?" he persisted. "Is prostitute not the right word? Do you prefer working girl or escort or something? I didn't mean to offend you and would like to hire you, no matter what you call yourself."

Everest took a step toward her, intent on kissing her pouty mouth. He figured as long as she was there, he might as well add to his bill--and he had several ideas in mind on how to do just that.

"But I'm not a whore! I'm your wife," she hissed.

CAUGHT

When he heard her words he stiffened. Whispering in disbelief, he growled tightly through his gritted teeth. "My what?"

"I'm your wife," Chloe snapped back, coming out of her shock. His nearness disconcerted her. Stuttering, she blurted out, "I'm not a hooker. I'm your wife. We got married that night in Vegas."

"I don't believe you." Everest lost his good humor. "Are you trying to get more money out of me? I'll pay what I owe, but I will not be part of some twisted blackmail."

"How dare you? I don't need your money." Chloe fumed. She poked him in the chest with her finger. It didn't phase the hard muscle. "And I'm not lying."

"I say you are," he broke in. He studied her through narrowed lashes. "I think I would remember getting married."

"See this cheap ring?" Chloe dug in her pocket and held out the dull piece of metal for his inspection. "And I have the certificate in my purse."

"Let me see it," Everest ordered. He was surprised at how easily she stood up to him. Most people cowered away from him in fright when he was angry. He hid his smile. Taking the ring from her hand, he fingered the cheap atrocity knowing he would never give it to a woman. The ring was already bent out of shape. He would have laughed if the situation weren't so dire. "This looks like it came from those kiddy machines at the grocery store."

Chloe walked to her purse and pulled out a folded piece of paper.

"Wait," Everest suddenly brightened. "Is this some kind of role playing thing? I didn't drunkenly promise to pay you something if you did this, did I? Did I actually buy you a plane ticket down here? I must confess this has never been one of my fantasies, but hey, who am I to complain? Just tell me--"

"For the last time, Mr. Beaumont, I'm not a prostitute. I'm not a call girl. I'm not even an escort." She handed the marriage certificate to him with shaking hands. "If you call me a whore one more time, I will deck you."

Everest shot her a bemused smile. He would like to see her try. The idea excited him and he licked his lips. Glancing at the bedroom, he sighed. Then, turning to the paper in his hand, he read it over.

"What kind of joke is this? This can't be legal. It says here that we got married at the Church of Elvis. That can't be a real place." Everest stared at the worn certificate in disbelief. It looked as if the woman before him had read it a great many times. He perused the black ink on the paper. It was his signature on the certificate. "If this isn't a role game, I'm insulted."

"It's a very real place. I looked up the chapel. I even looked up the Elvis who did the ceremony. He remembered us quite fondly from the evening before. He said that we were the only couple who came in that night and that we both tipped him very well. He asked how my husband was doing and he wanted to know if we were over our benders."

Everest swallowed, saying nothing.

"And it would seem that we couldn't take our hands off each other. Elvis thanked us for the show and says he knows we are going to make it for the long haul." Chloe gave an un-amused sniff. "I saw his credentials. I had my lawyer look them up too. It's a legal and binding contract. We are married."

"I can't believe that I would've gotten married at a place called the Church of Elvis." Everest handed her the certificate in bewilderment.

"Me, neither." Chloe sighed as she folded the certificate up and stuck it in her purse. "It really is quite insulting."

"So, what do we do now?" asked Everest as he sat back down. He couldn't fathom that he was married. But, as he witnessed her solemn face, he knew it was true. Hurriedly, he continued before she could answer, "So what were you talking about when you said you work at home? I mean if you are not a prostitute."

"Well, my name is Chloe Masters. I'm a writer. Grandpa mentioned you might have read one of my books." Chloe blushed as she thought of it. It was always embarrassing to meet a fan. She liked knowing they were out there, but didn't like to meet them because she never knew how to graciously handle the praise. She had always hated the book signings and the autograph parties her editor father used to make her do.

Everest was quiet for a moment. He had indeed read most of her work. Without a television, reading was one of his only forms of entertainment. In fact he had almost every novel she had ever written on his bookshelf--even the early years that weren't widely printed. He found them sensitive and moving. Clearing his throat, he said, "Yeah, I've read a couple. I found them to be diverting."

"Thank you." Chloe's color deepened. She wondered if by the word diverting he meant amusing, in a horrible way. He didn't really make it sound like a compliment and he definitely didn't look like her typical fan.

"So what do we do now?" Everest queried again.

"I had my lawyer draw up divorce papers. I figured I could come here, have you sign them, and be on my way." Chloe spoke professionally as if she was pitching an idea to her new editor. "You're welcome to read over them. They simply state that we both leave the marriage with what we brought into it. And, if you prefer, I will pay you a small cash settlement for your troubles and your silence. I have it all here in my briefcase. I presume a certified check will be sufficient. I think you will find it more than fair. This kind of scandalous publicity would not be good for my career."

Everest eyed her in shock. "I'm an honorable person. I don't need to be paid for my silence."

Chloe was taken aback by his sudden anger. "I didn't mean--"

"But didn't you? You think you can come here and treat me like I have no pride? I'll have you know I don't need your money. I don't want it." Everest stood up and towered over her.

"I didn't mean to insult you. My lawyer thought to put that clause in. Really, she is only trying to protect me. She didn't know what kind of a man you would be. For all I could remember, you were a backwoods militant leader with an army of anti-government radicals. Not that that is a bad thing if you are." Chloe gave him as sheepish grin. He smiled halfheartedly at her wit. She took a step toward him and put a hand gently on his arm. "I was drunk. I couldn't remember what kind of man you were. Please, don't be insulted."

Everest felt his heartbeat quicken at her touch. He lifted his hand to brush her hair from her face. Looking deep into the gentleness of her blue eyes he slowly leaned down, intent on kissing her. The fact that she had slept with him willingly excited him even more. After such a satisfying encounter, why wouldn't she want to do it again? It wasn't as if her 'fans' would find out. Her reputation would be safe.

Chloe felt his hand on face and saw his lips moving slowly toward her. Her mouth was pulled to him by a magnetic force she could not fight or understand. She closed her eyes as his lips brushed hers softly, testing the smoothness of her response. He ran his hands into her hair, pulling her mouth more firmly against his parted lips. He deepened the kiss, flicking his tongue along the outer rim of her mouth's opening. She moaned in stunned surprise against him.

Murmuring along her lips, he said, "Well, as long as we're still married...."

Chloe groaned as he pulled her more firmly against him. His rigid manhood pressed wantonly into her soft center and she could feel his hot length pulsing to be free of his denim jeans. She trembled as his hand began to move over her body, pushing seductively hard into her flesh. His chest pressed into her sensitive breasts, rubbing the peaks into hard points. His member thrust shamelessly into her and he bent her back over his arm. His passionate desires took her by surprise. He was confident that she would not deny him.

Chloe felt her thighs part at his persistent pressure and was rewarded with a wanton thrust to her hips. Her business suit was no barrier to his ardor as he lowered his hand to unbutton her suit jacket. Exposing the thin white linen shirt, he growled at the perfect breasts straining against a lacy bra underneath. The pretty undergarments beckoned his lips and he began to unbutton the blouse.

He was so warm to the touch. She felt the erotic beat of his heart against hers. She no longer could question what had made her sleep with him. He was amazing. Gasping in pleasure as his lips left hers to explore her neck, she moaned.

"Shoot!"

Chloe froze. She lifted her head to look behind her. Grandpa's voice had come from the kitchen and she could hear his hurried footfall disappearing to the other side of the house.

"One moment," Everest whispered next to her, not at all embarrassed about being caught. He gave one last longing glance to her breasts before letting her go. Strolling to the kitchen, he looked inside. It was empty. Their intruder was gone. When he turned to her, a blush lined her features. She had covered herself back up and was sitting in his chair.

"What were you doing in Vegas?" he asked quietly when she refused to meet his eyes. He could sense her nervousness through her jittery movements. His body urged him to pick up where he left off, but he could see she was going to need some convincing. Knowing that the pleasure was always sweeter when put off a bit, he forced himself to say, "Were you there for business? I seem to remember you calling my room."

The deep liquid pools of his eyes entranced Chloe. She lifted her hands to her hair to absently rub her temple. Without thinking, she said truthfully, "No, I was there to get married. I was supposed to call room 358. Instead I called your room number 258--a silly mistake."

"So you are engaged?" asked Everest, as he dropped his hands to his sides. He didn't move toward her.

Chloe was disappointed by his withdrawal. Her body swam in lightheaded protest. "Well, kind of. I mean not really anymore."

Everest was baffled by her answer. "Either you are engaged or you are not. Which is it?"

"I suppose I am technically," answered Chloe as she thought of Paul, a man she had never met. "But, I don't think you can be both married and engaged."

"I see." Everest backed farther away from her. His eyes glowed with a fiery light.

"There is one more thing," Chloe said as he pulled away from her. Her lips still ached from his kisses and her loins trembled with such intensity that she was shocked by her own wantonness. "I told Grandpa we were married and he told a waitress named Gladys. I think that she told the rest of the town. I didn't mean for that to happen, but it was the only way I could get Grandpa to take me up here."

Everest groaned, suddenly glad to have another reason to be angry with her. It would keep him from pulling another man's woman into his arms.

"I'm sorry." Chloe made a move to touch him, hoping he would kiss her again. Lowly, she murmured, "I'll do whatever it takes to make it right."

"I'll talk to him. You've done enough." He jerked away from her hand, sore at having to deny his passion. He knew he would have to service himself if he were to ever get to sleep that night. "Grandpa is in the spare room. You can have my bed. I'll sleep in here."

Chloe began to protest, but was cut off by his hard frown.

"I'll not have you accusing me again of being a bad host." Everest turned his cool gaze toward her, effectively ending the conversation. "I'll go over and sign your papers first thing in the morning. I trust you brought me a copy of everything."

"Yes ... fine ... perfect," Chloe stuttered in response.

"Good." He ushered her to his bedroom, saying, "There's a shirt on that chair if you need something to sleep in. No one will bother you here so feel free to make yourself comfortable."

Chloe nodded in understanding. As he shut the door behind her with a heavy thud, she sighed in frustration. What just happened?

Crossing over to the chair, she lifted his shirt from the top of a neatly folded pile of fresh laundry. Unable to resist, she pressed the shirt to her nose and breathed deeply of its earthy scent.

Gliding the shirt down her throat, she lightly ran the cloth over her swollen breasts to the throbbing ache of her lower stomach. Her body burned, stinging with a fierce need to be fulfilled. She shivered uncontrollably.

Stripping quickly out of her clothing, she crawled into his bed wearing only her bra and panties. His scent overwhelmed her as she lay in his blankets, hugging his shirt to her chest. The smell only tortured her more until her loins melted with an insistent fire. Knowing she would never fall asleep with such torments flowing in her veins, she quietly lowered her hand over her flat stomach to reach inside her lacy panties.

Taking his shirt, she bit into the soft material to keep from crying out. With painstakingly slow movements so the bed would not squeak, she stroked her fire until the throbbing transformed into trembling liberation. Muffling her cry into his shirt, her eyes closed and she saw Everest's handsome face thrusting before her. Her lips moved, remembering his hot kisses. Her hips jerked in bittersweet release, aching in denial of full gratification.

With a cry, she pulled the shirt from her lips and ran it to cover her stomach. Holding her breath, her body ached for Everest's hold, but she refused to seek him out. She didn't know what was happening between them and she wasn't planning on staying around long enough to find out.

Chapter Four

Chloe had a hard time sleeping in his home. The outside was too quiet compared to the noisy lullaby of the city streets. The only consistent sound she could detect was the faint hum of insects and not too many of those. Sometime in the night hours she thought she heard a howling wolf outside the bedroom window. She'd been convinced for about an hour that it was going to get into the house and eat her.

Everest's kiss had left her with a longing so intense that it shook her to the core. The large bed smelled of his virile mountain scent, of outdoors and fresh air, of pine trees and snow banks. She wished that he had continued to touch her, knowing that it was better he hadn't. How could she allow this man to get involved with her crazy life? How could he understand the

CAUGHT

circumstances around her impending marriage to Paul? She didn't even understand it at times.

Morning came slowly and she was up shortly after dawn. Her head swam with the haze of little sleep and she could feel her frustrated emotions surfacing. Remembering Everest's remark about her ill chosen attire, she dug through her bags until she found a pullover sweater and a pair of blue jeans. The outfit was more suited for the territory. Putting her dress shoes into one of the suitcases, she pulled out a pair of hiking boots. She had just bought them for the trip and they felt uncomfortably stiff against her feet.

Pulling her hair back into a makeshift bun she wished she could take a shower. She imagined she could still smell his aroma on her body and tried to cover the memory by spraying a strong perfume on her clothes. Then, out of spite, she sprayed a few squirts on his bed, hoping it would torture him in the nights to come, just as his scent had tortured her. She applied a small amount of makeup and made his bed.

Everest's bedroom was as sparsely decorated as the rest of his home. All the furniture was made of wood and looked to be of fine craftsmanship. The walls, the ceiling, the floors--all of it was wood. The home was too large to call a cabin and too woodsy to call a mansion. Chloe decided she thought it was more like a one-man lodge.

Tiredly, Chloe wondered if it was too early to leave the bedroom. She couldn't hear anyone stirring. Finally, after little debate she decided she would try to make some coffee. Under the circumstances, she hardly doubted Everest would mind her poking around the kitchen.

She pulled open the door to the bedroom and made her way into the living room directly outside of it. She had expected to see Everest asleep on the floor but was surprised to find that he was already gone and his blankets were neatly folded on a chair. The neatness was something she was quickly coming to associate with the mountain man. His house was immaculate.

Across the room a light shone from the kitchen, so she made her way to it. Inside the kitchen was empty. The coffeepot was half full and a clean cup was set beside it. She took the hint and helped herself. The coffee was plain but good. It was not of the exotic flavors she had grown used to in New York. She sighed. Things were so much simpler in the mountains.

After peeking outside, she saw that she was alone in the house. Both the jeep and Everest's old pickup were gone. Taking her time, she slowly wandered about his home. The layout was quite simple. There was the living room where they had sat in front of the fireplace, a small den, a large bathroom, the kitchen and the two bedrooms. Everything was beautifully unrefined. There was also a locked room off the kitchen. Chloe wondered why a man living alone in the mountains would feel the need to lock anything.

Hearing an engine roaring outside she rushed to the window. It was Everest in his pickup. Chloe went to the front door and held it open. Snow had begun to fall, blanketing the front porch like little diamonds. She shivered as the cool breeze filtered through the holes in her knit sweater.

Everest climbed out of the truck. Chloe felt her breath catch. He stared at her for a brief moment before jogging to the door. She stepped out of his way. He stopped to stomp his feet on the porch, shaking the snow off of his boots. She backed up and watched as he closed the door behind him.

"Where's Grandpa?" Chloe asked lightly, belying the twittering of her stomach and the fact that she was unnerved being completely alone with him.

"I think you'd better sit down." Everest motioned to the fireplace as he took off his coat. He detected the heavy scent of her perfume on the air. The smell was out of place in his rugged home and his gut automatically stiffened in pleasure. He ignored his body's unsubtle hinting and refused to let the scent affect him.

"Why?" Chloe did as his suggested. "What's happening?"

"Grandpa is gone." Everest said, bending to throw another log on the fire. "He left early this morning."

"Then how am I to get back to Miner's Cove? He said he'd take me." Chloe eyed Everest in disbelief. "He is coming back, right?"

"Well, eventually he will." Everest shook his head and gave a short laugh. "I am afraid you're going to be my guest for a short while."

"What do you mean? Why can't you take me back?" Chloe breathed in growing fear. "I can't stay here. I have a deadline. I have to get married."

"Did you forget? You are married." Everest kept his expression blank. His throat tightened bitterly. "Don't you think he'll wait for you?"

"This is insane. I don't know what kind of game you're playing at, but I won't be a part of it. I want to go back to Miner's Cove now." Chloe grew suddenly afraid. She prayed that he wasn't one of the stalking fans she had always feared. "Either you take me or I'll walk."

Everest laughed at her determination. "Unless you know a way to fly over several hundred feet of unsteady snow, I would say you're not going anywhere. Besides, an untried city girl like you would be dead within ten minutes in those elements."

"You can't keep me here. I have friends, very powerful ones. They know where I am. They'll not let you get away with kidnapping me." Chloe stood and began to back away from him. His laughter cut her off. His eyes flashed with mirth.

"I don't want you here any more than you want to be here, lady." Everest leaned back on the chair and crossed his arms. "Believe me, if there were a way to get you out of here, I would do it. If I thought I could make it, I'd throw you over the snow bank."

"Then why are you trying to trap me here?" Chloe asked, unsure. His firm lips made her tremble. She might not remember their night of shared passion, but her body seemed to just fine.

"I am not trying to trap you." Everest shook his head in amusement. "Are all writers as dramatic as you are?"

"I am not dramatic," Chloe huffed. "What would you have me think? You come back alone saying that I can't leave. You have yet to give me a decent explanation as to why."

"If you would calm down long enough to have a simple conversation, I could tell you." Everest's calm grated her nerves. Despite the inconvenience of her presence, he found her confused rage intriguing. He chuckled to himself, thinking he must indeed be getting bored living all by himself. This woman came attached to more problems than he wanted to deal with.

Chloe moved back to the chair, afraid that she was being irrational. The man before her threw her off guard. His very nearness rattled her brain. She wanted him, of that she was very certain. But even though he was her husband, she knew she couldn't have him. She didn't know him and he didn't know her. It took all of her willpower to look calm. "Please, tell me what's going on."

Everest smiled at her obvious self-control.

"It would seem that Grandpa has got it into his head that we are married." He raised a sarcastic eyebrow. "I forget who told him."

Chloe said nothing. She gave a guilt-ridden glance to the floor.

"He takes marriage very seriously and for some reason thinks that we are perfect together." Everest's features remained blank.

"What?" Chloe sat back in shock. Secretly, she was pleased by the compliment. "Did he say that?"

"No, he wrote it," Everest dug a hand into his pocket, "in a note he left early this morning. Would you like me to read it?"

Chloe nodded, unable to answer. She ignored the paper, unable to focus on anything but the subtle movements of his firm lips.

"To my dear grandchildren," Everest cleared his throat. "By the way, Grandpa is also my actual grandfather. And Gladys, the meddling waitress, is his wife."

"Naturally, why wouldn't she be?" Chloe nodded again through her bewilderment. She wondered if his entire family was in the habit of disappearing and leaving notes.

"Anyway," Everest continued. "To my dear grandchildren. It does my old heart good to see two young people find each other in such an unrelenting world. I would hate to think that you didn't give your marriage the best shot it deserved. So in the spirit of meddling grandparents everywhere, I am taking it upon myself to get involved. Should you like, you would discover that an avalanche occurred shortly after my crossing Old Miner's Pass this same morning. You will also find that I have borrowed the mattress from the spare room. Good luck, see you in a few months. If in that time you find you are still not suitable for one another, I will gladly stand aside. But, until then, Grandpa. Oh, and we would like some great-grandkids if you have nothing better to do this winter."

Chloe shook her head. "That's impossible. How could he know an avalanche was going to start? He told me they were unpredictable."

"Grandpa is a trained observer of avalanches. He can tell when they are close to happening and we did have some wild storms the last couple of weeks." Everest folded the note and slipped it back into his pocket.

"He can predict the exact time?" Chloe asked disbelieving.

"No," Everest answered.

"Then we can still make it." Chloe's eyes turned hopeful.

"No."

"But you just said that Grandpa can't tell." Chloe stood, growing completely frustrated at his nonchalant attitude. "Come on, let's go."

"That's where I went this morning." Everest sighed. Then, standing, he yawned. "I need some coffee."

Chloe followed him as he went to the kitchen. "Then you saw it?"

CAUGHT

"Yes. I saw it." Everest grabbed a clean cup from the cabinet and poured himself a drink. Everest sighed, before continuing, "Do you remember passing a white clearing of snow that was devoid of trees?"

"Where there was an avalanche a couple years back?" Chloe waited for his nod. "Grandpa pointed it out yesterday."

"That was Old Miner's Pass. My guess is that Grandpa shot his rifle up at the snow and encouraged another avalanche." Everest took a drink.

Chloe stared at him in disbelief. He acted as if this kind of behavior was normal. Maybe it was here in the mountains, but not where she was from. "You're telling me he purposely snowed us in? Anything could happen to us. We could die up here. What if there were people in that pass?"

"There's no one except us within several miles of that pass." Everest saw her mounting fear and resisted the urge to comfort her. He had to remind himself that married to him or not, she belonged to another man. And Everest was not the kind of person to stand in the way of such things. "We have plenty of supplies to last us. He made sure of that yesterday, unless you plan on dying from boredom."

Chloe considered that for a moment. "Can I at least use your telephone to call my lawyer and editor? I have many obligations. I can't just disappear."

"Don't have one," Everest answered. He took a sip of coffee. "If people need to get a hold of me they call Grandpa and he gets me the message."

"Of course, why would you have a phone?" Chloe muttered under her heated breath. "It's only the twenty-first century."

Everest pretended not to hear her.

"What about a two-way radio or a telegraph?" Chloe questioned sharply. "Or perchance a smoke stack I can use to signal the surrounding tribes?"

"I do have a two-way radio, but it won't work after an avalanche. There is no way of communicating to the outside world. Besides, the only person who can receive messages from it is Grandpa." Everest smiled ruefully at her wit. "And I don't think he'll answer me right away."

"Naturally." Chloe sighed. Then with a gleam in her eye, she said, "Wait, I have my cell phone."

Everest laughed and shook his head. "Won't work."

Chloe grinned shrewdly at that. Her tone was a bit gloating, as she declared, "It bounces off of a satellite. It will work."

"Feel free to try. It'll give you something to do." Everest set his cup in the sink and rinsed it out. "But the signal first goes to a tower and then a satellite. There are no towers around here. And, before you ask, the cable lines will be down so there will be no working place to plug in a modem to send emails. We are effectively cut off from the rest of the world."

"How about the smoke signal?" Chloe mumbled, as she sunk wearily into a chair. She glared at him as he shook his head to her rhetorical question. "Then I'm trapped here."

"Only for a few months, worst case three. I am sure your fiancé will wait for you." Everest didn't know why the idea of her with another man aggravated him. "It really isn't so bad. Hey, maybe you'll be able to get some work done without any distractions."

"Yeah, he'll wait." Chloe laid her head on the table. Paul would wait, but in two months it would be too late. Her father's will was clear. It stipulated that she had to be married by her thirtieth birthday. That was in four weeks. "Any chance we could be out of here in four weeks?"

"A slim one," Everest answered. Suddenly, he grew edgy at the notion of her staying with him. This was going to be the longest winter of his life. Walking to the kitchen door he turned to her. "Make yourself at home. Food is in the pantry. I'm going to chop some firewood and bring it to the porch."

Chloe nodded her head without looking up. Her blue eyes glared into the grains of the hard wood table. What was she going to do?

* * * *

It was a long and boring day for Chloe. Everest spent most of the morning outside cutting firewood. She watched him for only a moment before forcing herself to turn away. He was too damned sexy swinging his thick arms over his head with the ax. Then he had disappeared into one of the outer sheds. Around noon, he came in for a sandwich and then left again. The worst part was, he did all of this with hardly a word to her.

Chloe didn't know what to do. She was bored out of her mind and the only thing she could think of involved Everest. Cursing her dirty mind, she tried to keep herself busy.

He had said to make herself at home, but she didn't know what that meant. She had wanted to unpack her clothes, but didn't know where to put them. She knew she should work on her new novel, but couldn't get into it. She usually worked on a large table, spreading the mess of her research papers around her living room in miniature stacks of organization. Though, to every one else it looked like a tree exploded.

She doubted Everest would welcome such a mess into his neatly organized life. He was perhaps the cleanest man she had ever met. But what else did he have to do, being trapped alone in the mountains all year round?

So instead she spent the hours wandering his home, familiarizing herself with her surroundings. Even the man's kitchen and bathroom cabinets were neatly arranged and organized to annoying perfection. Chloe thought of her own messy apartment and was ashamed. Then, with nothing better to do, she decided she would try cooking. She wasn't a gourmet chef, but surely she could handle a simple meal for two. She had snooped through the kitchen so she had a basic idea where he kept everything. Everest would have to come back to eat sometime and she felt she had better do something to make her stay with him as painless as possible.

Everest hadn't asked her to invade his home or his privacy. She had to remind herself that he was a man used to being alone. Their marriage, after all, was mostly her fault. She shouldn't have drunk so much on the plane. She shouldn't have dialed the wrong room number. She should have met Paul before they were to be married.

Sighing, Chloe knew it was doing her no good to dwell on what was already done. Instead, she tried to concentrate on what she needed to do. Only, she wasn't sure what that was.

* * * *

Everest tightened a loosened bolt on the power generator. He had spent most of the morning doing maintenance on the old generators and plumbing system. Without constant attention they could stop working, the pipes would freeze, and he would be stuck without electricity and water. He had survived without the comforts before, but didn't think that his houseguest would be so inclined.

Everest could tell immediately that the city woman didn't belong in this world. She didn't seem prone to the type of hard work it took to survive in the wilderness. She was pampered and rich--one could tell that by merely looking at her, from her designer jeans to her turtleneck sweaters. And yesterday she had been in a tailored business suit.

Everest marveled that he could have mistaken her for a high dollar prostitute. Thinking of her outraged expression when he had offered her money brought a smile to his face. She was going to be quite a diverting amusement if anything.

Deciding that he was finished, he grabbed a towel hanging on the shed wall. He slowly wiped his hands. The shed was kept warm, so the insulated pipes wouldn't freeze as they poked above ground. Slipping on his coat, he opened the door and made the trek to the house.

The snow drifted silently from the purpling sky, keeping in spirit of the mild autumn snowfall that had been plaguing the mountains. Everest smiled in distraction, loving the gentle falling flakes. He stomped his feet on the porch before going inside.

"Hello."

Everest froze as he heard a cheery voice calling from his kitchen. For a moment the sound took him by surprise. He was not used to noise in his home, especially not of a feminine nature. Astonished that she sounded so pleasant, he shrugged out of his coat. He had expected her to be moping.

"Hello," he answered carefully. His stomach growled as he smelled food. Needlessly, he asked, "Did you make something?"

"Yeah, an omelet." Chloe came to the kitchen door and leaned against the frame. She wiped her hands on one of his towels. The scene made him a bit uncomfortable. She paused, before admitting, "I hope you don't mind. I didn't have too much to do so I thought I'd make dinner."

"That's fine, I told you to make yourself at home." Everest gave her a hesitant nod as he hung up his coat. There was an awkward silence that neither one of them knew how to fill.

Finally, she offered weakly, "I wasn't sure what you liked."

"That's fine. I don't expect you to cook for me. I'll grab a sandwich." Everest bent over and pulled off his boots. Clumps of snow fell on the floor.

"I meant that I didn't know what to put in yours, or if you even liked eggs. I assumed you did because there were so many of them in the refrigerator." Chloe stopped talking with a little groan. She wondered what the point was in trying. The man didn't seem to engage in conversation too often. Every time he spoke to her it was like pulling teeth to get anything out of him.

"Thank you," he answered in a murmur, as he crossed over to the kitchen in wool socks.

Chloe swept her lashes down over her eyes. His body turned to the side as he passed, brushing up against hers. A pretty blush fanned over her cheeks at the contact and she swallowed as she looked up into his steady gaze.

CAUGHT

His shirt was warm. It threw off an intense heat from his chest that jumped onto her tingling skin. With only a hairsbreadth of space between their bodies, Chloe swayed slightly toward him. Her breasts grazed lightly into his chest. She watched as his narrowed eyes dipped to her mouth in question. She licked her lips, waiting breathlessly for his touch.

His hands rose, lightly caressing her arms in a soft stroke. Her skin instantly blossomed in gooseflesh. Stiffening suddenly, he mumbled, "Excuse me."

Everest hurriedly moved past. He seemed to say all the right, polite things, but Chloe wanted more. She wanted him to engage in a conversation with her. She wanted him to come back and finish what she read in his lustful eyes.

Frustrated, she followed him to the table, grabbing a plate from the countertop on the way. As he sat, she set a plate before him. Then, going to the sink she got him a glass of water. With a wary smile, she said, "Grandpa did take the mattress out of the spare room."

"Hmm," Everest acknowledged as he took a bite. He acted like nothing happened. Nonchalantly, he shrugged and answered, "He said he was going to."

"I didn't know if I was supposed to unpack, but I moved my bags in there. His clothes are in the dressers." Chloe watched him take another bite without comment. She ground her teeth in frustration. "Is that where you would like my things?"

"The spare room's fine," he said, not looking at her. His eyes stayed focused on his plate.

"And how are we going to sleep?" she persisted. A blush fanned her cheeks at his sharp gaze.

"Same as last night, I suppose." He again shrugged, seemingly not giving it much thought.

"I'll take the floor, if you don't mind. I don't want to impose on you by taking your bed. This is your home. I am trying to respect that." Chloe sighed in frustration. He didn't seem to be listening. She cocked her head to the side to better study his face.

After a short time he looked up and wiped his mouth with a napkin. He considered her intensely until she looked away. Smiling at the pink tint lining her skin, he uttered, "No imposition. Take the bed. I can behave like a gentleman. And you might as well put your bags in there with you."

"Fine." Chloe wanted to throw the towel at his apathetic head, but she doubted it would change his attitude. Instead, she twisted it in her hands.

"This was good," he said, pointing to his empty plate. In a low, steady voice he mumbled, "Thanks."

Chloe shivered. Somehow, she didn't believe him. He acted so distant. "I have to meet a deadline. Would you like me to set up my office in your den or your bedroom?"

"Den's fine. You can use my computer if you like." Everest stood and brought his plate to the sink.

"I have a laptop," she answered in terse politeness. Chloe laid the towel by the sink. She had already cleaned her dirty dishes and put them away. Turning abruptly, she left.

Everest's eyebrows shot up in surprise as she stormed out. He didn't know what he could have done to make her so angry. He had answered her questions, though he knew he could have been more talkative. She was just so incredibly desirable that he was hard-pressed not to jump over the table and pull her into his arms. Smiling, he rinsed the plate and put it away. With a soft laugh, he went to his locked door and pulled the key from his pocket. Turning it in the latch, his grin widened as he went to work.

Chapter Five

"Where is she, Devon?" Paul Lucas tilted his thin, aristocratic nose in the air. His slender body stayed remarkably still under the brusque movement. "I waited for her in Vegas for a week. She never called. What kind of a business arrangement is this?"

Devon studied the attractive man before her. He was everything Chloe had asked for and yet she doubted her friend knew what those requests had added up to. Devon didn't care for his pompous attitude. "I explained to you on the phone that she had an emergency meeting with her editors and then she had to fly to London. It was unavoidable. And as far as a business arrangement goes, we have no contract. I told you she could back out at anytime. You agreed to those terms."

"Are you telling me she is backing out?" Paul was an elegant man, well dressed and from a good family. His overly groomed appearance gave the impression of spoiled money. He now sat on the edge of Devon's desk. "I will sue for damages. My guess is she won't like the publicity and will settle out of court."

CAUGHT

Devon stood up in outrage. "I never said that she changed her mind. How dare you make threats? You have no proof of the arrangement. You have no case."

"That is where you are wrong." Paul laughed. "I have plenty of proof. I tape record all of my conversations, especially the ones in hotel rooms--in Vegas."

Devon shut her mouth and glared at him.

"I would think you'd better find my blushing bride quickly. I'm not a patient man." Paul stood and wiped his hands together.

"How long are you giving me?" Devon inquired.

"One week," Paul answered. "You should be able to get her on a flight back here by then."

"I need two." Devon tilted her chin up.

"Done. But I want word in one." Paul leaned forward to tweak her chin. "And don't tell my bride of this new arrangement. I wouldn't want her thinking less of me."

"Get out of my office." Devon pointed her shaking hand to the door.

Paul laughed, but leisurely did as she commanded.

* * * *

A few days passed since her first night at the lodge, as Chloe now thought of Everest's mountain home. She spent most of her days in the den, organizing her research to start on her new novel. She was really behind schedule and found it difficult to work in the strange surroundings with the ever looming presence of such a virile man. She tried to keep her mess to a minimum, so as not to upset Everest's neat and organized life. She was amazed to discover that he was clean all the time, and had yet to see him leave messes sit for more than the time it took for him to clean it up. At home, she barely even made her bed in the morning. In fact, she couldn't recall ever making her bed since she lived on her own.

Everest pretty much kept to himself. She only saw him at dinner when she cooked for him. So far she had only made him egg dishes. She was afraid that she was soon going to have to confess that eggs were all she knew how to prepare.

Chloe had no inkling as to what Everest did during the day, because she locked herself in the den and worked nonstop. He never interrupted her and he never asked to see what she was doing. She was grateful for the privacy, but did desire human contact every once in a while. As far as contact was concerned, she wanted more from Everest then his conversation.

Hell, she thought in womanly frustration. *I don't care if a single word is uttered from his lips, so long as his body does the actual talking.*

Deciding that it was about time to cook dinner, she let loose a long gush of air. Instantly, her limbs shook with a nervous excitement. She shut off her laptop and closed her notebook. Going to the kitchen, she noticed Everest was gone. He always disappeared this time of day. She wished that he would tell her where he went and what he did, but when she tried to talk to him he would only give her brief answers. Being a writer, she was very curious by nature and his closed-mouthed approach wore her thin.

Grabbing eggs out of the refrigerator she decided on scrambled with bacon. She had to admit she was growing tired of eggs. But it wasn't exactly like she could order out for anything or call one of her father's maids. And she definitely wasn't about to fix him one of her experimental cooking dishes. He might be frustrating, but she didn't want to kill him.

It took her only a moment to prepare and she set the plates on the table. With perfect timing, Everest walked in as he had every night. Chloe felt her breath catch. All frustration melted from her when she looked at him, to be replaced by an intense longing. Her flesh began to tingle, making her body ache. She was never going to last three months. Could a person die from sexual frustration? What had happened to her? She'd never been this wanton before.

Everest eyed the plates, but said nothing. He didn't seem to notice her turmoil.

"How was your day?" Chloe asked, knowing she was going to get a one-word answer.

"Fine," he said. His voice sent chills over her spine.

"Mine, too." Chloe sat down and stabbed an egg. Taking a bite, she sat her fork down and grimaced at the plate.

Everest eyed her disinterest before smiling devilishly. "Novel not going well?"

Chloe looked up in surprise. He was actually talking to her? She almost didn't know how to answer.

"No," she stammered. "It's fine. I'm behind schedule, but it's coming."

"Hmm." He mumbled as he ate. "Not hungry?"

"No," Chloe answered. She finally was granted her wish for conversation and now she didn't know what to say to him. His rapt attention made her tremble with an unwavering desire to rip off his clothes.

Hell, thought Chloe, *I want to rip off his clothes when he's not talking to me. I am a very bad girl.*

Everest sat his fork down and leaned back in his chair. His handsome gaze lit with amusement. He crossed his arms over his chest. "You know, I like other things besides eggs. Not that I am complaining."

Chloe giggled, relieved that someone finally had said it.

"Something amusing?" Everest asked, amazed by the way her laughter bubbled from her storm-colored gaze. His eyes went to her finely arched lips. He longed to kiss her. Every time she was near him, he could smell the sweet scent of her perfume and he didn't think he could put off his desires much longer. His loins urged him to possess her, trying to take over his mind with its persistent insanity. During the night he would awaken, rock hard and ready for action. Once he had even caught himself at the bedroom door before jerking fully awake.

"No." Chloe breathed as she wiped a tear from her eye. Humbly, she admitted, "It's the only thing I know how to make. My father didn't think it necessary for me to learn. So in the morning when he was gone the maids would show me how to make breakfast. But we only got to the eggs before he found out. And I was so close to graduating to pancakes."

Everest laughed softly at the lively way she told her story. Her eyes sparkled with mischief.

Chloe smile faded at his masculine laugh. It was really the first time that she had heard it, other than to poke fun at her when she first arrived.

"Something the matter?" he inquired.

"Ah, no," Chloe lied. His laugh had disturbed her. Its deep melody shook her insides until she thought she might melt. The tension between their bodies was palpable.

"What do you say I cook tomorrow? We can have steak." Everest smiled as he picked up his fork and began to eat.

Chloe forced a smile to her tight lips and nodded her head, knowing the conversation was over.

* * * *

Chloe waited in nervous anticipation all day. She felt like a schoolgirl going on a date for the first time. The sound of his masculine laughter stayed in her head and she remembered his passionately gentle kiss from the first night of her stay. She wanted him. There was no way around it. She wanted him like she had wanted no one else. And she didn't know what to do about it.

She knew that she had Paul waiting for her. She knew that she would be divorcing Everest and that there was no way that they could stay together. The biggest reason being, he didn't want it. The second being she couldn't see their lifestyles working together. She was a rich girl from New York with a career and a life. He was a country boy from the mountains and she wasn't sure what he did for a living or if he even worked.

She took her time getting dressed. Her wardrobe didn't give her many options and she was getting down to her last outfit. She needed to ask him about the laundry. Chloe wished that she had packed her more comfortable stay-at-home clothes. She was tired of the nice sweaters and the designer jeans. She wanted her sweats and T-shirts.

Just when she thought she could wait no longer, it was time. She moved to the kitchen, led by the smell of steaks on a grill. Leaning by the frame of the door, her breath deepened. Everest stood over the stove. He had pulled down a section above the flat burners that she hadn't even noticed before. It was an artfully arranged makeshift grill.

"That looks really good," Chloe admitted, her tone a bit husky.

Everest turned at the sound of her sultry voice. "You're early."

"I couldn't wait. I smelled it in the den." Chloe blushed. "Can I help?"

"No, I don't need eggs." Everest shot her a captivating grin as he continued about his work.

It took Chloe a moment to realize he teased her. She smiled back and sat down at the table. She watched quietly as he finished preparing their plates.

"Here you go," he said, setting her meal in front of her.

Suddenly, Chloe froze as she thought of Everest's dead horse. Poking the steak lightly, she asked in hesitation, "What kind of meat is this?"

Everest eyed her warily, "Cow."

"Oh, good," she sighed with a relieved smile.

Everest tried to smile but only managed to stare at her in confusion. When she didn't elaborate, he slowly turned his attention to the plate. With a chuckle, he asked lightly, "Have a vendetta against cows?"

"No," Chloe blushed as she cut open the baked potato. She refused to answer.

Everything was delicious. The meat was juicy and flavorful and the potato had a piece of bacon tucked inside and wasn't cooked in a microwave. Chloe nodded her thanks as he handed her a tub of butter. Quietly, he took a bite. They ate in their customary silence.

Halfway through the meal, Chloe caught Everest studying her with a strange intensity.

"This is really wonderful," she said, wiping her mouth daintily with a napkin.

"What are you writing about?" he asked, letting his curiosity show. He dropped his fork and leaned forward.

Chloe smiled. "This time I'm writing about a woman in Tennessee who gives her baby up for adoption and then tries to reclaim her when she is older."

"Interesting." Everest gave her a sexy half smile. Steepling his fingers thoughtfully under his chin, he studied her. "Does she get her back?"

"No. She was a drug addict and prostitute so the courts decide to leave the child with her adoptive parents," Chloe whispered in response to his seductive tone. Her heart began to beat erratically under the pleasure of his straightforward attention. With a barbaric man like Everest, there was none of the games the men of civilization played.

"Then what happens?" Everest leaned closer as if in confidence. His eyes narrowed languidly as they dipped to her panting lips.

"You'll have to buy the book," Chloe hushed back. For a moment, she thought he might try and kiss her. His eyes stayed on her mouth.

"I promise I won't tell," persuaded Everest with a handsome grin.

"The mother kidnaps her," she answered.

"And?" he persisted. Everest leaned closer. His gaze seductively captured hers.

"And eventually she's caught and the girl is brought back to her real family, but not before learning a few of life's tough lessons."

"Any money if I sell this to a tabloid?" Everest gave her a self-satisfied smile and raised an eyebrow. Sitting back in his chair, he crossed his arms over the expanse of his Olympian chest.

"Oh." Chloe sat back in shock, the seductive mood completely broken. "Is that how you make your money?"

Everest laughed at her seriousness. "I was joking, Chloe."

Chloe liked the way he said her name. "So that isn't how you make your money?"

"Why don't you just ask me if you want to know?" Everest's smile remained devilishly intact.

"Fine, what do you do?" Chloe gave him a silly look. "I have yet to see you work."

"I have been working for the last two days. You've just been too busy to notice." Everest kept his pleasant expression.

"Really." That caught her by surprise. "Doing what? Ranching?"

"I'll show you." Everest stood and held out his hand.

Chloe jolted at the sudden offer and took his outstretched hand hesitantly. It was so strong and warm, just like she knew him to be. She followed him as he led her across the kitchen to the locked door. Her eyes strayed to his backside.

"You work in there?" she asked absently.

"Yes." He laughed at her tone and glanced over his shoulder. Her blue gaze darted up guiltily to meet his. Everest smiled. Her cheeks pinkened.

"Are you a spy?" she questioned coyly. Her lashes batted over her eyes in a fluttering wave. A half smile languidly curled his lips. Her heart began to race in feminine excitement.

"Hardly," he put forth. "Though, you are about to see all my closely guarded secrets."

Chloe giggled in return. "I doubt it."

"Just wait." Everest held up a finger. He pulled a key out of his front pocket and turned it in the lock. Pushing the door open, he felt Chloe peeking around his shoulder. She stepped close to his back.

"It looks like a workshop," she gasped in surprise. "I knew it. You're Santa Claus and you are taking over for Grandpa."

"It is and I am," he answered seriously.

"Where are the elves?"

"They're on strike. Damned unions."

"Hmm." Chloe pretended to study him. "Wait, you can't be him. Where is your white beard?"

Everest laughed. The sound was throaty as it hit her ears. Chloe shivered in uncontrollable pleasure. She had to turn away from his probing gaze.

"This is what I do. In the summer I take orders and in the winter I make furniture, clocks, trunks--whatever. And when I don't have orders, I make things on spec to sell the next summer or keep them for the house. It keeps me very busy."

"Beaumont," Chloe said in surprise. "You make the Beaumont clocks. My father gave me one for my twenty-fifth birthday. I love it. It's my favorite piece. I keep it in my living room. Everybody who is anybody in New York owns a Beaumont."

Everest cleared his throat in discomfort. "Yes, well. That's me."

"I can't believe it. I thought you were a rancher or farmer of some sort since you were always gone. Maybe even an international spy." Chloe started to walk around the room. She lightly touched an unfinished clock. "I never imagined...."

"No, this is it. The big mystery." Everest came up behind her. She could feel his heat scorching her back. In a low hush, he murmured behind her head, "Disappointed?"

"Not at all." Chloe smiled as she made her way around the large work area. There were unfinished chairs, a table, more clocks and some blueprints. "What are these? Future plans?"

"Yes, everything I have ever designed is in this filing cabinet. And these," he said reaching over her shoulder, "are my latest designs. I'm working on this one right now."

Chloe turned at his nearness to come face to face with his chest. He smelled of cedar, the whole workshop did. She lifted her eyes to him. Hoarsely, she uttered, "Any money in it if I sell it to the tabloids?"

Everest shook his head. "I'm afraid not."

"Is that what you were doing in Vegas? Taking orders?" she asked quietly, trying to keep her gaze from meeting his lips. Her breath instantly became ragged, painful gulps. Her mouth tingled.

"No," he responded in a quiet voice. "Chilton Enterprises out of Chicago wanted to buy the rights to my work and mass produce it in an overseas plant. I told them no. I take pride in what's mine."

Chloe felt a chill at his words. They left her with the impression that he would be that possessive with anything he considered his, even women. The idea thrilled her. Her eyes fluttered to his workbench, wondering if he would throw her over the dust covered table in his passion and take her from behind. Her heart pounded wildly at the wickedness of her mind. Swallowing guiltily, she asked, "Is that why you keep it locked up? So no one can steal your ideas?"

"No, nothing that exotic. This room gets dusty and the door is specially sealed to keep the dust from entering the other parts of the house," he answered. "Plus this room is fire proofed. That way if my house burns down I haven't lost my livelihood."

Chloe wanted to laugh although it made perfect sense. "So that's why I can't hear you working?"

"Yes. I suppose it is." His voice grew so soft she had to strain to hear it.

"Everest?" she whispered in a low, pleading hush, as her eyes finally trailed to his firmly irresistible mouth. Her expression turned serious.

Everest liked the way she said his name, like a breathy plea. His groin began to tighten at her nearness. In a low powerful growl, he answered, "Yes?"

Chloe was unable to stop herself. She lifted her hand to touch the stubble of his face. She rubbed her palm against the coarse surface of his jaw and moved it into the soft folds of his hair. Pulling him toward her, she leaned up for his kiss.

Everest saw her desire and put a hand to her mouth to stop her. With gut-wrenching slowness, he gently took her hand out of his hair. "We can't, you're engaged."

He let go of her and moved to the door. His body protested. His blood slowed to weaken his limbs.

His words held a cold finality. Chloe was mortified. His rejection was blatantly real as it slapped her across the face and tightened her heart. She followed him, confused. When she passed, she stopped near him. Without daring to look directly at him, she said, "I'm sorry. It won't happen again. Goodnight."

Everest watched her go, wanting to follow her, wanting to take her into his arms. He wanted her terribly. But she was engaged. She belonged to another man. He had been the 'other man' before and wasn't about to be the cause of that kind of pain to someone else. No matter how badly he ached to possess her.

"I'm sorry, too, Chloe," he whispered, as he turned to lock the door. She didn't hear him. He listened as she shut herself in the bedroom. Going slowly to the table, he gathered the dirty plates. He wished things could have been different between them. But they weren't. And he couldn't live with the guilt of taking a woman who belonged to another.

Chapter Six

Chloe was doing her best to ignore him and Everest wasn't sure he could blame her. In the last week he had only seen her the few

CAUGHT

times that she came out of the office, once to do laundry and a few other times to get something to eat from the kitchen. She said even less to him. It was like she wasn't even there. Everest had to admit he was missing their time together in the evening. He felt bad that she had taken his refusal of her kiss so hard, but what was he to do? She belonged to another man, at least technically.

Everest wondered why she was even engaged at all. She didn't seem to miss the guy, she never talked about him. And he knew it was none of his business.

It had been seven days since their last meal together and he marked each one off in his head in agonizing detail. Everest was beginning to long for her company, which was strange since he was used to being alone. His manhood stayed in a constant state of half arousal and he found himself wanting to masturbate at the oddest moments. Occasionally, he did. It was starting to affect his work. Already he was behind schedule. Not that it mattered. His clients would wait for the best.

Putting the sandpaper he had been staring at for at least an hour down, he made up his mind to go and talk to her. He decided that the only way he was going to get any peace of mind was to make amends with her.

He found her hard at work at her laptop. She didn't even see him in the doorway as he watched her. She was focused on what she was doing, unlike him. His stomach tightened into a regretful knot. She was coping fine without his company.

"Chloe?" he asked softly. "Are you hungry?"

Chloe jolted at his words, but didn't look at him. Trying to hide her utter embarrassment, she pretended to keep typing. Shortly, she said, "Not right now. I'm too busy. Behind schedule."

Everest nodded his head, disappointed that she was ignoring him. "Anything I can help you with?"

Chloe did look up at that. He was leaning against the doorframe, his blue flannel shirt covered with sawdust. Light sprinkles blanketed his usually clean hair. He was amazingly handsome in his disheveled state. She took a deep breath, trying to keep the images of his kiss from her mind. It had already occupied too much of it as of late.

"There is one thing," she said.

"Name it." Everest smiled, relieved that she didn't appear angry and sad that she didn't seem to be as sexually frustrated as he.

"I want to borrow one of your shirts and sweat pants if you have them. Or maybe the clothes Grandpa left in the spare room.

I don't think he'd mind since it's his fault I'm stranded here with nothing but dress clothes." She smiled at his look of surprise. "You didn't honestly think I like dressing up every day of my life did you?"

"No. Well, I guess I did," he chuckled boyishly.

"Actually, I'm a slob," she said in matter of fact tone. Smiling absently as she turned back to the screen, she typed a few words. "I hate cleaning. I hate wearing dresses and I especially hate doing dishes. You do own sweats, don't you?"

He watched her ability to hold a conversation and focus on her work at the same time in wonderment. "Yes, though they might be too big."

"That's perfect." She glanced up and then continued with her work. "One more thing."

"Yes?"

"I want your permission to make a mess of this office. I need to spread out. I work better that way." She grinned at his pained look. For a moment her eyes softened and sparkled. "I promise to return everything to normal when I am done."

Everest noticed she didn't say 'when I leave'. With a consenting nod, he said, "All right."

"Thank you." Chloe nodded, refusing to look at him.

As soon as he turned to leave, Chloe took a deep tortured breath and let it out slowly. His very nearness was hard for her. He looked so damned alluring standing there, that she had wanted to try to seduce him again. But she wasn't foolish. He was just being nice to her.

Leaning in her chair, she looked out the door. She made sure he was gone before moving her index finger to the keypad to delete the pages of typed nonsense.

* * * *

Quickly drying off, Chloe wrapped an oversized towel around her body. The mornings in Montana were extremely chilly. Even though the rest of the lodge was warm, the bathroom always stayed cold, especially after a shower.

Grabbing her dirty clothes off of the floor, she hugged them to her chest. She had once again forgotten to bring a change of clothes to the bathroom with her. At home, she was used to being able to walk through her house however she pleased. Sighing, she knew she was going to have to make a run for it. Not that she expected Everest to be around. He was probably hard at work.

CAUGHT

Things had been good between them since his peace offering the day before. She had been at the lodge for nearly two weeks and she couldn't believe how well she had adjusted to the new lifestyle. Everest was right. She had been able to get a lot more work done, after she had grown used to the silence.

Her impending birthday did weigh heavily on her mind. She knew she owed it to a lot of people to get married. She did her best not to think of it. There was nothing she could do snowed in on a mountain. She only hoped Devon could find a clause to extend her time period. Her father was so careful with details, surely there would be some clause to protect her should she get in an accident. And being snowed in was certainly an accident.

Chloe poked her head out of the bathroom and around the corner. Seeing she was alone, she made a run for the bedroom door. Since she held the dirty laundry and the towel she found it hard to maneuver the doorknob.

"Oh, sorry."

Chloe froze when she heard Everest behind her. Licking her dry lips, she swallowed nervously. She refused to turn around to face him.

"Do you need some help?" he inquired gruffly. Everest cleared his throat. She heard him take an uncertain step toward her. Her body ached fiercely. Her limbs shook and she felt like she wanted to cry out from the agonizing pain of her need.

Chloe turned and gave him a guilty look. She felt too exposed under his intense gaze. "No. I forgot to bring my clothes with me to the bathroom."

"Let me get the door for you." Everest came toward her. His eyes strayed to the wet tops of her exposed breasts. They were the color of silken cream.

Chloe pulled the towel closer to her, unaware that it pressed her breasts up to show a disarming amount of cleavage. She stepped aside. She could smell the fresh scent of his flesh as his thick neck neared her. She shivered, aching to drop the towel and touch him.

Everest leaned down and pushed open the door. Little beads of water sprinkled her skin, beckoning him to lick them off of her. He refused the temptation. Her wet hair brushed against his shoulder and the scent of herbal flowers drifted up to him. It was the same smell as her shampoo. She had left it in the shower and he couldn't stop himself from smelling it. It seemed she was leaving little pieces of herself everywhere in his home. He was beginning to not even mind her little messes.

"Were you looking for me?" she asked, not wanting to leave his nearness. The bedroom door creaked slowly open drawing their minds instantly to the warm bed within. Chloe was surprised when he didn't back immediately away.

"Yes." Everest smiled down at her, not remembering why he had sought her out.

Chloe gazed deeply into his piercing hazel-green orbs, mesmerized by the strength of emotion she saw in them. Under the rugged, hard surface Everest was a deeply passionate man.

"Why?" Chloe whispered in breathless awe. Her throat became dry and she swallowed nervously. She refused to come on to him again. She wondered if he even realized how beguiling his nearness was or how disconcerting.

Everest stared at her lips, unable to answer for a moment. He could almost see the sparks that lit between their heated bodies. He clenched his fists to keep from touching her.

"Oh," he mumbled, stepping back. He shook his head as if to clear it. "I wanted an opinion on something, a New Yorker's opinion."

"Oh," Chloe echoed in disappointment. Cocking her head cutely to the side, she inquired, "Give me a minute?"

"Take as long as you need. I'll be in the workshop." Everest averted his gaze and quickly left the room. He wasn't sure he could calm his desires and he had the feeling that they were burning dangerously out of control. Taking a deep breath, he tried to slow his rapid pulse. He didn't know how he was going to last the rest of her time at his home. If he saw her in a towel again, his guess was he wouldn't last at all.

* * * *

Chloe threw his large flannel over her tank undershirt and tied the drawstring at her waist. The sweats were rather big, but felt wonderful. Feeling very relaxed, she left the bedroom. Her hair was still wet from her shower and she brushed it back away from her face. She was starting to feel more like her normal self.

She was extremely comfortable in the lodge. Everest's quiet solitude soothed her in an odd way. She felt safe there, as long as he was near. He had left the lodge only once to check the mountain pass. They were still snowed in. Neither one of them had thought it would be otherwise.

It had been unsettling to be caught in her towel, and she couldn't help but notice Everest's violent reaction to her near naked state. Chloe scolded herself for being ridiculously hopeful. She usually paid little attention to her baser needs, discovering at a young age that sex in theory was usually better than the real thing. But, with Everest, she began to doubt the logic. Every fiber in her pulled to be with him. No doubt that is how she got into her current situation. Drunk she would be no match for his animalistic allure.

Hell, thought Chloe with a wry lift to her head, *I'm no match for it sober.*

She felt honored that Everest would seek her opinion about his work. It was one of the greatest compliments he could have paid to her. Not wanting to keep him waiting and more truthfully wanting to see him again, she made her way to his workshop. She knocked on the door even though it was cracked open.

"Come in, Chloe."

Chloe pushed open the door. His voice was soft like a gentle caress, but low like a rumbling mountain storm. Her eyes immediately picked him out of the room, sweeping over his gladiator-like form before he glanced to her. She smiled innocently at him, a blush barely visible underneath her white skin.

Everest leaned over a clock, sanding its grooves with a fine paper. She watched the powerfully precise movements of his strong hand and the straining motions of his muscular arm. Her smile widened when he finished and looked fully at her.

"I see you got them to fit," he said eyeing her outfit. She looked damned sexy in his clothing, more so than when she was dressed up. The sweats belonged to Grandpa though he never wore them, but the flannel was his. For a moment his gaze got trapped at her narrow waist as it tapered off into the sweatpants. The tie string hung in a small loop, enticing his fingers to loosen it with a bold flick.

"Yeah. What are you working on?" she asked as she moved toward him, only wanting to get closer. The faint stirring of dust settled in the air. It fell about him like a mist through the light of his work lamp.

"This one is almost done," he admitted. "I only have to polish it and put in the timepiece."

"Will you show me?" she asked, intrigued.

Everest looked at her in astonishment. In his disbelief, he questioned, "You really want to learn?"

"Yeah," Chloe laughed at his doubtful expression. "It would be fun to say that I got to help with a Beaumont. It would give me a story to tell at all those boring New York parties the publishers put on."

"All right. Come over here." Everest led her to a drafting table. "This is where I put the inside of the clock together. I've already done that."

Chloe nodded. She was studying his face instead of his hands.

"And then you just insert this into here," he instructed, not bothering to look away from her. Chloe nodded again.

"Then what?" she sighed, her words whispered past his neck to caress him under the ear.

"Chloe." Everest let go of the clock pieces and turned fully toward her. "You know we shouldn't do this. It's wrong."

"What are we doing?" she questioned innocently. Her eyes hardened slightly, but her smile stayed persistently intact. "You're teaching me to build a clock. Can I help it if I'm an inattentive student?"

Everest ignored her vague humor with a grim shake of his head.

"You have to feel it as I do." Everest took a step away from her. "It's not right, you're engaged."

"Oh, you mean Paul." Chloe took a step after him, stalking him boldly. She couldn't stop herself. He admitted he wanted her, which was more than her body could shrug off. If he didn't desire her, that would be different. But she could see no reason why they should torture themselves if they both wanted the same thing.

"I don't understand you. You say it like it's no big deal. You are engaged, Chloe. It's a very big deal." Everest didn't back away again. He found himself almost not caring.

Chloe took another step to him. "Let me tell you something about Paul. I have never met him. I will owe him no loyalty until we are married. And then, according to his lawyers, loyalty is optional as long as I am discreet."

"You're telling me you have never met your future husband?" Everest shook his head in disbelief. It did make sense. The way she hardly thought to mention him, the way she was able to marry the wrong man and not know it until it was too late. "Then, why?"

"Why would I throw my life away, you mean?" Chloe let loose a frustrated sigh. She didn't want to discuss it, but she didn't want to lie to him either. "My father sort of arranged the marriage. I don't have a choice."

"Everyone has a choice. We're not in the Middle Ages. Besides, I thought you said that your father was dead." Everest took a step back and was brought up against the table.

Chloe didn't pursue him. "How can I even begin to explain? I don't have a choice. I have to marry Paul. If I don't I won't get my inheritance."

"So you're marrying him for money," Everest concluded in disgust. He had thought she was better than that. It proved he really didn't know her.

"No, I'm marrying for my inheritance," Chloe flung defensively back at him. She was angry he doubted her character so easily. Hissing under her breath in aggravation, she said, "I didn't say I was to inherit money."

"Then what?" Everest questioned. "What inheritance is so important that you would give up your happiness for it?"

"I will get some money, but I don't care about that. Part of the will's stipulation is that I am not to talk about it," Chloe frowned before dejectedly adding, "with anyone but my lawyer."

"Then don't tell me." He turned to leave her.

"Wait," Chloe snapped a little too harshly. Lowering her voice, but not her hard tone, she stated, "Let me finish."

"What?" He turned back to her. He placed his hand defiantly on his hips.

"I am going to tell you on your promise that you will never mention it. I'm taking you at your word." Chloe felt her insides shake. She had a hard time trusting men and she was taking one of the biggest risks of her life in telling him.

"I give you my word." Everest knew he should tell her he didn't care. He should tell her not to risk it if it was that important. But he couldn't do it. He found himself needing to know.

"My father's will stated that I had to marry by my thirtieth birthday and bear a child by my thirty-second birthday, unless it was medically proven I could not have children or was having a hard time conceiving. In such a case, I would have to provide medically documented proof that I had been trying for at least a year and would continue to try." Chloe closed her eyes and turned away from him. "My future husband had to be tested for fertility before the match was made."

"And the inheritance?" he asked quietly. The very idea of such a strong-armed will made him physically ill. What kind of father would do such a thing?

"My father's publishing house, his printing warehouses, and a couple dozen other businesses he owns, his entire estate and one hundred million dollars." Chloe answered. "All to be given out in time allotments throughout the marriage, or upon the birth of children, or under proven necessity, et cetera, et cetera. There is a bunch of legal clauses as to the disbursements. But after ten years of marriage we will be allowed to divorce and the entire remaining inheritance will be mine. My husband will be given an ample pension, if you will, for time served and we'll be allowed to go our separate ways."

"So you are marrying for money," Everest concluded. Stiffly, he added, "I'm glad that I'm not a part of that arrangement."

Chloe shook her head. Somehow she had known he would look down on it as she had. She was relieved that his character was such that he hadn't even thought to get in on the deal himself. "No, not just the money. I have plenty of my own. But, if I don't do it, a lot of people will lose their jobs. A lot of people I care about and have grown up around. If I don't do it the businesses will be torn apart, sold to the highest bidder and the some eighty thousand plus workers turned out on the streets. I can't allow that to happen."

"I see." Everest found his opinion of her changing, though he couldn't tell her. Her fate was sealed. She was to marry Paul. And in doing so she was giving one of the ultimate sacrifices-- her happiness.

Chloe turned to him, desperate to not have him hate her. Tears brimmed over in her eyes. "Do you think ill of me? I wouldn't blame you if you did. This is a disgusting mess."

"No, Chloe." Everest shook his head and took a step toward her. She looked so alone in the world. He wished he could have a moment with her father, so he could teach the bastard a couple lessons about love, compassion and family. He wrapped his arms around her narrow shoulders to comfort her. "I admire the sacrifice you're making."

"You're angry?" Chloe shook in his light embrace. He felt so safe and warm. She was glad he understood that for her it was a sacrifice, not a blessing. Yes, she would never want for money. But what was that to her? She had everything she could ever need, a home and a solid career. Well, she had almost everything. She didn't have a true family. Her father had made sure of that in life and would continue to guarantee it in death.

"No, not angry," he lied. "I'm just glad that I don't have to be a part of it. How could he do that to you? His own child?"

Chloe nodded tensely in understanding. The wet strands of her hair loosened to frame her oval face. "You can't blame my father. I don't. You have to understand that he thought he was doing me a favor. I'm his only child. I hardly ever dated and I work all the time. This was the only way he knew he could force my hand.

He understood that I would not let eighty thousand people get turned out onto the street. His factories employ whole towns in the Midwest. He was trying to give me a push. He thought that if I hadn't done it by myself by the time I turned thirty, then it was his turn to do it for me. In his own way he thought he was doing me a favor."

With a tight tilt of his jaw Everest acknowledged her assessment, but didn't agree with her. He was mortified that a father would treat his child in such a callous, controlling manner. "Did you know about the will before he died?"

"No. And I do wish things could have been different between my father and I," she admitted sadly. Everest had said that he would never be a part of such an atrocity. She couldn't blame him. He was an honorable man, very respectable.

Everest knew her father was making her marry Paul. He wondered who Paul was to her father--a business partner or a rich friend's son? He hugged Chloe tighter against the hard length of his unyielding form. He didn't want to know.

Suddenly, she became aware of the solid block of his chest as it relaxed into her softer body. His unmoving muscles bent into her gentle flesh, molding it to his will. His heart beat steady and sure against her as she leaned into him. She felt right in his embrace. Everest was unlike any man she had ever met. Truthfully, except for movies, she didn't think such men were possible. He was incredibly sexy, rugged, strong, smart and even charming when he chose to be. He had a smile that could melt an arctic glacier and eyes that shifted between the green of grass and the woodsy color of a worn mountain trail.

Chloe had grown to love it in the mountainous country, with this silent mountain man. She didn't know when it happened, but she had started to fall in love with her husband. Under the circumstances, that wasn't a good thing. Instinctively she knew he was stubborn and proud. He would not be a part of her father's plot. He could never know she cared for him. It was better in the long run for both of them. Her heart pounded dully with the realization. She hugged him closer to her, ignoring the sudden pain in her chest. They could not be together. He would never know if she did it for the sake of the will, and she would never truly know if he did it for the money.

Chapter Seven

"Paul, I told you she was with an editor and then she would be flying to London." Devon eyed the snappy young aristocrat as he sat on the corner of her desk. She wanted to kick him off with the spiked heel of her designer boot. "She never made it to London. The editor lives in Northern Montana. There was an avalanche and she's snowed in. I contacted a local expert, Clark Beaumont. He said it could be anywhere from four weeks to four months until they're gotten out. More than likely it will be the latter. He says that there is no way to contact them in the meantime."

Paul ran a frustrated hand through his hair. "Then I will wait. But, as soon as she is back, we will be married."

"But, Paul, that's just the thing. She won't have the money in four weeks. Her inheritance needs to be collected by her thirtieth birthday. She will be snowed in way past when that happens. There is no money to get, you've lost."

Paul glared at her condescending tone. "I need her money."

"Why?" Devon shot back.

"That's not your concern," Paul hissed. His eyes fired at her in poisonous darts.

"Well, there isn't going to be any money. She doesn't have a cent to her name without her father's estate." Devon gloated.

"What about her career?" Paul asked.

"Please. Daddy published all of her books. Do you think she got paid? Daddy's money is all she had. She squandered what was hers. She thought her father was going to provide for her when he was gone." Devon shrugged her shoulders. "Sorry, but Chloe will be lucky to even get a contract when she gets back."

Paul laughed, unwilling to let go of his gift horse so easily. "Pack your luggage. We're flying to Montana."

Devon looked up in shock.

"You didn't think a Lucas would give up so easily, did you?" Paul stood. "We're going to find a way to get her out of there. And we will be married, mark my word--even if we have to do it over a damned walkie-talkie through a snow drift."

* * * *

"I should get to work." Chloe pulled back from the steel of Everest's embrace. With agonizing slowness, she dropped her hands over the bulging folds of his flannel. Her body ached to hold him. His nearness tortured her heating limbs. A violent longing curled inside her midsection. She could feel her body growing moist with desire. Every primal urge inside her pushed to rip the flannel from his muscular body, to lean over his workbench and demand he take her amidst the flying sawdust.

Trembling, she pulled away completely. When he didn't stop her, she moved to leave. It was the hardest thing she had ever done, walking out on him. But it would have been impossible to stay and not touch him.

"What am I doing?" Everest cursed under his breath as he watched her leave the workshop. His loins had grown painfully heavy and his heart thudded in loud protest to echo in his ears. Flashes of their shared night of passion assaulted his brain. She had been wild that night. They had come together all over the hotel room--the floor, the absurdly heart-shaped couch, the mini-bar, over the side of a table, the shower, even against the windows leading to the balcony. Growling at the sudden onslaught of memories, imagined or not, he stalked after her. He was unable to deny his need for her any longer. Right or wrong, he would possess her. And consequences be damned!

"Chloe," his voice was deadly in its passion. He caught up to her in the living room. His hand reached for her arm, twirling her around to face him. Panting heavily, he growled.

Chloe jolted, startled by the intimate sound.

Everest didn't miss a beat. As her lips parted in surprise, he gathered her into his arms. He pressed his lips to hers in a rough kiss that stole her breath and fluttered her heart. His hands trailed insistently up her shivering arms to grasp the back of her head. Running his fingers into her dampened locks, he groaned fiercely against her mouth.

"Are you sure?" She gasped when he freed her lips. His eyes bore into hers with the intensity of a winter storm. The hazel-green depths revealed his arduous need for her as he ground himself intimately into her hips. She felt the hard length of his arousal burning through the sweatpants. She could deny him nothing. He was controlling her.

Everest didn't answer except to lift her feet off the floor in an easy sweep of his arms. He refused to let her go. Lowering his passionate mouth, he kissed her again. Chloe moaned as she wrapped her arms about his neck. He carried her backwards to the fireplace. Kneeling, he laid her onto the bearskin rug and gathered her fully into his determined embrace.

Chloe shuddered in the envelopment of his solid arms, matching his passion with her own. Her flannel was still unbuttoned so he ran his hand freely to the tank underneath, caressing her waist with his searching fingers.

Supporting his massive weight with his arm, his mouth forced her over onto her back. Once underneath him, his tremendous form trapped her to the floor. His legs settled around her thighs. Chloe couldn't move. He grazed his lips across her neck and shoulder as he made his way farther down in rapturously tormenting caresses. The heat of the fire burned into her skin as his tongue flicked over the exposed line of her collarbone.

With her soft gasp of delight, his explorations grew bolder. Everest pulled up her undershirt to fondle the taut skin of her flat stomach. Her muscles tensed. A low, primal vibration began in Everest's throat to reverberate seductively against her skin as he devoured her quivering flesh. Chloe gasped. Her head pressed into the fur as she arched her stomach to meet his mouth. His passion began to frighten her with the full force of its intensity.

Lifting her up, he pushed the flannel from her shoulders and watched as it slid gracefully off her slender arms. Her fingers shook with nervous energy as she untucked his shirt and started to work on the buttons. Finding a white undershirt beneath the flannel, she ran her hand underneath the thinner material. His chest was strong and smooth and she tested her fingers along the hot contours of his muscles. His heart beat in a solid rhythm--confident and sure. She lifted the shirt to pull it over his head.

The motion disheveled his hair and she ran her fingers up into the disarray. She pulled his mouth once again to hers and felt his muscles stretch as he leaned her back. His hand slid underneath her sweats onto her buttocks. She gave a slight moan as he squeezed the tender globes. Her center jolted to throbbing heat, growing moist. She gasped in open-mouthed pants.

His body was new and familiar at the same time. She touched his perfect form in a massaging caress. There was not an ounce of fat on the muscular frame. Strong arms led to a virile chest that tapered to a narrow waist. Drawing her hands over every crevice, Chloe thrust her hips up, needing to feel him against her in raw urgency. She had felt him a million times in a dream and now that her fantasy was flesh she quivered before the fire of passion.

He pulled the drawstring of her sweats and ran his hand up to slip off her tank. He smiled devilishly, as he found the pink lacy bra she wore. He could see her budding nipples as they reached for him through the sheer fabric. Leaning down he licked her breast, just above the curve of the bra. Chloe gasped in pleasure. Never had she felt like this with a man. With every soft entreaty

CAUGHT

of her mouth, his lips became more insistent, pushing his tongue under the lace to taste the stiffened peaks.

Everest slowly moved his touches down her side and into her sweatpants. With a confident tug, he pulled the soft material down over her smooth hips. To his delight, he discovered a matching pair of feminine panties awaiting him. He smiled again as he moved down her length, pulling the sweats off her stocking feet. He ran his hands up and over her inner calf and then her outer thigh.

Chloe felt the soft warm fur beneath her and the heat of the scorching fire above her, a fire that had nothing to do with the blazing fireplace. Everest stopped on his way up to kiss over her hip, as he had her chest, in a long hot stroke of his tongue. She jerked in response, drawing an assured chuckle from him. The soft glow of orange light softened his hard features as his lips lowered to press a kiss on her flat stomach.

Caressing his way over her navel to her breasts, he gazed deeply into her eyes. With a playful glint radiating from his face, he gave her a slow half smile. He licked his firm lips and flicked the strap of her bra off of her shoulder. Chloe could not help but return his impish grin as he moved a finger lightly over her neck to the valley of her breasts.

She kicked off her socks. Pulling him to her, her thighs fell open. He settled more firmly against her. His sexy smile was driving her mad with its confidence. She could see he wanted her, but he held back to tease her mercilessly. He stroked and kindled her body with his firm touch until she thought she might explode. Her legs rubbed restlessly against the stiff material of his blue jeans. Hooking her feet around his waist, she pulled his hips toward her hot center. She let loose a shivering moan of ecstasy. His belt scraped against her delicate skin, its metal as hard as the rest of him. She wanted to feel him inside of her. She wanted to taste his fervent skin.

Their ragged breaths mingled. She glided her hands to his waist, feverishly undoing his belt buckle. She gazed up into his soft hazel-green eyes and the stern intensity of them pierced into the depths of her soul. Unasked questions filtered across the hazy orbs. His lips dipped to claim her mouth. Chloe trembled, panted, moaned.

Everest groaned as she lifted her legs to push his jeans off with her toes. She felt the hard, hot length of his manhood spring free of the denim to press heavily against her thigh. The hair on his legs tickled her feet. He wore cotton boxers that hugged his member like a second skin.

Everest became savage in his craving for her. He jerked roughly at her panties until he slid them off her long legs. Pulling his manhood free, just enough to enter her, he tugged her bra strap down over her shoulder to fully expose a ripe breast. The nipple peaked, yearning for his regard.

He could feel the hot wetness of her core beckoning him inside. He entered her hard, not bothering to fully remove his boxers. Chloe gasped at the suddenness of his thrust. His throbbing arousal stretched the velvety boundary of her center. The vastness of him filled her completely. He squeezed her exposed breast as he consumed her mouth with his own.

Tearing her lips away from his, she took a deep breath and let out a cry of passion. She felt him moving seductively hard within her. He withdrew from her with agonizing slowness only to thrust in long even strokes. Everest gritted his teeth in pleasure. Leaning up on his hands to gain better leverage, his buttocks flexed and tensed as he delved within her.

Unable to endure the slow, torturous rhythm he had started, she pushed him backwards, keeping him hard inside of her. She maneuvered onto his lap as she urged his manhood deeper still. She let out a loud cry of wanton pleasure.

Everest leaned back, enjoying her greedy passion. He let her control the movements of their joining, liking the way she commanded his body into submission. Her golden locks curled around her face, framing the beautiful roundness of her blue eyes. Chloe screamed, knowing no one could hear her. Everest's throaty groan joined hers as she rode the fiery length of his eager body. His head fell back as her rhythm grew more intense. She stroked the full length of his arousal within her moist velvet, pushing him to thrust deep and fast until his frenzied pace matched her own.

Chloe felt her body climb toward an unimaginable destination. Her loins racked and trembled until she thought she could take no more. Finally she reached her traumatic climax with a victorious yell. Everest was amazed at the passion with which she peaked. He grunted an almost painful release, spilling his seed deep within her.

Chloe felt as if the world was pulled out from underneath her. She held onto Everest, afraid that she would fall into the deep void if she let go. She rested her head against his steady shoulder as the last of the tremors racked her body.

Everest held her to him, not wanting to let go of her. He was afraid she wasn't real. His member stayed embedded deep within her. Her body sucked all the energy from him leaving him drained and immensely satisfied.

Chloe slowly came about to reality. As the earth righted itself, so did her sanity. And with her sanity came her embarrassment. She had always had so much control over her emotions when it came to sex. Never had she been moved to the kind of madness that Everest's sweet embrace invoked within her.

She took a deep breath, not knowing if she could lift her head from his shoulder. She was afraid of what she might see in his eyes. In her mind she saw him looking at her like a whore, like she did this kind of wanton thing all the time. In truth, she had only known a few men. She had always been too busy with her career for serious relationships. And somewhere in her life she had grown better at creating the fiction in her books than tending to the reality that was her existence.

Everest was puzzled by her sudden stillness and pushed her head up with his shoulder. An easy smile found his features. He felt her shift and move uncomfortably against him. She refused to look at him, which concerned him greatly.

"Chloe?" he whispered. Silently, he willed her not to regret what they had done.

"Ah, yeah." Chloe's voice trembled as she pushed off of him. She felt his member leave her. She declined to turn her face to him as she grabbed the flannel behind her. She slipped the shirt over her body, tugging the edges together to hide her nakedness.

Everest, sensing that something was not quite right, moved to his knees and grabbed her before she could move away. Pulling her around to face him, he uttered, "Wait. Look at me."

Chloe turned her nervous expression to him, unable to deny his command. Her mouth became suddenly dry. Her eyes grew round with unshed tears.

Everest saw the uncertainty in her countenance and frowned. "What's the matter?"

"I don't want you to think that I do that kind of thing often," Chloe stammered. Her cheeks blushed.

Everest smiled at her feminine insecurity. She always seemed so strong and yet here she was seeking his approval with the vulnerable tenderness of her eyes. Lightly, he ran his hand into her hair. He pulled her to his chest and kissed her gently on the lips. He felt his manhood stir as her lips parted to accept him.

Chuckling in amazement, he willed his naughty member to lower.

"I never thought that," he whispered against her mouth. He had to admit that he liked her like this, unsure. Her determined self-control was gone, as was her cool confidence. He felt as if he was seeing the real her for the first time. And he wanted to protect her. But even as he reveled in her emotions, he didn't want her to feel like she had to hide from him. Everest knew he was beginning to lose his heart and didn't like it. Nothing could come of it. The choice had been taken away from them and he was not about to burden her with his emotions.

"I know I'm being silly," Chloe said at last. She pulled away from him, looking deep into his concerned eyes. "Just as I know nothing will ever come of us. I know that we have no future and I didn't want you to think that I was taking this lightly, like I did it all the time."

"I know all of that, Chloe." Everest moved his head to nudge her. "I know that there can be no promises. Why don't we just see what happens? And when it's over, it's over. There will be no lies between us. We both know what has to be and that we will have no future. It doesn't mean we can't enjoy each others company while you're here."

Chloe nodded her head. She knew that for him it was just going to be a brief, albeit incredibly passionate, affair with a friend. For her it was going to be much more. It would be an affair of the heart. It was unlikely she would find love with Paul. She had never held any thought of that. And, after meeting Everest, she doubted any other man could ever compare.

"Besides, technically we aren't sinning. I mean we are married." Everest put forth with a small laugh. He watched her for a smile that never came.

"Yes, I think you're right." Chloe rested her head against him. If that is all he had to offer, that is what she would gladly take. Mumbling, she reluctantly agreed, "When it's over, it's over. Why not enjoy what we have?"

"Right," Everest asserted with a nod. His member began to stir again, waiting to be called into action. Chucking her under the chin, he asked, "Hungry?"

"Yeah, starved." Chloe grinned at him as he stood. With a lopsided devil-may-care smile, he yanked his cotton boxers over his manhood and held his hand out to her. She stood with his help and then moved to button her shirt, not bothering to pull on her pants. As Everest turned from her to go to the kitchen, she smiled wantonly at the movements of his firm buttocks. With a painful bite to her lip, she groaned inwardly. Already, her body began to stir. She wanted him again.

Everest barely made it to the kitchen before her hands were on his buttocks grasping him from behind. And when he turned he was ready for her, stiff and at attention. With a primal yell, he pushed her to the table. Laying her gently over the hard wood, he took her from behind.

* * * *

"Paul, what are you hoping to find here?" asked Devon as they pulled into Miner's Cove. In truth she was worried about her friend.

Devon wished she had convinced Chloe to contest her father's will when she found out about what Richard Masters had done. Then she wouldn't have engaged her best friend to a gold-digging aristocrat with a foul temper.

"I'm going to find a way to get her out of the mountains before her birthday. And you are going to help me." Paul turned the car in front of a fifties-style diner.

"Are you sure you want to eat here?" Devon queried sharply. Wearily, she glanced at the tall peak of a mountain that rose up over the town. Her words dripped with sarcasm as she uttered, "I doubt it will be up to your standards."

"It'll be just fine," Paul said in disdain. It was obvious he was dispirited by the town's lack of convenience. "We'll see what the locals have to say."

"Fine." Devon tried to stay calm. She hoped the locals didn't blow her cover for her friend. She wasn't sure what Paul was going to do when he found out Chloe had married the wrong man, was trapped in the mountains with him, and that she was not with her editor.

"Why would her editor choose to live here? It doesn't make sense." Paul grabbed a handkerchief and held it to his nose as he stepped toward the diner.

"I would think some people find it inspiring," Devon sighed. Though truthfully, she agreed with him. Montana was a far cry from the city. "You know, beautiful countryside, fresh air."

"Fresh air is overrated and if you want scenery I have some lovely paintings hanging in my home. One could stare at them all day." Paul pushed open the diner's door with the handkerchief.

"I am sure they could," muttered Devon under her breath with a sad shake of her head. She followed him inside.

Chapter Eight

"So you met Betsy. Did she ask you to take her with you?" Everest laughed heartily, making his chest rumble with the sound. "I don't know why she just doesn't leave by herself. No one has taken her up on her offer yet."

"Poor child," Chloe sighed. They were lying in front of the fireplace on the rug underneath a blanket. Chloe stretched out by his feet and looked at his smiling face. He was playing with her toes. "Do you all have to make fun of her?"

The last two days had been the best of her life. During the day they parted to work on their separate projects, or at least they tried. Occasionally one would find an excuse to interrupt the other, drawing from their duties to come together in the oddest places. At night they joined by the fire to make love and talk until they fell asleep in each other's arms. Everest's passion was insatiable, melting Chloe instantly each time. Chloe felt it was as if they had built a dream world around themselves and neither one of them wanted to destroy it. So as if by unspoken truce, they never mentioned her father again.

"Betsy has talked about leaving town since she was born. I don't think she'll ever go." Everest laughed harder as she poked her toe into his chest. Lifting it to his mouth, he kissed it.

"So you never wanted to leave?" Chloe laid her head down and stared thoughtfully up at the ceiling.

"My parents traveled a lot. They used to take me with them. So, after a while, I wanted to come back home and stay here. I waited until I was old enough to be on my own and moved back. I went to a trade school, learned carpentry and stayed with Grandpa. About seven years ago this property went up for sale. I spent the next several years building this house." Everest felt her move up beside him.

"So you actually built this house on your own?" asked Chloe in amazement. "I mean Grandpa had said that you built this house, but I thought that he meant you had it built."

"After I drew up the blueprints, I did have some help," he admitted as he moved his arm so she could lie on it. "I oversaw the progress and did some of the carpentry. I still need to finish the upstairs and build a staircase."

Chloe thought about that for a moment. "You know what this place needs is some decorations. Like curtains and a few pictures. I think red curtains in here and pale yellow in the kitchen. Maybe I should get you some. It would liven the place up."

Chloe was so taken with her enthusiasm she didn't feel him stiffen beside her. Everest sat up. Part of him liked her decorating his home. It was a part he didn't want to admit to. She was talking as if she was going to be there forever. He listened a moment longer to her plans, before interrupting, "Don't do that."

"Why?" Chloe sat up, suddenly realizing what she had been saying. "Oh, I'm so sorry. I was just talking. I love your home how it is. I didn't mean anything by it."

Chloe ignored the hurt in her chest when she thought of how harshly he had taken her ideas. It felt as if he didn't want her to leave any mark that she had been here. She realized then that their affair was probably something for him to pass the time with. He didn't feel as seriously about it as she did. The sudden insight hurt her deeply.

Everest stood up and pulled on his pants. "It's fine."

"Everest?" Chloe pulled the blanket around her shoulders and moved to touch his arm.

"Chloe, it's fine. Leave it." He pulled away from her. "I've got to go out and check on the generators. It feels like it's getting colder in here."

Chloe watched him leave, trying not to let tears overwhelm her. She had tried to get too intimate. This was a temporary fling for both of them. Apparently Everest wanted it to be nothing more.

Chloe moved a trembling fist to cover her mouth as a swift pain consumed her chest. She felt the sting of tears make their way down her face. There was no chance of his loving her and her heart was breaking because of it. He hadn't given her any reason to hope and yet she had. She was in love with her husband and there was nothing she could do about it.

* * * *

After the initial shock of his abrupt departure from her wore off, Chloe was left feeling numb. He had been justified in his anger, but that didn't mean she had to like it. Everest had gone straight to his own bed after checking on the generators without a single word to her and when she woke up the next morning alone on the fur she found that he was already hard at work.

"Well," Chloe thought, "two can play this game."

She went to work, intent on ignoring him. But she couldn't ignore that he was there, across the house. Or that she had to do something to calm his anger toward her. She hated to admit it, but he might be the only shot she had at fulfilling the stipulations of her father's will.

She hadn't wanted to think of it before, but his anger had given her pause. The will said nothing about her having to live under the same roof as her husband. So what if he lived on the other side of the world, as long as they were married and there were no scandals. The only snag she could see in her plan was that Everest would have to get her pregnant. She didn't know how willing he would be to do that, though the motivation was definitely there. She wasn't sure how he even felt about children and then there was the small thing about him finding her father's will detestable.

Chloe flipped off her laptop. She had stared at the screen for several hours, not typing a single word. Her mind raced with ways to convince Everest to keep the marriage.

Deciding that it would come to her when the time was right, she went to make amends with him. He had to at least start talking to her if she was to accomplish anything. A slow smile came to her lips as she thought of more interesting ways to assuage his injured pride.

She went to his workshop and found the door locked. He wasn't in the house, which could only mean he was out in the shed working on the generator. Chloe was astonished at how much attention that thing seemed to need.

She grabbed one of Everest's lightweight jackets off the coat rack. She realized this was going to be the first time she had left the house since her arrival. Going out onto the front lawn, she took a look around. The sunlit snow glistened like diamond crystals. She scooped up some white powder into her bare hands and formed it into a hard ball.

Bouncing the snowball lightly, she traded it back and forth between her two freezing palms. His property was really breathtaking. A mischievous smile formed on her lips as she looked at the shed.

"Everest Beaumont!" she yelled at the door. "Get out here right now!"

She leaned down and packed another snowball together, holding the wet missiles in her cold hands as she started for the shed door.

CAUGHT

"Everest! I want to talk to you!" she yelled louder. Readying her arm, she lifted it to take aim. "I'm calling you out!"

She crept closer to the shed, wondering why he wasn't answering her.

"Everest!" she screamed again.

"Is that so?"

Chloe froze as she heard him behind her and felt a snowball hit her in the nape of the neck. Wet moisture dripped down her back underneath the light jacket she had stolen from him. With a look of disdain, she slowly turned around to face her attacker. Smirking through a look of feigned anger, she shook her head in warning.

"Planning a surprise attack?" He chuckled as she turned to face him. His lips curled into a devilish smile and his hair was tied back in a ponytail. In his hand he roguishly bounced another snowball.

"Why you," she mumbled darkly before charging him. Chloe immediately launched her ammunition at his head. Both shots missed. She leaned down to reload.

Before she stood she was hit again in the shoulder. Her face turned red at his laughter. She threw and missed again. Everest chuckled even harder. He charged her as she knelt to grab more snow.

Chloe stood up in time to get knocked to the ground. Rotating in the air, he padded her fall with his weight. She felt the stiff snow crunch underneath her head as Everest landed to the side of her.

"Looking for me?" he whispered with a nuzzle and bite to her ear. Leaning over her, his hazel-green gaze drifted to her parted lips. Smiling, he studied her pink cheeks and red nose.

"No." Chloe breathed in his nearness. "I wasn't. I was innocently taking a walk when I was shamelessly attacked."

Everest laughed, white puffs escaped his mouth. Touching his nose to hers, he asked, "What did you want?"

Chloe beamed innocently up into his smug face and grabbed a handful of snow. She crashed it into his temple. "To do this."

"Ouch," he whined as he rolled off of her in mock pain. Feigning injury, he questioned, "What was that for?"

"For being a dolt," Chloe answered as she sat up. She placed her hands defiantly on her hips, ignoring the snow that stuck to her head and shoulders.

"I know. I'm sorry." Everest sighed as he looked up at her. Gently, he caressed her cheek with his cold fingers. He had spent most of the morning walking around his land thinking of their situation. He could not deny that he had feelings for the captivating woman before him. That is why he had gotten so angry. He wasn't upset with her. He was outraged by her situation.

"Don't think that just because you say you're sorry that I will automatically forgive you." Chloe brushed off her arms. Powdery snow fell from her like sawdust. "You'll have to work for my forgiveness."

Everest answered her challenge with a sultry smirk through narrowed eyes. Pulling on her jacket so she fell back, he moved his leg on top of her. Brushing a snowflake off the tip of her reddened nose with cold fingers, he leaned down to kiss her.

Chloe moaned as every ounce of anger thawed into the snow. She forgot that she wanted to talk to him. Murmuring contentedly against his mouth, she uttered, "Do you think our lips are going to freeze together?"

"Only if you have braces on," he grumbled seriously. She hit his back without breaking the kiss. Everest laughed as he pulled away. She gave a soft moan of protest. "Does this mean I'm forgiven?"

Chloe nodded. Her blue eyes drifted to his firm mouth. Her body stirred and began to heat, despite the press of cold snow. He leaned down to kiss her again. Mumbling against his increasingly passionate mouth, she breathed, "Which building is closest?"

Everest growled, entranced by her forward confidence and amazed that their desires had yet to dim. The more he had her, the more he needed to do it again. She was his addiction. He nodded his head toward the shed. Chloe shot him a coy look, her eyes shining with promise. Without words, she stood and grabbed him by his coat. Walking backwards, she led him to the door. Then, leaning against it, she pulled him in for a kiss.

Reaching up, Everest pulled the latch to let the door fall open. Chloe gasped as she fell back. Righting herself, she looked around. She slid the jacket from her shoulders before setting it aside on a worktable. Then, going to a large metal contraption, she asked, "Is this the generator that has been giving you so much trouble?"

Everest closed and latched the door before coming up behind her. All amusement faded from his eyes as he looked down at her tightly fitted blue jeans. His hand grasped the firm curve of her buttocks and squeezed his fingers near her hot center. Chloe groaned a low, throaty sound.

"Get out of those wet pants." Everest whispered his command hotly into her ear. "I would hate for you to get sick. I'm not much of a nurse."

Before she could respond, his hands found the tender flesh of her flat stomach. Chloe shivered. His fingers caressed her with the deft precision of a carpenter planing wood. His callused palms skimmed over her ribcage before finding the button to her jeans. With a deft flick, he unfastened the obstructive clothing and began to unzip.

Chloe didn't turn, liking the feel of him behind her. As he moved his burning caresses over the curve of her pelvic bone, he pulled her buttocks to press along the hardened length of his arousal. She raised her hands over her head, caressing the silken strands of his shoulder length hair. Leaning her head on his shoulder, she cried out in pleasure when he found her neck with his mind-numbing kisses.

And then suddenly, he was gone. Chloe grew dizzy at his absence, falling forward to press her hands on two metal pipes that came out of the ground and connected to the generator. The metal was warm under her chilled palms. She tried to control her ragged breaths, but her body ached for the feel of him and her flesh shivered in need of his impassioned touch.

A strong hand found the curve of her back, caressing in a dominant stroke up her spine. With a snap, he unhooked her bra underneath the sweater. As his hands found her hips, he slid the wet denim down her length, exposing the athletic curve of her beautiful legs. Everest growled, a bestial sound coming from his lips as he cornered his prey. Chloe couldn't move. Her pants trapped her legs about her ankles.

"Don't move your hands," Everest ordered. Chloe gripped the pipes fiercely. She felt so exposed bending over in front of him.

He didn't wait for her to answer. Lightly, he began kissing her firm buttocks. His tongue flicked over the sensitive flesh before biting it gently. Chloe swayed on her feet. Everest grabbed her hips to hold her still. He licked the quivering flesh of her other cheek. His hands ran over her skin in kneading strokes. Firmly, he spread her legs wide so his tongue could lap her sweet nectar.

Chloe bucked and tried to stand up, suddenly feeling self-conscious. She moved as if to turn to him.

"Tsk, tsk," Everest mumbled, a little disappointed. He held her hips firmly with one hand.

Chloe could feel him moving around behind her. Without hurting her, his hand grabbed her hair to pull her neck back in a steadfast motion. Chloe shivered at his domineering hold. It both excited and frightened her. Slowly his hands lifted hers above her head to pull off her sweater and bra. The chilled air hit her breasts to instantly peak her nipples into hardened beacons. Everest took their offerings with teasing fingertips. The aching mounds strained for more attention but were denied.

Again he grabbed her hair. With an unrelenting shove, he pushed her forward so she was again forced to hold onto the pipes. And then he was all around her. His hand caressed the length of her arms. His lips sought the sweet partings of hers. His breath grazed the frantic pulse at her neck. Parting her narrowed lids, Chloe saw the hard length of his erection looking up at her. Licking her lips, she thought of taking his member into her mouth to excite him.

But she had no time to lean over. As Everest chuckled mischievously, he let her go. Chloe tried to raise her hand to follow him, but gasped when she discovered he had bound her wrists to the pipes with his belt. She hadn't even noticed his plan through the distracting fog he created with her skin.

"Are you scared?" he whispered ominously from behind.

Chloe nodded and then shook her head. Confused, she pleaded, "Kiss me."

Everest obliged, trailing his lips over her naked back. Chloe could feel his hands over every inch of her burning form. Through small glimpses as she leaned over, she saw his bared feet. They were strong like the rest of him. His legs were lightly covered with hair, but they too were powerfully built. In her minds eye, she could see his brawny chest, flexing and bowing with every commanding move of his upper torso.

Finally, his exploring led his fingers to the scorching urgency of her center fire. Parting her slick entrance from behind, he massaged her womanhood open with callused fingers. Her trembling form melted over his hand to ease his way with the sweet liquid of her desire. Everest growled at her potent heat. Chloe bucked her hips against his fingers as he slipped one inside of her. It glided easily in the warmth. Joining it with a second finger, he began to force her to ride his hand. Leaning his head against her, his lips bit and soothed her slender neck.

"That's it," he muttered along her flesh. "Come on, baby."

Chloe's wrists pulled at the ties. She couldn't think beyond the burning need of her hot core. Tossing her head back, she screamed as she neared her snow-melting climax. Everest felt her convulse against his hand to pour her pleasure sweetly over him. As the tension left her body and she began to slump forward, Everest chuckled.

"Oh, no," he whispered with much greedy promise, "not yet."

Chloe lifted her weakened head. She felt him come behind her. His hands held fast to her hips. With a swift stroke he was in her, embedded completely in the moist heat he had created. Chloe gasped as he wildly began to thrust in her. He controlled her hips so he could ride her like an untamed mare.

Again the intensity climbed inside of her. Her weakened body could do nothing to resist as he pushed her higher and higher. Then, with a fiercely barbaric yell, he met his release inside her quivering loins. At the same time of his release, Chloe's scream echoed his as she again reached the pinnacle of his touch.

Chapter Nine

Everest slung his arm around Chloe's shoulders, completely sated. She smiled up at him through her lashes. After their lovemaking, they had quickly realized how cold it was out in the shed. Covering themselves the best they could, they ran to the house and straight to a steaming shower. Everest had been insatiable, bringing Chloe to climax another two times in the shower until she protested for a rest.

They sat curled on the couch in front of a toasty fire. Chloe thought mournfully of her neglected work, but was too happy to leave the gentle hold of Everest's arms. She had the rest of her life to fight deadlines and only a short time to spend with Everest. Nuzzling closer to him, she giggled lightly.

"Hmm," he mumbled against her hair. He planted a soft kiss on her drying locks.

"I was just thinking about how all of this came about," she sighed. "Who would have guessed dialing a wrong hotel room could be so enjoyable?"

Everest frowned, "Yeah, but I would've rather met you under different circumstances, not facing the terms of your father's damnable will."

Chloe tensed. Her smile faded. She couldn't answer. Through the soft crackling of a fire, Chloe heard a soft noise coming from the distance. She pushed at his chest to sit up. "Is that an airplane?"

"Where?" Everest sat up. He went to the window and peered out into the evening sky. He had been concentrating on Chloe and hadn't noticed the sound. Squinting, he said, "No, I think it's a helicopter."

Chloe joined him by the window. Everest grabbed a coat and tossed it to her before slinging one over his shoulders. As he opened the door to his home, a helicopter flew into view. Chloe followed him out onto the porch.

"What's it doing out here? Do you think it's going to land?" she questioned.

"It looks like it," he replied darkly, confirming both of their unspoken fears. "Quick, cover your head."

Chloe ducked her head and lifted her arms to protect her face. Everest moved over to shield her body with his own. The helicopter blew snow onto the porch as it made its decent. When finally it landed and the engine turned off, Everest stepped aside. The couple quickly brushed off their arms.

"It's Devon, my lawyer," Chloe yelled over the dying engine as she saw the logo on the aircraft. "The helicopter belongs to her firm."

Everest watched as a slender woman in a business suit and trench coat emerged from the helicopter. Devon lifted her sunglasses to cover her eyes. Her curly red hair was tamed into a neat, businesslike bun. She carried a briefcase with her.

"Devon!" Chloe yelled, as she ran out to meet her friend. "What are you doing here?"

"I was worried about you. Are you all right?" Devon gave her a quick hug as they ran for the door. Then, once on the porch, she looked expectantly at Everest.

"Devon Wentworth, this is Everest Beaumont," Chloe began with a quick gesture of introduction. "Everest, Devon."

"Pleased to meet you ma'am," Everest greeted politely. The pools of his eyes remained dispassionately calm, but his insides shook with anger--anger that the woman had dared to interrupt their time together. But, knowing that it was for the best that she had, he said nothing.

"Likewise," Devon tilted her head appreciatively at Everest. She leaned over to whisper in Chloe's ear as the lush mountain man turned around to open the door for them. "Perhaps I came too soon."

CAUGHT

Chloe nudged Devon in the side and tried not to giggle. Her cheeks stained with a blush as Devon winked knowingly.

"Please, come in." He turned stiffly to hold open the door.

"Do you mind if my pilot joins us?" Devon asked as she waved to the man.

"Not at all," he assented.

The pilot shook his head at the offer and lit a cigarette by the helicopter. Reaching behind him, he held up a thermos of coffee.

Once inside, Devon took off her black trench coat and matching leather gloves. Chloe hung them on the coat rack by her borrowed jacket.

"I'll leave you two alone," Everest stated. He opened the door to go back outside. "Chloe, coffee's in the kitchen if you would like some."

"Thank you," Chloe mumbled as he left. She wondered at his surly behavior. She already knew there would be coffee in the kitchen. There had been every day since she had been there.

"Well, well." Devon laughed as soon as he was out of earshot. "Not quite what we expected is he?"

"Nothing like we expected." Chloe let loose a girlish sigh. Heat colored her cheeks with the knowledge of what she had spent the entire day doing. She led Devon into the kitchen and motioned for her to take a chair. A concerned frown marred Chloe's features, as she inquired, "What are you doing here?"

"I came to warn you about Paul," answered Devon carefully. She sat at the wood table as Chloe poured her a cup of coffee. Her gaze became guarded, as she uttered, "He's on his way here to rescue you. We went to that little town, Miner's Cove. Well, thankfully no one told him anything. But he was able to learn where this house was from a waitress. Anyway, he left yesterday to charter a helicopter."

"How does he know where I am?" Chloe asked, puzzled. She searched the cabinet for some creamer. Finding some, she poured it into Devon's mug.

"He has been trying to force our hand," Devon returned bluntly. "He's not the man we thought he was. I'm sorry, Chloe. I used every resource I had to check him out. He has a clean record, but I guess there is no accounting for personality."

"How bad?" Chloe became alarmed. Her face paled.

"He's pretty dead set on marrying you," admitted Devon with a sad grimace. "I think he might need the money."

"He can have it," Chloe interjected. "I don't care."

"Have you got the divorce papers signed yet?" Devon questioned sharply as she ignored her interruption.

Chloe had forgotten about the papers she had brought with her. Neither one of them had felt the need to mention them. They were still in her briefcase. "No, but I can."

"Hmm. Why don't you tell me about this Everest?" Devon gave a secretive half smile. Chloe set the coffee in front of her before turning to pour her own. "How much does he suspect?"

"I told him everything," Chloe admitted. She watched as Devon took a sip out of her mug. Her friend didn't seem surprised. Carefully, she added, "I had to."

"Oh, my God, Chloe! You're completely taken with him." Devon sat back in her chair in surprise. "Does he know?"

"No," Chloe stated in a hushed tone. "And he won't want to hear it either."

"Does he want the money?" Devon asked, hopeful. "Is he going to stay married to you?"

"No. He thinks what we're doing is deplorable," Chloe mumbled. "He said that he doesn't want to be a part of it. And I don't blame him. I don't want any part of it. However, I don't have a choice."

"Even more reason to like him." Devon sighed, disappointed. "Well, listen. I have an idea. Paul would make a decent enough husband, as long as you lived on separate coasts. But I don't think it will have to come down to that."

"What are you planning?"

"We need to keep the option of Paul open," Devon answered. "So when he gets here go back with him. But tell him that you have to get directly to New York to make sure your father's will was legal. You're a writer, make up something."

"And how will I explain Everest?" Chloe questioned.

"I already told him that Everest was your editor. You got called away to an emergency meeting and before you could leave you got snowed in." Devon laughed sheepishly. "I also kind of told him Everest was gay so he wouldn't get jealous."

"How could he be jealous over me? He hasn't met me." Chloe stood up. "Want some more coffee?"

"Love it." Devon followed her with her mug. "Oh, you know, it's that whole male ego, pride thing."

Chloe groaned.

"You know this place isn't half bad. I would go crazy here in a week, but I could see you liking it. You are into this solitude thing."

"What do you mean?" Chloe handed her back her cup.

"You always have been, Chloe." Devon took a drink. "Got any whiskey?"

"No," Chloe answered with a distracted chuckle. "I think Everest and I have both learned our lesson about drinking."

"Too bad." Devon set the cup down, before continuing where she left off, "You always wrote better when you weren't disturbed, even in college."

Chloe laughed at the reminder. "I know. You and Eve used to drive me nuts with your constant talking."

"I remember."

They stood in silence for a moment.

"Chloe?" Devon asked.

"What?"

"Are you in love with him? Really in love?"

Chloe nodded her head. "Yes, but that can't be helped right now. He doesn't feel the same way I do. And if he did ... well he just doesn't."

"Have you told him?" Devon persisted. She was a sharp judge of character and could tell Everest didn't appreciate having his winter rendezvous interrupted by her visit. She could see his obvious possessiveness of her friend.

"There's no point," Chloe snapped. Then, lightening her tone, she said, "Sorry, I am under a lot of stress. Can you just tell me what it is you have planned?"

"Fine. Have Everest tell Paul he is your editor. Leave with Paul and tell him about New York. Then we stall. I still have all the paperwork on the other candidates. If we can't get you another husband in eight days, you'll have to marry Paul. You turn thirty in nine days."

"Don't remind me. How come everyone's thirtieth isn't this stressful? It should be enough that I'm getting older." Chloe set her mug down, untouched.

"I know it." Devon nodded in agreement. "That is the best I can come up with. Unless you can work it out with Everest?"

"No," Chloe sighed in grim denial. "There is no hope of that."

"Chloe," Devon began.

"No." Chloe held up her hand to block any argument her friend might try to make. "I don't want to hear it. There's no future for me here."

Devon nodded, "Then you'll go back to New York with Paul?"

"Why can't I come with you? Get a hold of him and tell him to meet us back there."

"We don't want Paul to know I was here," Devon returned truthfully. "I should be going. He will most likely come sometime tomorrow. My people discovered he has rented a helicopter for noon."

"All right, I'll see you in a day or so." Chloe gave her friend a hug as she followed her into the living room.

Devon grabbed her coat. "Fine. I'll be waiting in New York. Call my office first thing."

Chloe waved as Devon ran out to the helicopter. Her friend motioned briefly. As they took off, Chloe sadly closed the door to block the whirlwind of snow. Suddenly, her nose wrinkled with the violent force of her unshed tears. A ragged breath escaped her suffocating lungs in an unsteady sob. This was to be her last night with Everest.

Chapter Ten

Everest watched the helicopter leave from his place within the woods. He sat on a rock that jutted out over a cliff. Before him were the snowy peaks and the narrow valleys of the Montana mountain range. Trees hid the valleys, but he knew that they were there. Before his horse had died, he rode all along the countryside.

Everest had thought of showing Chloe the place. The spot was one of his favorites. He came here often. In fact, it was where he was when Chloe called to him earlier.

He wanted to bring her to this place with him, so he could tell her how he truly felt about her. He wanted her to know that he would wait ten years for her. He wanted to tell her he understood about Paul. That he understood her obligation to the numerous people whose livelihoods she was trying to protect. He wanted to tell her that he loved her and always would.

He watched the helicopter disappear with a heavy heart. Chloe hadn't even thought to say good-bye to him. He would have heard her if she had tried to call to him. Everest kicked at the ground in anger. He was too late. She was gone.

* * * *

Chloe wondered where Everest had gotten to. She searched for him in the shed and in the old barn. She called to him within the trees and received no answer. The old pickup was still parked in its usual spot.

Unable to find him, she went inside to wait. In the distance she heard the loud barking of animals which she could only imagine to be the lonely sound of wolves. Shivering in fear, she stared out the kitchen window. Through the onslaught of night, she willed him to come home. Her heart ached as she looked up into the darkening sky. The sun was setting in a myriad of beautiful purples and blues, but its beauty had no affect on her sorrow.

Sighing, she moved before the blazing fire. She knew it would do no good to look for him. He was the mountain man, not she. As the fire slowly started to burn out, she threw another log in the fireplace. She waited for hours for him to return. She waited until her eyes could barely stay open. Finally, she moved to his bedroom to lie in the comforts of his bed. Curling into a ball, she fought to stay awake. Everest never came home and she was unable to resist the sweet oblivion of rest as sleep came to claim her.

* * * *

Everest heard the second helicopter long before it landed. Looking out his kitchen window, he stiffened. At first his heart leapt, thinking Chloe changed her mind and came back to him. Then, with a grim shake of his head, he remembered that the divorce papers still were unsigned.

It was late morning. He hadn't slept. It was well past midnight when he returned home to fall exhausted on his floor before the fire.

Deciding it best to get it over with, he drew an icy mask over his features. He made his way slowly to the front door and opened it. To his surprise a different helicopter landed. Chloe had been right. There were many important people obviously looking for her. It had been a long time since his mountain had seen so many visitors.

"Everest?"

He froze as the voice came directly from behind him. Turning slowly in the opened doorway, he spotted Chloe coming from his bedroom. For a moment his heart skipped. She had stayed. She sent her attorney back to New York and stayed with him. But even from across the room he could tell by the look on her face that she would not be staying forever.

"What time is it?" she sleepily yawned.

"About eleven," he responded.

Chloe's face paled. She looked over his shoulder with a gasp. Turning quickly, she darted into the bedroom to quickly pull on a pair of slacks. Everest watched her for a moment before leaving to storm out of the house.

His step slowed as he landed on the snow-packed ground. A finely tailored young man jumped down from the helicopter as a pilot held open the door for him. To Everest the man looked like every other stiff necked, rich suit he had ever seen--boys as old as men that had too much money and not enough sense to use it. He could only guess that this was Paul.

"Well, no use in intruding," Everest fumed to himself as he strode rudely over the snow-covered yard toward his barn. He ignored the questioning look on Paul's face as he passed him. Stopping when hidden within the limbs of evergreens, he took a deep breath. Then, glancing over his shoulder, he saw Chloe on the porch. She wore one of her classier outfits. Her face froze with a smile. He imagined her eyes sparkled like sapphires from underneath her sweeping lashes. Everest felt as if he had been kicked in the gut. And, as Paul walked confidently forward to greet her, he growled, "I wouldn't want to impose on the happy couple."

* * * *

Chloe forced a pleasant smile to her lips as the young man reached his hand out to her. Her eyes darted over the distance to look for Everest. She couldn't see him. She expected him to be waiting for her, but he was already gone when she emerged from the bedroom. Biting her lips, she cursed herself for oversleeping. She needed to talk to Everest, to explain.

Hesitantly, she smoothed down the sleeves of her sweater. Paul was everything she had asked of Devon in a husband. It only proved that she should stop thinking of real people as characters in a novel. For, if she wrote Paul, she would have had him killed off in the first scene in some stupid accident.

She could see by the obnoxious bounce of his head, and the playfully amused way he surveyed the mountainside home, that he was not her type--not in a friend and definitely not as a husband or lover. Her flesh crawled as he came near her.

Chloe berated herself for not being fair to him. True, he was no Everest, but that didn't mean she had to judge him so harshly. He might, after all, end up being the face that she woke up to every morning. She shivered at the thought of having his children. Would they walk like he did? Would they act so self-important? The very idea instantly repulsed her.

"May I help you?" Chloe inquired tautly, remembering she was not to know who he was or why he came. "I'm afraid that Mr. Beaumont is away from the house for a time."

"Chloe?" Paul's voice laughed in familiarity. "Devon didn't tell me you were as lovely as your pictures. I'm your fiancé, Paul Lucas."

"Oh, of course!" Chloe gushed in forced politeness. "How did you find me?"

"When one is as resourceful as I, they find a way," he put forth smoothly.

"Right," Chloe allowed in a slow drawl. She tried to not let her repulsion show. His charm oozed off of him like a snake. No, she thought, that was not fair to the snakes.

"I wasn't aware that you were sent a picture of me."

"Oh, I picked up one of your silly little woman novels. Or rather, I had my secretary do it." Paul smiled as he looped his arm into hers.

Silly what! Chloe fumed as he began to lead her to the house. Her mouth dropped open, speechless.

"Let's get your belongings so we can go," he stated with assurance. "I can't believe that you would actually like staying here. How horrible it must have been to be trapped!"

Chloe wondered at his presumption. She hadn't invited him into the house nor had she offered to leave with him. "Should we see if your pilot would like some coffee?"

"No," Paul began in puzzlement before he smiled, as if addressing a delightful eccentricity he had discovered in his fiancée. "I don't assume we will be here long. After all, I am here to rescue you from this dreadful, ah, shall we say ... homey retreat. No doubt you will want to go somewhere and relax after having been snowed in this wasteland. I must say I was quite unnerved to discover you were stranded. How dreadful it must have been for you."

"I like it here. I was thinking of buying a place in the mountains," Chloe answered under tight lips.

"Oh, I've been warned how emotional writers can be. No doubt the whimsy will pass once you're around decent society again. I think that after the immediate ceremony we should purchase a house in the Swiss countryside--that is if you insist on wanting mountains." Paul smiled and touched her cheek briefly before walking into Everest's home. Over his shoulder, he called, "Though let's not discuss it until I've gotten you to my spa. No doubt a good massage and sea weed wrap will clear your head."

Chloe tried not to balk. She wondered what she would have thought about this man if she met him before her affair with Everest. Would she be judging him so brutally? Would his condescending tone annoy her so drastically? Did all the men in her social circle act in such a way? The answers resounded in her brain in a penetrable, *yes!*

"Well, I can't leave here right now." Chloe hurried as she followed Paul in. She panicked as she remembered his plan. "I have a lot of work that still needs to be done. Maybe you should go on ahead of me."

"Chloe, dear, after we're married there is no reason for you to work. If you are worried about an advance they gave you for writing, we will simply pay it back." Paul waved his hand in the air, disregarding her protest.

"But I enjoy working." Chloe tried not to act as affronted as she felt. "I have no intention of stopping."

"Yes, well." Paul's long nose shot up in irritation. It was obvious he had qualms about a wife of his being employed. He shuddered at the utter humiliation before waving his hand to dismiss her as he would a servant.

Chloe shut her eyes as Paul took a step toward her. She forced herself to think of all the people whose lives were going to be affected by her father's decrees. She remembered Devon's advice to keep Paul in the sidelines in case she could not find his replacement in time.

"Let's not fight." Chloe gave him a small smile. She saw him eyeing her lips and swallowed over her dry mouth. He was going to kiss her. Chloe froze, forcing herself to hold still. Closing her eyes, she gulped, doing her best not to flinch.

* * * *

Everest watched as Chloe turned one of her most charming smiles to her fiancé. He had gotten inside the barn only to turn right back around and follow the couple into the house. He wasn't about to give up without some sort of a fight. But, as he stood in the frame of the kitchen door, he knew that he hadn't a choice but to let her go. Paul leaned forward to press his lips against hers.

Everest's gut tightened and twitched. His fists balled into hard masses. Chloe didn't back away from the man. He didn't want to bear witness to the tender moment between the couple and found he had little choice to do much else. Perhaps the affair had been only of the body for Chloe. He steeled his face as he cleared his throat in disgust.

Chloe jumped and turned quickly to him. Her lips pursed tightly together, trying to rid them of Paul's taste.

"Everest, you're back," she stammered. She could barely meet his damning face.

"Yes, I'm back." Everest searched the deceitful woman before him. He looked for any trace of the woman he imagined to care for. Abruptly, he stated, "Are you leaving?"

It wasn't a question but a demand. She saw it in the cold depths of his icy gaze.

"You must be Chloe's editor. I've heard much about you."

Everest turned his probing gaze to the thin man who stood possessively next to Chloe. He nodded in slight confusion, unable to reach out to take his hand.

Editor? Everest fumed.

Chloe ignored Paul, her heart longed to grab Everest and never let him go. And she could have, if he but gave her a hint of affection.

"I'm Paul, Chloe's husband."

"Husband?" Everest hissed under his breath. He raised an eyebrow and turned to Chloe.

Paul moved in front of her before she could answer. "Yes. Husband. I thank you so much for looking after her. If there is a way that we can repay you and your boyfriend for the trouble, please, don't hesitate to mention it."

Boyfriend?!! Everest glared at Chloe. Just what had she been saying to her beloved husband before he had walked in? What kind of game was she playing at? His body tensed in a fiery outrage.

Chloe felt sickened by Paul's words. She had no reason to deny them though. They would be true soon enough. Tears threatened her gaze and she blinked them back. Shooting Everest a helpless look of apology, she started to open her mouth. But her words were cut off by his chilling voice.

"Actually, she has been a bit of an inconvenience to *us*. We would really like our privacy back. It's part of the reason we live so far up in these mountains." Everest took a deep breath, only beginning to feel vindicated. "Can I help you to the helicopter?"

"Ah, splendid." Paul turned and smiled at Chloe. He lifted a possessive hand to her frozen cheek. She didn't meet his gaze. He didn't notice. "Then your work is all done here, dearest. No doubt your editor can see to whatever it was you were worried about needing to finish."

Everest cringed at the pet name that fell so easily from the man's lips. There was no way that Chloe just now met the man before her. No doubt she had found herself married to him by accident and didn't want to tell her real husband about it.

"Mr. Beaumont." Paul didn't offer his hand to the discourteous host again. "It was a pleasure. Chloe, get your things. We should be back in Vegas by tomorrow."

"But I have to go to New York first," Chloe broke in, distracted. Her eyes pled silently to Everest. He stared coldly back. Weakly, she said, "I should have a meeting with Devon."

"We'll discuss that in the helicopter." Paul put his hand on her back and began to lead her to the door.

"Paul," Chloe glanced to her fiancé. Trying not to cry, she swallowed, "Go on ahead. I just have to grab one bag."

Paul nodded and made his way to the awaiting helicopter. Chloe watched as he stood by the door and waited for the pilot to open it for him. The pilot had to climb out of his seat and run around the helicopter before Paul would get in.

Shaking her head at the ostentatious display, Chloe slowly turned her sad smile to Everest. "Can you believe the--"

"What?" Everest interrupted darkly. His brows furrowed in a harsh line. "Can I believe you had the audacity to lie to me? Although, why should I be so offended by it? You obviously lie to your husband on quite a regular basis. But, hey, what does my opinion matter? I'm just a one night stand."

Her smile faded. Her mouth gaped open in surprise at his outrage. She had hoped that maybe Everest would find Paul's attitude as amusing as she had. There was no way she would be marrying the man now that she had met him. She would just have to contest the will. Devon had said it was a vague possibility. However, it was a chance she would have to take. She wondered if the people whose jobs were on the line feel the same way.

"I think I was right in my first assumption of you," he hissed. "You might not get paid, but you are still a whore."

Chloe felt her heart drop from her chest to shatter on the floor. Her face paled. The wide bewilderment of her blue eyes filled with tears.

"I see you have nothing to say for yourself." Everest moved away from her in disgust. Angrily, he shot, "Get your bags and leave."

"But," Chloe began. She saw by his face that it was over. The pain was unbearable, burning her nose, filling her eyes. Her stomach lurched until she thought she was dying. She wanted to cry out from the pain, but couldn't make a sound. There would be nothing that she could say to make it right. Even if it was Devon who lied to Paul, Chloe knew that she was still at fault for letting him believe the lies. With a hollow forming in the pit of her stomach, she squeezed her eyes shut and uttered weakly, "Yes, Everest. I'll go."

She heard the humbled words as they left her throat and knew it was the only good-bye he would allow her to say. Gazing at his handsome face, she shivered. His features hardened into an unfeeling mask, his eyes glared at her from their hazel-green depth until she could feel his hatred in every pore. A pain choked her words, making her limbs weaken with the need to lash out at the unfairness of her world. Chloe hid her tears as she ran quickly to her room. She grabbed her bag, not wanting to pay any credence to the pain she felt in her chest. Gasping, her heart refused to beat.

When she came out of the bedroom he was gone. No good-bye, no last look. He was gone. Chloe didn't bother to call out to him. She knew it would do no good. He was too proud a man to be mixed in such business as hers. She had been a fool to dream that it might be otherwise.

Seeing Paul's impatient face as it shone through the glaring window of the helicopter, she knew that she could never want to marry him. But if she couldn't have Everest, did it matter? What was her unhappiness compared to the lives of so many? With each footstep she took, she heard the snow crunched underneath her boots. The footwear had just started to get worn in.

"Thanks, Dad," she expressed sarcastically into the slight breeze hoping he would hear her so close to the heavens. Chloe tried to smile as she approached the helicopter, but her heart didn't feel it. Her eyes dulled and she knew she might never be happy again.

Chapter Eleven

"Is Paul with you?" Devon looked hazily out of her upscale apartment door. The strong smell of her French perfume was a pleasant change from the stench of the taxi Chloe had spent the last forty minutes in.

"No. Thank goodness." Chloe walked past Devon. She set her traveling bag on the floor and sat on the expensive, yet highly comfortable, couch. "Where in the world did you dig him up?"

"Yes," Devon drawled. "Not one of my finer accomplishments."

Chloe laughed wryly in agreement, unable to do much else.

Devon sighed as she took a chair across from her friend. She crossed her legs and tugged the belt of her silk robe. Reaching to grab a comb, she pulled it through her wet, tangled curls. "Was it all that terrible?"

"You mean his excessive babbling about his favorite topic? Or the fact that his favorite topic was himself?" Chloe took a deep breath and closed her eyes. She leaned back to lie on the couch. She was just glad to be rid of both men right now.

"Most men are like that Chloe. You just haven't dated enough of them to find it out." Devon sighed. "Coffee?"

"No." Chloe kept her eyes shut. "Can I sleep here tonight? I think Paul knows where I live and I don't want him there waiting for me. He might try to redecorate."

"Yeah, fine," Devon allowed. "But I didn't give him the address."

"I know. I did. It was the only way I could get him to agree to let me come here alone. No doubt he will be there when I get home. Maybe I'll never go home." Chloe laughed childishly at the thought. "Do you think he would notice?"

"Honestly. It couldn't have been as bad as all that." Devon shook her head. Chloe, being a writer, was always a bit dramatic.

"Hey, I haven't been a social outcast. Just because I haven't dated for awhile doesn't mean I don't know what men are like. I write them every day." Chloe opened one eye and shot her friend a belatedly scathing expression.

"No, you write fictional men. There's a big difference. You write about the loser who doesn't pay child support. Or the pimp who abuses his hos." Devon chuckled when Chloe scrunched up her face in displeasure.

"I have never written one word about a pimp. Though I think that will be my next book." Chloe did open her eyes that time, but only to roll them at her friend. Sarcastically, she mumbled, "Thanks."

"Please," Devon shot back, matching her tone. "The men in your books are the way you want them to be. People aren't like that. They are unpredictable and they don't always get what they deserve. Besides, I wouldn't date any of the men you write about. If I want a good beating, I'll join kick boxing."

"Maybe you should tell Paul I have a history of beating my men. That should change his mind." Chloe gave a cynical smirk. "I think I could take him."

Devon grimaced. Chloe didn't see.

"Devon, Paul is just," Chloe paused trying to find the right phrase. Then, lacking anything better, she mumbled dejectedly, "not Mr. Right."

"Mr. Right?" Devon shot back with authority. "Let me tell you something about that little number. Mr. Right doesn't always say the right thing or laugh when he is supposed to, support you when he is supposed to. He isn't handsome. He's nowhere near Prince Charming. Mr. Right is just a man--a man who you get along with a little better than the rest. And sometimes, he's the man willing to marry you to fulfill the stipulations of your father's will."

"I know all that," Chloe answered, though she didn't agree. Her friend's outlook was too bleak to accept. "But I don't think that man is Paul. There has to be someone else. There has to be a way to get Paul to go away."

"Are you sure you want him to change his mind? Did something more happen between you and Everest?" Devon's eyes turned hopeful. "If it has, you can blow Paul off. He might be mad, but if he tries to go public we'll just show the world how happy you and Everest are. It will only be a small public relations nightmare by that point. And maybe it will boost book sales, controversy always does."

"How can you berate personal relationships with such cynicism and then be the optimist about this?" Chloe chuckled halfheartedly. The pain in her chest hadn't lessened since leaving Montana. His face was painted permanently on the canvas of her mind. He thought she was a whore. She felt so wretched. Chloe turned her back on her friend and curled up into a ball.

"Hardly," Devon sighed. "Does that mean you didn't work things out with him?"

"No. I believe his parting words were something to the effect of get out of my house--*now*." Chloe took a deep, ragged breath. Her nose burned with the need to cry. She felt the tears welling up in her chest as she remembered his words. He had been so angry and not only that, he'd been so disappointed.

"Fine. Forget him. We will find someone else--if not Paul, then someone." Devon's tone turned professional. "How much does anyone really know about the man they're going to marry? We can find you a husband. The way I figure, it's a fifty-fifty chance. And I will write a pre-nup so airtight that ... well, you get the idea."

Chloe didn't want to think of it, but she really had no choice. Time was running out.

"First things, first. Where are the divorce papers?" Devon held out her hand. "I'll have them pushed through first thing. I have a judge who owes me a favor."

"Oh, no, I forgot them. I forgot my laptop, all my notes. I can't believe it!" Chloe sat up with a jolt. "I didn't have him sign them. He was so angry with me. Paul told him we were married and Everest must have thought I was cheating on my husband with him."

"What?" Devon shot in disbelief. She was a firm believer in work first, play later. "You were at his house how long and they didn't get signed?"

"I know," Chloe sighed in dejection. The time had gone so fast, but for the most part it was the most cherished time of her life.

"How could I have been so foolish? You really are in love with him. And not just love sex love. But love love, the real thing." Devon shook her damp curls in bewilderment.

"I don't want to talk about it. He doesn't care for me. In fact, I think loathe might be more appropriate a term--disgust, better." Chloe took a deep breath. She pressed at her temple to stop its throbbing. "Is there any way to divorce him without going back for the papers?"

"No, not in the time frame we have left."

"Then you'll have to do it for me. You have to go back there for me. Please, as my friend," Chloe begged.

"No, as your friend I think you should do it. Go to him. Try to patch things up. I still think that if you stayed with him it would be the easiest solution to this whole mess. You would have a husband who would be great for procreation purposes. And, as far as Paul goes, we can handle that."

"Then go as my paid lawyer. I don't want to see him. Ever," Chloe lied.

"Is something else bothering you?" Devon asked. "You don't seem yourself. Are you sick?"

"Yeah, I think I am coming down with the flu. I didn't have the best attire with me for the mountain climate." Chloe waved her hand in dismissal of the question, thinking of their little wet romp in the snow. "I don't have the luxury of thinking about it now. I can spend the next ten years of my married life being sick."

Devon nodded. She happened to agree that they lacked time. "Fine, I will get the papers for you. It'll have to wait for two days. In the mean time you have to decide whom you want to marry-- whether it's Paul or some nobody off the street."

"Paul told me that I can quit my career after we are married. He said that no wife of his has to work." Chloe laughed derisively. "And he had to have the pilot help him into the helicopter. He couldn't even get his own door."

Devon shook her head. "I know, I already said that I was sorry. That's what you get when you pick a husband out of a stack of financial reports."

"As my lawyer, should I marry Paul?" Chloe sighed. "Is that my best bet?"

"As your lawyer, keep him in the sidelines." Devon stood up and moved to place her hand on Chloe's shoulder. She leaned over to press her hand to the back of Chloe's head. She was pretty warm. "As your friend, I don't know what to tell you."

"I know, Devon, I stopped understanding this whole thing months ago." Chloe closed her eyes as she shook her head. "I don't understand why my father would be so unrelenting in this. He's the one who pushed me to work hard--to travel all the time, going from book signing to book tour. It was that reason I never had a meaningful relationship. No man could ever trust me to be faithful when I was gone. And what man would wait three months for a woman he'd only just met? It was impossible so I stopped trying."

"Chloe," Devon began with a frustrated sigh. She pursed her lips tightly together. There was nothing else she could say.

* * * *

"What?" Grandpa's voice boomed and crackled from the old speaker. Everest strained to hear over the halting words, "How ... the world ... she ... your ... wife ... you mean gone."

"Grandpa, you're breaking up," Everest returned with a push of the handset button, "I can't hear you."

For a moment there was crackling silence. Everest grimaced as his grandfather's voice boomed over the speaker.

"I said, what do you mean she's gone?"

Everest frowned at the irritation in the old man's voice. He knew his grandmother would be standing right behind Grandpa listening to every word. With a sigh, he answered, "Grandpa, she has two husbands. Her real husband came and picked her up."

"Real husband?" His grandmother's shocked voice revealed her presence. Everest chuckled without amusement.

"Yeah, grandma," he replied. "Our marriage was a mistake."

"I never," his grandmother's voice began to rise in outrage before the speaker went dead. Everest frowned. He knew his grandfather had taken his finger off the button so he wouldn't hear them arguing.

When the sound came back, Grandpa said, "Quiet Gladys. You don't mean that rich feller who was here looking for her do you, son?"

"Paul," Gladys chimed in helpfully.

"Yes, yes, Paul." Grandpa affirmed to quiet his wife.

"Yeah, Grandpa, that's him," Everest put forth with a firm click of the button. "That's Chloe's husband. He flew a helicopter up here to rescue her. She told him that I was her editor."

Everest refused to tell his grandparents what else she had said about him. With a frown deeply embedded on his brow, he growled, "Boyfriend my ass."

"What?" Grandpa hollered.

"Nothing," Everest said back with a boyish grin of mischief.

"Oh," Grandpa began.

"Here, give that to me."

Everest listened. There was a struggle for the handset on the other end. He shook his head with a smile. His grandparents had finally answered his call, though he had dutifully tried every day since the avalanche.

"Hey, son, it's grandma," Gladys said unnecessarily. "Paul can't be her husband."

Everest froze. The smile of amusement that had begun to line his lips at hearing his grandparents argue faded. His heart stopped.

"Everest," Gladys inquired when her grandson didn't respond.

"Yeah, I'm here," he stated. "What do you mean he's not her husband?"

"That Paul was here in Miner's Cove a few days ago. He was here with this red-haired attorney from New York."

"That's Chloe's lawyer friend," Everest clarified.

"Well, this Paul, he kept asking a lot of questions--too many questions for a married man to be asking about his wife." Gladys shushed her husband when he tried to interrupt. "No one but Betsy told him anything."

Everest forced a chuckle for the sake of his grandma, before saying, "What? That she wanted to go with him?"

CAUGHT

"He took her, son," Grandpa stated. Gladys shushed him again.

"Yeah, Everest, Betsy's gone to New York with him. He bought her a first class ticket. She said they were going to get married and live in LA." Gladys paused. "So he can't be married to Chloe and marry Betsy."

Everest frowned. Something was not right. Just want kind of marriage did Chloe have anyway? No wonder she was more than happy to get snowed in with him. Her husband was as unfaithful as she was. He swallowed down his regret, before saying, "Grandma, did you ever think that maybe he was lying to Betsy to sleep with her. Or that maybe Betsy didn't want to tell you the truth. That she was finally leaving the diner on her own."

"I saw him give her the ticket," Gladys asserted. "Besides, Betsy would have no reason to lie to me. I've been telling her to go for years."

Everest sighed knowing that with the girl gone his grandma would be losing her only help in the restaurant. "All right, but there's nothing I can do about it now. I'm still snowed in. I drove by the pass this morning, it looks as if it might be several more weeks until I can make it out of here."

"Yeah, I estimate about the same," Grandpa put in.

"Do you want me to contact her?" Gladys offered. "I can give her a message for you."

"No." Everest thought of the divorce papers he had found in his bedroom near her laptop. He had finally sat down and read them. They were quite generous terms that included a one-time check settlement of fifty thousand dollars. She had forgotten to get them when she left. With a confidence he didn't feel, he claimed, "I'll see her soon enough."

"All right, son." Grandpa had taken the hand piece from his wife. She didn't argue, as he asked, "Are you all right on supplies?"

"Yeah, I'm fine," Everest responded, standing from his chair. Leaning over the table, he said, "I'll contact you in a few days, out."

"All right, son," Grandpa repeated. "Out."

Everest shut off the two-way. Standing, he frowned. It didn't make sense. Had Chloe told him the truth from the beginning? Or was Paul really the husband she was trying to keep the truth of her indiscretions from? Everest wanted to believe her. He had been so angry the day she left. But what if she didn't lie? And then again, what if she had?

Shaking his head, he crossed through the house to his den. The house seemed so empty without her. The isolation had never bothered him before. Everest frowned. Going to the bookshelf, he pulled a book from its orderly place. Looking at the front cover, he read the finely scrolled words, "The Ashes of Littleton by Chloe Masters."

Flipping the hard cover over, he stiffened as he saw her grinning face. It was an older picture, her hair had been shorter and she sat in an office chair with a furry white cat on her lap. Everest smiled when he noticed the cat's bright blue eyes were slightly cross-eyed. Tracing his finger over the smooth line of her cheek, he sighed at the photograph. Before he had paid the picture little mind, choosing instead to read the novel. Now he wondered how he could have ever resisted looking at the beautiful woman on the glossy cover.

Carrying the novel with him back to his couch, he sat in front of the fire. He stared at her shining face for a long moment before leaning back and opening her book.

Chapter Twelve

Chloe walked despondently through the bright casino, by the endless rows of slot machines and blackjack tables. Her stride was proud as she lifted her head high into the air. She passed a waitress offering free drinks without a second glance. Today, she would meet with Paul Lucas. And she would do it dead sober so there would be no mistakes. Smoothing the black jacket of her finely cut business suit over her skirt, she hid her frown. She drew her face into a blank mask.

"Chloe! Chloe Beaumont! What a small world!"

Chloe froze in confusion at the excited voice. Stopping, she looked around. Seeing a woman coming directly at her, she smiled slightly. Then, as recognition dawned on her, she uttered, "Betsy? From Miner's Cove? What are you doing here?"

"I left Miner's Cove," Betsy asserted with a pleased grin. Her hair swept up to the nape of her neck in sleek fashion. Her makeup was toned down and her clothes looked to be of a very fine quality, though not overly rich. "And I'm never going back."

CAUGHT

"Well, what are you doing in Vegas?" Chloe questioned. For a moment her heart stopped. She glanced over the casino looking for Everest. She couldn't see him.

"I've come to land me a rich husband," the woman said without embarrassment. "I figured Vegas would be the perfect place."

"Good for you, Betsy," Chloe said, though she wasn't sure she meant it. Then, with a polite smile, she uttered, "I'm sorry, but I have to go. I hope everything goes well for you."

"I'm sure it will," the woman mumbled. Betsy opened her purse to pull out a piece of chewing gum. Popping it into her mouth, she waved over a waitress to order a drink. An easy smile formed on her catlike lips. Then, turning, she watched Chloe walk away.

* * * *

Chloe paused before knocking. She waited patiently as she heard Paul coming to the door. Opening it, he stared out at her in surprise. A towel wrapped around his waist and his wet hair was slicked back from his face.

Holding the door in his hand, he shot, "Chloe, what are you doing here so early? I thought the wedding was set for tonight."

"It is," Chloe answered. "But I came to talk to you about the will. There's something I need to discuss with you."

"Can't it wait?" Paul inquired. He pulled the towel closer to his flat waist to keep it from falling. Grinning slyly, he stated, "I'm not even dressed."

"Sure," mumbled Chloe. His half naked state had no effect on her whatsoever. With a frown, she asked, "Can you meet me downstairs in the lounge?"

"Ah, yeah, sure." Paul began to close the door. Before the wood shut all the way, he uttered, "I'll be down in fifteen."

"Fine," came her stiff reply.

Paul watched her leave through a slight crack before turning around to the bed. A slender woman arched her buttocks into the air. Her dark skin and raven black hair reflected off the mirrored ceiling to give Paul ample view of her naked form. She slightly parted her legs in invitation when she noticed his attention. With a naughty come-hither smile, she cocked her head for him to join her. Licking his lips in devious pleasure, he had to shake his head, denying the naked prostitute.

"I can't, Maria," he growled. "I need you to go."

"Oh, no," Maria whined. Her voice was thick. She dipped her finger in her mouth to suck on it gently before moving to touch her breast. She lightly circled the wet tip over her dark nipple.

Instantly, the bud peaked. She moaned and spread her legs wider. "You can't leave me."

Paul growled, liking the trashy appeal of the prostitute. He didn't even care that her name was probably not Maria. His loins tightened in instant arousal. His towel rose to reveal the imprint of his ready member. Maria giggled excitedly and wiggled her breasts enticingly before him. "I have to--business. But listen, I want you to keep tomorrow night open. Have that friend of yours ready, the one with the big tits."

"But, what 'bout me? Are you goin' to leave your little Maria all hot for you?" the prostitute asked with a lustful glance at the man's crotch. With an insistent whimper, she begged, "Come on. I'll let you do me like you like it, dirty man."

Paul groaned as the woman turned her tanned backside to him and spread her cheeks. Without further protest he threw the towel from his waist and hopped behind her on the silk-covered bed.

* * * *

Chloe sighed. Taking a sip of her lemon water, she looked at her watch. Paul was ten minutes late. As another waitress tried to approach her with a tray laden with alcohol, she held up her hand in denial. The plump woman backed away with a pout but soon turned to another customer who accepted her offerings.

Chloe looked around the fancy lounge. Even the bar had slot machines in it. She had chosen a private table in the back, away from the noise of the main room. Frowning, she lifted her wrist to look at her watch again. But, before she could check the time, she saw Paul in the entryway. He stopped the plump girl with the tray to order a drink. Then, scanning the lounge for his fiancée, he nodded in her direction.

Chloe stood politely as he came over to the table. As he took a seat across from her, she smiled.

"So, what's all this about?" inquired Paul pleasantly. The waitress brought his drink. Reaching into his coat pocket, he pulled out a bill and laid it on her tray.

When she was gone, Chloe said, "I need to go over a few details of the will. I wanted to make sure that you still wanted to go through with this."

"Of course I do," Paul answered, as if affronted.

"Good," Chloe tried to force a smile and failed. Taking a sip of water, she said, "Not many people would like the terms of it."

"Terms?" Paul inquired with a slight raise of his brow. He took a drink of bourbon. "You mean the fact that we have to have a kid in the first two years? I already know of a great private school that we can send him to the moment he turns five. And before that we can hire a nanny. There is no reason to be inconvenienced by it. My parents hardly took a hand in raising me and I'm fine."

Chloe swallowed her displeasure. "Sure, there is that. Also, I have to keep working. It's a stipulation. I got the impression you didn't want me to work after tonight, but I have to. If I don't, we don't get any money."

"Oh," Paul muttered. Then, thinking that his wife might be gone all the time on book tours and such, he smiled kindly. Lying, he said, "I just meant to imply that you didn't have to. But, if it's what you want, I will support you."

"That is so kind of you," Chloe preened through her teeth. She narrowed her gaze into shaded slits. Paul didn't notice. With a smirk beginning to form, she said, "But, there is more."

"Whatever it is, I am sure we can find a way to make it work," he said. Lifting his glass, he ordered another drink before his first was finished.

"I am sure you are right," Chloe answered. Leaning back in her chair, she waited for the waitress to return.

* * * *

"What are you doing here, Chloe? I thought you changed your mind," Paul slurred drunkenly from the suite's doorway. His suit was slightly crumpled and he hesitantly brushed down the sleeves. Glancing back at the bed, he waved the red haired woman out of view with a grimace. His eyes grew wide as she shot him a defiant look.

The prostitute ran soundlessly to the bathroom. Spinning back to the hall, he looked at the covered figure that silently held out her hand to him. Squinting, he stared at her trembling fingers before taking them in his own. He took a deep, irritated breath, "Is it time for the wedding?"

"Yeah, Paul, it's time. Come on, I have a bottle of whiskey out in the limo for us. I think we're going to need it."

Chapter Thirteen

Chloe frowned as she shut the last of her suitcases. Taking a last glance around her New York apartment bedroom, she sighed in thought. Outside her window she saw a stray cat crawl over the fire escape. She watched it hop down from a railway before scurrying past.

Chloe took a deep breath and let it out slowly. Seeing a sock on her cleaned floor, she bent over to pick it up and threw it into a laundry basket. After getting back she had cleaned her entire apartment until it sparkled. She sadly thought of Everest and his lodge. Then, going to her vanity, she lifted the lid to her makeup case and hurriedly threw in several small bottles of perfume, an extra lipstick and her nail file.

Grabbing the case in one hand, she lifted her suitcase off her bed with the other. She carried them into the living room and set them by the door. Inside, she felt dead. The Vegas trip had gone exactly like planned. Paul had been predictable. Shaking her head, she refused to think about it. It was over.

Wandering into her kitchen, she stopped at the box she had left on her counter. She opened the lid and dug through its contents. Hesitantly, she pulled out her research notes. Devon had brought them back with her from Montana. Packing the notes in her briefcase, she carried it over to sit with the rest of her luggage. Going back to the box, she threw the empty container away.

Chloe stared at the discarded package, trying not to cry. It was hard though. She felt a sob gather in her chest as she thought of Everest. Betsy might have wanted to get out of Miner's Cove, but Chloe wanted to spend the rest of her life there.

She missed the mountain haven. The city only seemed noisy and irritating to her now that she was back. Before, the smell of the streets had never bothered her. Now she found herself longing for the fresh, clean scent of a snowdrift and the stout odor of burning wood in a fireplace. Her body longed for all the times and places she had never made love to Everest on the mountain. His embrace still burned her skin, branding her and forever ruining her for another man's touch.

Shaking herself out of her self-pitying trance, she eyed her airplane ticket. Opening it, she scanned the bold print.

"Switzerland," she mumbled, "first class, no layover."

Seeing her purse, she pulled it to her and shoved the ticket inside. Then, pausing, she pulled out a worn piece of paper. Her hands shook as she unfolded it. It was her wedding certificate to Everest. She knew she should throw it into the trash or even a file somewhere that no one would ever see. Tracing the firm strokes of his precise handwriting, she smiled in remembrance. It was neat and orderly like the rest of him.

CAUGHT

Going over to her briefcase, she rummaged through it until she found the divorce papers. His signature stood out boldly from them, matching the wedding certificate perfectly. Folding them together, she put them away.

"Yeah," she hollered when the doorbell rang. Taking a few steps to the door, she pulled it open. Seeing Devon, she smiled and waved her in.

Devon eyed the suitcases wearily as she walked around them. "Are you all packed?"

"Yeah, I leave tonight." Chloe went back to the kitchen to grab her purse. Setting it by the luggage, she motioned Devon into the living room.

"Wow, did you hire a maid?" Devon asked in amazement as she looked around.

Chloe laughed wryly, "No, I finally picked up."

"Picked up?" Devon shot in skepticism. "I'd say you spent nearly ten hours on this place. I have never seen it so clean."

"Uh, thanks," Chloe muttered, as she rolled her eyes. "I just got in the habit when I was in Mon...."

Suddenly, Chloe stopped. Devon turned to her and frowned. Chloe's blue eye filled with pain as she squeezed them shut. Behind her lids all she saw was the potent form of Everest's naked body as he came over her. Shivering, she turned away.

"Did you ever try to talk to him?" asked Devon, all the time knowing Chloe hadn't. There was no way to get a hold of him in the mountains.

"No," Chloe stated. Her tone left no room for argument. "And I won't. He made himself clear. He doesn't want anything to do with me. If he did he would have sent a note or something with you."

"Chloe," Devon interrupted, "he doesn't know me. A man like that wouldn't send a personal note with a complete stranger. Maybe he wants to talk to you."

"No," Chloe denied with a firm shake of her head. "It's over."

"I don't think it has to be that way."

"Did he say something to you?" Chloe asked, a little too eagerly. Her eyes sparked with hope for a moment before going dead.

"Chloe, I am one of the best attorney's in the state. I read jurors, judges and witnesses. But, Everest Beaumont? I couldn't read a damned thing." Devon let loose a frustrated moan. "Chloe, if he feels for you even half of what you feel for him then it's worth giving it a try. Maybe you can work something out. Maybe later--"

"Don't. Do not say that maybe later we can be together. I can't afford to think of that. It wasn't meant to be. I can't.... It's too late for that."

Suddenly, Chloe began to cry. She hid her face in her hands. Shaking her head against the pain, she fell over to bury her face into the cushion of her couch. Hitting the soft material in frustration, she shot angrily, "I can't think of it. You don't know how bad it hurts to think of it. Damn it, Devon. I love him. I love his smile, his quietness. I love that he makes his own clocks and doesn't sell out to big business. I love that he eats eggs no matter how many times I cook them for him. And I love the way he looks, the sexy half smile he gets when he wants me."

Devon listened quietly. Slowly, she stood. "All right, I won't push. I just want to see you happy."

"I know," Chloe's voice was hoarse in her misery. Sitting up, she swallowed down a sob and turned her glistening eyes to Devon. "I'll be fine. I just need a little time to adjust."

"I came to say good-bye and good luck. I'll leave the address at your hotel in Switzerland when you get there."

"Thanks."

"Oh, I almost forgot to tell you about Paul," shot Devon with a smile suddenly forming on her amused face.

"What?" Chloe queried, confused. A feeling of dread curled in her stomach.

"That night you left him in Vegas he got married to another woman. I guess he got drunk and she showed up at his door wearing a wedding veil. He thought it was you." Devon started laughing so hard that she had to stop to take a calming breath. "The next day he called my office blaming me for setting him up. But I swear I know nothing about it. It's too bad. I'd like to be able to say I did it to him."

"Who?" Chloe asked in amazement.

"It was that waitress from Miner's Cove. Somehow she followed him to Vegas." Devon shook her head at the irony. "I guess his family has threatened to disown him and without a prenuptial, he's pretty much screwed."

"You mean Betsy?" Chloe shook her head, bewildered. Unable to stop herself, she giggled. "I guess she got her rich husband after all."

CAUGHT

"What did you tell him to make him change his mind anyway?" asked Devon when they were able to stop laughing long enough to speak.

"I told him the other stipulations to the will," Chloe mumbled. Her cheeks turned red with embarrassment. "The ones you forgot to mention--the one in the last amendment."

"What other stipulations? I told him everything that was required." Devon came back to her chair and sat down. She narrowed her gaze in confusion.

"Oh, that he had to work a nine to five at the Kansas City office for six of the ten years. You see my father was really big into work ethic and he wanted to make sure my husband would be too." Chloe chuckled before trying to force an innocent expression to her face. She failed miserably. "I also said that in total we had to have at least six children and they had to live with us until their eighteenth birthday."

Devon shook her head in astonishment. "You are quite a writer Chloe. I never would have thought of that, but I can't believe that was enough to put him off. He seemed to want the money pretty badly. What else did you tell him? And what are you not telling me?"

Chloe gulped. Her face paled a little in color before she looked Devon in the eyes. Licking her lips that had suddenly gone dry, she whispered, "I'm pregnant."

"What?" Devon sat straight up in her chair.

"Yeah, I found out before I got on the flight to marry Paul. I couldn't do it. When I told him that I was pregnant with Everest's child, he went crazy. I told him that in order to get the money he would have to claim the child as his own and that the child would be his heir. I guess male vanity won out over greed and Paul refused to go through with it. When I saw him last he was drinking himself into oblivion."

"You're pregnant?" broke in Devon, stunned. She barely heard the rest of the confession. "With Everest's baby?"

"Yes." Chloe shrugged her shoulders insecurely as Devon shot across the room to give her a hug. Muttering through her uncertain tears, she said, "So you see. I can't see him right now. I have to figure out what is best."

"But, with the baby?"

"He's too honorable. With the baby, he'll be with me for the baby. I'll never know if he would want to be with me for me. So first, I go to Switzerland to speak with dad's lawyer. I'll see if there is a way to get an extension and if there's not, I'll contest the will. I am sure he'll want to come to some sort of terms instead of seeing all of his commission held up on a technicality. Then, after that mess is straightened up, I'll think about what to do with Everest. By then the snow should have cleared enough to get up to his house."

"If it isn't, I'll fly you there myself," Devon asserted. "I can't believe you're having a baby!"

"Me neither." Chloe chucked insecurely as Devon pulled her into another hug. As her friend held her, she began to cry. But this time the tears were full of hope.

Chapter Fourteen

Zipping the suitcase over her new business suit, Chloe sighed. It was late, but the cab wouldn't be arriving for another ten minutes. Going to her bathroom, she grabbed a hair tie and pulled back her hair to the nape of her neck. Closing her eyes briefly, she yawned. It was late, almost midnight. Hopefully the airport wouldn't be too busy and she could check in fairly easily. Then she would be able to sleep on the plane.

She eyed her light gray T-shirt and blue jeans in the mirror. She refused to dress up for a fight across the Atlantic Ocean. Hearing the doorbell ring, she frowned. The cab was early. Going to the door, she flung it open.

"Cab?" a short man with a red cap asked in a gruff Bronx accent. The man looked nervously over his shoulder before tilting his jaw up in the air. "You call?"

"Yeah, that's me," Chloe answered. Turning around, she grabbed her purse. "Just let me get the lights and I'll be ready."

"Fine," the man grumbled. He looked curiously into her home and stepped in. "These goin' down, or what?"

"Yeah, all that." Chloe motioned to the luggage before rushing to the bathroom to hit the lights. Yelling over her shoulder, she said, "I'll take the two smaller bags down with me."

"Whatever you say, lady," the man hollered.

Chloe stepped across the hall to her small kitchen. She flipped the switch before coming back into her living room. Without looking up, she went straight to her bags.

"Can I help you with that?"

Chloe froze. Everest's voice poured over her body like a gentle rainstorm. Unable to believe her ears, she stood. Her purse slid from her shoulder to the floor with a crash. She ignored it. Her eyes rounded as she realized it wasn't a dream. Everest was standing in her living room. He wore a dark suit, his hair was tied back to the nape of his neck and he was holding a bouquet of red roses. His firm lips curled into an expectant smile.

"Uh, no," Chloe finally managed to choke out in wonder. Her heart started to race. It pounded frantically in her chest.

"Are you going somewhere?" he asked softly.

Chloe shivered and nodded her head. In a whisper, she hushed, "Switzerland."

Everest frowned slightly.

"What are you doing here?" questioned Chloe, puzzled. She wanted to jump into his arms and pull him to her lips, but she held back. Her body pulsed with the need to feel him. She had missed him so much.

"I came to wish you a happy birthday," he stated simply, as he held out the flowers to her. Whispering, he said, "Happy birthday, Chloe."

Chloe took the flowers. Her hand trembled as she drew them to her nose. She couldn't smell them as she tried to shakily breathe in their heady scent. It was the only gift she had received for her birthday. Everyone else had forgotten. "But, what are you doing in New York? How did you get here?"

"I called Grandpa on the two-way and had him send a helicopter over the drift. I booked a flight and came straight from the airport." Suddenly, he frowned.

"But, why?" she queried.

"You're not happy to see me." The statement was matter-of-fact. His eyes lost some of their shine as his face hardened. "Maybe I should go."

"No, wait." Chloe shot forward, her hand reaching out to stop him. She didn't dare to touch him, not yet. Her hand trembled and hung in midair. Turning, she laid the flowers on a small table by the front door. "I just--"

"Chloe, I love you," he burst all of a sudden.

"Oh, how romantic," the cab driver stated sarcastically from the door. "Miss, are you ready?"

"Can you give me one moment," Chloe replied breathlessly as she held up her hand. She didn't look at the little man, but kept her disbelieving gaze on Everest.

"All right, but if we are late for your flight it's your fault." The man leaned against the doorframe and waited.

Everest frowned. Reaching into his pocket, he handed the man a hundred-dollar bill. "Wait in the cab. She'll be down in a minute."

The man took the money and shrugged like it was no big thing. But he did leave.

When he was gone, Chloe whispered, "What did you say?"

"I said I love you, Chloe. That is why I am here. I came to find you." He took a hesitant step forward and eyed her pale face. She didn't look too well. Maybe she had missed him like he had her. "I came to tell you that I would wait for you. I'll wait ten years until you can divorce that prick."

"You'd do that?" she asked, dumbfounded. Her blue eyes rounded in amazement. Her hands trembled.

"Hell," Everest declared, "I have already waited my entire life to find you. Ten years will be nothing."

Chloe felt her heart race a bit more. The piercing light of his hazel-green gaze bore into her soul until it left it quivering with need. His handsome face was hard with emotion, but she could see the truth of his words in his eyes.

"But," she began.

"No buts," he broke in. Taking another step, he lifted his hand to her cheek. He couldn't deny his body the simple touch and was pleased when she didn't back away. "I don't care what the next ten years brings you. I'll wait. If you lose a leg or fall into a coma, I don't care. I'm coming to get you. At that time, if I have to sell my place in the mountains and move to New York, I'll do it. I'll do it for you."

"But," she tried again. Her love bubbled from her throat to choke her words.

"I'll take your child like it was my own and we'll add a baby or two and live as a family. I know why you are doing it. I know about the people you'll be helping. And no matter how much I hate it, I love you even more for your selflessness." Everest gazed deeply into her eyes. Her cheeks had colored prettily into a blush as he spoke. With an amazed smile, he noticed her toy machine wedding band hanging on a chain on her neck. Reaching into his pocket, he pulled out a small jewelry box.

Chloe gasped as she read the intent in his eyes. Numbly, she started to nod her head before he even spoke.

"Chloe, will you marry me?" he asked, before adding with a sheepish grin, "Again and in exactly ten years from this very moment?"

Chloe tried to nod but could barely move. Her breath caught in her constricted throat. He opened the box to present her with a thin gold band lined with diamonds. Tears came to her eyes, as she hushed, "The child is yours, not Paul's."

Everest narrowed his gaze, straining to hear her. Believing to understand, he nodded, "Yeah, the child will be mine."

Chloe felt tears line her eyes. Nothing was coming out of her mouth right. Finally, she managed to tilt her jaw, and said louder, "I don't have to marry you again."

Everest frowned, confused. Standing, he looked at her. She began to sniff harder.

"Yes, I will marry you," she finally blurted. She flung her arms around him to press kisses to his handsome face. A smile crossed over his perfect features that took her breath away. He didn't understand anything else she had said, but the last sentence was enough.

"I'll wait for you." Everest swore, beaming with the bittersweet pleasure of it. "And if you ever have a need of me all you have to do is send word. I'll come to you."

"I need you," she whispered. "Oh, how I need you, Everest. I need you every day."

Everest smiled, unable to resist her. He knew it was wrong, knew she had married Paul. But he couldn't stop himself. His need for her was too strong. It defied all logic. Cupping her face, he kissed her lips passionately.

"Do you have to leave for your honeymoon right away?" he asked thinking of the man downstairs waiting for her. "Will you miss your plane? I don't want to cause you any problems."

Chloe let go of him. Everest watched as she crossed over to the window. Pulling it open, she screamed down into the street, "Bring my bags back up, I'm not going anywhere!"

The cab driver's curses were lost as she turned back to him. Lightly she said, "I'm not going anywhere but Montana."

"Chloe?" he questioned with a hesitant smile. "How?"

Finding her words at last, she smiled happily. "I didn't marry Paul. I couldn't. I don't love him. I love you. I'm on my way to contest the will. My father's attorney is vacationing in Switzerland."

"Then, I'll go with you. We'll fight it together."

"But, don't you see?" she put forth as she moved to him. "We already have. Our divorce isn't final. I never sent in the final papers. I couldn't do it. I tried, but I couldn't. So we don't have to get married, we already are."

Everest rushed over, gathering her into his excited arms to kiss her. He lifted her necklace to study the cheap ring. Grabbing his hand, she held it tight over the bent metal band. "But you deserve a wedding. You deserve more than a minister dressed like Elvis and this."

"I don't want a wedding. I want you. I hate being in public. I just want to go home with you. I want to go back to Montana." Chloe breathed softly against his slanting lips. "Take me home."

Everest leaned over to deepen the kiss. His tongue edged the line of her velvet entrance before pulling back with a questioning glance to her flat stomach. "What did you mean when you said the child was mine?"

"Where do you want these bags?"

Letting go of Everest, she motioned to the floor, "There's good.

She absently grabbed two hundred-dollar bills from her purse and handed it to him. "Now go away."

The driver smiled, nodded and left. It was the easiest money he'd ever made.

She ignored the cab driver as she went back to her husband's arms. Whispering into his stunned face, she said, "I'm pregnant."

Everest growled happily, taking her into his strong embrace. With a squeal of delight escaping her lips, he lifted her into the air. His lips were on her mouth, her cheeks, her neck. Chloe groaned passionately as his hands moved over her firm backside in a solid caress.

"Oh, my!"

Chloe turned at the shocked exclamation. Seeing an elderly neighbor lady, she giggled.

"You should be ashamed--" began the woman in outrage.

Everest let go of Chloe and slammed the door, cutting off the woman's words with a hard thud. When they were finally alone, he directed his stalking growl toward her.

"I would defend your honor," he began.

"Bedroom's this way, mountain man," she broke in boldly. Her eyes shone with intense sexual promise. She giggled and squealed as Everest charged her and lifted her up into his arms. Carrying her as if she was no more than a feather, he began unfastening her blue jeans.

CAUGHT

Chloe ran her fingers to untie his hair. The silky brown waves crashed seductively over her fingers. Sighing huskily, she said, "You look very nice in a suit."

Growling, he responded, "I look better underneath it."

Chloe moaned at his confidence as he passed into her room. Dropping her to the floor, he threw off his jacket. Then he began tugging at his tie.

"Let me," she voiced lowly. With gentle urgency she began to undress him. Throwing the tie over her shoulder, she said, "You know, we really should get a dog. Mountain men should always have a dog."

"Mmmhmm," he nodded. Her hands skimmed to his waist to unbuckle his pants. "Whatever you want."

At that decree, she raised a naughty eyebrow. "Oh, really."

"Mmm," he nodded his assent. Her hand found the hard length of his member bulging beneath his cotton briefs.

Chloe fell to her knees. Looking up at him, she said, "There is one thing I have got to know before this goes any further."

"What's that?" he questioned. He thrust his manhood wickedly toward her mouth. Chloe freed the large erection. Everest groaned.

"Did you really eat your own horse after an avalanche?" she asked. "I mean you wouldn't expect me to, would you?"

Everest brows shot up in surprise. However, his manhood didn't lessen in its willingness. Chuckling, he said with a teasing light in his deep gaze, "No. It died of old age."

Chloe moaned in wanton delight. Leaning over she grabbed him firmly by his perfectly masculine hips. Her fingernails grazed his buttocks as she sucked him into her mouth. Everest hollered in virile rapture, reveling in the feel of the tender satin of her slick mouth. And there were no more words, only the groaning passions of two people madly in love.

THE END

Printed in the United States
36228LVS00006B/67-426